DEADLY FARE

A SERIAL KILLER THRILLER

DAVID LISCIO

To all the innocents who have died at the hands of a serial killer.

CHAPTER 1

June 1985
Boston, Massachusetts

ALL GYPSIES AREN'T FROM ROMANIA

Rainy nights at Logan Airport were usually best, the women eager to get inside his cab, not paying much attention to whether it was licensed or why the roof TAXI sign barely glowed.

For Luddy Pugano, this particular curbside pickup seemed as though it would work out much like two others earlier in the year – one during a January snowstorm and another amid an early-March cold snap that brought sleet and plunged Boston temperatures to below freezing. He had put the young woman's two suitcases in the trunk. Fake packages wrapped in brown paper filled the back seat so the fare was invited to sit up front, relax and pick a radio station. Once she appeared at ease, he'd slammed her head against the dashboard, then poked her menacingly with the tip of a clamming knife while driving to a deserted industrial lot in Eastie within earshot of the runways. But somehow this one had managed to squiggle out of his beefy arms. His leather belt was still cinched around her neck as she cast aside her thin trenchcoat and clawed her way up the muddy embankment to the highway.

The woman couldn't believe this was happening to her. She was a sophisticated sales rep flying into Boston to sell medical devices at three hospitals and heading home the

1

next day – at least that was the plan. Abduction by a weirdo cabbie who clearly was trying to kill her was something that happened to other people. She didn't dare look back. The mud was slippery but she was determined to get away. This wasn't how she would allow herself to die, so she climbed, yanking clumps of weedy grass as she put every last bit of energy into reaching the highway. Her gray pinstriped dress was torn at the neckline and she was shoeless, her hair disheveled, her bruised and muddied face a mask of sheer terror as she flagged down passing cars for help. She waved wildly at three drivers who kept on going, their tires hissing on the rain-soaked roadway. "What the hell? Why doesn't anybody stop? Am I some sort of Kitty Genovese? A tragic headline in the making?"

She thought her heart would burst through her chest as a fourth vehicle – which in the dark resembled a police cruiser with a driver-side spotlight -- switched on its directional signals and pulled over onto the road shoulder. Her face showed relief for a fraction of a second until she realized the worst had happened. It was him.

The woman tried to scream but no sound came out, her vocal cords compressed by the leather belt that flapped from her neck. The rain spattered her face and mixed with the coppery taste of blood on her lips as she stepped back against the metal guardrail. The driver's door opened and a large, barrel-chested man got out. The woman noticed he wore a dark hooded sweatshirt and knit watch cap. Despite her willingness not to die along the shoulder of a highway, she felt a paralyzing wave of fear wash over her from throat to toes.

The cabbie rushed toward her and reached for her arms, raised in self-defense. He'd grabbed her just as a BMW sedan pulled alongside the cab. A silver-haired man in business suit and necktie rolled down the passenger-side window and shouted over the sound of a plane taking off, asking if everything was all right. The woman felt the grip on her arms loosen as the cabbie turned and bolted. She watched in disbelief as he clumsily folded himself back into

2

the driver's seat, spinning the rear tires on the wet pavement as he roared away into the night. She saw the red taillights getting smaller as she leaned her weight against the guardrail and sobbed uncontrollably.

The woman's suitcases were mostly filled with medical device samples, branded coffee cups, pens and notepads. Luddy tossed them into a dumpster behind a gas station. During the following week, he scoured the newspapers for any reference to an attempted abduction at Logan Airport, just as he had done after the other two grabs, but there were no stories. An attempted abduction wasn't exactly news in Boston, not like a murder. The police had previously recorded two similar incidents at the airport as missing person cases. To the news reporters who covered the city's crime beat, none seemed worth the airtime or page space, so the public remained unaware of the danger. Only State Police Detective Lt. Hannah Summers, after interviewing the woman who had escaped, theorized the three cases might be related. She wrote a report that was read by her commanding officer with great amusement and summarily tossed aside.

CHAPTER 2

July 1985
Boston, Massachusetts

*IT'S ALWAYS A SLOW NEWS DAY RIGHT
BEFORE THE BIG STORY BREAKS*

The Boston Tribune newsroom was teeming with
reporters and editors clacking away on their desktop
computers while talking on the phone or bantering with each
other. It was a warm summer afternoon and at least six hours
remained before deadline so only the newbies were showing
any signs of concern. Reporter Rane Bryson sauntered into
the sprawling, florescent-lit room, tossed his suit jacket over
the back of his chair and flipped his middle finger at Paige
Williston, the leggy blonde photographer waiting near his
desk.

"And equal greetings to you, Mr. Bryson. Glad you
could lower yourself to enter the building where us mere
mortals toil away."

"It sucks being a super hero."

"If only your bosses knew it. They might pay you an
extra ten bucks a week."

"Doubtful, Willi," he said, grinning and clearly glad
to see her. "But since you're such a suck-up to the powers-
that-be around here, maybe you can put in a good word for
me."

Paige pulled up a rolling desk chair. "You won't want
to hear this and don't shoot the messenger. But we've got an

interview with the police commissioner and the mayor at four o'clock about the increase in drive-by shootings. After that we're supposed to meet with some commercial fishermen at Fort Point Channel who claim they're being booted out by greedy real estate developers."

"We're on it, Willi. Maybe the police commissioner will announce a grant for bulletproof vests for every resident in Roxbury. You can get a photo of Raybo strapping on the Kevlar and I can interview concerned moms because the vests don't come in petite sizes or pastel colors."

Paige ran her fingers through her short-cropped whitish blonde hair highlighted with two purple streaks. "Let's just get it over with," she said, adjusting the hem of her mint-green mini-dress that had ridden well above mid-thigh.

Rane eyed her shapely legs outlined in shear pink stockings and capped by black Doc Marten boots. Paige dressed sexy and tough, but Rane knew she was all sentimental mush, which is why he liked her so much.

"Give me ten minutes to pull together some challenging questions for the mayor and those fishermen and we'll head out for City Hall and the waterfront," he said. "Your ride or mine?"

"I'll drive, yours only has two wheels," she said, pulling a palm-size oval mirror from her camera bag to inspect the plum color on her pouty lips. "Besides, I just had the oil changed."

"Oh Christ. Will that bucket of bolts make it to Government Center or are we better off taking my bike?"

Paige smiled. "My car helps increase social awareness of the need for more public transportation. People see it and immediately know it shouldn't be on the road. Makes them appreciate the T."

"You scare me sometimes, Willi. Next you'll have all of us riding the bus."

"Never that," she quipped. "I draw the line at trains."

As Paige assembled her photo gear, Rane read the messages left for him on small pink paper slips by the newsroom editorial assistants. Nothing urgent. The writers in this section of the newsroom were standing around joking about the anonymous threats reporter Barry Schwartz had received by phone and U.S. mail after writing a story about a large Boston family that until very recently had collected welfare payments despite owning two Mercedes and annually vacationing in Aruba. The calls and letters vowed to kill Schwartz and were somewhat believable given the number of crimes the family members had committed over the past 20 years. With typical gallows humor, a couple of reporters had crafted a dozen stand-up cardboard signs that read, "I'm not Barry Schwartz" and placed them on every desk except for his.

"Time for you to start wearing a flak jacket," Rane yelled over to Schwartz who had just entered the room and discovered the prank. Judging by the expression on Schwartz' face he wasn't amused. Paige snapped a few photos of Schwartz that were later hung on the newsroom bulletin board with the words "Marked for Death?" scrawled beneath in black marker pen.

The interior of Paige's small Japanese sedan was a landfill of yellowed newspapers, Styrofoam coffee cups, books, magazines, scattered clothing and photography equipment. She tossed several items into the backseat as Rane brushed piles of crumbs off the front passenger seat and got inside. He noticed several of the pressmen were on break, sitting and smoking on the loading dock, their eyes locked on Paige.

"I think you have an audience," he said, nodding toward the loading dock.

Paige gave him a mischievous smile as she purposely leaned far into the small car's backseat to load her photo gear, knowing it would hike her dress to her cheeks.

"You are so fucking bad," Rane said.

"You love it. Don't kid yourself."

"Now those poor guys are all going home to drink heavily and chase their wives around the kitchen table."

6

"You're an asshole."

"Just drive."

Paige backed out of the employee parking lot, tapping the bumpers of two cars before straightening the wheel and heading onto the highway.

"Do you always park by Braille?"

"Not everyone has a motorcycle that fits in small spaces."

En route to City Hall they discussed how to get away from the pack of newspaper and television reporters who would be headed to the same press conference. Rane reached into his pocket and showed Paige the three 9mm bullets he'd brought along as props for any photo op they might encounter. The other photographers would undoubtedly get a picture of the mayor talking at a podium with a poster about the dangers of drive-by shootings as backdrop. Rane, making the most of his successful third year at the Tribune since relocating from a mid-sized daily in New Hampshire, strived for something different.

At the press conference, the mayor gave his spiel and the pack reacted as predicted, satisfied with the podium shot and pre-packaged quotes from the mayor's press office. Francis Roache, the new police commissioner, followed up the mayor's comments and was promptly escorted out of City Hall by his aides, assuring the media he'd be holding another press conference within a day or two. Roache had tactfully diverted questions about what many insiders knew was an ongoing FBI investigation into Boston Police Department corruption. When the press event was over, Rane approached the mayor and quickly explained that he needed to show him something important.

Caught unaware, the mayor registered his surprise as he gazed upon the three brass bullets in Rane's outstretched palm.

"How do we keep these from killing people, Mr. Mayor? These are the real enemy," Rane said.

Paige clicked the shutter several times as the flustered official stuttered to answer the unscripted question. Finally, the mayor said, "Nobody should have those. We need to crack down on guns. I'll be talking more about this to the police commissioner in the coming days."

"Have you ever fired a handgun, sir?"

The mayor didn't answer. Rane deftly dropped one of the brass 9mm rounds into the mayor's palm. The mayor inspected the bullet as though he'd never seen or held one, holding it like a Fenway Park peanut. Paige's camera clicked again.

Back in the car, Paige scribbled some notes on a pad that she stuffed into her camera bag. "You're such a news whore," she needled.

"Thank you very much. If I had left it up to you, we'd have a shot of the mayor picking his nose behind a podium instead of him holding up a bullet."

"I guess that makes you a genius," she conceded, swerving around a parked bus as she headed for Fort Point Channel.

"I prefer super hero."

"Super zero is more like it," she said. "If you had any brains, you wouldn't be in the news business. You'd be out making money in PR. I'm sure Kaleigh would agree."

Rane glanced at Paige. "Touché," he said, feeling a bit uneasy from Paige's mention of Kaleigh.

The press conference at Fort Point Channel wasn't much different in set up. A gaggle of raggedly-dressed commercial fishermen stood next to a shirt-and-tie lawyer sporting a cheap toupee, who announced his clients were being evicted because a super-wealthy real estate mogul planned to dock private yachts in a new marina next to luxury condos, replacing their rickety boat slips and dilapidated fish storehouses. Several reporters and photographers recorded every word the lawyer and the fishermen had to say, but the story would likely get 15 seconds of airtime or two paragraphs in the Tribune's news brief section.

Sensing all news value from the event had been exhausted, Paige sourly complained, "Are we done here?"

8

Rane asked one of the lobstermen if he and Paige could come aboard the boat. Paige shot him a look that said don't do this, let's go back to the newsroom so that I can process my film and punch out on time. But Rane, sympathetic to their plight, ignored her silent plea. The fisherman nodded, eying them warily. Once aboard, Rane tactfully approached the topic of where the lobster fleet might relocate if evicted and what changes that might bring to the fishermen and their families. Did they have a plan? Had they approached their congressman for help?

The lobsterman admitted he had no idea where the fleet might end up or how his family would survive. Maybe Gloucester, but that was 25 miles east, and might as well be the other side of the world. His eyes were glassy when Rane asked him to open a keeper crate and hold up two of the biggest lobsters from the day's catch. Paige was ready with her camera and as the crustaceans were lifted from the crate, water dripping from their shiny dark green carapaces, she clicked away, framing the bearded man's weathered face between the two lobsters.

The fisherman tossed the lobsters into a cardboard box and handed it to Rane. "Here ya go. These are yours. Don't know when you'll get them this fresh again if we're booted out."

Rane knew instinctively he had the story angle, which wasn't *"Big developer ousts fishermen,"* but *"Big developer denies fresh seafood to public."* That would get many more readers pissed off.

"I can't take those," he said.

The fisherman grimaced. "I'll be pissed if you don't."

It was past 9 p.m. when Rane left the newsroom. He hoped the lobsters were still alive and kickin' in the small refrigerator where several reporters and editors routinely stored their pathetic lunch bags and Tupperware leftovers. Paige had made it clear she wanted no part in cooking or eating them. Kaleigh was even less excited when Rane walked into his apartment and announced he intended to boil the groggy creatures as a late-evening snack.

She had waited patiently for his arrival, anticipating they might simply fall into bed. Instead, Rane was boiling water and heating a skillet of butter.

CHAPTER 3

August 1985
Boston, Massachusetts

HOMECOMINGS ARE FOR QUEENS,
NOT SOLDIERS

Emmett Decker had seen all he wanted of the Middle
East's high-tension cities, North Africa's unforgiving deserts
and the unpredictable banana republics of Central America.
He was psyched to return to the simple life he had once
known in the rugged hills of Pennsylvania, even if it meant
spending hours each week mending his war wounds at the
Veterans' Administration Hospital in Pittsburgh.

Shot twice during firefights with Syrian soldiers
and later hit with shrapnel during a clash with Iraq's
Revolutionary Guards, Decker had earned his pay as an Army
Special Forces Ranger. He had parachuted into places where
other soldiers dared not tread, called in artillery coordinates
for high-value targets, lugged his long-barrel Barrett M107
sniper rifle on dozens of missions, came very close to dying
on several occasions, and decided after many months in
Sandland that the U.S. Central Command hadn't a clue about
what to do with Lebanon.

He'd been in Beirut in '83 as part of the Multinational
Peacekeeping Force when a suicide bomber attacked the U.S.
embassy. It came as a personal shock because he knew a few
of the CIA staffers -- the ones he referred to as his spook
friends – who were among the 63 people killed. Some very

talented people died that day, he thought.

When the U.S. and French military barracks were attacked with a massive truck bomb several months later, he was in Syria as part of a covert mission, but several of the 220 Marines killed had been friends or acquaintances. He'd also lost a fellow Army Ranger.

The Middle East had sucked, plain as that. The mission was unclear, the Multinational Force was a revolving door in which you never knew if the Italians were staying or leaving, if the Israelis or the PLO were going to commit yet another atrocious act to keep the fires of hatred burning. Some weeks he was paired with French special ops troops with whom he didn't share a common language, not even the metric system, and on others he was simply left to his own devices so that he became sort of a lone wolf, calling in by satphone, reporting kills and troop movements, awaiting orders that never came. Just a fuckin' circus is how he described it to friends, family, counselors and anyone else who asked. No, it wasn't Vietnam. Nothing like World War II, that's for sure. Not even a declared war. Not a declared anything. Hardly ever saw the enemy or maybe he just hadn't recognized them, even when they were in the crosshairs. And the ones he had killed, well, he hoped they were the enemy. Too late to think they weren't.

On one miserably hot day near the Syrian border, he pulled the trigger on a target while listening to Prince sing *When Doves Cry* on his new Sony Discman CD player. Another time, on a night mission, he located his target while grooving to Springsteen's *Dancing in the Dark*. The memory of those kills left him feeling unsettled. How was it that music always found its way to the battleground? He'd tried to listen to the new song by Cindi Lauper and her rally cry to girls who just want to have fun -- he certainly wasn't opposed to that -- but the sound of her voice grated on him.

Decker swore if he heard Nena sing *99 Luftballons* one more time, he'd track her down himself and let a bullet end it. Music just didn't fit in Lebanon where fun was a remote concept. Dancing, singing, drinking and dining in

12

chic restaurants might have been part of Beirut nightlife when it was known as the Paris of the Middle East, but that was before the bullets started flying and the Green Line dividing Christian and Muslim territory became a no-man's land.

Instead, Beirut had become a world of snipers, including some who killed for sport. He'd heard about the laundry woman shot dead by one heartless gunman whose faith varied, depending on who was telling the story. The old woman was attempting to take down her white bedsheets and pillowcases from the clothesline she'd strung on the rubble-strewn roof of her apartment building. Twice she'd been agile enough to avoid the bullets that ripped chunks of concrete from the wall directly above her head. She had managed to snag two bedsheets and was attempting the pillowcases when a .50-cal. round took off most of her head. Pure madness. In Beirut, it was all-out war, 24-7.

After six years of military life, when the time came to re-up again or leave the service, Decker picked the latter. He was 28 and without a clue to where his life might take root. He could have returned to Pennsylvania but one of his Ranger buddies lived in Boston, Massachusetts so he thought he'd give it a whirl -- different city, new start, finish out his rehab for PTSD and battle wounds, get honorably discharged, fold away his uniform and find a job like the rest of the schmucks in his generation.

At least one thing was different. The girls he met in the Boston clubs seemed intrigued by his uniform, which was a complete reversal of the horror stories he had heard about troops returning from Vietnam. People had spit on those poor guys or tossed fake blood. So he took to wearing his tan desert cammies, often benefiting from free train and taxi rides, drinks, dinner and admission to dance clubs, not that he would ever ask for or want such favors. But it seemed to make people feel good to help a soldier. He was also given passes to movie theatres, Fenway Park, and several local museums, which is how he met Kaleigh Adams.

CHAPTER 4

August 1985
Boston, Massachusetts

A SUMMER HARVEST SURPRISE

A farmer found the body while working his field. It
was August. The young woman had been there nearly a week,
at least that's what the detectives guessed, and the corpse was
decomposing in the blistering heat, the stench overpowering.
The more experienced cops and EMTs had already dabbed
their nostrils with Vicks VapoRub to cut down the smell and
were waiting around for further instructions from the medical
examiner.

Rane knew two of the state cops and they
acknowledged each other's presence with a nod or mock
salute. Clutching his narrow, spiral-bound notepad, Rane
asked the medical examiner if he thought the victim had been
strangled with rope or twine because he had glimpsed the
furrows on her neck moments before investigators spread a
yellow plastic tarp over the body. These were ligature marks
in the parlance of those who deal with the dead.

"You weren't supposed to be here before the police,"
the medical examiner snarled, giving Rane a reprimanding
look before adding that nothing more would be known until
an autopsy was done. The procedure was scheduled for first
thing in the morning at the regional morgue just south of
Boston.

Rane persisted, asking whether any weapons had

14

been found. It was obvious that insects and small animals had already gotten to the body like some Discovery Channel special.

Rane asked, "Were there any indications who might have killed her?" It was a question designed to catch the medical examiner off guard and perhaps trick him into giving up a tidbit of information gleaned from the detectives. After all, Rane knew the medical examiner was there to determine how the woman died, not who might have killed her.

The medical examiner itched his bony chin thoughtfully. "I never said anybody killed her. You should leave before the police arrest you for trespassing at a crime scene."

"I thought you just said there was no crime."

"Don't put words in my mouth. I'm sure there will be a press conference of some sort for you folks later on."

Rane sensed it was time to leave before trouble descended. A uniformed state trooper in campaign hat and tall boots was marching his way with a pissed-off look on his face. Besides, it was already getting dark. He drove the 20 miles back downtown to the newspaper and filed a brief story with the night news editor. Rane's suggested headline: *Topsfield Farmer Finds Young Woman's Body While Harvesting Corn.*

Below the headline, he typed, By Rane Bryson, Tribune Staff.

The night editor looked up briefly from his desktop computer, took a drag off the cigarette that had been burning in the ashtray and cynically quipped, "Who gives a shit?"

Rane shrugged. "Not you, that's for sure."

"You got that right. Unless she's related to the fuckin' Kennedys, this story isn't going up front."

"Never underestimate the Kennedys when it comes to dead women."

"Go home, Bryson."

Rane already knew that a potential suburban murder story without any juicy details wasn't going on Page 1 and would likely find its place deep inside the tabloid next to a furniture ad. It was just another crime story and the paper was already full of them – robberies, drug killings, drive-by shootings, gang warfare, domestic violence. He knew from stories he'd written that there had been 211 murders in Massachusetts the previous year and the 1985 rate was already on track to surpass it.

Rane went home to sleep, feeling jittery as he closed his eyes and pictured the bloated woman in the red dress amid the healthy green cornstalks. He wondered who was looking for her right now, still expecting her to walk through the door with a bright smile, or to at least come home. She was about the same age as Kaleigh, who thankfully was only inches away, sleeping peacefully in his bed.

Two nights later there was a big tenement house fire in Roxbury, an impoverished neighborhood known mostly for its pimps, hookers, expensive cocaine and discount crack. Three people were killed – a father and two children. The bodies were badly burned.

Rane heard the story first-hand from two Boston firefighters he occasionally drank with at Nemo's -- a pleasantly rundown neighborhood bar in Eastie that was feeling the strains of gentrification. The place was a few blocks from his loft in a former industrial building. The firefighters who were on duty during the blaze said the bodies literally started falling apart as they were loaded onto the Stokes baskets. It was an ugly scene, they said - another tragedy, third-floor tenement, no fire escape, no sprinklers, no smoke alarms, no way to save them. Maybe they were sleeping and died of smoke inhalation, they said, at least that might be merciful, but who the fuck knows?

The bodies were brought to the regional morgue and placed on stainless tables in a refrigerated room alongside the dead woman from the cornfield. They were the latest corpses to arrive and were not yet stored in long metal drawers. Rane and the gaggle of print, radio and television reporters who routinely covered Boston's police and fire news referred to these victims and others like them as toe tags. Gallows humor was ever present among the jaded press corps.

16

The following morning, two pathology interns in their blue doctor scrubs were hunched over, holding their stomachs and vomiting into a plastic wastebasket. The way Rane heard it from one of his hospital snitches there had been competition over who would hold the basket. The young doctors had swung open the heavy doors, eager to cut and stitch, only to find the refrigeration had failed during the night and their fresh cadavers were now four mounds of glistening maggots.

By the time Rane arrived, a janitor was mopping up the mess on the hallway tiles but refused to enter the room. He had heard what lay beyond the door and asked his boss to call an exterminator. Twenty minutes later a lanky kid with greasy hair came strolling in with a spray tank harnessed to his back. He stunk of reefer, sweat and unwashed clothes.

"Got to give this place a double dose of my special mix," he explained proudly. "It's illegal. I could lose my license for it, but there ain't no way you're going to kill those fuckers if you don't double dose 'em."

The exterminator put on his mask and sprayed the room, then closed the door and taped on a warning sign.

Rane casually approached the interns, wondering if some wily defense lawyer would one day use the extermination to eliminate evidence. The intern still dabbing his chin with a handkerchief explained how he had tried to brush off the maggots with his clipboard. He wanted to see what was left of the young woman's face and neck without distraction. Dried blood had left her hair pasted to her scalp. It was hard to tell where one strand ended and another began. But it was obvious that a lock of hair had been removed with some sort of sharp instrument. He made Rane promise not to repeat what he had said. Rane vowed not to say a word about the missing tuft or their weak stomachs.

At Boston Police Department headquarters less than a mile from the Tribune, the typically busy squad of homicide detectives was sitting around, feet up on their desks, reading the daily newspapers. One detective wearing a shoulder holster was cleaning his .38 Special. He nodded to Rane and

17

went back to inspecting the revolver's shiny cylinders.

Rane had entered the squad room after climbing a back stairwell. He knew his way around the station because he could be trusted with sensitive information, unlike many of his journalistic colleagues who frequently burned bridges in the name of being first to break a story, then wondered why the cops shooed them away at every turn.

Rane was hoping for scuttlebutt because crime news travels like lightning through the law enforcement community. He had several pressing questions for Harry Simms, the captain of detectives, a thin, bespectacled man in his early 60s who'd been part of the bloodiest fighting in Europe during World War II and whom he'd come to respect in the three years since he began working at the Tribune.

Rane knew the Boston Police Department would not concern itself with a body found in a rural town 20 miles away. But somebody in the squad room might have heard from the state troopers who had gone to the scene. And if so, had those investigators identified the victim? Was anything known about her? Had there been any speculation on the cause of death?

Rane wanted to know because he needed a story and couldn't go back to the newsroom without something to write. He was well aware the smaller dailies on the North Shore would chase the dead-girl-found-in-field story and very often they beat their metropolitan rivals to the punch. In the rural areas, that sort of news made for more interesting reading than another report on the Grange meeting, dairy prices or the upcoming church fair.

"Nothing to get all fired up about, Geraldo," said Capt. Simms, referencing the mustachioed TV journalist Geraldo Rivera, an ongoing rub about Rane's blond hair, beard and moustache. "If nobody reports her missing from the city, then there's no use in us going out and busting our ass. Right now it's somebody else's problem."

"Thought you might have heard something," said Rane, who understood that Boston Police detectives generally stayed within their jurisdiction, which stopped at the city line.

18

The Suffolk County district attorney, whose office housed a unit of State Police major crime detectives, might take a mild interest, but because the body was found in abutting Essex County in the outlying town of Topsfield, the district attorney and state troopers from that jurisdiction would spearhead the investigation.

"Maybe you can ask the troopers yourself," said Capt. Simms. "We're waiting for three of them from Essex County to get here. There's a big bust going down this afternoon – joint narcotics task force. If they score, that'll get you some headlines."

Rane couldn't depend on it. If the bust didn't happen, he'd be scrambling. He was on his own and whatever story he found would be told in words without accompanying pictures -- unless the city editor at the tabloid cut loose a photographer from the grinding daily schedule of political favor grip-and-grins, chamber-of-commerce ribbon cuttings and pseudo events with little or no news value. Rane had witnessed how a photographer's time could be misspent on what he and other journalists called firing-squad photos – line 'em up and shoot 'em, mostly politicians armed with ceremonial shovels, fake handshakes and smiles, closing deals that meant nothing to the average reader – at least not to those who read the Tribune. Goddamn baby kissers. As the newsroom saying went, some of those politicians have attended more groundbreakings than a family of woodchucks.

Acting on a hunch, Rane rode his '71 Triumph Bonneville motorcycle back to the cornfield, where highways quickly become country roads, overhead lights are few and far between, and pieces of rusted farm machinery punctuate the tall grass near the fence lines. The farmer was there on his tractor. The ground was soft and the big green John Deere's tires left their impression in the crushed soil. Rane waved and approached but the farmer didn't immediately stop. Several minutes later he returned from the far end of the field, put the tractor in neutral, spat chewing tobacco and in a perplexed tone asked, "What the hell do you want?"

Rane broke into his I'm-no-city-slicker routine, doing his best to act like a country boy. The farmer seemed to buy it. He talked briefly about the weather and the sweet corn and then about the dead woman he had found. He was angry with the police. "How am I supposed to work my field when they got it all roped off down the far end with that yellow tape? And what for? She's not there anymore."

The yellow plastic crime scene tape was tied to the sturdiest cornstalks and created a generous perimeter around where the body was found. The farmer drank from a water jug, swished his mouth and spat out a stream.

"If she had lain there another couple of days, nature would have taken care of everything," he said without a hint of emotion.

The farmer drank again, rinsed and spat. He capped the jug, set it back of the seat and put the tractor into gear. The machine lurched forward. Rane stepped out of the path of the big tires. The farmer shifted again and without as much of a nod drove the snorting tractor down the sloping field. Rane watched him go, staring at the place amid the withering cornstalks where he had first spotted the body. It had been just a patch of vibrant color until he had stopped for a closer look – chalky blue arms and legs sticking out from a short red dress.

CHAPTER 5

September 1985
Boston, Massachusetts

BORN TO BE WILD

The sun was strong, the air windless, and Rane's white Oxford shirt with the sleeves rolled up was soaked through the back. He fired up his Triumph in the Tribune parking lot and waited for Paige to tuck her extra camera lenses into a small backpack. It was a slow news day so the city editor had instructed them to cruise the streets looking for possible stories. Rane interpreted streets as anything paved, which included the roads leading out of the city and into the countryside. After two hours of fruitlessly searching Boston's neighborhoods, Rane steered the bike north over the Tobin Bridge. They inhaled the salty air, refreshing compared to the city smog with its diesel fumes, smokestacks and gridlocked traffic.

Paige had her arms wrapped around Rane's chest. She shouted above the road noise. "Do you think we should be getting this far out of the city? What if something big happens?"

"Our instructions were to phone in every two hours, even if nothing is brewing. So that's what we'll do. And if they ask where we are, we'll say on our way back to the newsroom unless they want us to keep cruising."

Rane stopped the bike at a gas station and used a payphone to call the city editor. "Find a story and get pictures," the man said grouchily. Rane hung up and saluted the phone. "We're good," he announced to Paige, gesturing for her to climb aboard. "Let's have some fun in the sun."

Rane roared north onto Interstate 95, then exited for Route 133 that would take them along the back roads through the quaint New England towns of Rowley, Essex and Ipswich. It was pushing 90 degrees when they pulled into the Windy Tavern, a biker bar known regionally for its funky neon signs, fresh clams, cold beer and panoramic ocean views. The bar was perched on a hill overlooking acres of tall grass leading down to the sea, and living up to its name, the wind was blowing through the unpaved parking lot in warm gusts.

"Come here often?"

"Absolutely," said Rane. "Can't beat the ambiance created by tattooed and toothless bikers playing darts and eating broken glass."

"So I should thank you for bringing me here?"

"Consider it a once-in-a-lifetime experience, which is what I thought it would be until I started coming here every few weeks."

The interior of the Windy Tavern was actually a comfortable drinking establishment and in midafternoon was nearly empty with the exception of two biker couples seated in a cushioned booth along the windows. The walls were painted green with varnished wood trim, the ceilings tall, the U-shaped bar both efficient and social. Rane ordered two Budweisers. Nobody paid special attention to Rane and Paige who wore what in the Windy Tavern might be considered city clothes.

Rane couldn't stop thinking about the dead woman in the cornfield, whoever she was, currently laying supine in a metal drawer and labeled Unknown Homicide Victim.

It had taken him two weeks of cajoling and cashing in favors to get an unofficial, abridged and redacted copy of the autopsy report because the information was sealed as part of the ongoing murder investigation. Answers to questions he had asked the first day were all affirmative. The woman

22

had been sexually assaulted – slashed in the stomach and upper thighs and choked with some sort of twine or wire. But what had killed her was something long and pointed, more like a filet knife or an icepick. When he pressed the media spokesman for the Essex County district attorney for details, he got the expected "no comment." At that point, Rane had lost his cool and accused the spokesman of being irresponsible and unconcerned both about the dead woman and the public's right to know there was a killer on the loose. "What good is a spokesman who doesn't speak?" he had snarled.

Rane had been equally unpleasant to the medical examiner, insinuating that the older man had perhaps worked the job too long and outlived his usefulness.

"What's with you? The girl was too old to be a runaway," the coroner had angrily responded. "Judging by her tattoos and the track marks on her arms, she was probably a working girl and I'll bet her pimp isn't going to report her missing. But if you go and write what I just said, I'll make sure you lose your job. The people of your generation just have no respect."

Paige could see Rane was lost in thought as he gazed out the big picture windows to the sea. "Let me in," she said.

"Sorry, Willi. I've just been pissed off that the cops won't talk about that girl in the field. Even Andy Mac has been quiet," he said, referring to one of his closest police sources. "That tells me there's something more to it."

Paige raised her bottle. "To the girl in the cornfield," she said. "Whoever she may be."

"No, to you, Willi."

"Why to me?"

"Because you and I are so much alike it's scary. Tormented by the same demons, I guess. Just think about the people we work with. Would any of them cut out on a beautiful day to take a ride in the country and drink a few beers?

"Probably not."

"Definitely not. That's why you're the best."

"You've got a special place in my heart as well," she answered, clinking their bottles together. "I guess that means we should probably get a couple shots of tequila."

Rane laughed, leaned in and kissed her on the forehead.

"That's all I get, a kiss on the forehead? Who the fuck are you, the Pope?"

"Bless you, my daughter," he jested, making the sign of the cross on her forehead with his thumb.

Paige gave him a peck on the lips, which he returned with a quick probing kiss. "That's better," she said. "Let's get that tequila."

One of the bikers' girlfriends wandered over toward the jukebox. "You know what we want to hear," her boyfriend commanded.

The girl, no older than eighteen, grinned mischievously. "Definitely," she said, dropping coins into the machine. Seconds later, Madonna could be heard belting out *Physical Attraction*, which only seemed to emphasize the connection between Rane and Paige who used the moment to stare deeply into each other's eyes. But the song selection caused uproar at the booth. The biker scowled. "What the fuck did you just play? What kind of shit is that?"

The girl giggled. "It's Madonna. Just try and listen."

"I don't want to listen to that shit." He shook his head and banged his beer bottle on the table so that the contents sloshed over the rim.

When the song was over, the jukebox came alive with *Burning Up* from the same album, further incensing the biker who strutted to the jukebox and kicked it with his heavy black Harley Davidson boots until the needle skidded across the record and the song stopped.

"Happy now," he growled. The girl folded her arms in protest.

The biker dropped several coins into the slot. "Let's hear some real music."

The jukebox did as instructed by playing Twisted Sister's *Live to Ride, Ride to Live,* Meatloaf's *Bat out of Hell* and Judas Priest's *Freewheel Burning*. The songs seemed to put the bikers in a better mood. The playlist ended with Steppenwolf's *Born to be Wild* and the two men sang along out of tune, encouraging their girlfriends to join them.

After three beers and two tequilas, Rane and Paige were in happy mode. Rane again called the news desk. Luckily the assignment board was still clean. He promised to check in again as scheduled, saying he was nearby, just west of the city at the Newton line and listening to the police-fire radio.

Out at the front entrance of the Windy Tavern, the westerly wind was a blast furnace, picking up heat as it moved over the land toward the ocean. The temperature was approaching three digits. Rane took off his shirt and stuffed it into one of the saddlebags. He gave Paige a full-tooth smile and strummed an air guitar, singing a mumbled rendition of *Born to be Wild*.

Paige laughed. "Let's ride."

A mile down the single-lane road flanked by cornfields and uncut hay, Rane pulled the bike off the shoulder, kicked off his leather loafers, removed his khaki trousers and underwear and stood there naked.

"Well?"

"Well, what?"

Rane strummed the air guitar. "Born to be…."

"Please, spare me," Paige said, cutting him off. "You really want to do this?"

Paige yanked her sleeveless lime green halter top over her head, unclipped her bra and shimmied her small breasts. "The things I do for," she said.

Rane shook his head in approval.

"What?"

"More, Willi."

Paige wiggled out of her ankle-high boots and black stretch pants.

Rane clucked his tongue and swept an arm along the horizon. Not a farm or house was in sight for what seemed miles in all directions.

"Come on, Willi. Be part of the wildlife."

Paige removed her panties and twirled them around her finger. Rane's eyebrows rose. He collected their clothing, stuffed as much as possible into the saddlebags and tied Paige's pack to the seat backrest.

"Let's do it," Rane said, hopping on the bike. He fired up the throaty Triumph.

Paige got on the bike and coiled her arms around him. She was thrilled that they were naked.

"Don't we need our helmets?"

"Fuck the helmets," he said.

The bike took off like a rocket, purring along the country road, the hot wind caressing their bodies. The road dipped and climbed, the bike leaning into each curve as Rane expertly adjusted the throttle. He let out a rebel yell and Paige echoed it.

"Thanks," Paige shouted into his ear.

"For what?"

"For doing this. If it wasn't for you, I'd never know what this feels like to ride naked." She held on tight and playfully grabbed a few strands of his sparse blond chest hair.

Rane pushed the throttle and the bike responded, hitting 80 mph on the straightaways and ramping back on the corners. It was dangerous and exhilarating. Paige pressed her nipples into his bare back as they rode. They were both sweating and sticky. Rane was first to spot the tractor and hay wagon heading toward them. "We've got company."

Paige stiffened. "What?"

"Hay wagon."

Paige burst out laughing, raised her arms over her head and let out a whoop.

The bike blew past the tractor driven by an old man and what was likely his grandson. Both marveled at the sight of the naked, good-looking couple barreling past on a motorcycle.

Rane slowed and steered the bike onto the dirt shoulder. "Do you think they know your parents?"

"Fuck you," she said, appreciating his sarcasm.

Paige got off the bike and started pulling her clothes from the saddlebag but Rane stopped her. He extended a hand and she clasped it, following him into the field. In seconds they were rolling atop the prickly hay. Rane lay on his back, ignoring the discomfort. Paige kneeled between his legs and took him in her mouth. He was already hard as she crawled forward, arched her back and slid down onto him. Paige thrust her hips until she knew Rane was no longer in control and rotated them until he came inside her. At those moments, she felt he would always be hers. She wanted them to last forever.

The sound of a motor wafted across the fields. "I think I hear a car," she said.

"So what? They can't see us in here."

"Our clothes. My cameras. They're on the bike. If I lose my cameras, I'm done."

Paige ran toward the parked Triumph and dressed faster than a firefighter. Rane was still naked, standing in the field, arms raised to the sun.

"You're going to get sunburned in certain places and believe me, you'll wish you hadn't."

Rane reluctantly got dressed. A few miles down the road they found a phone booth outside a country store that was advertising sweet corn and cold beer.

"We should get a sixpack."

Paige shook her head. "We've had enough," she said. "Call the newsroom and make sure we still have jobs."

As it turned out, the city editor was anticipating Rane's call. Paige had forgotten to check her beeper.

"Drive-by shooting in Roxbury. Two dead. You better get down there," the man on the other end of the line gruffly advised.

"On it," said Rane. "Can you give me the address?"

"Thought you were listening to the police radio?"

"I heard it, but the transmission was garbled. We're on our way."

The city editor passed along the address of the shooting. Rane knew he was at least 45 minutes, maybe more, from the crime scene. He called the spokesman for Suffolk County District Attorney Joe Sanders and milked a few details, but it was evident the media guy was holding a grudge from their previous conversation when Rane had demanded information that wasn't contained in the press release.

The cops and the crime scene tape were still at the scene when Rane shut down the bike. Paige immediately began shooting. Rane begged one of the Boston cops he knew to let Paige through the yellow tape so that she could get a shot of the chalked body outlines and the numbered plaques that identified the location of each spent shell casing. Paige knew it wasn't a Pulitzer, but it was better than returning to the newsroom with nothing.

"We're fucked," she said.

"No, we're not. Be thankful that our competitors are frightened of this neighborhood. They'll be waiting to be spoon fed by the DA's office. We'll talk to some neighbors, get some quotes and photos, and it'll look like we were here when the gangbangers were unloading."

Rane had the police radio pressed against his ear when Paige shouted his name.

"What did you say?"

Paige smiled at him. "I love you."

CHAPTER 6

October 1985
Marblehead, Massachusetts

DEATH WORE A COSTUME ON HALLOWEEN

It was Halloween, which in New England can mean a balmy evening of costumed fun and frolicking for thousands of children and teenagers, or a frozen precursor to winter that keeps everybody inside.

As the cops say, weather is the best policeman.

Only this year, it was 70-plus degrees and people were crowding the beaches, mostly to stroll, picnic or exercise their dogs. When Rane heard the coded call come over the police radio in the newsroom, he waved to Paige and they headed straight for Marblehead, a well-to-do coastal town about 40 minutes north, filled with pedigreed Yankees, new money, recreational sailors and commercial fishermen.

At first it sounded routine. Man walking dog finds body on beach. Not something they hadn't heard before. But a buzz was already channeling through the small town, with coffee shop rumors and those she-couldn't-possibly-be-from-here comments often made by people convinced that crime will never set foot in their privileged community. There was no shortage of moronic comments, including, "Maybe it was just a Halloween stunt" and "I used to be a nurse, did they check her pulse?"

The victim was a young woman – mid-twenties, long dark hair, naked, badly bruised. She had washed in with the tide at Devereux Beach, the sea bottom apparently rattled loose by an earlier coastal storm. Her body had been weighted with two 20-pound Danforth anchors and about 10 feet of galvanized chain. A single lobster trap with a tri-colored buoy and coil of seaweed-coated pot warp line was woven into the tangled mess, preventing the anchor tines from gripping the sea bottom. The storm had done the rest.

The State Police and a few Marblehead cops were spreading a plastic tarp over the body when Paige and Rane arrived. Paige got some decent photos with a 300mm telephoto lens, detailed shots but not so graphic the editors would shy away from publishing them. The usual gawkers were there, trying to get as close as possible to the body, thrilled and frightened at the same time. The body was coated with sand and seaweed, the skin a bluish tone.

Sgt. Andre Macusovich, a massive state trooper and homicide detective in his early 40s assigned to the Essex County district attorney's office, scowled as Paige and Rane approached. "Get the fuck out of here," he barked.

"Just visiting," Rane said with a smirk.

"Then at least wait over by my cruiser. You guys are like fuckin' buzzards." He shook his head in distain at Paige's pink mini-skirt, leopard-spotted blouse, faded denim jacket, fishnet stockings and Doc Marten boots. His unspoken question was readily apparent: What the fuck are you supposed to be?

Paige brushed back her cropped flaxen hair, the streaky purple highlights catching the sun, and returned the state trooper's comment with a sassy smile. Half an hour later, with at least ten local uniformed cops cordoning off the beach, the medical examiner's black panel truck arrived. Four EMTs and paramedics who had responded to the scene by ambulance along with the Fire Department set the body in a Stokes basket, carried it to the parking lot and set it atop a gurney. The stretcher wheels dug into the sand, making it difficult to roll, but the body was eventually placed inside the medical examiner's truck. It was all quite the show, the news helicopters whirling overhead getting the best footage.

Several newspaper photographers and TV cameramen from the metro and regional stations were on scene, taking B roll and recording whatever comments locals and potential witnesses were dumb enough to offer. The story had some sizzle because it was creepy and had happened on Halloween in a wealthy community where crime was a rarity.

Macusovich, known to his friends as Andy Mac, ignored the reporters who thrust their microphones and spiral-bound notepads toward him, demanding comment. He had no patience for them. In fact, if it were not illegal, he would break their cameras over their heads and kick their asses all the way back to Boston or wherever else they came from. Paige and Rane were waiting near the trunk of his unmarked cruiser.

"Not much I can tell you," he said, punching Rane roughly in the shoulder with his massive fist, an odd sign of affection.

Macusovich and Rane had tiptoed around each other when they first met at a series of crime scenes nearly three years ago. The muscular, gruff-tempered trooper had mockingly labeled the blond-bearded news reporter Rane from Maine, suggesting the unruly facial hair made him look like a Down East hillbilly. Rane had bought him a Dunkin' Donuts coffee that he reluctantly accepted. It turned out they shared a passion for motorcycles, handguns and military history, and Rane often felt the barriers breaking down as they discussed Caesar, Grant, Rommel, Patton. Their last talk a few weeks earlier ended in argument over the lax security that had led to the deaths of hundreds of U.S. Marines in a barracks bombing in Beirut. The two-year anniversary of that dark day in 1983 had just passed.

During that conversation, Rane had asked his police detective friend, "Who the fuck was watching the gate when those two ragheads came barreling through with their explosives-packed truck screaming God is Great or Allah Akbar or whatever the fuck it is they yell?"

Macusovich was an ex-Marine and, as the saying goes, there's no such thing -- once a Marine, always a

Marine. So he wasn't about to criticize the sentries. Better to blame the intelligence community for its failure to warn the troops of impending danger.

But today the subject wasn't military strategy. It was current events -- the body of a young woman on the beach tangled in boat anchors, chain and seaweed.

"She might have drowned from the weight holding her underwater, but my guess is she was dead before she went over the side. The lab will be able to tell," said Macusovich. "We're talking to the harbormaster and as many fisherman as possible. We want to know if any of them happened to notice anything unusual out on the water recently."

"Any ID?"

"Nothing -- at least not yet. We'll try for dental records. One thing's for sure, somebody's missing a couple of anchors. And hey, fuckhead, don't print that."

Rane's story and the least graphic of Paige's photos ran in the next day's paper, but the story was buried deep inside, sharing space with a couple of department store ads. Most of the reporters and editors respectfully referred to Paige as Paige One because her skillful images frequently appeared on the front page of the tabloid.

A newsroom joke, started by Rane, went that her folks lived in a log hut in Appalachia and were so illiterate they couldn't spell Page, hence dooming her to work as a photographer instead of a writer. She had countered that his parents were such backwoods Maine inbreds they actually believed Rane was the correct way to spell the word for water falling from clouds. And so it went, the two of them busting on each other day in, day out, more like brother and sister than co-workers, thoroughly enjoying each other's company.

The onslaught of winter in early November cut short any further exploration of the sea bottom off Marblehead, so the body remained at the regional morgue like the others, labeled Unknown Homicide Victim with a numbered toe tag.

The foul weather also pushed people indoors, so Nemo's was packed on weeknights as well as weekends. Rane occasionally met up with Kaleigh at the bar after work,

32

which for her was anytime after 6 p.m., unless the museum was holding a special evening event. It was difficult to know when Rane's workday might end, the deadlines frequently shifting with breaking news and the gathering of updated details for stories already published. When not at Nemo's they hung out at Rane's apartment with its loft layout and plate glass windows. Kaleigh liked the place far better than the tiny box she rented with two other young women in Back Bay, home of blueblood New Englanders who seemed to scowl at anyone who dared a sidewalk greeting. She stayed overnight at Rane's so often that many pieces of her clothing were now in his bedroom closet. The thought of their clothes sharing the same space made her smile. In some ways, it felt like they were married, or at least living together. Rane sometimes referred to the two of them as the OMC or old married couple. It had been well over a year since they'd first met at a party and immediately fell into lust. Kaleigh stayed at Rane's apartment that first night and didn't leave for three days, during which they'd made rapturous love, listened to music, ordered a stream of takeout, caught up on work and then repeated the cycle. By the time she left, she'd almost forgotten what it was like to put on clothes, content to wear nothing more than one of his white, button-down Oxford shirts. She'd never gotten serious about someone with such a wild streak. In fact, she'd never met a young man whose passion for living brought such thrills and danger. Her past lovers were boys from her Connecticut high school and those in college, after which she dated a string of suitors who mostly bored her to tears. And then Rane had come along and everything was different. She'd never felt so in love. He might be a bit on the crazy side, like the night they broke into an abandoned state asylum because Rane wanted to have a look around, but there was never any question whether life with him would be exciting. It promised a rollercoaster ride. Besides, she thought he was undeniably handsome and his flair for the dramatic had become the topic of many conversations among the crowd at Nemo's as well as in the newsroom.

Kaleigh knew her parents would certainly disapprove, especially if they knew he drove a motorcycle and had a handgun that he was licensed to carry. Didn't she understand that the only acceptable suitors were doctors, estate lawyers, successful stockbrokers or, better still, trust fund offspring of the most established families who could give her elevated social standing and financial security in one sweet package?

Whenever Kaleigh's thoughts wandered in that direction, she felt compelled to head downtown to Filene's Basement and buy the sexiest lingerie on the rack, intending to solidify her relationship with Rane and make him want her like no other woman. She was determined not to become the boring, freckle-faced girl next door who rode English saddle and played tennis like a pro but hadn't a thought in her head beyond easy-to-cook recipes and picking out baby names. And just to make sure she was on the right track, she often did things to surprise herself, and perhaps Rane even more. She didn't want to be just another couple like so many others she knew, young men and women already following the course their parents had taken, enmeshed in roles that put him in the living room drinking beer and watching football with the guys every Friday night while she made popcorn and pizza and chit-chatted in the kitchen with their spouses and girlfriends. She wanted more than that and promised herself if it didn't happen, she wouldn't be to blame. Some days, it seemed to be working, especially when she stretched her imagination and her daring.

A few weeks earlier, she had used her key to enter Rane's apartment for the first time, the one he'd handed her in a manner that seemed somewhat reluctant, as though it might not be such a smart idea. Kaleigh let herself in and efficiently prepared two shrimp cocktails, an elaborate fruit salad and chilled a bottle of respectable champagne. She lit candles throughout the living room, arranged throw pillows and blankets on the couch, and piped some of his favorite jazz music through the apartment's six speakers. When Rane arrived shortly after 9 p.m., she met him at the door completely naked, holding two glasses of champagne, and the look in his eyes left no doubt she'd made a lasting impression. They wasted no time making love on the couch and, with their sexual hunger sated and appetites aroused they devoured the shrimp and salad. As they finished the champagne, Rane talked about his day at the paper. He was obsessed with reporting on the most recent murder story and she listened attentively, disappointed when he didn't seem interested in how she'd spent her hours at the museum.

Nonetheless, riding the tide of victory, she'd orchestrated another special event the following Friday night at his apartment, including a bubble bath for two and a hot-oil massage for him. She spent a chunk of her weekly paycheck on a bottle Chateauneuf de Pape that she was sure he'd appreciate. The French red wine gave them a buzz and Kaleigh found herself talking far more than Rane, then wondering if she'd talked too much or whether he simply wasn't interested in what she had to say. Sometimes she wondered if he listened to her at all.

When Rane announced he was going to Chicago on short notice for a journalism seminar on organized crime and then to Miami for a weeklong investigative reporter's conference in February, Kaleigh felt sad but imagined how strongly they'd pine for each other in mutual absence. After all, wasn't it true that absence makes the heart grow fonder? She'd never been able to accept the out-of-sight, out-of-mind perspective. Love conquered all, she thought. She was convinced he'd miss her like crazy, even while basking in the Florida sunshine while she slogged through Boston's ice and snow.

CHAPTER 7

January 1986
Boston, Massachusetts

THE DAY JENNY LEHMAN DISAPPEARED

She had long dark hair, bright white teeth, big lively brown eyes, a backpack slung over her shoulder and a bulging suitcase at her side. Luddy Pugano pulled the dark blue Ford Crown Vic to the curb where dozens of Logan Airport passengers were craning their necks waiting for rides. He wondered if she would notice his car had no city taxi medallion affixed to the trunk lid, no name or telephone number stenciled on the doors. A magnetic, three-dimensional sign on the roof spelled TAXI and a spotlight was attached to the driver's door.

Luddy put on his most winning smile, which he sensed made him look somewhat boyish and non-threatening, wondering if he still smelled like clams and fish guts from his hours in the seafood market. He was self-conscious about the odor and his temper flared whenever the guys from the neighborhood called him Shucker, or occasionally You Mother Shucker. He rolled down the passenger window and flashed a sincere smile. "Your lucky day. I was just about to call it quits and then you came out."

Luddy did a quick assessment of the woman – educated and rich, judging by the expensive puffy down jacket, Tufts University sweatshirt, purposefully tattered jeans and Frye cowboy boots. She was probably a bit flakey, definitely more flower child than business type, which meant she would be more likely to trust him.

"Hop in and enjoy the ride," he said, trying his best at being charming while watching her every move in the rearview mirror as she climbed into the back seat. He tossed her suitcase in the trunk and headed for the exit. He often made small talk with passengers, though some didn't seem to appreciate it.

Jenny Lehman gave him the address of her apartment near the Tufts campus in Medford and began searching the contents of her backpack.

"Heading back to school?"

"Yes."

"Did you enjoy your Christmas break?"

"I did. My family and I went to the Bahamas. It was lovely."

"Never been there myself, but it sounds beautiful. Must be 1,200 miles from here, maybe more."

"Oh, I'm not sure. That's the problem with flying. You don't get a sense of what's between where you took off from and where you landed. There's no journey, if you get what I mean."

Luddy imagined her on the beach in a string bikini, lying in the pink sand, drinking some sort of coconut rum beverage while soaking up the sun. He envisioned himself in a white linen suit, pant legs fashionably rolled up, walking barefoot along the water's edge to where she lay relaxed, the palm fronds rustling in the breeze. In his mind, she motioned for him to join her beneath the trees where she dropped her bathing suit and ran into the surf. Luddy saw himself toss the linen suit aside and strut casually to the water. Soon they were frolicking in the waves until he was hard enough to enter her. He tried to hold that thought but couldn't stop wondering whether the beach sand would make doing it uncomfortable or even painful for both of them. He had no experience in beach sex.

Jenny Lehman knew it was usually a half-hour ride from the airport to her apartment in Medford on the rim of the campus, maybe a few minutes longer with traffic. When she looked up from her notebook filled with scribbling that promised to help her pass the upcoming biology exam, she noticed the steel girders of the Tobin Bridge.

"Why are we heading north across the bridge? Medford is the other way," she asked.

Luddy was shaken from his reverie. The dark-haired girl had just been telling him how much she loved him, begging him to take her there in the waves. "This is actually a shortcut," he said. "There are some big detours tonight because of the snow and several accidents, but this will get us there faster."

Luddy focused on her face in the mirror, his dark, deep-set eyes unblinking. She thought the direction of travel odd but didn't seem suspect, at least not until the dark blue sedan veered off the highway near the north end of the bridge and zigzagged into an industrial neighborhood of cargo containers, oil tanks, cranes and other machinery.

Before she could say another word, Luddy was out of the car and opening the back door. In seconds he was on top of her, his thick, sausage-like fingers pressed over her mouth while he slipped a cord around her neck. She kicked and tried to scream but the cord kept growing tighter. In those painful last moments, Jenny Lehman saw her father's face, urging her to pay attention to her whereabouts at all times and be less trusting because not everyone is filled with love and goodness. Was this precisely the fate he worried so much about? Was it really happening and not just a bad dream? Would she never see her family again? The body atop her was heavy, pinning her to the car seat. She caught a whiff of fish as she suffocated.

When she no longer breathed, Luddy removed her boots, jeans and underwear and felt himself inside her. He lay atop her warm body for what seemed an eternity but was actually less than five minutes, inhaling her flowery perfume. He savored the moment, thinking if he had asked for a date, she would have laughed in his face as so many other women had. Oh, come on, fat boy. Who you kidding? You've got a zero chance in hell with a girl like that. She's a rich bitch and you're a poor, ignorant slob who rakes clams, sells fish bait and drives a gypsy cab.

Maybe so, he thought, but now she's mine. My Little Beach Blossom.

Luddy ejaculated inside the woman, eyes shut tight, his mind on a beach in the Bahamas. Semen spilled onto his trousers and the backseat blanket as he withdrew. Panic set in unexpectedly. Sure, he was always on the prowl, looking for opportunities, but it was late in the day and most of the busy flights had already landed. He hadn't expected to come across a sweet hippie chick whose naiveté was her death sentence. He had to get rid of the body. But he wasn't going to repeat what had happened three months ago off Marblehead where he was less familiar with the waters. That woman, whom he now thought of as Nature Girl, had fought desperately, deeply scratching his face until she was knocked out by a flurry of heavy punches. He had thought she was going to be an easy mark. She'd been taking pictures along the East Boston waterfront and offered him $100 on the spot to take her out to photograph seabirds – what Luddy assumed were purple-peckered pelicans or something of the sort. She hadn't even made a call to anyone, just climbed aboard his skiff at the dock like it was the most natural thing to do. She even complimented him on his cabin cruiser once they reached the harbor mooring and clambered aboard, telling him her father's yacht had the same warm and lustrous interior wood. Luddy considered selling her expensive Nikon cameras and telephoto lens to a local pawnbroker, but in the end he decided to toss the equipment overboard. It seemed such a waste.

Luddy was breathing heavily as he glanced around the derelict industrial waterfront but there was nobody in sight. This certainly isn't yacht-clubby Marblehead where Nature Girl went over the side, he said to himself. No Ralph Lauren designer clothes in this hood.

Droplets of sweat had beaded on his face despite the chill temperature. He zipped his pants and stuffed the woman's cowboy boots, jeans and underwear into a paper grocery sack.

Luddy had parked the Crown Vic within the dark shadows cast by the towering steel oil tanks. He could hear the nearby docks creaking with the tide and it settled his mood. This was Eastie -- home turf. He knew every alley, bar and backroom, every street punk, wannabe gangster, made OC guy, bookie and bartender. It was in most respects a closed community. Across the harbor a different story was being played out as tall cranes gave birth to glitzy highrises and swank hotels in downtown Boston, but in Eastie things were grittier, the crime and violence an everyday occurrence, the residents tired and frustrated from being just out of reach of the American Dream.

Luddy stumbled toward the dock, clamored into his small skiff and pulled the outboard cord. Nothing. Maybe it was the change in temperature causing condensation within the fuel tank, but for whatever reason the outboard on the aluminum tender had proven difficult to start ever since the winter's first snowstorm.

Once he had the outboard running he left it idling, tied to the pier in the dark. The woman's body was heavy considering she was so petite. The corpse seemed as though it had stiffened, but Luddy knew it was too soon after death for that to occur. Maybe his mind was playing tricks, he thought. Maybe the release he had felt minutes earlier had left him low on energy and mentally clouded. He had hoped to enjoy the sated feeling longer but he had to get rid of the body before first light. He rolled her in the worn wool blanket that had covered the back seat of the cab and dragged her to the water's edge. Her body thumped into the bottom of the skiff and he quietly puttered out toward his battered wooden cabin cruiser moored in the harbor.

Luddy was proud of the boat, his floating second home that he named *Sea Bitch*, the letters stenciled across the transom. He told himself this lovely dark-haired young woman, this Beach Blossom, would have enjoyed being aboard, if only things were different. Maybe she would have sunbathed nude on the deck and made him breakfast in the small galley. They could have had fresh-brewed coffee and slices of warm Italian bread slathered with butter. He could have taught her how to catch striper or maybe even a yellow-fin tuna. And he certainly could have shown her how to shuck clams with the short, stiff blade. He even imagined her as his date for New Year's Eve, which had come and gone a few weeks earlier. But like all New Year's Eves, he'd sat home with his mother, Celeste, in their cramped apartment, she insisting he drink a shot of anisette followed by a small glass of golden liquor in which fresh cherries had marinated for more than a year. On their small television, they'd watched the ball drop in Times Square as they ate an entire plate of Italian pastries, with Luddy hogging the cannoli. That night in the cramped apartment, he vowed to end the tradition, one way or another. Next year would be different.

The college girl's body lay sprawled in the cockpit, partially covered by the blanket. Getting her over the gunwale wasn't easy. By the time he finished, Luddy was again huffing and puffing. He went below, sat at the galley's fold-down wood table and poured himself a plastic tumbler of cheap vodka mixed with lemonade. He knew it was a mistake but he needed a drink badly. He made a second one, greedily gulped it and fell asleep on the settee. When he awoke two hours later, he was shivering cold. He opened the sliding door to the cockpit where a light snow was falling and looked down at the teak floor. The woman's eyes and mouth were open but she hadn't moved. He physically shrank back in fear, taking a few seconds to realize she was dead.

Sometime after midnight he steered the cabin cruiser toward the open sea, past Boston Harbor Light on Little Brewster Island where chunks of ice floated with the tide and he continued southeast toward Stellwagen Bank. When he was well beyond the shallow bank he threw her puffy jacket, cowboy boots and other clothing overboard, cutting them to shreds with his filet knife. He snipped a lock of her hair and cut the Tufts University sweatshirt into rags. Then he went to work on her body -- hands, feet, head, then arms, legs, torso in pieces. It was more difficult than he had remembered, particularly cutting through the bones with a hacksaw. It gave him new respect for the butcher he talked to nearly every day in the meat market near the waterfront. The man's white apron was always spattered with blood, the knives and cleavers gleaming under the florescent lights.

The cockpit was a bloody mess, but after a few hours, the body was gone along with the knives and hacksaw. He had slashed the blanket into strips and tossed that over the side as well, then swabbed the deck with soapy seawater and bleach. As the sun crept over the horizon, he tightly held the small crucifix around his neck and prayed the sharks, crabs, lobsters and other marine life would devour every bit of this woman who never would have dated him or invited him to her home. Goodbye my Beach Blossom, he sing-songed aloud before praying the boat's aging engine would not stall because he had no anchors to keep from drifting.

Shucking clams at the waterfront market later that morning, he kept a close eye on the TV news, concerned there might be a missing person story. But there was only coverage of the space shuttle that had blown apart moments before takeoff from Cape Canaveral in Florida, killing all seven astronauts aboard, including first-ever teacher-in-space Christa McAuliffe. The spacecraft had exploded over the ocean, the horror televised live for the world to see.

The Chyron generator on the TV screen made it clear in white letters that this was Jan. 28, 1986, as though trying to burn the date in the minds of viewers. President Reagan was shown repeatedly, offering his condolences to the families of the dead.

"We've grown used to wonders in this century. It's hard to dazzle us. But for 25 years the United States space program has been doing just that. We've grown used to the idea of space, and perhaps we forget that we've only just begun. We're still pioneers. They, the members of the Challenger crew, were pioneers," the President reassured the

42

nation in his melodic Hollywood voice.

Since the launch had been televised live, the President also felt he had to address any trauma it might have caused to those watching. So he continued,

"And I want to say something to the schoolchildren of America who were watching the coverage of the shuttle's takeoff. I know it is hard to understand, but sometimes, painful things like this happen. It's all part of the process of exploration and discovery. It's all part of taking a chance and expanding man's horizons. The future doesn't belong to the fainthearted; it belongs to the brave. The Challenger crew was pulling us into the future, and we'll continue to follow them."

Luddy craned his neck to see the snowy television screen. "More feed for the fishes," he remarked to nobody in particular as he fileted a heavy haddock, staring back into its impenetrable eyes.

That evening, exhausted from lack of sleep but still in overdrive, Luddy went to Mass at the Most Holy Redeemer Church in Maverick Square, inhaling the incense while basking in the quiet and the warm candlelight glow. He kneeled and reflexively made the Sign of the Cross, recalling his years as an altar boy when, like the priests, he was on stage and somehow closer to God. Each time the Sanctus bells chimed, he felt an electric current race through his body and he secretly hoped one of the older priests would say the words in Latin, that mystical tongue he yearned to hear as an altar boy. He was angry when the Catholic Church did away with Latin in favor of what he recognized as a bunch of folk-singing wimps. Guitars had no place on the altar, only bells and chimes. Still, the priests – even the non-traditional ones who seemed not to care about their frocks and collars -- were always kind, appreciative of his presence at Mass, just as the elementary school nuns had singled him out for praise because his knowledge of geography was unrivaled among his classmates. Oceans. Deserts. Fields. Lakes. Rivers. Marshes. Mountains. All these places were so different, yet so magical. He knew the names of at least 60 countries and facts about their culture, climate, economy, government and, of course, geography. It could have been such a beautiful world, but it wasn't, at least not for Luddy who told himself God had spent six days creating each and every person and place, a grand story that made his Bible sing, and then gone on to ruin it all on the very last day by introducing Eve.

The creation of women had destroyed everything, tainted everything, he thought. Would God accept a blood sacrifice in return for remaking the world without Eve? Other religions certainly did. The Aztecs killed dozens of virgins each year, cutting out their hearts with jade or onyx knives and letting their blood spill down the sides of stepped pyramids.

Sister Mary Margaret had told everyone at the school that Luddy had a real knack for geography, for memorizing countries, reading maps and learning about all the special places in the world. She had singled him out and he relished the attention, feeling his self-pride swell whenever she entered a room in a swirl of white nun's habit. But all that had changed one day when he told her how Father Gallagher had hurt him. First she said she didn't want to hear about it and then insisted he must be mistaken, that the Holy Father would never do such a thing. Then she called him a liar. After that day, she no longer mentioned Luddy's ability to read maps, nor did she ever praise him again for any accomplishment. If he raised his hand in class, she wouldn't call on him. And whenever he stood to say he needed to use the toilet, she ordered him to sit down, be quiet and pray to God for the ability to control his bowels.

CHAPTER 8

January 1986
Boston, Massachusetts

SATURDAY MUSINGS

State Police Detective Lt. Hannah Summers felt the
hair rise almost imperceptibly on the back of her neck as she
lay on the couch reading the missing-person report on Jenny
Lehman who was last seen at Logan Airport days earlier.

The story sounded eerily familiar. Summers had
begun tracking possible abductions and missing person
cases involving women in the Boston metropolitan area soon
after joining the State Police unit in Suffolk County. She
felt an affinity with these victims, perhaps because she was
under 30, attractive, intelligent, trained in self-defense and
convinced it was possible to avoid such a fate. She tossed
the report into her leather bag on the upholstered chair
and promised herself she'd write copious notes on how an
undeniable pattern was emerging. She'd attach the notes and
bring them to the attention of her commanding officer, Maj.
Michael Delaney, first thing Monday morning.

As Summers brewed a pot of coffee she envisioned
the smug Delaney smiling condescendingly as she explained
the similarities of two Logan Airport disappearances and how
they might be related to the Jenny Lehman case as well as the
attempted abduction of medical device saleswoman Nancy
Perlman, knowing all the while her report would go unread.

Summers recognized Delaney as a chauvinist, a law-and-order type who suffers from what a sociologist had freshly dubbed "linkage blindness" – an affliction among homicide investigators that left them unable to connect similar killings. She wanted to shout at him, remind him that the cops who do believe there's a serial killer out there think he looks like Jason from *Friday the 13th* -- a movie she'd seen out of curiosity.

With steaming mug in hand, Summers gazed out the window at Ivy Street in Brookline, the tree branches laden with new-fallen snow. A small boy was shoveling the sidewalk and Summers studied the way he joyously tossed the snow into the street. She continued to ask herself, "Who should we be looking for?"

The detective recalled from a criminology course that the typical serial killer is white, male, somewhere in age between mid-twenties and mid-forties, works alone and projects a nice-guy image. If the researchers were correct, these psychopaths tended to target prostitutes, young boys and girls, and the naïve or trusting person. Their goal: stalk, capture and control.

Incensed, she asked herself, "Why the fuck can't Delaney see that? We shouldn't be out looking for Freddy Kruger in *Nightmare on Elm Street*. We're not going to find a guy with metal claws. We should be out looking for another Ted Bundy who, thankfully, is behind bars in a Florida penitentiary."

Summers had faced this sort of opposition before, mostly as a recruit at the State Police Academy, where she assumed the harassment was due to the fact that she was young, female, good looking, outspoken and sexually uninterested in her classmates. She now added to that blacklist the often-heard refrain that she had far less experience than the other State Police detectives assigned to the Suffolk County district attorney and had been promoted simply because she was a woman who fulfilled the human resources quota.

46

Summers flopped down on the couch in her pajamas, appreciative of the day off. She wasn't in the mood to dress in slacks, police polo shirt, windbreaker and sturdy boots, the 9mm Sig Sauer an unwelcome weight to her left side.

Summers nudged her bare feet against a stack of books that teetered precariously on her side table. She didn't flinch when the books cascaded to the carpet that was awash in unread travel, fashion and entertainment magazines. She pawed through the glossy pages, trying to find some significance in the trials and tribulations of movie stars and celebrities, people who seemed so removed from her world where knives, bullets, baseball bats and poison often spelled the difference between life and death. When she had flung the last magazine aside, she expertly wove her honey blonde hair into a French braid and began writing notes about Jenny Lehman and the other women who had disappeared after landing at Logan Airport. Soon her analytical abilities were in overdrive. She nearly jumped when the phone rang. It was the doctor.

At 27, Summers sensed she was just starting out on a big adventure, but for the past two years her relationship with renowned neurosurgeon Dr. Chandler Hughes had left her feeling stifled, unappreciated and oftentimes belittled. They had met when the doctor gave testimony at a criminal trial in which Summers was among the investigators.

Although she was attracted to his intellect, surgical skill and, in some smaller way, his social standing, he often chided her. He was the quintessential type-A personality, confident and brash, adept at making everyone think his word was God-like. But after two years she no longer yearned for him sexually. In fact, she had begun to cringe at the notion that they might spend another night together. He was in his late-forties, almost a different generation, and there were times she felt like a child in his arms. He occasionally surprised her with additional attention during their lovemaking, but it never registered a 10 on what her girlfriends called the Erotic Richter Scale. In fact, it was barely a tremor.

Summers thought back on the times they had sex and how after it was over, she would still be revved up and wanting, but the esteemed doctor was fast asleep, snoring lightly, a satisfied expression on his face as though he had sated the kingdom's nymphomaniac.

Summers listened as the doctor made it clear he was coming over to her apartment once his last surgery was completed for the day to talk about rekindling their relationship. As he put it, she would be making a huge mistake by refusing to see him.

When the doctor finished speaking, Summers said with finality, "Chandler, you and I both know we're done. Just let it go."

Summers hung up the phone and drained what remained of her coffee into the sink. She put on running clothes and a quilted vest and jogged three miles under the warm winter sun, trying to burn off the doctor's existence. When she encountered an indoor farmers' market she bought a blue orchid for her apartment. The vendor put two clear bags over the top of the plant to protect it against frost nip, forcing Summers to walk back home or chance ruining the delicate petals. By the time she returned it was noon, so she poured herself a lowball glass of Kentucky bourbon.

Summers held the glass to the window so that the sunlight passed through the amber liquid. She wondered how she'd gotten here, sipping whisky at noon. She blamed it, in part, on her hard-drinking co-workers, and imagined what her parents back in Kansas City, Missouri, would think if they could see her in a crystal ball.

Despite her misgivings, Summers sipped until the bourbon was gone, poured another, and happily gazed upon the non-events that were occurring along her neighborhood street. She also thought about the doctor and how he could be such a dick, a trait she found many men possessed.

Hannah Summers had been the queen of her high school prom, a title she hadn't strived for, but even back then she sensed there was something wrong with her king. The boy had been kind and gentle, and certainly handsome, but it seemed to Summers he was lacking both intellect and cool. She found it discouraging. It wasn't so much the lack of intellect, although that did bother her a bit. More so, it was the lack of cool. She recalled someone famous had once said, "It doesn't matter how much money you have, you can't buy cool." She wholeheartedly agreed.

Summers shook her head in desperation and recalled thinking at the time, "If this fool tries to grope me without having a conversation first, I might have to punch him in the balls so hard he never forgets."

College days weren't that much different. Once again, the young men tended toward athletic and good looking, but in bed they were mostly slam, bam, thank you mam. The notion that she might never find a suitable partner depressed her, but she vowed to make the most of her day out of the office. She finished what remained in the glass and enthusiastically swung open her closet doors.

As was her indulgence on her day off, if the weather cooperated she would don a dress and heels and allow her honey-blonde hair to cascade down her back, the waves no longer tamed by elastic bands or elaborate knots. She'd take her weekly mental-health walk to nearby Hall's Pond nature sanctuary and, depending on the season, study the trees, flowers, birds and, her favorite subject – the turtles. She had no idea why, but even as a little girl she loved turtles. She missed them in winter.

The dress she had in mind was flowery, girly, summery and hung slightly off her shoulders, tapered at the waist and swirled outward from her hips in a display of color. She simply wanted to feel feminine instead of like one of the guys. She also wanted to leave her badge and gun at home and remember what it felt like to be a civilian, unconcerned with criminal activity and the safety of society. But for that dress she'd have to wait until spring.

Instead, it was early afternoon when she donned boots, jeans, thick sweater and wool coat. She strolled toward Hall's Pond and ten minutes later was lingering on the wooden footbridge. The sanctuary was nearly empty on this January day and Summers embraced the solitude as she listened to the chirping birds and honking geese, a gentle wind creaking the bare branches of towering maples and oaks. She wondered if the frogs, snakes and the other creatures she normally saw in springtime were asleep under the mud, paired off as though waiting to board Noah's Ark. If that was so, where did the singles, those without partners like Hannah Summers, go when the Ark arrived?

Summers admitted to herself that she liked being in control, that she enjoyed rules and expected both friends and enemies to play by them. It was this sort of thinking that brought an end to at least two romances during her college days and more recently with Chandler Hughes. None of those men seemed capable of playing by the rules.

Whenever she fantasized about the perfect guy, he was always kind and caring, and law-abiding, of course, but also handsome, hunky, macho, self confident, tall enough to look down at her five-foot-seven frame, and in no way feel intimidated by her intelligence, marksmanship, daring, and her natural abilities when it came to police work. She grinned at the thought, adding for good measure that this ideal man would also enjoy reading books and traveling the world with her. She seriously doubted he was out there.

CHAPTER 9

February 1986
Boston, Massachusetts

A MUSEUM TREASURE

Decker first met Kaleigh Adams on a warm summer day in August. People were bitching about the heat, and all he could think of was how much hotter it had been in the desert -- 110 Fahrenheit in the shade, if you could find some. Six months had gone by since that first chance meeting.

Decker knew Kaleigh was seeing someone else but that didn't deter him from returning often to the Institute of Contemporary Art on Northern Avenue, a five-minute walk from Fort Point Channel where the local lobster boat fleet was moored. She had noticed him right away and they had chatted briefly as she worked setting up an exhibit. Decker's attention was riveted by her long, silky chestnut hair that had an almost Lady Godiva quality about it, the strands spreading across her back as she kneeled on the floor and hammered a nail into plywood. During his second and third visit they had ended up talking for over an hour, much to her boss' displeasure.

Decker knew he wanted her friendship and perhaps something more, but his feelings were tangled. It had been a while since he felt honestly interested in a woman. The fun and games he'd enjoyed between deployments, in places like Singapore and Bangkok, amounted to little more than drunken bouts of flirtation and meaningless sex. There certainly hadn't been much to get excited about in Burka Land where the women were shrouded head to toe.

Kaleigh called him her warrior arts patron, which he found flattering. She was curious about the experiences he had endured in the Middle East and South America. She knew Rane would be put out by these long conversations with Decker, but she felt a need to know more about the hostilities in Lebanon than what was broadcast on the evening news. It was such a mess over there. She didn't know which country to believe anymore or which was good and evil. Besides, she found Decker undeniably alluring – tall, fit, handsome, muscular, with piercing blue eyes and thick black hair shaved close to the scalp in military fashion. Since those early talks Decker had allowed his hair to grow and his chiseled facial features to cover over with loose stubble. Kaleigh said it made him look rugged. To her, he was exotic because he was a soldier and she'd never known one before. He also had an insatiable thirst to learn more about art. Actually, Decker seemed interested in knowing more about every subject, which drew her to him. He usually was carrying a book with the pages dog-eared over. Kaleigh appreciated his inquisitiveness and told him so numerous times. She had immediately noticed he walked with a slight limp but was tactful enough not to mention it. She also understood that beneath that martial exterior was a sensitive young man who had seen and done things not by choice but due to circumstance. She mentioned him in passing during two conversations with Rane, but as usual he was obsessed with chasing news stories and somewhat less attentive to her interests. Rane was always, to use her word, intense. And while she certainly preferred that sort of man to a dullard, she couldn't help wishing he would sometimes just relax, slow down, stop talking, and simply revel in the quiet beauty of the moment.

As a museum exhibition space designer, Kaleigh appreciated the importance of putting art on display in an interactive way, knowing that it often takes more than simply hanging a few paintings on the walls and inviting the public to come see them. She loved art and she continued to paint big, wild, vibrant canvases that included colorful birds, reptiles, fish and distorted human faces. She also spent freely on fashionable clothes, and many of those pieces were unfortunately flecked with paint, evidence of those days or nights when the muse had struck and she grabbed hold of paints and brushes, forgetting she was clad in expensive designer wear.

Her parents had advised she give up painting, which they called nonsense, and concentrate on a career in business, law or medicine. She wanted none of those and was especially sensitive to the possibility of living the way her parents and their friends did in Darien, Connecticut. To her, it was a wealthy place without a soul. For years growing up she'd watched the army of briefcase-toting men leave their neat and comfortable homes in early morning, drive to the nearby train station and board the commuter rail for Manhattan. They'd usually return around 7 p.m.

During the day, scores of fashionable, well-groomed wives would sate their boredom by playing golf or tennis, drinking, having sex with the golf or tennis pro, or, if they were desperate, the landscapers or pool boys. Kaleigh wanted no part of it, though she often wondered if her mother was among those women who carried on. After all, they'd had a nanny to keep her and her brothers occupied so mom had plenty of free time.

On his most recent visit to the museum, Decker gave Kaleigh a necklace he had purchased from a street vendor in Beirut. It was a series of blue glass stones each framed by a setting of scrap metal pounded into a crude shape, but the overall result was surprisingly elegant.

Kaleigh immediately refused the gift but Decker insisted, saying her listening to his stories just about every week did more to cure his PTSD than a room filled with shrinks in white lab coats at the VA hospital. She felt the same way and actually blushed when he asked if he might see how she looked wearing the necklace.

When the necklace was fastened, Decker stepped

back and smiled, flashing the perfect white teeth that Kaleigh had also noticed the first time they met. Neither seemed to know what the giving of this necklace meant so they wrote it off to gratitude, payment for services rendered – young woman helps guide struggling soldier as he reenters society. End of story. But both of them felt the currents that were already present and now being channeled by a piece of Middle Eastern folk jewelry.

That day marked the first and only time they'd gone to Perk, an artsy coffee house on A Street a five-minute walk from the museum. They sat at a small table in the window, really not saying all that much, mostly watching people pass by along the sidewalk and silently enjoying each other's company. Kaleigh felt peaceful around Decker. He exuded a calm that she found rejuvenating rather than draining. She also found herself telling him things she would never have told Rane because he would probably be furious.

When she told Decker she was earning extra money at the museum one night a week by modeling for a group of art students, he never flinched, but a thin smile creased his lips as his eyes bore into hers. Decker wondered what Kaleigh looked like without her clothes. He imagined her up on a broad pedestal or dais, kneeling perhaps, or seated on a low stool, her position frozen until asked to readjust after group consent. Was she self-conscious at all? Was it about the challenge, the thrill, the money, or maybe all of those combined?

"Is it weird when people are just looking at you and drawing or painting you?"

"I don't really think about it when I'm doing it. I sort of tune them all out," she said, breaking into laughter as she recalled a former college roommate who occasionally worked as a nightclub stripper. "She told me she never looked out at the crowd. She only focused over the top of them as she did her performance and never responded to the guys up front who were trying hard to get her attention. She just didn't care and she never let them stuff dollar bills in her G-string. She didn't want their grubby hands touching her skin."

54

"Well, I've never known a nude model before. Maybe I should take up painting."

Kaleigh frowned. "It's not that exciting, believe me."

Decker knew he could easily debate her on that point, but he kept silent and simply smiled. He was still having difficulty adjusting to civilian life after so many years in the Middle East where women most often were draped in heavy clothing. The sight of a mini-skirt and halter top was enough to make him stir with desire.

Four hours went by in a blur as they swapped stories while gazing out at the snow-covered street. They'd moved on to wine, ordered a plate of cheeses, fruit and a baguette, and finished by settling their stomachs with cognac, swirling and sipping from bulbous glass snifters.

Kaleigh sensed the second round of cognac might be a mistake but it had been a challenging week at the museum and besides, Rane was in Miami at the investigative reporters' conference. He had seemed eager to leave, taking a cab to the airport two hours before the flight was scheduled to depart.

It was well into evening when a trio of folk musicians stepped onto a small stage and began strumming love songs to the audience, which was mostly couples. The lyrics were all about love and passion and being sure you find the right heart to match your own. It was a little awkward for Kaleigh because she was pretty sure Rane was the one, but here she was with Decker pouring out her feelings, wants, dreams and desires like a burst watershed.

It was approaching midnight when Kaleigh's mood changed without warning. She grew reserved and pensive. "I should go," she mumbled, sliding back her chair and feeling unsteady. Her hands were braced against the table edge. Decker reached across and placed his hands atop hers but immediately withdrew them as tension registered in Kaleigh's eyes.

"I have to get a cab."

"No need for that. I'll drive you. I have my roommate Dogman's car. It's in the lot next to the museum."

Kaleigh crinkled her eyebrows at the unusual name. "Dogman?"

"It's a long story. I'll tell you some other time. Right now I want to talk more about you. We've only scratched the surface."

Kaleigh blushed, though Decker couldn't see her face under the hood of her coat. Snow was falling lightly as they stepped into the night and walked toward Northern Avenue. The sidewalk was slippery so Kaleigh held onto Decker's coat sleeve. When both of them nearly fell she ended up in Decker's arms and they laughed a bit too loud because it was the only way to ignore the fact that their bodies were pressed together.

The beat-up Volvo sedan was covered with snow. Decker started the engine, put on the heater and told Kaleigh to get inside. He brushed the windows with his coat sleeve because he wasn't wearing gloves, then sat beside Kaleigh as the car interior slowly warmed. It was so cold they could see vapor as they exhaled, which got them laughing over whose breath was most impressive.

Kaleigh allowed herself to look directly into Decker's eyes. "You're full of hot air, Decker."

"Why thank you. You're full of compliments tonight."

Decker brushed the chestnut strands of hair from her eyes and leaned toward her. She recoiled. "Rane's coming home tomorrow."

"And?"

"And I shouldn't be here with you."

"We're not doing anything wrong."

"I know that, but it feels like we are."

"Kaleigh, you're the best friend I've got in Boston."

"You're right. We're friends. We can be friends." She clutched the necklace. "And thank you so much for this. It's beautiful. Are you sure you want me to have it?"

Decker grinned, amused by her words. "I'm sure," he said. "The jeweler in Beirut might not have known it at the time, but he was making it for you."

They barely spoke during the drive to Kaleigh's Back Bay apartment. Kaleigh hummed and rubbed the necklace stones as she gazed out the window.

"You have arrived, mademoiselle," Decker announced as he pulled the car to the curb.

Kaleigh stepped out and closed the door. Decker was just about to shift the transmission into gear when Kaleigh scurried around the front of the car and knocked on the driver's window. A fluffy snow was falling as Decker rolled down the glass. "Thanks, Decker. You're sweet."

Before he could respond, she leaned in through the open window with both arms outstretched. She coiled her arms around Decker's neck, pressed her lips to his and kissed him far more passionately than she'd intended. Decker was surprised, but he gladly went with it. After Kaleigh broke away she stood for a moment staring at his dark hair, dazzling blue eyes and freshly-kissed lips.

"Goodnight, Decker," she said, and literally hopped up the steps to her front door like a schoolgirl.

CHAPTER 10

March 1986
Las Vegas, Nevada

LAST CHANCE IN SIN CITY

Luddy Pugano could hardly believe his luck when in March with dirty snow still piled high along every street in Eastie he won a three-day, all-inclusive trip to Las Vegas. He had reluctantly contributed $20 to the raffle at Nemo's and suddenly he was holding the winning ticket.

It had been a tough winter for the draggermen, gillnetters and longliners as powerful offshore storms claimed thousands of dollars worth of expensive gear or, in many cases, sank their boats. The lobstermen turned to catching fluke, flounder and the occasional haddock, but more often remained idle as they awaited the return of spring. The slim harvest put them in foul spirits and fights often erupted in the bars and streets of Eastie, especially when the dragger crews returned from two weeks at sea.

Luddy had been in a funk, haunted by the woman he'd dismembered aboard *Sea Bitch.* He was nearly broke, despite his job at the seafood market, his occasional clam raking, and the inflated fares he collected while driving his gypsy cab. Together the jobs brought in just enough to pay the rent, heat and electric bills in the Jeffries Point tenement he shared with his mother. Luddy made sure he stashed a few dollars aside to spend at Nemo's. Celeste usually bought the groceries with her government check. Although she was a skilled seamstress willing to take in work at home, Luddy's presence seemed to scare off the women who stayed for a fitting and never returned.

Luddy convinced himself the dour circumstances were the result of God getting back at him for killing that girl, the smiling hippie chick, the one who had seemed so stunned when she realized she had stepped inside his murderous nest and there was nothing she could do about it. The thought of God's vengeance depressed him further, but the feel of a ticket to Las Vegas in his pocket made him smile. He would no longer have to say he had never been to Vegas, already convinced he was the last man of his generation to miss out on that big adventure.

Rubbing the ticket in his pocket, Luddy felt his luck had changed. He told his boss at the fish market he would fly out and back without missing more than one workday.

Outside the airliner window he could see the desert just as he had pictured it – brown, wide and empty for miles around. It was no wonder gangsters in the 1920s had sought out this place to run their gambling, bootlegging and prostitution empires. It was hard to reach by ground transportation, no law enforcement for miles around, plenty of booze and lots of pretty girls looking for work.

The all-inclusive trip offered bus transportation to a less-than-glamorous hotel but Luddy was certain he had slept in worse places. The charter bus was scheduled to make at least a dozen stops along the 15-mile route between the airport and the hotel, something the tour operator had neglected to mention, but Luddy decided he wouldn't complain and just enjoy the ride. When the bus pulled into an isolated strip mall flanked by a no-name casino and a few seedy motels, Luddy picked up his carryon suitcase and went inside the convenience store where he bought a six-pack of Coors and some Slim Jims. He never left his suitcase behind -- force of habit. He had stolen plenty of them when their owners briefly stepped away, especially at the airport.

The young, olive-skinned woman in front of him on the cashier line was talking to an elderly couple debating which lottery tickets to purchase. Luddy wanted to say, 'Buy the fucking tickets and let other people get to the checkout, you rubes.' He was impatient, shifting from one foot to the other as the couple examined each game ticket and discussed whether they should buy the $10 or $20 chances or maybe just stick with $5.

When he caught the dark-haired young woman looking at him he stopped shifting and smiled widely. As always, he did a quick assessment: clogs, tank top, denim shorts, hair pulled back into a ponytail, cradling a bag of Lay's potato chips and a liter of diet Dr. Pepper soda.

Luddy followed her with his eyes as she left the store and got into a small, non-descript sedan. When he stepped into the parking lot she was still there, an exasperated expression on her face. The starter was grinding but the engine wasn't turning over.

Luddy concentrated on approaching her with the biggest, friendliest smile he could muster. He hoped to exude the innocence and boyishness of an altar boy.

"Sounds like trouble. Can I help?"

"Oh, I don't know," she said. "I'll probably have to call the rental company or maybe AAA."

Without hesitation, Luddy deftly reached inside the car and unlocked the hood. The carburetor smelled flooded, gas fumes evaporating on the heated engine block. He sensed it would start once the excess fuel was gone. To pass the time, he fiddled with the wires and air filter while the woman sat in the car.

"Give it a try now," he said.

The engine started after a short gasp. Luddy closed the hood with a victorious nod and suggested she allow him to test drive the sedan to make certain it was running properly. As the woman exited the driver's seat. Luddy quickly tossed his suitcase and beer onto the rear seat and got behind the steering wheel. Seconds later she was seated next to him. Luddy revved the engine.

"Sounds good, but we should just drive around a little bit to make sure the fuel line stays clear and everything else is OK. I don't want to chance you breaking down around these parts. Who knows what's out there – snakes, scorpions, you name it."

The woman seemed suddenly frightened, but was grateful for his concern. She introduced herself -- Suzie Milano from Massachusetts. Luddy extended his hand. "Rudy Thompson."

They talked openly and she was comforted to learn that he, too, was from Massachusetts. Her family was from Cape Cod. Luddy told her he lived in the Berkshires near a farm that raised llamas -- all very back-to-nature. He thought she'd appreciate knowing that.

Suzie opened the bag of potato chips and handed it to Luddy. He stuffed a few chips in his mouth as he drove, talking and chewing at the same time. He was worried about getting back to the bus before it departed. Suzie offered to drive him to The Strip in Vegas where she'd been promised a job as a cocktail waitress.

"No need for that. I've already paid for the bus ticket." He turned off the main road onto an unpaved track. "If I cut across here, we'll come out back at the store." Suzie reached over and touched his arm. "Where are you going? Let's get back on the main road. It's going to be dark soon."

"You're right. I just have to find a place to turn around. Got to make sure there's enough room for a three-point turn because the sand is soft on the road shoulders. Don't want to sink into the ditch and get stuck."

A few minutes later, Luddy cranked the wheel to the left, put the car in reverse and began backing up. When he tried to move forward the wheels spun, just as he knew they would.

"Shit," he said. "I think the back tires are digging into the sand. I might have to put something under them for traction."

"Oh, god. I'll walk back to the store. There's a phone booth there. I can call for a tow truck."

"Just stay calm. I'll have us out of here in no time."

Luddy unzipped his suitcase, pulled out a Boston Celtics sweatshirt and stuffed it in front of the right rear tire. He knew the sweatshirt wouldn't provide adequate traction, but it seemed like a good prop that might show the young woman he was doing everything possible to save the day. He told her to stand away from the car as he revved the engine in neutral and put on the emergency break amid the noise. He slipped the transmission into drive and the rear wheels spun, tossing the sweatshirt out beyond the rear bumper, but the car didn't move.

The young woman picked up the sweatshirt, inspecting it for damage. "Sorry you had to ruin your sweatshirt," she said, brushing off the soil.

As she handed it to Luddy he smashed a full beer bottle over her skull. She was stunned and it took a few seconds for her to collapse in the sand. Luddy was feeling the rush. Blood was oozing from the woman's forehead. Beer foam was running down the side of the car. He spotted a roundish rock and ran toward in. It was about the size of a football. The woman was starting to move in the sand, moaning and holding her head. Luddy brought down the rock, knowing it would probably spatter him with blood. After that she didn't move. He switched off the car engine and dragged her body about forty yards into the desert twilight. She was pretty enough, though not as stunningly beautiful as Nature Girl, the photographer who had wanted to take pictures of seabirds.

Suzie Milano had lost her clogs while being dragged. Luddy kneeled along side her, breathing hard. He unsnapped her jean shorts and pulled off her underwear. He liked the fact that they were plain white. For several minutes he stared at the dark patch between her legs, pushing his face close and inhaling. Luddy removed her tank top and bra so that she lay naked and motionless in the sand. He ran back to the car and pulled two beers from the six-pack.

For the next half hour he sat next to Suzie Milano's body, savoring each sip of beer as his hands roved over her curves. He hoped too much time hadn't passed because he no longer felt aroused, but he had an idea how to fix that.

Luddy cuddled her body as though laying spoon fashion in a bed. He ran his hand through the blood on her forehead and then stroked himself until he was hard. Seconds later he was thrusting inside her, thrilled that he had finally made it to the desert. He told himself she was probably a hooker – sweet on the outside but a licentious whore within who deserved no better. Some trick at one of the hotels down on The Strip was probably still waiting for her to show up -- $50 for a blowjob, $150 for the night. Tough shit for him. If it wasn't that trick, it would have been another sucker signed up for a lap dance in some strip joint, some bald-headed Tupperware salesman groping her tits and coming in his pants as she writhed against his crotch.

Sipping his Coors in the car, Luddy though, well, my Sweet Desert Girl, I saved you from that fate and made certain you never have to go back to that shithole where they give you no respect, that cesspool of sickness and evil, dancers and strippers, stage shows and casinos, roulette wheels and card tables, drinking and drugging, pornography and endless blowjobs, fucking in alleyways so shamelessly that even the homeless turn their heads. No, he thought, my dear Sweet Desert Girl, you will not go back to that.

It took hours to scrape a hole deep enough to bury her body and then cover it with loose stones, but by dawn the task was done and Luddy was singing along with a country station on the car radio as he approached the outskirts of Vegas. The feel of her hair in his front pocket made him smile.

CHAPTER 11

April 1986
Boston, Massachusetts

*ANIMALS GATHER AT THE WATERING HOLE
AFTER DARK*

Nemo's was crowded the night Luddy returned to
East Boston. He had taken a cab home from Logan Airport
and closely watched the odometer the entire way to make
sure the driver didn't try to cheat him. He didn't like the
feeling of being a passenger in the backseat but it made him
better understand what it was like for his customers.

Luddy sat on his favorite barstool in the far corner,
scanning the room for people he knew so that he could tell
them about his trip to Vegas. But the only faces he recognized
were the nameless ones, mostly in their late twenties or early
thirties, new to the neighborhood, trendy assholes who paid
four times as much as their apartments were worth and in
turn priced out the people who had lived amid the cramped
and hilly streets of Eastie their entire lives.

The television over the bar was showing stock footage
of planes taking off and landing at Logan Airport. WCVB
news anchor Susan Wornick was talking but the audio
was low so Luddy tried to read her lips. He froze when a
photograph of Jenny Lehman's smiling face appeared on the
screen with the word "Missing" beneath it. He wanted to hear
the report but Bubby was at the other end of the bar, paying
close attention to the new customers.

Luddy moved closer to the TV. The Lehman family was offering a $50,000 reward for information about their daughter's whereabouts. At least five television news reporters were holding microphones toward a striking but perplexed-looking young woman with dark blonde hair held back by a ponytail. The woman was dressed in black slacks and a blue windbreaker. A gold police badge in a leather case hung from a lanyard around her neck.

The TV studio's Chyron text generator identified her as State Police Detective Lt. Hannah Summers. Luddy strained to hear. He only caught bits and pieces.

"...last seen at Logan Airport collecting her suitcase from the baggage carousel...Eastern Airlines flight... January...Maryland...Tufts student."

The Chyron machine printed the 800-number to call with information about Jenny Lehman.

Summers knew the Suffolk County district attorney would be unhappy about the demeanor she had affected with the news media, but her experiences with reporters over the past three years made her wary. She was often misquoted or her words were taken out of context, used as sound bites to sensationalize a story. Despite this opinion, she needed the reporters to spread the word about Jenny Lehman who had vanished in January and, based on national crime statistics, was probably dead. Four months was a long time in these situations. She hoped for a few new leads on what already had become a cold case, now added to those of Karen Gilmore and Darlene Parks, both of whom were last seen at Logan Airport before they vanished. A killer was undoubtedly out there and Summers felt compelled to pursue the case, but she didn't even have a body.

Summers sensed Jenny Lehman's parents must have clout in the circles of power because they'd been able to stir the media to action. Maybe it was simply the fact that they were offering $50,000 for information leading to their daughter's whereabouts or to the arrest of anyone responsible for her disappearance. The TV stations and newspapers had already exhausted the missing-good-looking-grad student angle as well as the look-over-your-shoulder-at-the-airport scare story. The campus-mystery angle hadn't gotten very far because there was no indication Jenny Lehman's disappearance had anything to do with her enrollment at Tufts University.

Luddy wondered if anyone would call the 800-number and, if so, what they might say. He hadn't mentioned a word about the murder to anyone, not even a veiled brag to the other gypsy cab drivers. He wanted them to understand and perhaps envy the elation he had felt when killing her, but he was too cunning to offer more than a knowing smile if the subject of Jenny Lehman's disappearance came up in conversation.

Luddy wanted more information but the pretty blonde police detective was already off the screen, replaced by a commercial for a new kind of mop. He cursed the strangers who preferred the jukebox to the TV. He returned to his corner stool and glared at them, wishing they'd never discovered Nemo's or his neighborhood.

Luddy noticed the soldier in desert cammies at the opposite end of the bar had also stared intensely at the TV when the blonde police detective was being interviewed. The soldier was with some of the newer faces but Luddy sensed he was somehow different than the latest horde of urban settlers – not as spoiled or self-obsessed. He was chatting up a young woman with long, straight, glossy chestnut hair that reached the middle of her back. The woman had lively blue eyes, an upturned nose, an animated face and thin lips that revealed her straight white teeth and pink gums when she smiled.

She was wearing a deep-purple sleeveless mini-dress cut well above her knees, matching heels and a blue stone necklace. Luddy noticed there were flecks of paint near the hem of the dress and he wondered what sort of panties she was wearing. He imagined they were purple to match her dress. He wanted to touch her silky hair. The purple mini-dress seemed to be listening intently to every word the soldier in camouflage was saying. Every so often she cackled

66

loudly, a weird witch's laugh that didn't fit her appearance. The other guy with them had blond hair combed back and parted in the middle like Prince Valiant, with a scruffy beard and moustache. He was wearing a gray woolen two-piece suit. Luddy had seen him plenty of times over the past year. Apparently this guy, too, was part of the new crowd, the ones who looked upon people like him with disdain, as though they were uneducated slobs not worthy of living on these coastal hills overlooking the Boston skyline.

Luddy recalled hearing at the bar that the bearded guy was some hotshot newspaper reporter who had been writing regularly about organized crime in New England. He actually knew the guy's name and had to admit he liked reading the Tribune stories, which were accurate, detailed and exciting. He enjoyed reading about some of the powerful organized crime guys like Gennaro Angiulo, the made men, most of whom had done short time in the Charles Street Jail years earlier while awaiting trial for car theft, housebreaks and other crimes. He knew the more prominent OC guys had probably seen the inside of Walpole or some other East Coast maximum-security state prison where they send convicted murderers and rapists.

Luddy doubted any of them would remember him from Charles Street because he had tried to stay invisible while serving his short stint for car theft and attempted arson. There was no telling what the other felons in the cellblock might do if they found out he had badly beaten his mother and stole all the cash from her pocketbook. Word in the jail traveled fast. And he wasn't especially proud of the botched arson job in nearby Lynn that left him with burns and scars on his back, arms and chest. Those were troublesome days, dulled by Percocet, his favorite black beauties, along with the usual opiates so readily available on the streets of Eastie.

Sitting on his perch, Luddy surveyed the scene. The blond-bearded reporter was engaged in some sort of heated political conversation with two guys in suits whom he'd never seen before. More strangers. It wasn't very exciting, he thought, sort of like watching the Yule Log on TV during the Christmas season. But all of a sudden the reporter turned his attention away from the suits and put his arm around the purple mini-dress.

Kaleigh introduced Decker to Rane, explaining how they had met at the museum a few months back. Rane immediately went on the offensive, unloading a dozen questions at Decker about his uniform, deployment, the situation in Lebanon and what sort of action he had seen. After another round of beers and shots of Bushmills, which Rane demanded that Bubby put on his tab, he asked what Decker thought of the Beirut barracks bombing. How the fuck did that happen? Were the Marine sentries asleep or out banging the local Lebanese girls?

Although she was secretly pleased by his jealousy, Kaleigh urged him to back off, but Rane was clearly awaiting an answer from Soldier Boy, as he had begun referring to Decker.

When Decker revealed that he knew at least five of the Marines who had been killed in the bombing, Kaleigh assumed that would be enough to get Rane to ratchet down, but the information only seemed to prod him on.

"So does that mean the sleeping sentries were partly responsible for your friends' deaths?"

Decker stepped forward until he and Rane were inches apart. "If you weren't there, then there's no point in discussing it," said Decker, who clearly had no intention of backing down.

Rane smirked. "No, I wasn't there, but it sure looks like the sentries were asleep at the switch. The way I heard it, the rules of engagement prevented those guys from carrying loaded weapons. That seems like one fucked-up rule in a war zone."

Decker clenched his fists, which caused Kaleigh to inch closer to both men and rest a hand lightly on each of their shoulders. He relaxed at the feel of Kaleigh's fingers. Looking directly at Rane, he said, "CENTCOM didn't want sentries opening fire on the locals. That would only cause more trouble in what was already a bad situation.

68

What if there was a language problem or some other misunderstanding? What if the hajis in the truck were looking for help in an emergency and had gone to the Americans only to be gunned down? How would that play out in the media? You should know the answer to that better than anyone in this bar."

Rane pursed his lips as though convinced. "Fog of war," he said, and immediately felt trite for saying it.

"Rules of engagement," Decker countered. "If it was me, I'd have shot first and asked questions later. Like that old adage goes, better tried by 12 than carried by six."

At that moment, Rane noticed Kaleigh's necklace. He reached out and lightly clasped one of the blue stones between two fingers. "New? It looks good on you."

Decker gazed down at his boots. Kaleigh smoothly declared, "I got it at a flea market that the museum was running a while back. I'm not sure why I like it so much. This is the first time I've worn it."

Decker smirked, pleased by her ability to keep their little secret. Lifting his head, he signaled Bubby to bring another round. "That's a very nice necklace," he said, smiling at Kaleigh. "But I wouldn't know an emerald from an eggplant."

Luddy laid another $10 bill on the bar and, ensconced on his corner stool, intently studied the interactions of these strangers who had begun to occupy his world. He looked longingly at the young woman in the purple dress, memorizing the curve of her muscular calves, the lovely way her hips canted as she talked. He was pissed that Bubby served the soldier and the reporter before him. Where was her fucking loyalty? He imagined dragging her out to the back alley and pressing the dumpster lid against her tattooed neck until she promised to never again serve an outsider before serving him. Then he'd punch her meth-stained teeth, which would probably fall out. It was a simple matter of respect. Didn't she get it? How could she? She was too busy parading around in her Flashdance outfit, flirting with the soldier and trying to score tips.

Luddy wondered if it were true that women are attracted to men in uniform. He had never served in the military nor worked any job that required a uniform, like a cop, firefighter, EMT, or even a mailman. The Army had rejected him because of his clubfoot and arrhythmic heart. The closest he'd ever gotten to a uniform was as an altar boy at the Most Holy Redeemer Church in Maverick Square where he wore a black and white frock. He remembered how Father Gallagher once told him to wear only his underpants beneath the black frock, otherwise he might overheat during Mass and needlessly sweat. When the ceremony was over, Father Gallagher stood in the sacristy holding the trousers and weirdly joking that he wasn't going to return them because he liked to see the altar boys' in their underwear.

Luddy ordered another draft beer and nervously reached into the back pocket of his jeans. He unfolded a magazine article about things to do in Las Vegas. He had meant to read it. The cover photo showed The Strip in all its neon glory, with big hotels and fountains. Luddy crumpled the two pages into a ball and tossed it toward the trashcan behind the bar. The shot missed but Bubby deftly scooped it into the trash without looking at Luddy.

"Nice shot, Shucker. The Celtics definitely aren't in your future," she snickered.

Luddy gave her the malocchio – the Italian evil eye sign -- but Bubby ignored him.

"You're going to die an early death," Luddy warned.

The tension between Rane and Decker had simmered down. Rane was waxing eloquently about the feature series he was writing on the fate of Vietnam War veterans. What had they gone through in Southeast Asia? How had it changed them? What were they doing now? Seemed like a lot of them were drunks or drug addicts or going on incessantly about PTSD, or else it was Victor Charlie this and Ho Chi Minh that, he said.

Rane was obviously interested in their plight but short on sympathy. "We never heard the World War II guys whining on like that. They fought the Germans and the Japs,

70

saw some bad shit, then came home, had a family and got a job," he callously pontificated.

Decker's attention momentarily increased when Rane mentioned a certain soldier nicknamed Zilch who had lost all four limbs and was living at the VA hospital in Jamaica Plain.

According to Rane, the soldier was a second lieutenant who had stepped on a land mine that mostly likely had been rigged as a defensive perimeter by his own platoon. Or maybe it was a friendly grenade meant to kill him before his questionable command decisions got anyone else killed. War stories like that were always sketchy and ferreting the truth often impossible.

"Dumb fucker," Rane said.

Once again Decker tensed. "I know that guy Zilch. He got shot to bits saving his buddies in the Delta. From what I heard, he's got a drawer full of medals but won't show them to anybody."

Rane drew back and rested his arms on the bar. "I stand corrected, Soldier Boy. And now I need to crawl into my bed. Another big day in the world of journalism tomorrow." Without a word to anyone, including Kaleigh who was standing less than five feet away, Rane nonchalantly walked out of the bar and into the night.

"Rane?" she called. But he didn't look back.

Decker's eyes locked on Kaleigh who'd already found his gaze. Kaleigh shrugged as though to say I'm not sure where Rane is going or if he's coming back. Decker waved a $20 bill to again get Bubby's attention and ordered two Bombay gin and tonics with lime. He handed one to Kaleigh.

"I usually don't drink gin. You know I'm a lightweight."

"Maybe then just for tonight," he urged, clinking glasses. "You held up pretty well the last time we had a few together."

"That's not how I remember it."

"What do you remember about that night?"

Kaleigh smiled demurely and sipped at the gin. "This isn't half bad. I know you boys like your

71

Bushmills, but I'm not an Irish whisky fan."

"Mostly juniper berries," he said. "Certified by the Queen of England herself."

"Very Anglo. I could get used to this."

"I could, too," he said, clearly not talking about the gin.

An hour later, with no sign that Rane might return, Decker offered Kaleigh a ride home.

"I'll behave this time," she said.

"Please don't."

Luddy studied them as they left Nemo's. He imagined them fucking but in his mind he replaced the soldier with himself and thought of how much he'd like to tear off her purple dress. He was lost in this reverie until he heard Bubby's voice say, "Hey, you Mother Shucker, what are you lookin' at?"

Luddy cursed. "Just shut the fuck up and get me another beer."

The April night had turned cold and blustery, an icy east wind coming from the sea. Decker and Kaleigh were both glad to get inside Dogman's aging Volvo sedan. The music came on as soon as Decker started the engine and he immediately switched off the radio.

Kaleigh was about to ask what kind of music he preferred but Decker kissed her before she could say a word and she kissed him back. His lips found her neck and ears and he nibbled at them with a flurry of kisses while his left hand caressed her thighs beneath her dress. She moaned involuntarily.

"Don't, Decker, please. Not here. Not like this."

Decker pulled away, confused by the night's mixed messages. "Sorry. I've wanted to kiss you again ever since…"

She didn't let him finish. She pressed two fingers against his lips, then lifted her chin and kissed him. This time Decker didn't slip a hand beneath her dress. He simply responded to her kiss and waited to see whether she would break it off. When she didn't, he continued kissing her but

72

with more vigor, their tongues swirling and probing. A car backfired somewhere along the street, causing Decker to rip away and clench the dashboard, his eyes scanning quickly in all directions, his muscles tense. Kaleigh instinctively understood what was happening and Decker seemed embarrassed when he realized it.

"It's OK," she reassured, caressing his face. "I can't imagine what it was like over there."

After that they kissed until their lips were sore, then let out breathless laughs as they relaxed back in their seats.

"I haven't kissed a girl like that since I was 17," he said, gently poking her in the ribs. "A real make-out session."

Kaleigh cackled. "And I didn't even bring my Chap Stick," she said, adding, "Oh, Decker. What are we doing? We're supposed to be friends."

Decker paused before responding. He waited until her eyes were locked on his. "We are friends. That's the best part of it. Too many people who say they're in love only have the physical. They don't have the friendship, which when you think about it, is really the most important piece."

Decker framed her face between his palms. "When I was in the desert, it was all about friendship with the guys in the squad. 'I watch your back, you watch mine, and together we'll get out of this alive.' That's the kind of bond you never forget. You can't compare it to having sex with someone and saying you're close because you slept together. There has to be a deeper connection. There has to be friendship."

Kaleigh's mood had become far more serious. "Decker, I'm your friend. I've got your back."

Decker was silent, but Kaleigh saw tears spill from his eyes and down his cheeks. "I've got yours, too."

73

CHAPTER 12

May 1986
Boston, Massachusetts

THE MAN WHO THOUGHT HE WAS SIGMUND FREUD

Decker again borrowed Dogman's car to reach the VA hospital in Jamaica Plain. Dogman, whose real name was Freddie Morales, was an Army Ranger assigned as a K9 handler until a booby-trapped piano left him missing a leg and near death amid the battle-hardened streets of Beirut. Major, his German shepherd, had dragged him from the rubble that was shrouded by smoke and the smell of cordite. The others in the squad were dead. A medevac helicopter flew him from the war-ravaged city to an offshore hospital ship. Decker remembered that day as one of the bleakest in his deployment. He had heard the chaos on his radio and arrived on scene just as the medevac was about to dust off. He ran to the open doorway and hugged Morales, whose body was burned and bleeding, clear surgical tubes extending outward from his nose and arms. He tried not to focus on the missing leg and mangled arm. Major was crouched beside Morales who lay motionless on the stretcher.

After months of rehab in Germany, the wounded Ranger was honorably discharged from the Army on full disability pay and, in an unusual departure from military procedure, allowed to keep the shepherd. Dogman sensed the media had played a big role in that decision by running

74

stories about the heroic canine named Major who pulled his master from the throes of death. The public loves a good animal story. Going against the readers and viewers by splitting up man and dog could very well have been a military career-killer for the officer charged with making that decision.

Decker liked dogs, so he and Major became fast friends despite the animal's undying loyalty to his partner.

With his one reliable hand, Morales tried to give Decker $10 for gas but the soldier refused and was in no mood to argue. He never looked forward to these mental health sessions, figuring most of them were bullshit and only served to keep the government shrinks employed.

The rotund triage nurse flirted with Decker, as did her male assistant who took his blood pressure and other vitals. They inspected the scars where bullets had passed through his left leg and rib cage and renewed his prescription for painkillers. The nurses told Decker he was a hero in their eyes for having served in the military, especially in the Middle East where the danger seemed to grow each day. He instinctively winced whenever he heard those words: *Thank you for your service*. After all, they hadn't a clue about what he'd been through or what it was like to face death daily so that the folks back home could continue to eat at McDonald's, go to the movie theater or sports stadium, drink beer at backyard barbecues and tear around in their gas-guzzling Cadillacs without fear or worry that an enemy might be waiting to fire a bullet into their empty heads.

Decker smirked at a few of the questions the triage nurse read him from her clipboard. Did he drink more than two alcoholic beverages per day?

"Absolutely not," he answered.

Was he sexually active? Decker tried to remember what a naked woman looked like in his bed.

"Yes, ma'am. Very much so," he lied enthusiastically, which prompted the nurse to roll her eyes in amusement.

Decker fanned through three waiting-room magazines cover to cover – including Time and Newsweek.

He initially picked up the Sports Illustrated that promised the annual Swimsuit Edition inside, but when he flipped to the spread somebody had already ripped out the pages.

Well after the appointed time, Dr. Heinrich Vlotka met him in the waiting room, hand thrust out in friendly greeting. Decker shook the doctor's hand – clammy and weak. Vlotka was just over five feet, pudgy, overbearing and an unabashed know-it-all. He offered no apology for the delay.

"Let's see what we can do for you today," he said, ushering Decker down a hallway to his corner office. "If I recall our last visit, you were rather quiet."

Decker sat in a hardback chair, preferring it to the couch. He sat with his fingers clasped in his lap as the doctor fiddled with a manila folder bulging with documents.

Dr. Vlotka sifted through the file, mumbling to himself – "yes, yes, Sgt. Emmett Decker, Bowdoin College, bachelor's degree in the liberal arts, six years in the military, age 28, unmarried, no children, no religion specified, combat decorated, twice wounded in action."

Decker shifted in his chair, grunting and clearing his throat as though to say let's gets this parade started.

"So tell me, sergeant, are you getting out and mingling with people, or locking yourself away in your apartment?"

"What difference does it make?"

"Well, I'd like to hear that you are trying to normalize."

"Like that's going to happen," the soldier replied.

"Are you still having bad dreams?"

"Only about having to come here to see you."

The doctor ignored the comment. "Have you applied for any work?"

"Uncle Sam is still paying me. But yes, I've got a few things going."

"Such as?"

"Same stuff I was schooled in. Private surveillance work, keeping an eye on cheating spouses and back-injury claimants working heavy construction jobs."

"Interesting."

"I'm not carrying a rifle anymore, just in case you were wondering. The company gave me a camera instead. Much less messy."

Dr. Vlotka flashed a look of disdain. "Can we pick up where we left off about your duties with Special Forces? You never did tell me if you actually had to kill anyone?"

Decker was silent.

"Was there any hand-to-hand combat?"

"No. Nothing like that."

"Oh, I see. The killing was done from a distance then? Not a knife but a bullet?"

"That's right."

"So, you were far from these people, but still pulling a trigger. I imagine you value accuracy and professionalism. Did you experience any guilt?"

"I didn't think about it. I just did my job."

"Did you target any women or children?"

"Not if I could help it."

"Sergeant, are you angry that the government required you do these things?"

Decker laced his fingers and cracked the knuckles "It's what I was trained to do. I enlisted and volunteered for sniper school."

"Is that what you were, a sniper?"

"I did lots of things."

"There are some holes, let's call them omissions, from your military record. Would you care to share any details regarding your classified assignments following your deployment to Lebanon?"

"If they're classified, I can't share them."

"But you were in Lebanon?"

"If that piece of paper you're holding says I was in Lebanon, then I was in Lebanon."

"And what about after Lebanon? Where were you for at least the next 18 months? Everything in that part of your file is blacked out."

"Then I must have been blacked out."

"Sometimes these places in a person's file that have been obscured, well, they can be like little black boxes containing precisely the information I need to treat PTSD. And in your case, there are several little black boxes."

"If I told you what's in those little black boxes, I'd have to kill you."

Dr. Vlotka fidgeted in his chair and scrunched his face as though deep in thought. He pulled out a pad of paper and handed it to Decker. The pages contained a succession of inkblots.

"I will be administering the Rorschach test," said the doctor. "As you answer each question, I will record your answers and analyze them using psychological interpretations. This first phase is strictly free association. That means…"

"I know what free association means."

"Then just tell me what you think when I show you the image. I can assure we use very complex algorithms to reach our conclusions."

Dr. Vlotka showed Decker the first inkblot.

Decker remained silent.

"Well?"

"Looks like a gorgeous blonde with big tits."

"Please, Sgt. Decker. I'm trying to help."

Dr. Vlotka turned the page. "And this one?"

"Looks like a beautiful brunette with big tits."

Focusing directly on Decker, he diagnosed. "You're obviously fixated on breasts. You also seem very pent up. Do you masturbate? It can relieve tension."

Decker stood, his muscular legs pushing back the ·chair. "Are you fuckin' kidding me? Why the fuck would you want to know that?"

"Please sit down."

Decker sat, looking perplexed.

"Do you imagine killing people?"

"Only if they ask me if I masturbate."

The doctor stiffened in his chair, a bit unnerved by Decker's candid response. "I'm trying to get a sense of your mental well being. Please don't be insulted by my line of questioning," he said, reaching for a pen in his lab coat pocket. "There are many questions I need to ask you. For instance, do you love your mother? Did you and she have a loving relationship or were you at odds? These things can make a great difference in the way people behave. It can affect their entire attitude toward life."

"Sorry, doc. But this conversation is over. Personally, I think you're fucked in the head."

"You need to talk about these things."

Decker stared intensely, leaning forward until he was face-to-face with the little man, literally two inches from his nose. "No, I don't."

"Walking out of here won't do you any good."

Decker snugged on his black beret with its Ranger tab and jump wings. "Neither will staying here," he said.

"War does awful things to people."

"So do shrinks who work at the VA."

"Don't blame your doctors. The first step toward getting better is to admit you are sick."

"No, doc. You're the sick fuck. After this conversation, I feel a lot better just knowing I'm not like you."

CHAPTER 13

May 1986
Boston, Massachusetts

MODEL BEHAVIOR

Kaleigh was angled on a wooden stepladder that had been painted fire-engine red, her naked body extending the length of it in a languorous pose. She was facing sideways to the semi-circle of a dozen art students whose hands moved rapidly over their charcoal sketchpads. Her long chestnut hair was fanned across her back.

One of the students, a burly man in his early 40s wearing soiled jeans, sandals with socks and a gray, paint-spattered sweatshirt, seemed more intent on studying Kaleigh's body than drawing it. Twice he left his easel to walk completely around the subject under the pretense of gaining different perspectives. The man's behavior made Kaleigh uneasy because he repeatedly stopped and stared but she ignored him and fixed her eyes on the ceiling track lights.

Normally modeling in the nude didn't faze her because her body was trim and shapely. She was often the envy of her friends who wished for such firm breasts and perfectly proportioned hips. But this latest group of students definitely included a few strange birds. She was glad when the burly student returned to his easel. She watched him out of the corner of her eyes as he sat and began drawing enthusiastically with a stick of charcoal.

Kaleigh closed her eyes and resumed counting the

minutes until the session was over. Nearly an hour later, at precisely 8 p.m., Kaleigh deftly stepped off the ladder and donned a white terrycloth robe. She acknowledged only the gray-haired woman among the artists, who fished money from her purse and handed it to Kaleigh. The two women exchanged a few words and briefly laughed over some shared bit of humor. The other students packed their supplies and set cash or checks on a small table as they exited the gallery.

Kaleigh walked briskly toward a door that led to a small storage area she used as a dressing room. Clothing hooks and shelves lined both walls. A velour-covered, one-arm casting couch like you might find in a Hollywood producer's office dominated the far end of the small room. A single incandescent lightbulb hung from the ceiling by a wire, its red shade giving off a glow akin to a photographer's darkroom.

Once inside the room, Kaleigh peeked out to see if the students had left the gallery. She heard a last set of heavy footsteps growing fainter before she closed and bolted the door.

Kaleigh slipped on her bra, underwear, checkered mini-skirt, white angora sweater, black woolen leggings and faded white Converse hi-top sneakers. She stuffed the terrycloth robe into her backpack, slung it over her shoulder and opened the door. The long hallway was empty and most of the lights had been switched off or dimmed.

At the front desk, an elderly security guard stood and smiled. "Good evening, Miss," he said, glancing at his wristwatch as though prepared to lock the building for the night.

"Would you mind calling me a cab?"

"Certainly," he said.

Kaleigh gazed out at Boston Harbor while the security guard requested a cab.

"They're busy. Could be 20 minutes before they're here," he said.

"I know you're trying to close up. As long as I know they're coming, I'll just wait outside," she said.

The security guard locked the front doors. "I can wait here with you," he offered.

"Oh, thank you. That won't be necessary."

It was dark outside with plenty of shadow patches despite the museum's exterior lighting. Kaleigh leaned against one of the glass panels near the entrance. She was unnerved by the scruffily-dressed art student who had ogled her during the modeling session. The man was standing near the water's edge looking in her direction, sketchpad clamped beneath one arm. He began walking slowly toward the museum, hands stuffed into the pockets of his worn trenchcoat. Kaleigh felt her heartbeat quicken as the man picked up pace, staring directly at her. For once she wished she had a can of pepper spray.

Kaleigh's jaw dropped as Decker, seemingly out of nowhere, walked jauntily up the front steps beneath the cantilevered glass building. A canvas military satchel hung from his shoulder. He was wearing his black Ranger beret, which gave him a distinctly artsy and masculine appearance, enhanced by an all-black ensemble of T-shirt, jeans and lace-up leather boots.

He smiled warmly, flashing a perfect set of white teeth. "I was hoping I might catch you on your way out," he said.

Kaleigh felt her body physically unweight at the sight of Decker. It was pure relief. She knew the dubious art student would not approach as long as Decker was around. In fact, the man had already retreated to the harbor's edge and begun walking toward Northern Avenue.

"I called a cab," she said, trying not to show how excited she was by his presence.

Decker wrapped his arms around her. "I've been thinking about you day and night, thinking about kissing you and holding you and…"

Kaleigh cut him off. "OK, that's enough," she said, pushing him away. "So what are you doing here?"

"I've decided to become an artist. Pursue the bohemian life."

82

"That's good to know. I thought you'd come here to gawk, just like that other creep."

"You mean that guy standing down by the water? I noticed him eyeballing you."

"Very weird. He did more staring than sketching."

Just then the cab pulled up. Decker handed the driver a $10. "Ride's cancelled. This is for your trouble."

The cabbie gave Decker a fuck-you look but he took the $10 and drove off.

"That was my ride."

"I've got Dogman's car. Let's go get a drink."

Pressed deeply into the shadows beside the museum, Luddy watched as Kaleigh slipped an arm through Decker's and laid her head against his shoulder.

CHAPTER 14

May 1986
Boston, Massachusetts

A MADMAN ON THE LOOSE

Rane and Kaleigh were undeniably at odds. Although spring had officially arrived on the calendar, winter had not released its grip on New England and the weather was taking its toll on the general mood. The snow was like a houseguest who didn't realize the party was over and the time to leave long past.

Rane had been cranky and short-tempered, so their lovemaking was lackluster and their relationship frayed. They'd had big blowout during which Kaleigh told him she had modeled nude at the museum several times. Rane told her she was fucked up for doing it. An exhibitionist. A slut.

Despite their increasing disharmony, Kaleigh had convinced herself that Rane was what really mattered. He was "the guy" she was going to marry. She frequently fantasized about the life they would have together, maybe two kids, son and daughter, with a house surrounded by flower gardens and a white picket fence. Rane would be there for her at the end of every day, a Pulitzer Prize-winning author whose dedication to investigative journalism was admirable but whose *raison d'etre* was her and the children.

Kaleigh continued to stay at Rane's apartment at least three nights a week, but she was perplexed by his inability to listen to her concerns, her stories, or even how her work at the museum was going. When they went out on a dinner date, Rane automatically tuned into the conversation at the adjoining tables and was able to recite specific quotes uttered by pure strangers, no matter if it involved a love triangle, a stock market blunder, or some long-shrouded family secret. Such times made Kaleigh fume inside. It was almost as if Rane couldn't stop being a reporter, an information magnet, not for a minute. Such times made Kaleigh sad and she imagined what it would be like to sit across the table, enjoying great food and fine wine, with a man who focused only on her and what she had to say. She'd made an effort to avoid thinking about Decker but she couldn't get him out of her mind. If she were here with Decker, they'd be looking into each other's eyes, and if either told a story, the other would comment in a way that showed they had been listening and interested. They wouldn't give a shit what the people at the adjacent tables were talking about.

Much of Rane's foul mood related to conditions in the newsroom. For weeks he had argued with his news editors, pleading with them to lay off assigning him mundane stories and to let him devote his full time, energy and expertise to investigating a possible serial killer. He had been wound up about the prospect ever since his conversation with Macusovich, who made him promise not to speak a word about it to anyone.

According to the police sergeant, the FBI had taken an interest in the murders because kidnapping was involved, which is a federal offense. Things were definitely heating up. Investigators were pointing to a theory that over the past two years, the same killer had murdered at least three women, perhaps as many as 10, in Boston or along the North Shore. One of the women had lived to tell about the attack that occurred after she landed at Logan Airport and got into what she assumed was a legitimate taxicab. Nancy Perlman was a medical-device saleswoman based in Chicago, but since the attack she was taking some time off to settle her nerves.

Rane knew that Detective Summers had flown to Chicago to interview Perlman and filed a detailed report at

State Police headquarters. Just hearing second hand about the volume of information contained in the narrative, Rane gained plenty of respect for Summers' skill as an investigator. But Summers had refused Rane's request for an interview and would not answer any of his questions off the record.

Summers' report had come to Sgt. Macusovich's attention when he started looking at the murders as a whole and immediately identified a few common denominators. A pattern was evident, just as Summers had projected, but nobody among the State Police detectives in his Essex County homicide unit was about to go public with such a theory. It was too unsettling, unproven, and nobody on the unit wanted to be labeled a crackpot. The report had already caused some detectives to snicker at Summers.

According to Summers, Perlman had escaped with her life because a Good Samaritan had happened along in his car. Her tattered gray pinstriped dress was now part of the evidence collection, as were hair fibers and whatever skin beneath her fingernails she'd managed to tear from her attacker's face and arms. Unfortunately, the officers who responded to the scene had handled the evidence carelessly and already there were questions about the so-called unbroken chain of custody that must be maintained in such cases.

From what Macusovich could determine, the Boston Police homicide detectives on the case agreed the suspect was probably in his 40s and overweight, lived within 30 miles of Boston, and had connections among the cabbies working Logan Airport. The witness claimed her attacker had dark hair and sideburns but no beard, moustache or other facial hair, and scary eyes in deep sockets, so intense she felt as if they were burning a hole into her. She couldn't give a definitive answer about his height – maybe six feet.

Summers had noted in her report that the suspect obviously knew the terrain because he had driven the victim directly to a remote spot that those unfamiliar with the area around the airport might never have known about.

As for the possibility that the suspect was driving a gypsy cab, there were dozens of these vehicles slipping into the ranks of the legitimate airport cabs whose trunk lids bore an official city-issued medallion, their doors emblazoned with company names and phone numbers. Such non-descript vehicles were difficult to trace.

Rane convinced his editors to submit Freedom of Information Act requests for cases involving the abduction of women at Logan Airport during the past decade – all incident reports, letters, court transcripts and other correspondence. But the requests yielded little of value, partly because the police had no identities for some of the victims, and mostly because no confidential information would be released for cases still under investigation.

Realizing the official path was a dead end, Rane turned to his street sources for information, which included law enforcement officers equally frustrated by the situation. After all, some cops felt it would be beneficial to leak information about the investigation to the press, if only to unnerve the suspect and perhaps force him to make a mistake.

Rane managed to cobble together a story that essentially stated police were investigating at least three possible murders of young women over the past 16 months that had tenuous links to a gypsy cab driver at Logan Airport. He knew it was a long shot, but he also lumped those cases together with the woman found in the cornfield, the nature photographer who had washed up on a North Shore beach, and the disappearance of Jenny Lehman.

The story was certainly a stretch because he had no way of knowing whether the woman found on the beach in Marblehead had been inside a taxicab. Nor did he have any solid proof that the woman in the red dress whose body was abandoned in a cornfield had also encountered the phantom cabbie. But it was indisputable that these women – all brunettes in their mid-to-late twenties, had died violently within 20 miles of Boston in a relatively short timeframe, and their murders remained unsolved.

Rane was excited by the prospect of writing about a serial killer and his first story – accompanied by a police composite drawing of the suspect – brought in a flurry of letters and phone calls, including a package of information from a California group eager to link the slayings to the infamous Zodiac killer.

When he showed Macusovich the Zodiac letters, the seasoned cop smirked as he stuffed them back into the manila envelope.

"Nut cakes," he declared. "People love being part of a story like this, but most of them don't know their ass from a hole in the ground. You should have known that when you saw the California return address."

Rane was disappointed but vowed to find out more, so he reached out to a couple of local thugs known for their connections to organized crime. He'd met them in Suffolk Superior Court in Government Center during a lengthy arson trial he had been assigned to cover and, in some weird way, they'd found common ground. By the time the trial was over, they were on a first-name basis and at ease around Rane, convinced he wouldn't make the mistake of ratting them out if they uttered something compromising without thinking.

Rane knew them as Jimmy Two Cubes and Tommy "The Blade", one named for his stinginess when it came to buying ice to chill down beer, the other for his stealth and deftness with a knife. He didn't know their last names and wasn't even sure if their first names were actually those to which they answered. He did know that Jimmy Two Cubes was a meth head and that Blade once rode with the Hell's Angels in nearby Lynn and Salem, retiring with a pronounced limp after a near-fatal motorcycle mishap. He also knew they hung out near Jeffries Point where they ran numbers for a big-time Jewish bookie named Harry Ragansky. According to Rane's sources at the FBI, Ragansky was connected to the Italian Mafiosi in the North End and to the Irish mobsters in South Boston and Eastie, doing a brisk business for both families while trying to stay out of harm's way.

88

Rane went to Cavelli's bakery where he was a regular customer, figuring the owner might tell him where to find Blade and Jimmy Two Cubes, two wannabes known for their passion for biker drugs, sports betting and Italian pastries. The newspaper reporter earnestly said he wanted to place a sizable wager on the upcoming Red Sox game.

Franco Cavelli recognized Rane and knew he worked for the Trib. "You doing a story about running numbers in the neighborhood?"

"Not my style, Franco," said Rane. "If I did that, I'd have nowhere to bet."

The baker chuckled. "Forget Fenway. You're better off putting your money on the dogs at Wonderland."

"I might have to try that, but first I have to find Blade or Jimmy Two Cubes before the Sox go out on the field."

"I wouldn't know how those guys spend their day. They come here in the morning, pick up a box of cannoli and they're gone."

"You must have some idea."

"Try Saratoga Street."

Rane was already aware that Ragansky's betting parlor was in the basement of a rundown triple-decker off Saratoga Street, but he didn't know the exact address, even though it was common knowledge among the local gamblers. After driving back and forth along the street for nearly an hour, Rane found a building fitting the description and parked his motorcycle. The comings and goings told him he had the right place. Jimmy Two Cubes was furtively heading for the front door so Rane waited patiently until he reemerged. Ten minutes later, Rane spotted him pacing nervously on the sidewalk, a cigarette dangling from his thin lips. Rane walked over as though he were simply passing through the neighborhood.

"Hey, Jimmy Two Cubes," he said nonchalantly. "Haven't seen you since the trial. How's Blade these days?"

Jimmy Two Cubes acted as though he didn't recognize Rane, nervously cocking his head in every direction before he whispered, "What are you doing here?"

Rane explained that his boss at the newspaper was on the warpath because he hadn't brought back any information about who might be behind the murders that were putting the neighborhood on edge.

Jimmy Two Cubes responded in hushed tones, wringing his hands. "How the fuck should I know? The big guys are very unhappy about it. Not just Fergus, but Desmond, too. They don't want cops or newspaper reporters nosing around and causing trouble. They don't like all the attention."

"The big guys must have some idea who's responsible. If somebody farts in Eastie, Desmond O'Malley knows about it."

Jimmy Two Cubes nervously scratched both of his arms simultaneously. "Could be. But they wouldn't tell me even if they did. And nobody would ever know if they whacked somebody. That person would just disappear, you know what I'm sayin'?"

"I know how it works," said Rane. "I was just hoping you might point me in the right direction so that I could help find whoever's doing these things."

"Why don't you ask your copper friends? That trooper, Macusovich, has been asking questions all over the place."

"The cops don't tell me anything. I really don't think they care if the killer gets caught. They're more concerned with getting coffee and doughnuts."

"That's for sure. Fuckin' cops. They're all useless."

Jimmy Two Cubes drew up the hood of his sweatshirt, took several steps away from Rane, then turned and said, "I hear the one they're looking for lives in the neighborhood. O'Malley sent down the orders and Fergus Cavanagh is just trying to figure out what to do with him."

With that, Jimmy Two Cubes literally trotted along the sidewalk and ducked into an alleyway. Rane didn't follow. He knew that was everything he would get.

CHAPTER 15

May 1986
Boston, Massachusetts

WHEN THE STORY BREAKS

Luddy Pagano's face reddened as he read the story of the so-called Boston Butcher, his fingers clenched tightly around the edges of the newspaper. Although the story gave no precise descriptions, it made clear the police were looking at the possibility of a methodical serial killer at large in the Boston metro area. The story mentioned the killer was most likely male, of middle age and cunning enough to lure women into his clutches – all generalized characteristics that the cops and the public pretty much presumed.

The piece also included a quote from the police commissioner, warning women not to venture out alone at night and to report any suspicious activity. The killer was undoubtedly familiar with the city, the commissioner safely theorized.

Luddy cursed the blonde State Police detective for pursuing the investigation and putting the serial-killer thought into the minds of others – especially the news media and law enforcement officers who previously ignored the possibility. He vowed to make Lt. Hannah Summers pay for the misery she'd caused. He imagined striking her over the head with a tire iron, ripping the gold detective badge from its lanyard, cutting off her ponytail with a clamming knife and raping her until that in-control look on her face was transformed into pure fear.

Luddy spotted Rane Bryson's byline on the story, which contained a quote from Sgt. Macusovich, suggesting a gypsy cab driver working near Logan Airport could be linked to the disappearances and possibly the deaths. What he found most disturbing were the quotes from unnamed sources supposedly familiar with the activities of Boston's organized crime families. According to the story, the sources claimed the serial killer would soon be stopped not by the police, but by the underworld itself.

"When we find this guy, nobody will ever hear from him again," Bryson quoted one organized crime acolyte as having told him in a confidential interview. "People shouldn't have to be afraid to go out in this city."

Luddy tossed the newspaper aside and continued shucking clams, flipping the gooey innards into white plastic buckets that would later be sold to area seafood restaurants. As he worked he envisioned sticking Rane Bryson in the heart with his shucking knife's stiff three-inch blade, or maybe an ice pick. But that sort of death would be too quick and deprived of all enjoyment, he thought. Instead, he imagined the smug journalist hog-tied and gagged, only in this new vision he'd nicked several of Rane's veins with a filet knife to ensure slow but fatal bleeding, during which time his beautiful girlfriend would be repeatedly raped and ultimately slain before his eyes. He didn't know how she would die, but he already had six different scenarios in mind. He might even hang her from the ceiling and light her on fire, a thought that caused him to lose his concentration and deeply slice his thumb with the sharp blade.

Luddy cursed aloud, which caught the attention of several customers in the market. He scowled at them as he bundled his finger in a soiled rag. The television news was still droning on, but there had been only scant mention of the homicide investigations. Luddy knew that without pictures, a TV story wouldn't get much airtime.

When the seafood market closed for the day, he went straight to Nemo's.

"Shucker you stink," said Bubby, singing aloud as she wiped the rim of a cocktail glass.

"Fuck you. You're probably smelling your own cunt."

Bubby grinned, exposing her brownish teeth. She set a draft beer in front of him. "Why don't you shower after you leave that place?"

"Why should I? Who am I going to run into here, the fuckin' President? I don't think Cindy Crawford is going to walk through the door."

"It might help you make some friends."

"I've got friends. Plenty of them. And none of them complain that I smell. I'm a fuckin' rose."

"Just a suggestion."

"Well, keep it to yourself."

Luddy knew she was right and, in her own strange way, trying to be helpful. His clothes, hands, forearms, and most likely his face and hair, smelled strongly of fish. Perhaps in another era this might have been considered manly, but he knew those days were gone.

A slender, balding man in creased bluejeans, a pink golf shirt and tennis shoes sat down on the adjacent stool. Bubby greeted him cheerfully. He ordered a scotch and soda. His nose visibly twitched as he sipped and cast a sidelong look at Luddy. "Let me square up with you. I think I'll finish this at a table," he said politely.

Luddy's dark-set eyes locked onto the man with contempt. The man immediately stood, fidgeted with his wallet, gently laid a $5 bill on the bar and told Bubby to keep the change.

Luddy belched loudly. "Fuck you buddy." The man was already walking away and didn't turn around. Luddy glanced at Bubby, awaiting her comment.

"Thanks for losing me another customer."

"This place is full of assholes. More every day."

"Get over it. At least they spend money, not like some of the regulars who sit here all day nursing three or four $1 drafts and don't even leave a tip."

Luddy chugged the remainder of his beer, then pushed back his bar stool with such force it toppled to the floor with a loud clatter. Several customers looked over as he grudgingly picked it up and set it back in place. He flung a few singles on the bar and stomped out.

CHAPTER 16

June 1986
Boston, Massachusetts

WEDDING BELL BLUES

Luddy stared at himself in the mirror. He felt
awkward wearing dress slacks, collared shirt, necktie and
blazer. But he and his mother had been invited to a wedding
at a sprawling restaurant on Route 1 in Saugus and he was
obligated to attend. His mother had insisted, so Luddy dug
the clothes from his closet and sniffed them to check for the
smell of mothballs.

There were more than 400 people at the June wedding
with many guests of Italian heritage. The band played the
tarantella and other favorites, and the older guests danced
until they were exhausted. Then the younger crowd took
over, including the bride and groom who spun wildly to the
band's blaring disco. The groom was clearly intoxicated.
When he'd reached up his bride's thigh to remove her garter,
he went farther than what most guests expected, earning him
a friendly slap. Most of the bridal party found his impolite
move entertaining. Luddy's attention was riveted on a tall,
slender bridesmaid with dark brown hair that flowed across
her shoulders and down her back. The beautiful young
woman had danced repeatedly with the groom, wrapping
her arms tightly around his neck and grinding him with her
shapely hips. The flirtation had prompted comments from
the guest tables nearest the dance floor, but the groom didn't

seem to mind.

Luddy continued to watch, feeling the anger form in the pit of his stomach. His fists curled when the lithe brunette pushed two other women aside to catch the bridal bouquet, which she held above her head like a victory torch.

The groom twirled his bride's garter and sent it flying toward a horde of bachelors. With a captivating smile, a handsome man of Tuscan decent and bedroom eyes caught it in mid-air. He nonchalantly walked toward the beautiful woman holding the bouquet, extended a hand and helped her climb atop a chair.

Although the bridesmaid was intoxicated, she managed to balance while the good-looking stranger slipped the bride's garter over her high-heeled foot and up beyond her knee. The band churned out a sexy riff. Other men stopped dancing and gathered around. They began to clap as the garter was wriggled higher and the entire sleeve of the man's black tuxedo vanished beneath the gown. The bridesmaid, whose name was Rose Cavelli, flashed a dazzling smile and squealed with delight.

When the show was over, the dancing resumed and Rose Cavelli zigzagged toward the ladies' room in a nearby alcove. The groom followed and waited outside the door. When Rose emerged, wearing fresh makeup with crimson lipstick, the groom put out his hands to dance. Both were inebriated and kissed as they swayed to the music, pressing into each other. Rose planted a perfect outline of lips on his cheek. The groom dropped to his knees and announced he'd like the opportunity to remove the garter from her thigh. Rose shot him a sultry look that said go ahead. Just as he reached up beneath the gown his bride rounded the corner.

"Enough," the woman shouted, yanking off her veil and tossing it to the floor. "What the fuck is the matter with you two?" She glared at her supposed close friend Rose, who immediately stopped squirming and attempted to straighten the wrinkles in her dress but nearly fell over. The groom tried to stand and assist her but his wife shouted, "Mario, get your hands off of her. And Rose, get the fuck out of my wedding."

Rose burst into tears and ran back into the ladies' room. She tripped and broke one of her heels as she pulled open the door. The bandleader picked up on what was happening and immediately switched to a slower number that would bring couples together and perhaps calm the situation.

Luddy found Rose Cavelli sitting on a curb in the parking lot, clutching her high heels and smoking a cigarette. He introduced himself as a close family friend.

"I need to get out of here," she whined. "I need to go home but I came with the bridal party and now I'm stuck."

Luddy put on his most charming smile. He acted both shy and polite. He soon learned that her parents owned Cavelli's bakery and immediately offered her a ride. He hadn't seen her since she was a child.

As they talked, the bridal party began leaving along with most of the guests. Word quickly spread that the fun would continue at the groom's house a half mile away and everyone was invited – everyone but Rose Cavelli.

Luddy took her hand and ushered her toward his car, which was missing its TAXI roof sign. He was glad he'd washed and vacuumed it. Rose had trouble walking. Her feet dragged across the warm asphalt. Luddy put an arm around her but she pulled away.

"I'm going to call a cab."

"You don't need to do that. I live close by. We're neighbors."

Luddy noticed the sudden fear in the woman's eyes. "You can trust me. My mother will be coming with us," he said.

At that, Rose seemed relieved. Luddy opened the back door of the Crown Vic and told her to sit and wait while he retrieved his mother from the restaurant. "She's probably trying to take all the flower arrangements," he said.

Celeste had nothing to say to Rose on the ride to East Boston, though she knew the young woman's father, Franco, and mother Gloria, because they both worked at the family bakery. Celeste was feeling pious. She had seen Rose flirt and cause trouble at the wedding, an act she thought unforgivable without a visit to the confessional where Father Federico would dispense a lengthy penance. She wanted to strike Rose across the bottom with a cat-o-nine tail, just as her father had done to her whenever she was out of line.

Luddy could see Rose was disturbed by his mother's silence. "The guests are all going back to the family home in Saugus. Maybe you should go there and apologize," he suggested.

Rose seemed to be considering the idea as Luddy escorted his mother to the front door of their Jeffries Point tenement. "Momma, you go up and get in bed. I'm going to give this girl a ride back to Saugus so she can make things right."

Celeste nodded approval and pushed open the door. Luddy returned quickly to the car, worried the young woman might have had too much time to think and object to his plan. Rose was conflicted but finally agreed. Luddy assured her she was doing the right thing and that she'd feel much better the next morning.

Rose sat in the front seat and curled her legs beneath her dress. Luddy had difficulty keeping his eyes off the flesh exposed by the slit along her thigh. He drove north and exited onto Route 107, known locally as the Lynn Marsh Road. It was a dark stretch of two-lane highway flanked by tidal marsh. Luddy knew it well. He occasionally worked part-time at the Conley & Daggett commercial lobster pound on the east side of the road. Directly behind the ramshackle wooden building and saltwater pens was a narrow path of muddy sand leading to the water's edge. The path was nearly invisible amid the 10-foot tall bulrushes and groves of sumac.

Luddy jerked the steering wheel toward the unpaved parking lot, drove down the sandy path and turned off his headlights. Rose, who had been dozing, was suddenly awake. She pressed her back against the passenger door.

Luddy smiled. "We should talk about what you're going to say before we get there."

Rose clutched her broken shoe. "I know what to say. Let's just go."

Luddy switched off the engine and inched closer to her along the bench seat. She recoiled, but he continued until his knees were touching her legs.

Luddy leaned forward and tried to kiss her. "Get away from me," she said, pressing her hands against his chest.

When he tried again she slapped him hard. As the sting spread across his cheek he punched her full force in the face, knocking her head against the window. He grabbed the black silk scarf around her neck and twisted it until the material tightened into a garrote.

Rose tried to slip her fingers between her skin and the scarf, but Luddy was twisting it tighter. When he finally released the pressure, she struggled to breathe. Rose tried to swallow but was paralyzed by fear when she saw the undiluted evil in Luddy's eyes. She pleaded with him to stop, but it was as though Luddy were in a trance. He held the scarf with his left hand while his right tore away her underwear. Rose tried to squirm away but she was pinned by Luddy's 290 pounds atop her. She felt him spread her legs. Her long fingernails dug into his face. She clawed his ears, but after each attempt to fight back the garrote tightened until she had no more air, filling her with unbearable pain seconds before she lost consciousness. Luddy didn't notice that she had stopped fighting. He was in the full throes of rape and didn't look up until he was satisfied. Rose's head had slumped to one side and she had stopped breathing.

Nervousness set it as Luddy thought about how he would dispose of the body. He stripped off Rose's gown, bra and silk scarf, scooped up her purse and then dragged her body into the shallow, brackish water where the crabs were sure to find her. He wasn't thinking clearly. Rose's body floated face up atop the reeds, the black soil suspended in the water washing across her clear skin like so many flecks.

Luddy knew his chances of getting caught would increase if he left her in the marsh. Even if he obscured the impression of his car tires using a tree branch or whatever else might be handy, the police might find too much evidence. Then he remembered the roll-off dumpster behind the building that was filled with fish guts, lobster and crab shells, and whatever marine life waste had been tossed inside during the past 24 hours. The disposal company hauled it away before dawn each day. He didn't know if they did so on Sunday, but it was a better plan than leaving her body in the marsh. He snipped a lock of her hair and hoisted the young woman into the yaw of the dumpster.

Three days later, a bulldozer driver at the landfill in nearby Peabody found the body. The story made headlines because Rose Cavelli was strewn amid dozens of mannequins discarded by Filene's Basement, a popular department store in downtown Boston. Rane was among those reporters who covered the story, and it was he who tracked down the bulldozer driver for what became the most-repeated quote in the news.

"I thought she was a mannequin," the driver had told police and later repeated to Rane with more elaboration. "She was just lying there in the pile, her arms and legs spread at crazy angles just like the mannequins. At first I couldn't believe what I was seeing, but when I got closer, I realized it was a real person, and that she was dead."

CHAPTER 17

June 1986
Boston, Massachusetts

LOOKING OVER YOUR SHOULDER

As she walked home from the T station to her Back Bay apartment, Kaleigh sensed she was being followed. She tried to slough it off to her overactive imagination, but there was no ignoring the fact that women her age were being targeted in and around Boston. It seemed everyone was talking about Rose Cavelli and how she was last seen leaving a wedding with a guest who police had not publicly identified. It was such a horrible story with a ghoulish ending among mannequins in a landfill. Even Rane, who was accustomed to gruesomeness from working the police beat, had found the circumstances repulsive. Whoever had done that to her was beyond sick, Kaleigh thought.

Rane had told her about the weird phone calls he was getting at the paper, though he didn't mention the one deep-voiced caller who had advised he stop writing serial-killer stories if he wanted to keep his girlfriend healthy and alive. He figured it was just another nut job or somebody with a vested interest in the East Boston Chamber of Commerce, worried the stories would keep business away. He also considered it might be one of his colleagues pranking.

Later that night, Kaleigh's phone rang. There was heavy breathing on the other end that made her shiver. These weren't sexualized respirations. The sounds were more akin to nostril and mouth noises made by a large animal. She hung up and called Rane but he didn't pick up at his desk. She tried his apartment but there was no answer. She heard the clattering of trashcans in the alley and someone shined a spotlight on the apartment windows facing the street. When she looked out, a dark car pulled away with its lights off. She tried Rane again but no answer, so she called Decker. He answered on the first ring.

"Decker?"

"Kaleigh Adams, my favorite exhibition space designer, not to mention my favorite exhibitionist – I mean model."

She ignored his playful comments. "Decker, how would I know if somebody is following me, because I think there might be?"

Decker immediately grew serious. "Why do you think so? Did you see somebody or hear something?"

"I just got this feeling and then my phone rang. Nobody said anything on the other end, but I could hear breathing. It really freaked me out. It wasn't you, was it?"

"Stay there. I'm coming right over," he said, and before she could object the line went dead.

Ten minutes later, Decker was knocking on her apartment door. "It's me," he shouted.

Kaleigh didn't want to let him inside. If Rane found out she and Decker were at her place alone, there would be another big blowout. There would be suspicion and jealousy and other emotions that tend to destruct relationships.

"Hey. Do I have to kick in the door? That's what we did in Lebanon."

Kaleigh opened the door all the way but Decker didn't move. He just stood in the hallway staring at her.

"Well. You're here. You might as well come in. And thank you."

Decker smiled briefly with his eyes before he literally marched into the apartment, flicked on lights and checked every room. He even made certain the window locks were secure and the blinds pulled. When he was satisfied nobody had tried to break in, he returned to the living room where Kaleigh was seated on the couch.

"I appreciate your doing that. It's nice to have a friend."

"Yep. That's me. Your friend and good buddy. Glad to be of service. I figured you were in hiding. Haven't seen you around. Where are your roommates?"

"I'm not sure. Probably shopping or working late."

Decker flopped into one of the oversized marshmallow chairs. He wasn't in his cammies. Instead, he wore faded and ripped bluejeans, a black T-shirt with the message Eat Fish emblazoned across the front and a pair of scruffy Sperry Topsiders.

"It's so beautiful outside it's a shame to have to lock the windows, but I think you should keep them that way until we find out what's going on," he advised. "Let's take a walk. It might do you good."

Kaleigh glanced down at her flannel two-piece plaid pajamas. "I'm not exactly dressed for a walk around the neighborhood."

"I'll wait."

Kaleigh retreated into her bedroom and emerged two minutes later dressed in a black leotard, jumper and charcoal flats. Decker was loaded with questions as they strolled along Commonwealth Avenue on this mild June evening. Did she get a license plate number on the car that pulled away? Did her roommates have any known enemies, old boyfriends holding a grudge? Were any of them involved in occupations that might result in unsatisfied clients?

Kaleigh bristled with each question. "Let's get a few things straight," she finally unloaded. "Me and my roommates aren't spies, hookers, drug addicts, gamblers or anything that might resemble any of those things. We all work for a living, get a little rowdy on the weekend and basically lead normal lives."

"No offense," he said.

"None taken. We aren't so out of the ordinary that somebody would want to kill us. They'd have no reason."

"Some people don't need a reason. They just want to kill."

"Thanks for the pep talk."

"I'm not trying to be smart. I'm just saying there are psychopaths, sociopaths and every other kind of fucked-up individual out there who do harm only because it pleases them and suits their needs."

"And you think one of them might be interested in me?"

"I didn't say that. I'm just trying to figure out why somebody might be stalking you, calling you and shining a spotlight at your windows."

Decker could see she was trembling as her hands moved nervously through her hair. Her eyes welled with tears. He put his arms around her.

"Everything's going to be all right," he whispered into her ear. "We'll get this figured out."

"Do you think it's that weird guy from the art class?"

"Don't know. Could be. If you get me his name I'll check it out."

"I think I have it at work."

"Good. And what about Rane, does he have any enemies who might want to get to him through you?"

"Rane makes a lot of enemies in his job."

"I know that, but is there anyone in particular these days who he might have mentioned?"

Kaleigh knew Rane was getting plenty of phone calls and unsigned letters at work that were related to his recent stories about what appeared to be a string of serial murders. But most of those communications were anonymous.

Decker nodded. "What about your old boyfriends?"

"They were boys who were my friends. We parted ways without bad feelings. They were gentlemen. We were all going in different directions during and after college."

"What about between their departure and Rane's arrival?"

"What do you want, my sexual history?"

"I'm trying to help."

104

"Rane is the first man I've slept with since graduating college and moving to Boston. I guess you could say I had a dry spell."

"For three years?"

"Fuck you."

"Sorry."

"You should be."

"Look, this isn't easy for me. When we were in Lebanon and other countries that I'm not supposed to talk about, the guys in my squad were my best friends. We'd do anything for each other. I actually saw one guy give his life for three others when we came under attack while on patrol. It was that level of devotion. So when you and I agreed to become friends, well, I took it very seriously, knowing that I'd do whatever it took if you ever got into a jam. And now it looks like you might be in one."

"Decker, you know we're more than friends."

"But how can that be when you're just about living with Rane?"

Kaleigh's eyes filled with tears. "Please. I don't know. I'm so confused and now somebody is stalking me. I'm scared."

Decker pulled her head into his chest. "Don't worry. We'll get this sorted out."

The two-hour stroll seemed to calm Kaleigh down. When they returned to her apartment's front door, Decker caught a slight movement in his peripheral vision. A dead cat was hanging from the nearby fire escape. Kaleigh screamed.

"Stay behind me," he said, taking a few steps toward the limp calico. He examined the animal for a collar or ownership tag, but there was only the strand of monofilament fishing line that extended from the cat's neck to the wrought iron railing about eight feet above them. A trashcan rested on its side and Decker presumed whoever killed the cat had used it to reach the fire escape and tie off the line.

"Yours?"

Kaleigh shook her head. "I don't have a cat."

"What about your roommates?"

"No cats."

"Let's get inside."

Kaleigh was clearly distraught as she entered the apartment. One roommate was on her laptop at a small desk, the other reading a magazine on the couch. Kaleigh asked if either had seen the dead cat hanging in the alley. The roommates simultaneously returned incredulous stares that seemed to question the woman's sanity. No, they hadn't noticed any dead cats hanging in the alley.

Decker theorized that was perhaps because the alley wasn't well lighted, or else the animal had been hung after they arrived home.

Taylor Nelson seemed only mildly concerned as she checked out her lustrous auburn hair in the wall mirror. "If the landlord has to get rid of it, he'll probably charge us. He's such a dick," she said. "Then again, he should have fixed the broken light. Maybe then people wouldn't hang dead cats in our alley."

"How can you be like that? The poor little thing didn't deserve to die in such a horrible way," said Gina DeAngelis, who had been sipping a glass of wine and pecking at her keyboard when the commotion began. She had since walked to the window and was peering through the blinds. "Why would somebody do such a thing? We should call the police."

"They probably won't make it a priority," Decker explained, trying to veil his amusement at her suggestion.

Kaleigh realized she had not introduced Decker but both roommates were well aware of his presence the moment he entered the room. Gina, her skintight pink workout suit accentuating her perky breasts, snatched three different brands of beer from the refrigerator and held them out to Decker without saying a word.

Decker smiled at Gina with his eyes and chose the Pabst Blue Ribbon. "Much appreciated," he said, twisting off the cap.

Gina returned a flirtatious look and suggested he sit on the couch while they all discussed the situation. As Kaleigh recounted the details of her phantom stalker, Taylor

106

rolled her eyes in disbelief. "Everybody wants you, Kaleigh. We all know that," she said.

Gina feigned interest but her attention was obviously focused on Decker's biceps and firm abs. "Where do you go to the gym?"

"Yes. Tell me," said Taylor, a devout fashionista who hadn't been to a gym since her sophomore year in college. "You obviously work out."

Kaleigh stood and sighed, exasperated by the notion that nobody was taking her seriously, despite the fact that a dead cat was swaying outside the front door. She also realized she was feeling jealous because her roommates were fawning over Decker.

Decker drained the beer and diverted the talk away from physical fitness. Instead, he offered advice on how to secure their apartment against intruders, starting with installing extra locks on doors and windows, setting the lights on timers, leaving the television on or music playing when they weren't home, and many other strategies. Kaleigh's roommates were rapt as he spoke. Before he left, he gave both roommates his phone number and instructed them to call him anytime, day or night, if something was amiss, a gesture of chivalry that further incensed Kaleigh even though she knew it was the right thing to do.

It was after 11 p.m. when Rane phoned Kaleigh to say he'd received her messages. He apologized, explaining he had been busy chasing two breaking stories on deadline. Kaleigh knew that was the nature of the news business. She related the highlights of her evening, including the call to and subsequent visit by Decker.

Rane didn't respond immediately. After an awkward pause, he asked, "Why did you call him?"

"I tried to reach you but you were out on a story. I didn't know who else to call and I was really scared."

"Why didn't you call the police?"

"I thought they'd think I was crazy."

"And Decker didn't."

"No. He tried to help."

Rane was silent on the other end of the line as he thought about what to say next.

"You there?"

"Yes. I'm just trying to figure out who might have called you or shined that spotlight on your windows, not to mention leave behind a dead cat. I did get a couple of unusual calls at the paper this week from somebody who casually mentioned that he knew I had a girlfriend."

"Rane, why are you telling me this now? Don't you think you should have shared that detail as soon as you got it?"

"It didn't seem important. I get all sorts of odd calls."

"But this one involves me. Unless, of course, you have another girlfriend that they're referring to," Kaleigh snapped, then hung up the phone.

Rane immediately redialed. Gina moved to pick up the receiver but Kaleigh told her to let in ring.

"But what it it's for me?"

"It's not," Kaleigh snapped. "And if it is, they'll call back tomorrow."

"Easy for you to say when you have one gorgeous guy coming by to take you for a stroll around town and another calling as soon as he gets out of work. Must be nice."

"Decker and I are just friends."

Gina and Taylor traded glances and in unison rolled their eyes. "Well, now that he's given us his number, I guess we're his friends, too," said Taylor, smirking as she gulped her third glass of white wine.

"I think I'll call him tomorrow," Gina teased. "I want to make sure I understood what he was saying about dead-bolting the door so that nobody gets in. Do you think Decker would agree to sleep here, just until we're sure everything is OK?"

Kaleigh knew they were teasing her but she was still too upset from the night to appreciate the girl humor. She poured herself a glass of wine, extended the middle finger of her right hand toward both women seated on the couch, and without a word stomped off to her room.

108

Detective Summers had had an equally disturbing day. While jogging along Beacon Street she thought she saw a dark sedan following her. She spotted the vehicle again on her return route, parked on a side street in her neighborhood, but the driver sped off as she approached. The vehicle looked like a Ford but was too far away to get the license plate number. Summers didn't mention it to the other detectives at work the next day because they'd only accuse her of being paranoid. But that night she slept with her 9mm Sig Sauer under her pillow.

CHAPTER 18

June 1986
Boston, Massachusetts

COPS OF EVERY KIND

Rane ran into Macusovich at the municipal courthouse on Meridian Street in Eastie the next day. A paunchy man in his mid-40s with wavy light brown hair and long sideburns accompanied the State Police detective. Macusovich introduced him as FBI Agent Kevin Finley, assigned to the bureau's organized crime task force in Boston.

"Kevin has read all your stories," said Macusovich, nodding toward Finley who was wearing an expensive, two-piece, tailored suit, Italian leather shoes and Tommy Hilfiger sunglasses. "He's a fan."

"And?" Rane noticed the custom clothing as well as the gold Rolex Submariner on Finley's wrist. His first thought was cops usually wear Timex and crappy shoes.

Finley looked directly at Rane. "Your stories are well written."

"You an editor?"

"Hey, Rane," said Macusovich. "Kevin was just being friendly."

Finley continued. "Your stories contain lots of information and most of it is accurate, which is more than I can say for the majority of your colleagues in this great city. I was wondering if you left anything out that might help us."

Rane didn't like the guy. "I wish I had more details to put in them."

"Well, stick around and maybe we can get you something nobody else will have," the federal agent said. "We've got a few suspects regarding the recent homicides, but as you certainly know, there's a code of silence in this part of the city. People don't want to get involved."

Macusovich explained that the neighborhood gangsters, namely the bookmakers, extortionists, loansharks and enforcers, were feeling uneasy due to the increased police presence. In fact, one player in particular had dispatched his underlings to find out who was killing these women, and to put an end to it.

"You mean the guy who heads up the Chamber of Commerce?"

"Don't be a fuckhead," Macusovich said. "We're trying to give you a break."

The FBI agent locked eyes with Rane, "You ever heard of Fergus Cavanaugh?"

Rane smirked. "Fergus Cavanaugh," he said, repeating the name for emphasis. "Oh yeah. Ex-IRA operative suspected of a string of bombings in Belfast and the death of at least two British soldiers, but nobody could prove it and all the potential witnesses either went underground or literally are in the ground. I wrote a story about him a while back. These days he pretty much runs all the day-to-day organized crime activities in South Boston and Eastie. But he still answers to Desmond O'Malley. I guess he wanted to live in a place with more charm than Belfast."

Macusovich chimed in. "Well, Rane from Maine, you certainly know your shit when it comes to OC. Did you know his full name is Fergus Ultan Cavanaugh? That's why some people call him Fuck behind his back. His initials are FUC – get it? He can be one mean son of a bitch. But from what we hear, he's on our side when it comes to tracking down the person or persons responsible for the recent murders. But listen, fuckhead, you can't print that. Understand?"

Rane nodded.

"So what can I print?"

"You can say you have it on good authority that the Federal Bureau of Investigation has joined the State Police in this case and their pooled resources will lead to an arrest," said Macusovich.

"Sounds like a press release. Nobody will read it. And I won't write it."

"Well, you can word it however you want."

"That's not news. Nobody gives a shit if the feds and the state are working together on a case. What about Rose Cavelli?

Macusovich smiled at the FBI agent. "See, what did I tell you. He's sharp."

"OK, cut the flattery. You know it doesn't work."

"What about her? What do you want to know?"

"Beautiful young woman like that. Why would somebody want her dead?"

"That's what we're trying to find out."

Macusovich showed Rane a police photograph of Rose Cavelli's body amid the plastic, flesh-toned mannequins. There were deep furrows cut into her neck, as though she had been strangled. "Her parents showed me her highschool yearbook photo. Beautiful girl. Witnesses told us she'd had a lot to drink at a wedding on Route 1 and made a scene. Somebody apparently offered her a ride home but she never got there."

"And you think that person is the same person who murdered the other women?"

"We're not saying that," Macusovich answered. "But we have people under surveillance, guys who have done time for sexual assault and are back out on the street."

"The marks on her neck look a lot like those on the girl with the red dress who was found in the cornfield in Topsfield."

Macusovich bit softly into his lower lip, as though measuring what he was about to say. "Could be. But the girl in red wasn't wearing a scarf. And no, you can't print that either."

112

Rane slapped his spiral notebook closed. "Gentlemen, it has been a pleasure talking to you," he said sarcastically.

"We'd appreciate a call if you hear anything," said Agent Finley.

Rane knew he'd never call Finley. "I'll save myself a quarter and let you read about it in my next story."

CHAPTER 19

June 1986
Boston, Massachusetts

RELAXING IN THE MOUNTAINS

Luddy Pugano hated his small bedroom, but it was bigger than his mother's and the fire escape landing was right outside the only window. He had lived in the apartment his entire life, the only child of an unmarried Italian woman scorned for her indiscretion. He'd never met his merchant marine father and only asked about him when he felt the need, questions to which his mother replied, "You're better off not knowing. He was a bastard."

Yes, Luddy had thought at the time, my father was a bastard and so am I – the neighborhood *bastardo*. No father on the sidelines at my Little League games. Nobody to call dad or papa.

Luddy sprawled across the bed and loosened his belt, releasing a stomach bloated by an excess of alcohol and rich food. He was studying his collection of maps from throughout the world. Some of the maps were tattered and marked with inky scribbling. Several words clearly had been written with black marker on a New England roadmap: ocean, forest, field, river, mountain, marsh. After each were notations about cities, parks, campgrounds and special interest attractions. Taped to the New England campgrounds map was a yellowed newspaper clipping from the Manchester Union Leader about a rash of murders in and around those recreational areas and a reference by police to the so-called "Campground Killer."

Pigeons were cooing loudly on the fire escape. Luddy reached under his bed and pulled out a gas-fired pellet pistol. He quietly shot three birds dead before the others figured out what was going on and flew away. He enjoyed shooting them and figured he had killed hundreds since his early marksmanship days with his mother's Daisy pump-action BB rifle. Pigeons were dirty and noisy. He never understood why some people fed them bags of seed down by the waterfront on Marginal Street. Didn't they realize they were just helping to spread disease?

Celeste knocked on her son's bedroom door. The intrusion caused Luddy to clench his teeth.

"What do you want?"

"I want to talk to you."

"About what?"

"Let me in."

Luddy unlocked the door and opened it a few inches. Celeste looked intently at her son while trying to see beyond his shoulders into the room. "What happened to Rose after you left here with her?"

"How should I know? I gave her a ride back to the groom's house in Saugus. She wanted to go inside by herself. She told me to just let her off outside the party, so that's what I did and then I drove straight home."

"You know the police are going to come here. I'm surprised they haven't showed up already.
Luddy pressed against the door so that Celeste could no longer see his entire body. "Why would they come here?"

"They're going to want to speak with you. People saw us leave the wedding with Rose."

"Well, fuck them. I hope they find whoever killed that girl, but I've got nothing to tell them. After I dropped you off, I gave her a lift back to the groom's house in Saugus so that she could apologize. She went inside and didn't come back out. That's it."

"Luddy, are you sure you didn't have anything to do with this?"

With a linebacker's agility, Luddy yanked open the door, quickly closed it behind him and grabbed Celeste by the neck, lifting her frail body off the floor and pressing her against the wall. The frightened woman gasped for air. As though he had snapped out of a trance, Luddy released his mother and she slumped to the floor.

"Jesus Christ, Ma. You see what you made me do?"

The woman crawled toward the stairs.

"Let me help you up."

"No. Get away. Don't touch me. You've got a bad temper," she shouted, picking up the broken gold chain necklace with medallion of the Virgin Mary that lay on the floor.

Luddy looked at the medallion in his mother's hand. "I'm sorry. I'll get you a new one at the shrine."

"I don't know why I raised you. Your father didn't want you. He never came back," she said, waiting apprehensively for him to strike her. "I should have given you to the church and gotten on with my life."

Luddy ignored her. He rummaged in his closet, yanking out a sleeping bag, Army surplus backpack, battery-powered lantern, folding shovel, jackknife, Bowie knife, canteen, a nested set of aluminum cookware and worn workboots. He stuffed most of the items in a canvas duffle along with the pellet pistol. His car was parked in a nearby alley that left only inches to open the driver's door.

Once on I-93 north he studied the road map and headed for New Hampshire's White Mountains. Exhausted by the ocean, the coastal flatlands and saltmarsh, he looked forward to hiking the rocky peaks. With the exception of digging clams in the Revere and Winthrop saltmarshes or fishing from his cabin cruiser in Boston Harbor, he'd never been much of an outdoorsman. He preferred to spend his time in the neighborhood bars. And when he did go to New Hampshire in summer, his time was usually spent driving slowly through the various campgrounds, looking for

116

opportunities. If nothing of interest presented itself, he'd sleep in his car and head back to Eastie in the morning.

Luddy pulled the Crown Vic off I-93 at the Lincoln exit and stopped at a supermarket where he bought two cans of clam chowder, Slim Jims, a tin of mixed nuts, a package of Oreos, box of Cheez-Its, jars of peanut butter and jelly, an orange, a loaf of sliced white bread and a six pack of Budweiser cans. Soon he was barreling along the Kangamangus Highway, which cuts a scenic swath through the mountains all the way from Lincoln to Conway. He reached into the glovebox and gulped from a half pint of cheap vodka. He didn't like the taste, but he'd heard somewhere that doctors and lawyers drank vodka because it didn't smell in case they got pulled over by the cops. He didn't know if that was true, but he'd grown accustomed to the lighter-fluid taste. Before long the powerful Crown Vic was barreling along the winding Kangamangus, passing slow-moving Winnebago motor homes and station wagons filled with families like they were standing still. He nearly drove a camper van off the side of the road when he passed on a blind turn only to see a logging truck heading straight for him. The man in the camper van laid on his horn so Luddy flipped him the bird, thrusting his left arm out the driver's window in hopes the man could see the middle finger protruding above the roof.

All along the highway were signs pointing to trails, campsites and scenic overlooks. Luddy randomly picked a destination and after driving a few miles along a narrow road pulled into an unpaved parking lot where the hiking trail began. He was physically overweight and out of shape, but he plodded for over an hour along an easy trail that branched off the Kangamangus and gradually climbed the mountainside. He angrily slapped at the mosquitoes on his arms, wishing he'd worn a long-sleeve shirt. He was sweating profusely as he approached a clear stream that cascaded over a series of waterfalls. He had to admit that the scenery was absolutely beautiful.

Luddy rested his backpack on the sunbaked rock,

dipped his hands into the cool water and splashed his face. He had stopped thinking about Rose Cavelli and the law enforcement officers who might knock on his door. Up here in the mountains, he could let go and empty his mind of its dark thoughts. As the water spilled down his face, he heard singing coming from farther up the trail. It was a woman's voice. He listened. The words had something to do with feeling manic and not wanting to face work on Monday morning. He vaguely recognized the song from the pop radio stations and he could relate to the words because he, too, hated Mondays at the fish market, the way it made his clothes and hands stink no matter how much he washed them.

The young woman was startled to see Luddy kneeling on the flat rocks on the far side of the stream, the water glistening on his face and staining the front of his shirt. She was wearing cut-off bluejean shorts with a frayed hem, a tight black tank top that accentuated her plump breasts, hiking boots with florescent pink socks rolled down, and a Red Sox baseball cap. The backpack straps were pressing into her shoulders.

Luddy couldn't help but give her a lascivious look, which she found unnerving. He caught himself and flashed a friendly smile, all the while thinking he'd like to rip off her clothes and fuck her in the shallow stream with the water coursing around their bodies. She'd be his Mountain Mistress.

The woman glanced back toward the trail in the direction from which she'd come. Luddy wondered if she'd simply bolt, but she was at least 45 minutes from the nearest road even if walking at a steady pace. He stood and continued to smile.

"Hard to believe this water is good enough to drink," he said in the most casual tone he could fake, reaching for the plastic, military-style canteen tied to his backpack. "I was just going to get a refill."

The woman nodded but still hadn't spoken a word. She studied the stream, looking for a network of rocks that would allow her to stay dry as she crossed.

"You want help getting across?"

"No thanks. I can manage."

Fuck you, Luddy thought. Another self-reliant bitch.

Just then the pealing sound of laughter came from the trail – more voices. Another woman and two men emerged from the woods. His Mountain Mistress was obviously relieved to see them.

"Jenna," the other woman called out. "We can't keep up with you. You're like a machine."

"Way too much energy," one of the guys added. "We've got to teach her to slow down and smell the flowers, or at least the bear shit."

They all laughed. Luddy felt out of place, standing next to the stream, holding his canteen. His right hand instinctively rested on the handle of the big Bowie knife that hung from his belt. Both men noticed. The bigger of the two hooked his thumbs into his backpack straps and looked unflinchingly at Luddy. "How you doin' man? Enjoying the trail?"

"My favorite," Luddy replied. "Always a surprise on this one."

"Well, take it easy," the bigger man said, stepping gingerly from rock to rock until he was across the stream and about 10 feet from Luddy. The others followed, the smaller man nodding, the women keeping their eyes forward.

Luddy watched them disappear down the trail. He was nothing to them. He imagined following them and waiting until they'd pitched camp. After dark, he'd study them as they roasted marshmallows on the open fire. Then he'd sneak up on the men and stab them to death with his Bowie knife as they slept. He'd tie the women to trees and torture them, just as Robert Garrow had done a dozen years earlier in upstate New York.

Luddy decided not to fill his canteen, fearing the water contained parasites. He unwrapped a Slim Jim and gluttonously devoured it. Back on the trail, he walked a short distance until he found a clearing. He cursed himself for forgetting to bring his cheap Kmart pup tent, but he'd left home in a hurry. Now he'd literally have to sleep under the stars. The sky was clear but he hadn't listened to the forecast on the radio. He gathered a pile of twigs and branches but couldn't get a fire going. He eventually managed to light the Cheez-It box and used a cellophane-covered Slim Jim as starter fuel. He didn't have a can opener so he jabbed the Bowie knife into the top of the soup cans, making a gap wide enough to drink from. He set the cans in the flames until they began to bubble over, then sat cross-legged by the small fire, scooping hot soup into his mouth and cooling it with sips of Budweiser.

At nightfall he zipped the sleeping bag around him and stared up at the stars. The woods were alive with strange noises. Luddy clutched the Bowie knife and tried to sleep, but the surroundings filled him with fear. There were no ships sounding foghorns, no commercial jets roaring through the sky. He masturbated, thinking how different things might have turned out if his Mountain Mistress had been hiking alone. He imagined them living in a rustic cabin and making love each night under a blanket of furs, the pelts of animals he had slain for her.

A branch loudly snapping in the impenetrable darkness brought Luddy's revelry to a quick end as goosebumps spread over his body. He tightly held the knife and listened, praying it wasn't a hungry bear or mountain lion. He prayed – six Hail Marys, six Our Fathers, and an Act of Contrition for good measure. Hours passed before he finally fell asleep and in the morning his body was stiff and his feet ached but he ignored the pain, eager to get back to his car and out of the mountains. He'd spend the next night at a motel with hot running water and a breakfast menu.

CHAPTER 20

June 1986
Boston, Massachusetts

NEWSROOM NOTHINGNESS

Rane's stories about a potential serial killer on the loose in Boston were picked up by the nation's two largest news wire services, the Associated Press and United Press International. As a result, the stories appeared in several other newspapers in New England and across the country, as well as on television and radio stations.

The heat was on as the news media and local politicians grilled the Suffolk and Essex county district attorneys, both of whom held elected offices. What was being done to reign in this terror? Young women throughout metropolitan Boston were no longer leaving their homes after dark. Some weren't even going to work. Did they grasp the negative impact this situation was having on business?

As the old saying goes, shit flows down hill, and Detective Sgt. Andre Macusovich was swimming in it. His boss, the district attorney in Essex County, was demanding results. And over at FBI headquarters in Government Center, federal agent Kevin Finley was having an equally bad day. The situation was no different at the district attorney's office in Suffolk County, where Hannah Summers and other state troopers from the major crimes unit were being criticized for ineptitude and laziness.

In an unusual move, the state and federal lawmen whose agencies seldom trust one another, decided to pool their resources, calling in favors and interviewing every snitch living in the Boston area, but none seemed to know any more than they did. The rumor mill was churning, but its end product did nothing more than fuel gossip on the street.

Macusovich, Summers and Finley planned to attend Rose Cavelli's funeral, although her autopsied body remained at the regional morgue pending further investigation. As with any homicide case, they'd take special notice of who attended the church service and later the graveside prayers. They presumed the crowd would be comprised mostly of relatives, friends and bakery customers, but there was always the chance an unexpected face might show up. The preliminary autopsy results indicated death by strangulation.

Rane used those results as the angle for his next news story in which he repeatedly referred to the killer as the Boston Butcher. He dug up some background on the victim to fluff out the piece, mostly quotes from her highschool yearbook, club memberships, hobbies and employment history. He also mentioned that her parents owned the most popular bakery in Eastie, just in case it turned out the murder was in any way related to the business. It wasn't much, but with a story like this, the public was eager for any tidbit.

Now that the AP and UPI wire services had given attention to Rane's stories, his editors were waking up. Normally they were a pain in the ass, so deeply reliant on formula and advertising dollars that they habitually assigned top-gun reporters and photographers to ridiculous stories like the best beaches for celebrating summer, the hottest new holiday toys, the latest restaurant trends.

The closer it got to the end-of-year, the more unbearable the situation in the newsroom became, with assignments like: How to cook a Thanksgiving turkey to feed 20 friends and family; How to chop down your own Christmas tree; Where did the city buy the tall evergreen standing near Faneuil Hall and how many lights are strung on it?; What are poor orphan kids expecting from Santa this year?; Where are the most exclusive holiday parties being held and who's on the A-list?; and, of course, How many snow shovels were sold locally as the first major snowstorm approached?

Some days, it was enough to make Rane think seriously about quitting the profession, though he knew he never would. He loved being a reporter, the guy in the know, with access to just about anybody, anywhere, from the highest trappings of government to the inner world of privileged wealth, from racetracks and strip joints to military defense spending and organized crime syndicates. He had contacts in every quarter and an oversized Rolodex on his desk stuffed with tattered white cards, each one containing precious information. The other reporters at the paper, and many of those among the competition, admired his tenacity, writing skill and investigative know-how. They were impressed by his ability to nurture contacts in places where they found no admittance, and the sheer number of journalism awards he'd won since arriving in Boston. They were also envious.

CHAPTER 21

June 1986
Boston, Massachusetts

THE PROFESSOR WILL BE LATE FOR CLASS

Two days of heavy drinking and pill popping had taken its toll on Luddy. Twice he dozed off at the wheel as he drove south from New Hampshire's White Mountains and nearly went off the road into a ravine. He knew the police might have his home staked out, so he kept driving until he was approaching the access road to Logan Airport. He saw two marked State Police cruisers parked near the main terminal but the troopers didn't seem to recognize him or his Crown Vic, and then he reminded himself there wouldn't be an APB out unless the police had solid evidence that he had committed a crime. He might be a suspect, but no doubt there were others.

It was mid-afternoon as Luddy attached the magnetic taxi sign to the roof of the sedan and circled the terminals, not knowing what else to do. He thought of heading for the docks and taking his skiff out to *Sea Bitch* where he'd down a few beers and enjoy being on the water. But if he was a suspect, the police might be watching the boat. He was about to leave the airport loop when a tall, wiry woman in her late twenties or early thirties with rust-colored hair and a constellation of facial freckles flagged him down. She had four pieces of luggage, two of which resembled the protective metal cases used to transport musical instruments or delicate scientific equipment.

Luddy pulled over and popped the trunk lid. The woman abruptly explained that she was a biologist attending a very important conference at Northeastern University's Marine Science Center in Nahant. Did he know how to get there?

Luddy grinned. Oh yes, how many girls had he tried to kiss while parked on the sandy beach that ran along the causeway leading to the small peninsula? How many pairs of panties had he forcibly ripped while parked behind the dunes? How many runaways, usually in their teens, had tried to collect their fee from him, only to feel his fist strike their face, his thumbs squeeze their windpipe? Yes, he knew how to get to Nahant.

The biologist prattled on about the significance of her job. So many species were vanishing, she said. Overfishing was just about eliminating the native stock. There were dozens of different sea worms, and when it came to clams, well, there were countless more to study. But too many clam beds in the Boston area were being contaminated by pollution – usually industrial waste or human sewage. At least that's what she'd been told.

Luddy assured her there were still plenty of healthy clams in the tidal flats and salt marshes in Winthrop, Revere and Saugus, and even more in places farther north like Ipswich. The woman, who referred to herself as Professor Appleton, listened attentively as Luddy explained how the clams were harvested with rakes, rinsed with saltwater and sold at market. Depending on who was monitoring the activity and how many environmental police officers were on duty, the clams might need to undergo expensive ultraviolet treatment at a regional facility before being sold. But if nobody was looking, the clams went straight to market, even the contaminated ones. And if the buyers balked, there were always a few restaurants in Chinatown where regulations were lax and expectations even lower.

Professor Melanie Appleton thanked Luddy for his frank assessment and asked if he might serve as a guide during her stay, perhaps give a paid tour of the saltmarshes and tidal flats where she could collect samples. Would he be interested and, if so, be able to escort her tomorrow?

Luddy agreed. For $100 she'd buy his services for four hours -- starting two hours before dead low tide and extending for another two hours into the incoming tide. It would be the perfect opportunity to dig. The professor asked for his address and phone number, but Luddy told her not to worry, he'd pick her up at 4 p.m. outside the Lynn motel where she was spending the night.

Luddy popped some amphetamines and kept driving. He parked near Kaleigh's Back Bay apartment and watched the residents coming and going. He did the same on Ivy Street in Brookline, keeping a lookout for Hannah Summers, but he saw neither woman.

The next afternoon, Professor Appleton was standing under the carport of the seedy Harbour House Hotel on The Lynnway when Luddy arrived. His pullover shirt and jeans were a mass of wrinkles. He had slept briefly in the front seat of the red Ford pickup that he'd stolen from the long-term parking lot at the airport. He had covered himself with his sleeping bag, its woodsy smell conjuring images of wild creatures ready to pounce on him in the dark. It was exactly 4 p.m. and the sun was already in the western sky.

The professor was dressed in faded jeans, a mauve cotton short-sleeve blouse, a green photographer's vest and rubber Wellington boots. She had a daypack slung over her shoulder. In one hand she held a plastic pail with holes in the bottom and the other a sharp-tined, long-handled bull rake. She tossed the clamming gear into the truck bed, climbed into the front seat and clutched her daypack. Luddy hefted the professor's suitcase and a large Pelican case containing scientific equipment into the truck beside the clamming tools. He wended through the tangled streets of Lynn until he crossed the Fox Hill Bridge over the Saugus River and continued onto the Marsh Road, a straight and unlit stretch of blacktop where teenagers often raced their cars and met tragic fates.

Professor Appleton busied herself with the contents in her daypack as Luddy turned off the paved road and onto an expanse of wetlands, the view of which was shrouded by sand dunes and sea grass.

"This is where we get out," he said, still wearing his hiking boots.

"Don't you have rubber boots for clamming?"

"One of the guys stole my chest waders earlier this week."

"Oh, that's so unfortunate."

A flat-bottom aluminum boat with a long wooden pole lashed across the seats was tied to a scruffy sumac tree. Luddy undid the knots and pulled the boat into the shallows where the brackish water reached his knees. Professor Appleton followed close behind, carrying the bull rake and pail.

"Pull it closer so that I can get in," she said curtly.

Luddy gripped the narrow gunwale of the small boat as the professor rested her free hand on his shoulder and stepped aboard. The boat rocked unsteadily.

"My, my. Is this the only boat you have available?"

"This is it."

"Well, if this venture works out, the university can provide something more suitable."

"Sounds good."

Luddy clambered aboard, nearly spilling them both as he wrestled to gain his balance. He sat down clumsily on the seat nearest the bow, causing the boat to shudder.

"Easy does it," she instructed, her tone a reprimand as she handed him the long pole.

Luddy didn't like her attitude. She seemed too uppity, more so than when he first met her at the airport. She was ordering him around like a slave.

The afternoon sun was angled toward the water, giving the still expanses a mirrored surface. The mosquitoes and flies had arrived and Luddy shooed them away with little success. The bugs didn't seem to bother the professor who pulled a spray can of insect repellent from her vest and handed it to him. Luddy sprayed it lavishly on his head and arms, creating a thin fog, not stopping when the professor began to cough. He stood, checked his balance and poled the boat farther into the marsh until they reached a tidal flat where the hull came to a halt. He was sweating profusely and short of breath.

"Can we get out here?"

"Not unless you want to sink down into the mud."

"Well then?"

"Try here," he said, indicating the professor should thrust the multi-bladed rake into the muck and pull.

Melanie Appleton wasn't friendly or social. She was all business to the point of boring, so the act of removing her photo vest and blouse was anything but sexual. It was what was required to bring down her body temperature. She was overheated. Luddy's eyes were fixed on her white ribbed beater shirt and the fact that she wore no bra. He could see the nipples of her tiny breasts poking into the cloth and felt himself getting aroused.

The professor leaned over the gunwale and whacked the rake into the muck, using all of her strength to retrieve it. Nothing. But on the next try she got two clams and cheered at her success. "Bravo," she said. "I could get used to this."

Soon the tide was completely out, exposing more tidal flats. The mud gave off a rank odor. "Pole us over to that one," she commanded. "It looks like where clams might live."

Luddy pushed off on the pole and the boat nudged free of the mud bank. He poled toward the opposite exposure of fresh mud.

"I'd like to get out." Without warning Professor Appleton put a leg over the gunwale until her boot found the surface, then hoisted herself out of the boat and onto the mud bank.

"See that. I'm not sinking," she bragged. "Hand me the rake and the bucket."

Luddy did as he was told. The professor hacked at the mud with her rake for half an hour until the bucket was

128

brimming with clams. Her pulled-back red hair had come undone and the ringlets were jiggling in front of her face. She set the bucket in the boat.

"Take this," she ordered, handing Luddy the bull rake. She turned to face the sun and stretched her arms over her head and then outward. Luddy had no idea what sort of panties a woman like this might be wearing beneath her conservative tan cargo pants. Her beater shirt was soiled with muck. The skin just below her armpits glistened with perspiration. Luddy stood, his legs shaky from excitement. He wanted to reach out and touch her. It was eerily quiet in the marsh.

Professor Appleton turned, reached into the front pocket of her trousers and pulled out a $100 bill. "Job well done," she commended, handing him the folded bill. "And now you've been well rewarded. Everyone is happy."

Luddy took the money and tucked it in his back pocket, then brought the bull rake down on Melanie Appleton's head. The professor cried out and collapsed on the tidal flat. Luddy climbed out of the boat and kneeled at her feet. He pulled off her rubber boots and trousers, eager to see her panties, which were pink with yellow ducklings, more like something a child might wear. The professor was bleeding profusely, her legs cycling in the wet sand. Luddy pulled down his bluejeans and underwear. The professor began groaning in pain. Luddy grabbed the bull rake and raised it above his head, but decided to wait. He didn't want her to die, at least not yet. Torrents of blood were running down the professor's neck and shoulders.

Luddy pulled the blood-soaked white beater over her head so that she was naked and hacked off several strands of her hair with his clamming knife. The professor seemed to be looking at him in disbelief but he couldn't be sure. He let the entire weight of his body fall atop her and inserted himself, climaxing almost immediately. Then the reality of what he'd done took over. He looked all around, turning his body 360 degrees. Nobody was in sight. The woman moaned again so Luddy picked up the bull rake and struck her until she was quiet. He grinned at the sight of her, saying aloud, "No talking in class, Professor."

The tide had reversed and was now incoming, lifting the small boat so that it drifted off the mud bank. Luddy hoisted the professor's body over the gunwale and let it flop into the boat. He tossed the clothing beside her and began poling the boat toward where they'd first entered the saltmarsh.

Luddy dragged the professor's body to the pickup truck and hefted it into the cargo bed along with her clothing, the bull rake and pail. He covered her with the sleeping bag and spread the other equipment atop the mound. Blood was smeared on the tailgate and rear bumper. When Luddy opened the driver's door, his hands left bloody fingerprints on the handle. The same thing happened when he gripped the steering wheel. He was in full panic mode and knew he had to calm down, but more importantly his mistakes meant he had to get rid of the evidence. He had to torch the truck.

Luddy used sand to dry and remove the blood on his hands. He drove to a hardware store in Revere where he bought a five-gallon plastic jug, then filled it at a nearby gas station. The attendant eyed him suspiciously and asked, "Hey buddy, what happened to you?"

"I cut myself fixing the lawn mower, but the bleeding finally stopped. I'm fine."

Luddy's heart was beating so strongly he thought it would thump through his skin. He drove to a remote gravel quarry near the convergence of two major highways and parked the pickup behind the largest mountain of loose stone. He recalled one of the wannabe OC guys had told him cellophane potato chip bags were the best way to torch a motor vehicle. You filled the gas tank and stuffed the greasy bags under the dashboard near the firewall and lit them. Once the grease caught fire and spread, the vehicle went boom, leaving behind no trace of an accelerant other than the gas in the tank. But there was no time for that. And even if there had been, Luddy knew the police would eventually trace the vehicle identification number to the owner and then to the airport parking lot where he'd stolen it, but that could take days.

The professor's naked body lay twisted beneath the equipment in the truck bed. Luddy hauled her out by the feet and dragged her behind the gravel pile. He laid the bloody sleeping bag on the ground, rolled the professor atop it and poured out the five gallons of gasoline until the body and cloth bag were drenched.

The smell of gasoline brought back the memory of the botched arson job in Lynn several years earlier. He'd gotten a call from Fergus Cavanagh and was paid to set fire to an old brick industrial building so that the owner could collect the insurance. It was his third arson job in Lynn and he did exactly as instructed, doubling a heavy-duty plastic construction bag, filling it with several gallons of gasoline and securing it with a knot at the top. He tied a strong rope to the knot, tossed the rope over a wooden ceiling beam and lowered the gasoline-laden bag until it sagged less a foot off the floor. He plugged the timer into a wall outlet, and ran the extension cord to the cheap bread toaster, which was positioned directly beneath the bag. He set the timer for five minutes and pushed down the toaster lever. That should have been enough time for him to get out of the building and walk a block, but something went wrong. The timer malfunctioned and just as he turned to flee an explosion rocked the room. His body was hurled against the nearest brick wall, the flames incinerating his clothing. Bits of green plastic trash bag were embedded in his skin. He awoke in a Boston hospital burn unit where doctors explained he was lucky to be alive and where police ordered him held for questioning. When the police detectives finally left the hospital room, Celeste Pugano stood beside the hospital bed and shook her head slowly in disappointment. She pinched his cheek and said, *Stunod* – stupid.

Recalling the pain of that horrible night in Lynn and the lessons it taught, Luddy subconsciously massaged the thick scars on his neck. There were other ugly, raised scars from the burns on his back, arms and legs, which was one of the reasons he never wore shorts or went shirtless.

With the Lynn arson job fresh in mind, he realized he should have fashioned some sort of fuse to put distance between his cigarette lighter and Professor Appleton's corpse. He also sensed that soon it would be too late, that he had to act, because it was only a matter of time before some dog walker, birder or hiker would be traipsing through the quarry. So he tossed his lighter onto the sleeping bag and dropped to the ground. A flash preceded the initial explosion, which was more whoosh than bang. Luddy got to his feet just as the cloth went up in flames and a louder explosion echoed in the gravel quarry. He began running toward the truck as a plume of black smoke rose into the sky. Almost immediately he was out of breath and cursed his overweight body.

Luddy got behind the steering wheel and spun the tires in the loose gravel. When he reached the highway he drove under the speed limit, telling himself to relax, but dread was coursing through his veins like a virus. He could hear sirens in the distance getting louder and soon spotted the flashing emergency vehicles. He counted two Revere police cruisers and two fire engines. It wouldn't be long before the police and fire radios would start crackling with detailed information and the news satellite trucks would head for the scene.

Luddy knew he had to ditch the truck. He recalled a few street guys telling him about the deep spot in the Saugus River only a few miles from the Revere quarry. He drove the Marsh Road in the opposite direction toward Lynn and veered off onto Hamilton Street in Saugus where a section of guardrail was missing behind a seafood restaurant parking lot. He left the pickup in neutral at the edge of the river where it teetered on the brink. At the last second he dropped the transmission shifter into drive and with all his might he pushed the truck until it inched forward and went over the grassy bank and into the river. The truck floated for a few moments, causing Luddy to panic, but he calmed down as the chassis began to bubble and slowly sink into the inky water. From everything he had been told, the water in that stretch

132

of the river was over 40 feet deep. Every other year the Metropolitan District Commission Police dive team would locate the metal hulks, attach cables to a wrecker and wait to see what was inside them.

Occasionally the divers would find a body in the trunk or backseat, but more often the booty was dozens of thick, squirming black river eels that leapt from the hoisted vehicle back into the dark river.

Luddy used a payphone to call Elroy McGuinness, assuming the cabbie would be working the airport. He left a voice message on Elroy's beeper, asking as a favor to be picked up at a gas station near the Lynn-Saugus line. Luddy stood in the shadows of the adjacent used car sales lot and waited. It seemed like hours, but within 20 minutes a battered taxicab pulled to the curb.

A bellowing voice boomed out the passenger window. "Hey You Mother Shucker! What you doing here, pal?"

Luddy climbed inside the cab that was dense with cigarette smoke and shouted, "Go. Go. Go."

"Where we goin'?"

"The airport."

"Shit. I just came from there."

"I know that. I gotta get my car."

"Why's your car at the airport and you're here?"

"Long fuckin' story, Elroy, and not worth repeating. Just drive me to my car. I owe you big time."

CHAPTER 22

June 1986
Boston, Massachusetts

A VISIT TO MOMMA'S HOUSE

When a body gets torched, word on the street travels fast because very often it's related to ongoing criminal activities. Blade was first to hear and brought the news directly to Fergus Cavanaugh.

"The cops are all over the place. Looks like some lady got charred in the gravel pits. Our inside guys at the precinct will give us a call if something comes up. There's not much left of the body, so right now there's no ID."

As Blade continued his report, State Police Sgt. Andre Macusovich, accompanied by Lt. Hannah Summers and two uniformed troopers, knocked heavily on the door to Luddy and Celeste Pugano's apartment.

"Police," he shouted. "Please open the door."

Celeste Pugano, wearing a conservative dark green dress and an apron dusted with white flour, slowly opened the door. She put one hand to her lips as though aghast at the sight of police at her front door, while the other hand adjusted the grey bun of hair on the back of her head.

"We'd like to come in and have a look around," the sergeant announced gruffly, waving an official-looking document. "And we'd like to talk to your son, Luddy. Is he here?"

"He's not," Celeste said, opening the door. "But you're welcome to come in."

The uniformed troopers led the way into the apartment that smelled pleasantly of homemade tomato sauce and garlic, in contrast to the bathroom that emanated bleach fumes. The furniture was worn, the kitchen table had metal legs and a Formica surface, the four straight-back chairs a mishmash of designs. A wooden hutch in the living room was crowded with handmade dolls, as were the two end tables. As the troopers closed the front door, a white Lincoln Continental drove past and Fergus Cavanaugh glared out the backseat window.

The sergeant was abrupt. "Where's your son?"

"I don't know. I haven't seen him."

"He's not at work."

"It could be his day off. He doesn't tell me."

The sergeant noticed the bruises on Celeste's forearms. "What happened to your neck and arms?"

"I fell. I was trying to get something from one of the upper cabinets and I slipped off the chair. Luddy wanted to buy me one of those metal sticks with a grabber that are made for short people like me when they want to get something from the cupboard. But I told him no."

The sergeant ignored her explanation. "Did you attend a wedding in Saugus recently?"

"Yes, I did."

"Did your son attend as well?"

"Yes, Luddy was there. He drove me home."

"When do you expect him?"

"I really don't know. He might have gone camping."

"Does he often go camping?"

Celeste shrugged innocently, morphing into her Sweet Old Italian Lady persona. She moved slowly toward the refrigerator. "Would you gentlemen or the young lady like some cannoli?"

"No thank you," the sergeant said, cutting off the state trooper who seemed just about to accept the offer of pastries. "What makes you think he went camping?"

135

Celeste hesitated long enough to wordlessly tell the detective he was asking far too many questions without the presence of an attorney.

"If he's camping, where do you think might have gone?"

"I wouldn't know. He doesn't tell me when he's going. Sometimes he likes to drive up to New Hampshire or Maine. He likes to get out of the city, get some fresh air." She held open the white cardboard box of cannoli where the troopers could see its contents.

"Did he take his car?"

"If it's not where he usually parks it, he might have driven somewhere.

"Mind if we sit?"

"Not at all."

Sgt. Macusovich, Lt. Summers, the two troopers and Celeste settled into stuffed armchairs and couch in the cramped living room. Summers gave the sergeant a look that said his interrogation was too aggressive. Macusovich throttled back on his questioning and instead chatted about the neighborhood and how it had changed in recent years, particularly with the influx of new residents and money. Yuppies. It was difficult for the police to know what sort of problems these new people might bring, especially with all the cocaine use, which is why they relied on the longtime residents like her for information.

Summers stood and wandered toward the doll collection. She praised the craftsmanship and gently asked several questions about who had made the dolls and how long it had taken to collect them. The lieutenant sensed that beneath the grandmotherly countenance was a pit viper patiently waiting for the right moment to strike.

When the talk got around to Celeste's family history and Luddy's childhood, the sergeant's questioning regained its vigor. He had already heard lurid tales involving Luddy Pugano but he wanted the man's mother to confirm them.

"We know Luddy likes to keep the neighborhood orderly," he said. "We know he has tried to limit the number

136

of pigeons from the roofs and streets because they spread disease, and that he dealt with some problem dogs that residents were complaining about."

Celeste rubbed the dark tress of hair that she kept pressed between the pages of her Bible. "I know he doesn't like pigeons. And the dogs, well, those were pitbulls and they barked and barked and bit several children, so Luddy decided to take care of them because nobody else would. That dog officer we got around here, he's good for nothing. He's afraid of the dogs."

Summers grimaced as she tried to digest what Celeste was saying.

Macusovich pressed on. "We heard Luddy set them on fire. Is that true?"

"All I know is that the barking stopped and the children started playing in the streets again. The neighbors all agreed they could sleep better once those dogs were gone."

"I see. And did he also take care of the neighborhood cat problem?"

"Luddy may seem tough, but he's really an angel," said Celeste, who took note that Summers had rolled her eyes in disbelief.

Celeste looked directly at the lieutenant. "He can have a temper, but inside he's sweet. One time, when he was small, he found baby birds that were left to die out in the cold. He brought them inside and put them in the oven to warm them up. But of course he didn't understand that the oven temperature would get too hot," she said.

"I'm sure he's sweet, but we still have to talk to him," said Summers. "By the way, did you know Rose Cavelli?"

Celeste paused before she spoke. "I didn't really know her, only her family, the father and mother. It's very sad what happened."

Macusovich seemed annoyed by the fact that Summers was participating in the interview. In an effort to retake control, he asked, "Is Luddy still working at the fish market?"

"Oh, yes. He works very hard. You don't know how much detergent I go through trying to get the smell out of his clothes. Sometimes I have to use a little bit of bleach, but he gets angry because it fades his shirts."

Celeste shrugged, as in, what's a mother to do?

Once again, Summers fought the urge to roll her eyes. "Do you mind if we look around a bit more?"

"I don't think she'd mind," said Macusovich. "We'd like to go upstairs and see your son's room."

"Oh, the place is such a mess. I'm so embarrassed. I haven't even made my bed. But you let me clean up and you can come back tomorrow," she said.

Macusovich showed his frustration by exhaling with exaggerated effort thorough his nostrils. "Can we just take look in Luddy's room tonight?"

"I prefer you didn't," she said, standing and stepping toward the entrance door. "I'm feeling very tired, so if you wouldn't mind coming back tomorrow, I'll see you then."

Sgt. Macusovich recognized that Celeste Pugano understood the need for a search warrant, which they didn't have. The liberal judge had been a stickler for protocol, far exceeding the usual demand for probable cause. Macusovich had hoped to bluff his way in by brandishing a handful of police incident reports.

"I'm sorry for interrupting your evening," he said.

Celeste smiled coyly. "You all seem very nice. It's an interesting job you have, not like the work I did in the factories, same thing every day for years. I watch a lot of those police shows on television these days. The detectives, they usually have a piece of paper from the courthouse that says they can look around somebody's house."

Sgt. Macusovich knew very well Celeste was now playing him and that he had underestimated her. He felt foolish.

"We'll see you tomorrow morning, Mrs. Pugano," he said, mustering a forced smile. "We'll have everything that's required and you'll have time to look it all over."

"*Buona note*," she said.

138

Macusovich nodded. "Good night."

Summers extended a hand and Celeste shook it warmly, making unflinching eye contact. The two troopers returned to their barracks and Summers headed back to her Brookline apartment but Sgt. Macusovich kept the Pugano apartment under surveillance for the next two hours. He could see Celeste moving from room to room, but it was difficult to say precisely what she was doing.

Several cats were hissing and fighting in the narrow alley that divided the three-story apartment building where Celeste lived and a nearly identical structure. A neighbor with a bellowing voice cursed the felines from a third-floor window. Celeste had heard the hissing, screeching and moaning as well. She filled a small bowl with Prestone automotive anti-freeze, knowing the cats would drink for its sweetness, and set it just outside the back door where the fighting had been loudest.

Sgt. Macusovich thought he saw her drop a heavy object out her bedroom window, but he couldn't be sure in the dark. There had been an audible thud and the catfight stopped. He saw Celeste close the window. There was no sign of her son.

CHAPTER 23

June 1986
Boston, Massachusetts

REMEMBERING THE GOOD OLD DAYS

Celeste dimmed the lights, sat in her favorite stuffed chair and poured herself a cordial glass of anisette, sipping slowly as the liqueur warmed her insides. She closed her eyes and rubbed the lock of dark hair between her thumb and forefinger, then returned it to its place between the Bible pages. As the anisette took effect, she let her mind indulge in recollections that she usually kept buried.

How had she ended up in this squalid little apartment surrounded by well-meaning but poor and unintelligent people? She had always felt she deserved better, but from the start things went in a different direction. It all seemed so long ago it made her weary just to think about it, but then an image or voice would pass through her mind like a ghost and she'd stop to reflect, to examine it like a child might a new toy.

"Celeste is the best."

How many times had she heard the boys repeat that little jingle? At 12, when her breasts had not yet begun to grow, she'd let Lucca and Tony touch them under her new and only bra. The boys were thrilled and Celeste bathed in the glory of her newfound popularity among them.

Giovanni was the first to put a hand below her waist, although in that case it was up her skirt. He'd clumsily inserted a finger and Celeste was surprised to feel her nipples harden. After that, she let Giovanni put his fingers there, usually on Wednesdays after the lengthy catechism class they attended along with the public school kids. On the way home, they'd cut into the narrow alley behind the church where Celeste would stand against the brick wall while Giovanni caressed her. Giovanni was also the first boy to kiss her, though they seldom did and he never put his tongue in her mouth, although she expected it. The boy seemed more interested in exploring her body than kissing her lips.

Celeste sipped the licorice-flavored liqueur. "Fuck you, Giovanni, wherever you are today," she cursed aloud.

Her mind reel slowed as she recalled the outbreak of war, or more precisely, when the Japanese bombed Pearl Harbor on Dec. 7, 1941. She was 21 years old, working the assembly line at the Chelsea clock factory, spending her days making timepieces for the Navy's warships. The pay was terrible but it was loads of fun working with the other young women, many whom had never been allowed out of the house alone on a date before taking this job. On Friday nights, the girls from Eastie would gather at Santarpio's pizzeria on Chelsea Street or in the wooden booths of the soda fountain shop off Saratoga. The young men would join them and usually it was a good time unless somebody they knew had been killed in battle or was being drafted.

Gino Talenti was as handsome as they come, with lustrous black hair combed straight back, an athletic gait and a wise mouth. He was the neighborhood bad boy and Celeste gravitated to him like an ocean to the orbiting moon. For months they played out a wild romance, mostly in the cargo bed of Gino's father's fruit truck. Neither imagined the possibility of breaking apart, although Uncle Sam had different plans. It was obvious to everyone in the neighborhood that Gino Talenti, the easygoing bad boy who couldn't be tamed, had fallen deeply in love with Celeste Pugano, the pretty little firecracker.

When Gino decided to enlist in the Marines in the spring of '42, Celeste was devastated. She begged him not to

141

go. But Gino said, "If I wait around, I'll be drafted. I'll end up in the Army and I won't have any say about anything. At least in the Marines, I'll be with other guys who know their shit."

As war in the Pacific raged, Celeste felt as though she would go mad waiting for the next letter from the battlefront to arrive. At first, the letters were all about the perfection of their love, their devotion to each other, and how nothing would ever come between them, not even a war. They exchanged details of their mutual dream to get married and raise a family. But as the months blurred past, the frequency of Gino's letters slowed, and their content became darker.

Wherever on the pages Gino had mentioned his location or identified his unit by its military designation, the government censors had blackened it out. But even beneath the thick, black ink and the carefully chosen words, Celeste knew he was in hell. When Gino came home on furlough, Celeste literally thought she would float away from excitement. She met him at the South Station train terminal along with his parents. Outwardly, Gino was still the good-looking wise ass, and dressed in his Marine blues he was even more handsome than ever, but Celeste saw in his eyes that he had changed.

During those two blissful weeks, they made love twice a day, wherever they could find a place to be alone. Father Federico was hesitant to comply with their wishes to get married immediately. He urged them to wait until the war was over, until things were calmer so that they might think rationally rather than impulsively. War does odd things to people, the priest said. But they persisted, despite Father Federico's reservations and the disapproval expressed by both sets of parents.

The priest was concerned that they had had no time to attend the series of pre-nuptial lessons the Catholic Church requires for couples planning to marry. Nonetheless, given the circumstances, he relented and agreed to perform the ceremony after the last Mass on Sunday morning. A kind and generous man, he even gave them a wedding gift of brass

142

candlesticks.

Celeste wore her mother's wedding gown, which was lent begrudgingly. It was shoddily sewn and had begun to yellow with age. Gino's muscles had beefed out since joining the Marines so he borrowed a suit from Eddie DeMarco, his best man. Eddie was his oldest friend from the neighborhood, an extroverted jokester who'd recently become more quiet and introspective as he awaited orders from the U.S. Navy. Celeste asked Stella Rinaldo, her closest ally at the Chelsea clock factory, to be her maid of honor. The two women had known each other less than a year but Stella was a hell-raiser and party girl and they had become fast friends.

Matteo and Carlotta Pugano didn't attend their daughter's wedding ceremony or the reception, nor did Celeste's younger brother and sister. The small party was held in the church basement where the ceiling was festooned with paper streamers and the folding tables covered with pink paper, courtesy of the women's rosary prayer group.

There was no time for a honeymoon but Gino had accumulated enough military combat pay for the ferry ride and two nights at a hotel on Nantasket Beach in Hull, a small town that juts into the ocean just south of Boston.

When Gino again left to rejoin his outfit in the Pacific, Celeste was crushed. She moved in with his parents and slept on a cot in the hallway. She'd never felt more alone or lonely. During her lunch break at the factory, she scoured the newspapers for any mention of the war in the Pacific, which she knew was causing the deaths of thousands of Marines. She listened to the news radio broadcasts and paid close attention to the newsreels about the war that were shown at the local movie theater before the feature presentation. She came to dread the names of places like Guadalcanal and Tulagi where the Marines were taking heavy casualties.

She cried twice in the same week when two women on the assembly line learned their boyfriend and husband, respectively, had been killed in action. After that, she felt herself dry up inside until she was hollow.

On one particularly overcast day, her grim-faced

143

father-in-law gave her the news that Gino was listed as missing in action. The family had received a telegram. His words made her sick to her stomach. The last she'd heard, her husband's unit was somewhere near the Philippines. The news offered scant details about the Battle of Bataan, but it sounded frightening. That night she drank a half bottle of peach brandy and puked it up near the docks. She didn't report to work for three days, and when she returned, the foreman docked her pay and placed her on probation.

The Friday gatherings at Santarpio's and the soda shop had been replaced by drinking parties at different homes where couples paired off and vanished into the bedrooms. Celeste began imbibing heavily. Her world was coming unraveled. Depressed that she might never see Gino again, convinced he lay dead and rotting on some palm-fringed Pacific island, she went into a tailspin of partying that was meant to ease her pain and help her forget the love they once shared. It was at one of those parties early in '43 she met Nello Franchi, who was Eddie DeMarco's nattily-dressed cousin from New York.

Nello was like no man Celeste had ever met. He was handsome, educated, articulate, and about 10 years older than she, a sophisticated city slicker who emanated an air of mystery. When she asked him why he wasn't in the military, Nello smiled knowingly and quietly explained that he was involved with a top-secret government agency responsible for shipping important supplies to the troops. As he put it, "I can't tell you more than that. If I did, they'd throw me in jail." Reverting to the wartime slogan plastered on billboards throughout the city, he added, "Loose lips sink ships."

Nello always had a wad of cash and drove a new sedan, which was impressive given that production of civilian vehicles had slowed due to the demand for war materials. He told very few people where he was staying in the neighborhood. It was as though he were in hiding, but nobody seemed to know from whom.

Nello introduced Celeste to French champagne, which she found was to her liking. Occasionally they'd park Nello's

144

car near the waterfront and drink the bubbly while watching the harbor traffic. It all seemed very innocent until the night Nello started kissing her. She half-heartedly pushed him away but as soon as his arms were around her she responded by moaning with desire and thrusting her hips. Her precious silk stockings had ripped during their interlude and Celeste knew they'd be near impossible to replace because every bit of silk was needed to make parachutes for the nation's airborne troops. Nello brought her three new pairs the next day.

News that several U.S. servicemen had escaped from a Japanese prison camp in the Philippines gave Celeste new hope. The world was just finding out about the Bataan Death March and the atrocities committed against captured British and American troops by the Japanese. Celeste said three rosaries immediately after hearing the news, praying Gino was among the escapees. She lit a candle for him most days at the Most Holy Redeemer Church and recited the prayers she'd learned as a child. *Bless me father, for I have sinned.*

Father Federico often asked about Gino as a courtesy, knowing very well if the young man had been killed the local priest would have been among the first informed in the neighborhood so that he might console the grieving family. Once each week, Celeste went to church to confess her sins – too much drinking, cursing, taking the Lord's name in vain -- but she never told any of the priests about Nello, nor did she mention how hard she had fallen for a man about whom she knew so little.

Celeste was a lost soul with nowhere to turn. By spring, Nello had returned to his nebulous occupation in New York, promising to bring her a high-fashion dress on his next visit to Boston and more nylon stockings. Celeste found out from neighbors that Nello was involved with New York gangsters, bad people, dangerous people, some of whom wanted to harm him, which was why he was hiding out in Boston. She also heard and rejected news that Nello had a wife and two kids back in the big city. She convinced herself that Nello, a white knight, would return to Eastie, sweep her into his arms and together they'd live happily ever after.

Gino Talenti was a broken man when he returned that summer to his parent's East Boston apartment. A Japanese bullet had torn through his right leg and a piece of his left ear was missing. The war had damaged his spirit but he hoped the reunion with Celeste would make everything all right. Gino's parents had moved to a larger apartment and in a magnanimous gesture gave the newlyweds the tiny spare bedroom with its two windows facing the alley. Things seemed to be falling back into place as the weeks ticked by, and though their lovemaking lacked its previous ardor, Celeste's bouts of morning sickness suggested they had not been idle in bed.

When Celeste announced she was pregnant in late summer, her parents finally acknowledged the marriage. The Italian women in the neighborhood hosted two baby showers and their small room in the Talenti home was soon filled with a carriage, crib, blankets and boxes of clothing. Gino returned to his job helping his father on the fruit truck, picking up fresh produce at the wholesale market and delivering it to small grocery stores run mostly by Italian immigrants. Celeste's stomach swelled quickly and in December a baby girl with abundant black hair was born. Celeste named her Antoinette and told everyone to pray for the baby's health because it was so premature.

Still recovering from his war experience, Gino went about his days on the fruit truck with a sense that it was good to be alive. He was home in one piece instead of in a metal box and he tried not to think much past that feeling, but some of the guys in the neighborhood had begun to razz him about how the baby had been born only six months after he had returned home.

Celeste was always nervous whenever Gino cleaned his rifle and shotgun at the kitchen table, especially if they had been arguing, as they did often about finances and his depressive moods. Her fears worsened when he guzzled straight from a bottle of bourbon as he reamed the gun barrels with oiled cloth patches. It was as though he were in a trance,

146

methodically cleaning his weapons before the next round of bloodshed.

Once when she asked him what he was thinking, Gino chuckled and said, "I'm thinking about when I stuck my bayonet into some fuckin' Jap's eyeball so he'd stop yelling 'Banzai!' The little yellow fucker was insane. Even when he was dying, he kept whispering, 'Banzai' over and over. Never seen anything like it. Weirdest goddamn people."

Antoinette was four months old when Celeste's scream echoed through the tenements. Gino was staring out the bathroom window at the brick wall on the far side of the alley, hands at his sides. The baby lay face down in the bathtub. Celeste scooped Antoinette's small body from the water but there was no breathing, no pulse and the baby's skin was turning blue.

Gino glanced at his sobbing wife holding the limp infant. "Everybody thinks I'm a chump. Why didn't you tell me?"

When the police arrived, Celeste was certain she'd point a finger at her husband and accuse him of murder, call him a baby killer. Instead, she was riddled with guilt about him being cuckolded by her affair with Nello Franchi. It was a tragic accident, she swore. The police solemnly told Gino and Celeste that the funeral parlor would be notified. Celeste snipped a lock of Antoinette's black hair and tucked it between the pages of her Bible.

A week later, Gino Talenti boarded a westbound train and left no forwarding address. Celeste remained cloistered amid the tense atmosphere of the Talenti home. As far as the Talentis were concerned, their battle-fatigued son had failed to pay attention to his infant daughter in the bathtub and tragedy had struck. Now their son had left for parts unknown, compounding their suffering. But Celeste was still with them, a constant reminder of all the happiness their only granddaughter might have brought. Celeste knew she would have to find another place to live and she cursed Nello Franchi for abandoning her. She prayed he would realize he loved her more deeply than any other soul on this earth and show up at her door bearing flowers, champagne and elaborate plans for spending the rest of their days together. She would have Nello's baby. No, not just one. Babies. Lots of them.

The war in Europe and the Pacific continued to inflict its misery. Boston's Scollay Square, which was later demolished to make way for a drab cluster of concrete buildings known as Government Center, was a frenzied scene in the 1940s where soldiers and sailors spent their pent-up energy amid the bars, gambling halls and whorehouses. Celeste had been subtly asked to leave the Talenti home. She unsuccessfully tried to contact Nello Franchi who apparently had never lived at the address listed on his driver's license.

Reverting to her maiden name to rid herself of shame and all connection to the Talenti family, Celeste Pugano moved a dozen miles north to the shoe-manufacturing city of Lynn where she rented a room in a dilapidated Victorian mansion shared by several other single women. She took a job as a dishwasher in a local restaurant and later as a barkeep, but neither was enough to pay the rent and buy food. The first time a bar customer quietly asked Celeste if she would suck him off for $5, she just laughed at the ballsy ridiculousness of the offer. But a few weeks later when he asked again, she was already short on rent money and decided it wouldn't be so bad. Word spread among the customers and soon Celeste had a cast of regulars who met her in the back room of the bar.

"Celeste is the best," she heard one of them say.

When one of her more well-heeled customers suggested she might make far more money in Scollay Square where servicemen were literally tossing away their dollars before returning to the war, Celeste followed his advice. She found bartending at the Old Howard Theater both easy and lucrative. She spent her first paycheck on perfume and a few low-cut silk blouses she was certain the male customers would find intriguing. The theater manager promised her an opportunity to perform in one of the popular burlesque shows, but after bedding him three times Celeste knew she'd been hoodwinked.

Ludwig Barnes, a muscular merchant mariner with dark, deep-socketed eyes, a bulbous nose and worm-thick lips, was among those drawn to Celeste's cleavage. As she poured his drinks he told her stories of crossing the Atlantic in sight of other ships sinking in oily flames after being struck by German U-boat torpedoes. Within a week they were spending every spare moment together, Ludwig carefree with his pay, sensing the war was far from over and time was of the essence. Whenever they had sex in one of the Scollay Square hotels, Celeste imagined it was Nello Franchi inside her and she half expected to open her eyes and see him atop her amid the threadbare sheets. She nearly vomited when the doctor told her she was pregnant. She told Ludwig she was sure the baby was his and that she wanted an abortion. She had heard of a doctor in New Jersey's Pine Barrens who would perform the operation for $500. Ludwig frowned at the suggestion. Didn't she know that quack doctors often conducted these procedures using rusty coat hangers that would certainly leave her with serious infection if it didn't kill her?

Two days later, tears spilling from Ludwig's eyes, he handed her a stack of bills in different denominations, totaling just over $4,000, which was his entire life savings. Official deployment orders in hand, he squeezed her tightly before he stepped onto the gangway and boarded a gray-painted freighter laden with explosive war supplies bound for Europe. Celeste didn't return the hug. She felt dead inside and instinctively knew she'd never seen him again.

As months went by and Celeste's stomach swelled, she presumed her swarthy merchant mariner had gone to Davy Jones' locker, sunk to the bottom of the cold dark Atlantic by a German submarine. The newspapers were full of bad news in those days. Merchant ship convoys were being torpedoed by German wolf packs at a startling pace, some only a few miles from Boston Harbor.

Little Luddy was born by the time the allies entered Berlin and the atomic bombs were dropped on Hiroshima and Nagasaki, bringing hostilities to an end. Celeste had moved back to Eastie where she rented a tiny railroad flat and found work in a paint factory. Her parents still refused to acknowledge her presence, so she raised Luddy as a single mother. Apparently she hadn't done such a great job, she thought, given that her son was now a murder suspect and the police had visited her home.

As she dozed in her chair, Celeste dreamed of tankers and freighters plying the water of Boston Harbor and she saw herself as a little girl gazing out at the barges, industrial cranes and massive steel fuel tanks. She saw herself looking out at what she could only call home. Nello Franchi was there in her mind, too, seated nonchalantly in the driver's seat of his sedan with the plush velour interior, and together they were gazing across the water at the lights of downtown Boston and the Custom House Tower, then the city's tallest building at almost 500 feet.

Celeste itched her nose as she dozed in the chair, her mind reeling through the sights, sounds and smells of her girlhood. How had more than 60 years gone by so quickly? Why had she been unable to forge the kind of life she envisioned?

In the wee hours of the morning, with a warm summer dawn about to unveil itself over the Atlantic, an exhausted Luddy Pugano unlocked the front door and stepped inside the apartment. He stunk of acrid smoke and gasoline. Celeste appeared to be asleep on the couch. She opened her eyes and shook her head in disapproval.

"*Qui ce puzza,*" she said, remarking at the strong odor in the room. "You need to shower. The police were here looking for you and they're coming back."

CHAPTER 24

June 1986
Boston, Massachusetts

A MAN ON A MISSION

Decker knew something out of the ordinary was brewing when Bill Carrington, his boss at the private investigation and security service Executive Cover, told him to meet a new client at the Top of the Hub, the 360-degree restaurant near the roof of the towering Prudential Center. He was given a date, time and description of the man and woman who would be seated at a specific table.

Skip Lehman shook hands with Decker and introduced his wife, Cornelia. He was early 50s, fit and handsome, she a few years younger. Both were well dressed in expensive urban clothing. It was 9 a.m. and the sun basked downtown Boston in a golden glow. Decker nodded to the waitress who was holding a pot of steaming coffee and she poured him a cup.

Skip Lehman began speaking as soon the waitress was out of earshot. "This meeting never took place," he declared with authority. "I'm told you were briefed only that this involves a missing person."

"That's right."

"Well, it's not just a missing person. It's our daughter."

"I'm sorry to hear that, sir. Many times these cases have a way of clearing themselves up," said Decker, who knew as soon as he spoke that his words were a mistake. He was there to listen.

"If you're suggesting our daughter is some sort of runaway, you're mistaken. Jenny is the epitome of responsibility. She checks in with us regularly, sometimes more often than necessary."

"I don't doubt that for a moment, sir," said Decker. "If you have any information that's already on file, it would help get me started."

Skip Lehman opened his briefcase and slid a manila folder toward Decker. The folder held color and black-and-white photographs of Jenny Lehman. In addition to headshots there were photos of Jenny skiing, surfing and also backpacking in what appeared to be a mountainous country. There were neatly printed and alphabetized lists of every college roommate she'd had since freshman year at Tufts, every young man she dated, and the name of every male professor she might have had contact with. Many of the names were printed beside postage stamp-size photos of the person.

"We know she landed at Logan Airport. So whatever happened occurred sometime after the flight touched down and about 10 a.m. the next morning, when her roommates reported that she hadn't arrived as scheduled. The flight attendants described her as engaging and cheerful. We're talking a space of about 14 hours at most. I want to know what happened to my daughter during that time."

Decker sifted through the materials in the folder. He examined the list of legal and gypsy cab drivers who routinely picked up fares at the airport. Each entry listed the driver's work and home address and, if licensed, their taxi medallion number. He saw the names of every State Police officer assigned to the investigation or who worked the Troop F barracks at Logan Airport, as well as their respective duty shifts.

"You've assembled quite a lot of information here," said Decker, amazed by the comprehensive file.

"I had help," said Skip Lehman, choosing not to

explain that the assistance had come from close associates at Langley.

Decker abruptly stopped turning the pages when he reached the 8x10-inch color photograph of a blonde woman with green eyes. He couldn't pull away. It was as though an electrical current was connecting him to her face. He turned the photograph over. On the back side, the name Detective Lt. Hannah Summers was printed in block letters and beneath it the affiliation Massachusetts State Police.

Decker immediately matched her with the TV interview he'd seen in Nemo's about the reward offer for Jenny Lehman. Only during that interview, her long blonde hair wasn't spilling over her shoulders as it was in the photograph. Hannah Summers exuded a calm, natural beauty -- the girl-next-door who blossomed into something marvelous and didn't seem to realize it.

Skip Lehman noticed how much attention Decker had paid to the photograph. "Not your average cop," he said matter-of-factly. "Hard working and analytical."

Decker nodded, thinking, Hannah Summers could be a magazine model and instead she's a homicide cop.

According to Lehman, both the State Police and the Boston Police had been unable to locate his daughter or produce a single clue to her whereabouts. He had read every police report pertaining to the case. He noted Summers was in charge of the investigation in Boston and had written the most comprehensive summaries.

Lehman let out a burst of information about Summers, which showed the extent of his research and the hope he placed in her. Summers was assigned to the Suffolk County district attorney's office, so any major crime occurring in Boston fell into her domain. Her career file showed early promotion to detective and a keen ability for tracking down killers. She had solved two cold-case murders in the past year.

Lehman was captivated by her report that suggested the attempted abduction of Chicago-based medical device saleswoman Nancy Perlman might be related to the missing person cases of Karen Gilman and Darlene Parks.

According to Summers' report, all three women were brunettes in their twenties with long hair and traveling alone when they landed at Logan Airport. In all three instances the weather had been foul. Gilman, 25, was in Boston on a long layover from Frankfurt, Germany to Cincinnati when she decided on a whim to see some of the city. She had left a message saying as much on her parent's home phone. She never returned to the airport for her connecting flight.

Parks, 29, had flown from San Francisco to Boston to flee her husband after a long history of domestic abuse. She had planned to take a bus to New Hampshire where her sister was waiting to comfort her. Summers had checked with the bus company drivers who would have covered that route but they recalled no passenger matching Parks' description. The police in San Francisco had questioned Parks' husband multiple times until he was no longer a prime suspect.

Most of the police reports Lehman had obtained were typed on official forms with what he considered vital information left blank. But another narrative had caught his attention, written by Sgt. Andre Macusovich, a State Police detective assigned to the homicide unit in abutting Essex County. Macusovich was investigating the murder of a young woman whose body was dumped in a cornfield. The detective had speculated in his report that the woman found in the field was among the victims of a serial killer. He further noted that another woman's body had washed in with the tide in Marblehead, also in Essex County, during the final week of October, and the two cases bore similarities.

"Can you talk to Macusovich? His theory pretty much supports what this Lt. Summers has been saying all along in her reports."

Decker nodded.

"And Lt. Summers as well?"

"I'll reach out to both of them."

"I'd do it myself, but it seems the police don't want parents getting involved in the investigation."

"That's right," added Cornelia Lehman, who

154

for the first time looked up from the cup of tea she was methodically stirring. "We were told to stay out of it, to let the professionals handle it, but nothing has happened since Jenny disappeared in early January."

Cornelia Lehman glanced at her husband for support and to make certain he agreed with her statement, but Skip Lehman was suddenly mute. Decker could see the woman was stifling her tears. He pretended to study the panoramic view of the city while she searched her purse for a tissue. Skip Lehman shifted in his seat as though filled with boundless energy that was going unused and damaging his insides.

"We all spent a week together in the Bahamas during Jenny's school break over Christmas. She didn't seem any different. She wasn't pensive or depressed. If fact, I don't think I'd ever seen her happier. She was just buoyant," Lehman said.

Decker tried to smile as he asked, "What to you think was making her feel so happy?"

Skip Lehman's expression shifted from blank to cross. "Because she's a happy person. She loves the world. She trusts people. She's always saying people are essentially good with a few bad apples thrown in."

Decker nodded. "I simply meant, sir, that perhaps she'd recently received some good news -- maybe an excellent grade in one of her courses, or an important message from a boyfriend. Anything like that."

"Jenny is a straight-A student so getting an A in a course would not be reason to cheer. It would just be normal. I don't know about any steady boyfriend. Of course, she dates. She's a beautiful young woman."

All talk ceased when the waitress brought their breakfast, which Lehman had ordered earlier without any input from Decker. He was concerned that someone might suspect three people at a breakfast meeting with no food on their plates.

Of the more than 100 names Skip Lehman had included in his file, only six comprised his short list of suspects. He pulled a white index card from the breast pocket of his navy sport jacket and slid it across the table. Decker read the names, which meant little. Their occupations told more. One was a college professor at Tufts University who had frequently corresponded with Jenny and seemed to harbor more than an academic interest. Another was a former college student in his mid-twenties who had backpacked to various countries with Jenny, but their friendship apparently had cooled over the past year for unknown reasons. Two were Boston cabbies – neither licensed by the city. Witnesses claimed to have seen both cabbies at the airport the night Jenny disappeared. The fifth suspect was a groundskeeper and pool boy who had worked at the Lehman's Maryland home. Skip Lehman had fired him last fall after it became apparent the young man was smitten with Jenny and had begun to act obsessively, sending her flowers and letters and stalking her. The last suspect was Nikolas Ruskoff, who Lehman noted might have reason to harm his family as a way of getting to him, although no further explanation was offered.

Decker had his own set of questions for the Lehmans but he had to wait for the proper moment to ask. He turned the pages of the file, pretending to reexamine them. "So, you work for a global communications company?"

"I don't think it says that anywhere in the file."

"That's what I was told in the briefing."

"What else were you told?"

"That you have certain connections, people who might be able to assist you or those you hire in conducting a private investigation."

"Let's leave it at this. Money is no obstacle, nor is the law. My contacts may be able to offer logistical support, but only if absolutely needed."

"Understood."

"Did Bill discuss the terms of our verbal contract and how you would be compensated?"

"He told me to keep track of my hours. That's it."

"And are you comfortable with that arrangement?

Decker was about to say, 'As long as it's not minimum wage and I get double-time on holidays with a clothing allowance and coupons to Burger King' but then thought better of it. Instead, he paused and said, "I'd like to find your daughter, Mr. Lehman."

Skip Lehman seemed satisfied with that answer. "I looked at your military record. Special Forces commando. Plenty of Ranger black-ops experience. Weapons expert. Multiple commendations and medals. Bronze Star. Quite impressive. You have the sort of skills we were hoping to find in the right person. So we have a deal?"

"Yes, sir. Seems we do."

"I'll be in contact through Bill. Let's see if we can get these cops to stop dragging their feet."

With that, Skip Lehman rose from the table and his wife followed his cue. He and Decker shook hands. Cornelia Lehman held her purse with both hands and seemed far away in her thoughts. Decker lamented leaving behind heaping but untouched plates of pumpernickel toast, Belgian waffles, eggs Benedict, sausages and strips of bacon.

CHAPTER 25

June 1986
Boston, Massachusetts

WHISKY AND WORDS IN THE AFTERNOON

Rane got word that a torched body had been found in the Revere gravel quarry. He immediately made a dozen phone calls and tried to get anyone in a position of authority to possibly link the incident to the spate of killings. He also tried his street sources, including Frankie Tomatoes, who owned a greenhouse in a contaminated industrial lot in Everett where most of the neighborhood immigrants bought their fruits and vegetables.

Frankie Tomatoes, who had retired in his early seventies after a lifetime of crime, usually was a rich source of information if you brought him a bottle of Grappa and stroked his ego. But on this day, he had nothing to share. Nobody wanted to go on record. In fact, most of those in high office that Rane reached by phone didn't even want to talk. Nor did they want to piss him off because the next time a story arose in which they might be implicated, they would find no mercy in his pen.

Although the story he began writing lacked attribution, Rane had established what he believed were a few facts. This was no accident. The woman's body had been purposefully set afire since she most likely didn't do it herself in some aberrant act of self-immolation. He had called every police department in the metro region to ask about missing person reports. Nothing -- at least not yet.

The newspaper's final deadline wasn't until 9 p.m., which was eight hours away, so he decided to walk the streets of East Boston, asking questions of residents, shopkeepers and complete strangers. He also kept an eye out for Jimmy Two Cubes and Blade, just in case they had heard any news and felt like sharing.

Nemo's usually wasn't busy during the daylight hours, but Rane went inside and was surprised to see Blade sitting at the bar with a tough-looking blonde who had a long scar beneath her left eye and was questionably of legal drinking age. Rane sat a few barstools away and nodded. Bubby immediately appeared before him, set her elbows on the bar and framed her face with her hands. She smiled coyly.

"What brings you in before sunset? I thought you were a vampire."

"Only on weekends," he said.

Rane ordered a Bushmills on the rocks. It was early in the day, but nobody was keeping score. He told Bubby to get Blade and his companion a drink.

"They're having vodka Jello shots with beer chasers," she said.

Rane tried not to smile, but he found the situation amusing. "I didn't pick their poison," he said to Bubby.

Blade and his friend held up their shot glasses. "*Grazie mille.*"

"My pleasure," Rane said. "Not enough people around here enjoying themselves these days. I didn't know you speak Italian?"

"Nah. Just a few words I picked up at work."

Rane was about to comment on Blade's occupation but Bubby had already poured herself a shot of peppermint schnapps and raised her glass. "To Nemo's," she toasted. "May it stay the same when everything else around here is changing."

Blade's bottle-blonde friend Trisha clinked Bubby's shot glass so hard some of the schnapps spilled onto the bar. Bubby ignored the spill and tossed back the schnapps. Trisha sucked down a Jello shot and chased it with her Miller Lite.

"I hate all these fuckin' slant-eyed immigrants," she slurred, announcing proudly that she had been born and raised in Eastie and wasn't about to relocate. "Where the hell are they all coming from? And who the hell sent them here?"

Rane sipped his Irish whisky. "The American Indians who dug clams in the Belle Island Marsh hundreds of years ago probably felt the same way about the British settlers who arrived uninvited," he said.

Blade chuckled. "Instead of feeding those people turkey, stuffing and mashed potatoes at Thanksgiving, maybe the Indians should have taken out two or three of the leaders with bows and arrows. Then the rest of them settlers would have jumped in their boats and sailed back to England or wherever the fuck they came from."

Trisha punched Blade's tattooed arm. "You think popping people is the answer to everything."

Blade lifted her chin with the crooked forefinger of his right hand. "Why don't you shut the fuck up? You don't know what you're talking about."

Trisha pulled away and sulked but quickly rebounded by asking Bubby to change the television channel. As Bubby remotely went around the dial, Rane asked Trisha, "Don't you like watching the news?"

But Trisha wasn't listening. "Oh, oh. Stop right there," she told Bubby, pointing at the TV. A re-run of The Jetsons cartoon show had captivated her attention. "Don't you just love this show? It's so cool. Hey, Blade. I want one of those moving walkways so that I can exercise at home. You're always saying I'm fat. Do you think we can get one?"

Blade finished what remained of his beer but didn't respond. Bubby refilled Blade's glass and asked Rane if he needed to see the local news broadcast. "You news guys all copy each other anyway," she teased in her sassiest voice. "Everybody's got the same story."

"You got that right," Rane conceded. "Investigative repeating."

160

Bubby laughed, feeling witty because she got his joke, which Trisha missed entirely. But Trisha became immediately fascinated with the idea that Rane was a real-life newspaper reporter and she took the opportunity to ask him questions, which clearly annoyed Blade. As it turned out, both Blade and his blonde friend, and just about everyone else in the neighborhood, had read Rane's stories about the recent murders. Only Trisha hadn't matched the man to the byline.

Blade was wobbling on his barstool. His speech was slurred, but he didn't shy away when Rane asked him about the word on the street. What were the cops thinking? Did anyone have a clue about who killed Rose, the baker's daughter? Or why?

"The fuckin' girl is dead. That's all we know. But when we find out who did it, we're going to scorch that motherfucker," he said.

Trisha chugged her draft beer to the bottom, belched quietly with her hand over her mouth and apologized. "I knew Rose. We were in the same class at Central Catholic, but she was a lot smarter than me. She was always so pretty. The guys all loved her."

"What do you think happened to her?"

Blade shot Trisha a look that said shut your mouth. Trisha frowned.

"Another round of Jello shots and beer for this couple, and another Bushmills for me," said Rane.

Blade held up his hand in objection, but Bubby already had the drinks poured and was setting them on the bar.

"To all of us," Rane toasted. "And to Rose, and to figuring out who killed her."

Rane and Bubby clinked glasses. Trisha glanced at Blade as though seeking permission to drink. He nodded and everyone touched glasses without any more toasting.

"I heard Rose was kind of wild at the wedding before they found her," Trisha said. "Apparently Shucker gave her a ride home and that's the last time anybody seen her."

Blade uneasily slid from his bar stool to a standing position. "Don't listen to that shit," he warned Rane. "It's the vodka."

And then to Trisha, "You don't know what the fuck you're talking about. You always have the story ass backwards."

Trisha was incensed, her pride wounded. "Oh, yeah. Well I know lots of things that you don't," she retorted. "You wouldn't believe the things people tell me when I'm doing their hair."

Sensing an opening, Rane asked, "Who's Shucker?"

"Shucker's an asshole," said Trisha. "He gets ticked off over nothing. Thin skin, I guess. Personally, I think he's just weird, Lots of people say he's a real Mother Shucker."

Blade scowled. "Drink and shut up."

Trisha turned from him and faced Rane. "He works at the fish market and comes in here a lot. Lives with his mother, I think. You must have seen him. Usually sits on the corner stool and stares at people."

Rane nodded, envisioning the heavyset, brooding man who, now that he thought about it, often glared at him and his friends.

"Why do you say he's weird?"

"I knew him when I was a little kid. He was older. We were scared of him. He had these dark eyes like black marbles and if he looked at you, yikes! Run! And that's what we did!"

"Did he ever try to hurt you?"

"No. But we knew what he did to the animals."

Blade wobbled again, steadied himself against the bar and announced, "I gotta take a piss. Why don't you shut your trap while I'm gone."

Trisha made a face and Blade raised a hand as though he were about to slap her. Rane stood and said, "Whoa, whoa. I'll make sure she doesn't talk while your gone. I don't want to get in the middle of it."

"Good."

162

As soon as Blade began staggering toward the men's room, Trisha moved closer to Rane. She smelled of cigarettes and citrusy perfume, but she was nice.

"Shucker killed lots of pigeons. We all knew that. He shot them. We'd see their bodies in the alley behind his apartment. Actually, we still find them dead. And we all heard about the barking dogs that stopped barking after Shucker set them on fire. I think there were five or six of them. He set a lot of cats on fire, too. Poured gas on them. He really seemed to hate the cats more than the dogs. Somebody told me he had a parrot that could swear in Italian," she said. "From what I heard, he would bring the parrot out on his boat. But I'm not sure that's true. Sounds like it might be bullshit."

"What kind of boat?"

"I don't know what you call it, but he keeps it down by the abandoned docks off Meridian Street. It's really creepy around there. Lots of big oil tanks. Not someplace you'd go at night. I sure wouldn't. Maybe not even during the day."

Blade must have splashed his face with cold water in the men's room because the drops were turning dark on his shirt. He seemed suddenly more alert. Without ceremony, he grabbed Trisha by the arm. "Let's get out of here."

"OK, honey. Just don't squeeze my arm so hard."

Blade applied more pressure and began walking toward the door. His mood had clearly worsened. "Thanks for the drinks, Clark Kent."

"Any time," said Rane, as the couple pushed through the entrance door.

Bubby smiled. "They were mighty messed up. I think they were doing more than Jello shots. Probably Dexies."

"You might be right. Their pupils were dilated into big black dots."

"Blade likes his Black Beauties. He's not addicted or anything, but he needs them. He's different since he got out of prison."

Rane nodded as though he understood but didn't ask Bubby what had led to Blade's stint behind bars. Instead, he nursed the Bushmills and quietly watched the television

163

news. There weren't many details about the torched body at the Revere quarry. By now he had a buzz on but it wasn't enough to quell the frustration he was feeling inside about the story, his bosses at the newspaper, and his relationship with Kaleigh.

With scant information available, Rane returned to the newsroom and strung together a story that loosely linked the burned corpse to the spree of killings. His editors didn't like the lack of source attribution, but they ran the story anyway. Most readers didn't care if the sources were named or vaguely described. They just wanted entertainment. They wanted the dirty laundry.

CHAPTER 26

June 1986
Boston, Massachusetts

HIDE IF THE BOSS IS HAVING A BAD DAY

Fergus Cavanaugh was fuming. His Italian counterparts in the North End were spreading rumors – even making jokes – that he had lost control of his streets in Eastie. How could he allow a beautiful girl like Rose Cavelli to be murdered and not know who did it? How is it that some cocky newspaper reporter continues to write stories that could hurt the family, exposing the goings on in East Boston, and nobody is doing a thing to stop him?

Fergus Cavanaugh has no balls, they said. He should go back to the Land of Micks and spend the rest of his days drinking piss-warm Guinness and telling the gullible villagers about what a big mob boss he was in America.

"What the fuck do they want me to do? I can't just go out and kill a Trib reporter," he told Jimmy Two Cubes, who showed up at the office with Blade to confirm how many sports betting slips they had delivered to Harry Ragansky's bookmakers.

"I know, boss. I'm just telling you what the word is out on the street. People are saying things."

Jimmy Two Cubes paused, gazing up at the acoustic tile ceiling as though he'd had an epiphany. "Maybe you *can* kill him. I heard there was a reporter out in Arizona about 10 years ago who was writing things some people didn't want

165

him to write. They put sticks of dynamite in his car and that was the end of it."

"Jimmy."

"Yes, boss."

"Shut the fuck up. You're so stupid you didn't even know that this Trib reporter we're talking about gets around on a motorcycle. He doesn't drive a car. You can't blow up his car if he doesn't drive a car."

"Jimmy's only trying to help," said Blade. "Everybody knows you were the dynamite king back in Belfast, that you blew some of them British soldiers half way to Mars."

Fergus seemed lost in thought. He adjusted the mirror aviator shades that were balanced on his head, tapped his pen on the ratty wooden desk and lit a Parliament, puffing out a series of smoke rings.

"I don't know about bombing any newspaper guys, but I think we should talk to Shucker," Blade suggested.

"Shucker? You think Luddy Pugano is in this thing?"

Blade sensed Fergus' anger rising and knew first-hand how dangerous that mood could be. "I'm pretty sure, boss. He disappeared for a while right after Rose Cavelli was murdered."

Fergus set his burning cigarette on the edge of the desk, folded his hands in front of his face like a church steeple and touched the tips of his fingers to his lips. "Find out," he said. "But we gotta be sure. Shucker has done this family favors. Not the biggest ones, but big enough to show him some respect."

Before Blade could ask for details, Fergus told him about the disposal jobs Luddy had made possible aboard *Sea Bitch* over the years, mostly small-timers who'd violated the family trust in one way or another and paid the price. Luddy hadn't done the actual killing, but he had been present from start to finish. The bulk of those favors were done for Fergus' late boss, Cyrus McMacken, before he, too, disappeared. But Fergus was a stickler for tradition and mob etiquette dictated that you respected your elders, even after they were dead.

Fergus recalled the time Luddy helped hide one of McMacken's girlfriends aboard the *Sea Bitch* after Mrs. McMacken caught them screwing in the couple's Revere Beach pool house. Luddy had a side job cleaning swimming pools at the time and, lucky for McMacken, he was able to convince the angry wife to hand over the .357 magnum revolver she was aiming at her husband's testicles.

Fergus also knew well that Luddy had a few wet wires in his head that caused him to short out when least expected. And that he could be vicious, often without reason. He chuckled as he pictured the day McMacken found out Luddy had tried to put the moves on the boss' girlfriend while aboard the boat in Boston Harbor.

"McMacken had Shucker brought into the office. You had to see it. There's four guys holding him while the old man uses a filet knife to cut off Shucker's leather belt. Shucker has the fear of god in his eyes at this point and doesn't know the old man is just fucking with him," said Fergus, smiling and shaking his head as though still in disbelief. "Down goes Shucker's zipper, pants at his knees. McMacken is wearing these blue rubber gloves like the EMTs use on the ambulances and he's sawing with the long tapered blade so that Shucker's underwear has joined his pants below the knees. McMacken looks him dead in the eye, presses the razor-sharp knife hard against Shucker's pecker and says, 'Hey kid, I hear you were hitting on my girlfriend while she was visiting your boat. Is that true?"

Fergus was clearly enjoying the memory and having fun telling the story. "Shucker's face was white as a communion wafer. You should have seen him. Shakin' his head, eyes bulging out, and perspiring like a pig. McMacken looks him straight in the eye and says, 'There's plenty of broads to go around, so don't try to take mine. You want one, I'll buy you one.' Shucker just gulps. He has no fuckin' idea what to say. All of a sudden everyone in the office starts laughing hysterically, leaving Shucker standing there trying to pull up his pants and probably thinking to himself he just came a cunt hair from dying."

167

Fergus slapped the tabletop. He had tears in his eyes from laughing.

"And then everyone had a drink -- imagine that -- the best scotch in the house," he said. "Single malt. That was a good day."

Blade and Jimmy Two Cubes were grinning like idiots, mesmerized by Fergus' recollections, thrilled that he would share such tales with the likes of them.

Jimmy Two Cubes blurted out, "I'm surprised Shucker didn't wet his pants."

"Who said he didn't?"

"Next time I see Shucker, I'll ask him how it feels to have a knife against his prick."

"Don't you ever mention it," Fergus said sternly, "or you might find out yourself."

"I won't, boss. Don't you worry."

Fergus removed his aviator shades and made certain the men knew he was looking closely at them. "Shucker has done some real bad shit, things that may come back to us. People know he likes to cause pain and that he beat his mother more than once, which isn't a forgivable sin."

Fergus made the sign of the cross. "If he has killed without authorization, then we got a problem. A big problem."

Blade flicked his switchblade and twirled it so that the metal gleamed in the overhead light. "You want me to take care of him, just say the word."

"Me too," added Jimmy Two Cubes.

"Your loyalty is noted," said Fergus. "But let's see what the cops have to say about the torched body before we do anything."

CHAPTER 27

June 1986
Boston, Massachusetts

*GOOD FRIENDS, LOYAL DOGS,
AND COLD BEER*

Luddy presumed showing his face on the street and
at Nemo's would send a message to the police that he didn't
consider himself a suspect in hiding. Rose Cavelli might be
dead, but he had nothing to do with it. And he certainly didn't
know a thing about any torched body in Revere.

"Hey, Shucker. Cops have been lookin' for you," said
Bubby. "The big one, Sgt. MacSomething-or-Other, was in
around noon asking questions. He wanted to know what time
you usually stopped by."

"What did you tell him?"

"I told him you usually come in for a beer after you
get off work at the fish market," she said, setting a draft beer
in front of him.

"Well, I'm here."

Luddy wound his plump hands around the glass of
beer and studied the bubbles rising. Beer always helped
settle his nerves. He wondered what the cops had found at
the gravel quarry -- a burned body, mostly ashes, a few bone
fragments.

Before leaving his apartment he had methodically
scrubbed every part of his body in the shower, splashed Brut
cologne on his face, neck and wrists, and hoped it would

169

mask any residual smell of gasoline.

It was after 7 p.m. when Decker walked into Nemo's with Dogman and Major. They sidled up to the bar and the shepherd immediately moved to sniff Luddy who literally tried to kick the animal away.

"Hey, easy guy," said Decker. "He's friendly. Just checking you out."

The dog growled and Dogman yanked on the leash, giving a command in Spanish. The dog immediately flattened out on the floor at Dogman's feet.

Decker introduced Dogman to Bubby and ordered two Bombay gin tonics with lime.

Luddy narrowed his eyes. "Most people don't bring their dogs in here."

Decker glared back at Luddy. "Most people didn't fight a war and get saved by a dog. This dog."

Before Luddy could reply, Bubby looked directly at Dogman and blurted out, "Is that what happened to you?"

Dogman held up his mangled right hand, using it to tap his artificial leg.

"Wow," she said. "You really did get hurt. My brother's in the Army, but he got stationed in Germany. He said the most dangerous things there are Porsches and Mercedes going 120 mph, eating too much sausage and drinking until the sun comes up."

"Well, tell him to stay safe," said Decker, who carried the two drinks to a nearby table. Dogman and Major followed.

Four young women charged through the front door in a flurry of laughter. Two were in office attire, pencil skirts and man-tailored blazers with puffy shoulders. The third woman wore gym workout clothes and the last blue surgical scrubs and clogs. They were in happy-hour mode, ready to forget the workday with a little help from a pitcher of margaritas. As the women settled themselves at a table, the tall redhead in the Spandex workout suit introduced herself as Brenda and asked if she could pet the shepherd. "Sure thing," said Dogman, uttering a few syllables in a language that

170

definitely wasn't English. The dog got to its feet and wagged its tail at the woman as she petted his head. A second woman in the group asked if she, too, could say hello to the dog. Soon all four had joined in lively conversation with Decker and Dogman. The jukebox was loaded with dance music and several couples quickly took to the floor when Bubby cranked the volume. Bubby made certain they played *Maniac* from the *Flashdance* movie and when it came on she danced wildly behind the bar, adjusted her headband and swung her hair in a circle. Decker seemed suddenly perplexed by the music and finished his gin-and-tonic in one long gulp.

"I'd love to show you my breakdancing routine," said Dogman, smiling at the four women, extending his artificial leg and hiking up his pants so they could see the metal and plastic limb. He waited for the anticipated responses, including "Oh my God" and "I'm so sorry."

Dogman registered the expressions on their faces and grinned. "Maybe some other time we can do the Moonwalk. I'll show you how to glide in style," he joked, pushing through the momentary gloom. "The kids back in my village in the Dominican Republic are breaking before they start school. Must be in the blood."

The nurse engaged Dogman in medical talk related to his injuries, but she seemed especially interested in Decker. Her name was Amal Shahadi, a dark-eyed beauty of Lebanese birth whose parents had moved to the U.S. a dozen years earlier when she was 14. As soon as she learned the two soldiers had served in Lebanon, her interest multiplied. Within minutes they were comparing notes on the neighborhoods of Beirut, the country's cuisine and its troubled history. Decker bought two more gin and tonics and another pitcher of margaritas. He enjoyed talking about Beirut in a way that didn't involve patrol routes, casualties and the ever-present threat of death.

Over the next hour Nemo's filled to capacity. All the bar stools and every table were taken by the locals and many of the neighborhood's newer residents, leaving the latecomers to stand holding their drinks as they talked, watched the

171

television or played Keno. The mood was festive. A waitress brought baskets of popcorn to every table. Bubby worked her magic behind the bar so powerful drinks flowed efficiently from the taps and bottles.

Amal kneeled beside the dog. As she stroked its black fur her hand accidentally bumped into Decker's shin. He glanced down at her with intensity but didn't know what to say.

The two women in office attire had discarded their blazers and were dancing together, as were other women and six or seven couples. Amal extended a hand toward Decker. "Dance with me," she said, her white teeth luminescent amid her perfect olive skin.

"Go for it, Decker," yelled Dogman.

"Yes," the woman in the jogging suit chimed enthusiastically. "I'll stay here and chat. I've had enough exercise for one day. I'm sure your friend and I can keep each other entertained."

Decker seemed frozen. "I don't feel much like dancing," he said, which embarrassed Amal and made her withdraw. After two romping dance numbers off Warren Zevon's *Excitable Boy* album, the crowd whooping it up and singing along, the jukebox shifted gears to *Saving All My Love For You*, a new slow song by Whitney Houston. Decker looked directly at Amal as though trying to read her thoughts.

"Better?"

"Much better," he acknowledged, fighting to return from his momentary trip to the past where Billy Idol's *Rebel Yell* was pulsing through his headset as he found the target in the crosshairs. "Sometimes I get overloaded."

Amal bravely extended her hand and led him onto the dance floor. She put her arms around Decker's neck and he gently held her hips as she swayed in her surgical scrubs. She smelled of lavender. As Whitney Houston poured out her emotions, Amal rested her head against Decker's chest and closed her eyes. Decker relaxed and tried to flow with the music, his insides aroused by the heat from Amal's body pressing against him.

172

Decker's mind wandered as they danced. He imagined what it might have been like had he met a woman like Amal while stationed in Lebanon. She was beautiful without having to shout it or wear heavy makeup. Her body felt taught but not rigid. And when he momentarily gazed into her eyes, he felt unarmed and susceptible to whatever charms she might unveil.

Whitney Houston crooned and Decker whispered into Amal's ear that he hadn't come to Nemo's in search of a date but was counting lucky stars to have made her acquaintance. It was not so much her looks, which he certainly found pleasing, but the sound of her voice that had captivated him. He leaned in and told her, "When you speak, I hear a voice I've known all my life."

Amal smiled with her eyes. "You probably say that to all the girls."

"No. Life's too short to play games like that. But working in the ER, I'm sure you already know that."

Amal nodded. "I've seen too many people die."

"Me too."

Kaleigh didn't expect to see Decker at Nemo's and her mouth opened slightly at the sight of such a lovely woman dancing with him in the middle of the room. Rane was bumping through the crowd toward the bar, pulling her in tow. He slapped high-fives with two guys in collared shirts and chinos who worked at City Hall. They were leaning back against one of the thick pillars, drinking beer and eyeing the crowd. One of them shouted over the din, "Nice job on that mob story."

Rane smiled proudly. "Glad you liked it. More to follow."

Kaleigh couldn't help wondering about the blue surgical scrubs. She was focused on the woman's slender waist and the glimpse of olive skin that showed where the two-piece scrubs came together. When had this woman entered Decker's life? They'd probably met at the VA hospital. Decker hadn't been around much since he'd calmed her down the night the dead cat was found hanging outside her apartment. That was two months ago. She had called him a few times from the museum, choosing not to leave a message on the answering machine he shared with Dogman. Her roommates repeatedly asked what had become of the handsome soldier who so chivalrously rescued them, but she had no real answer.

Kaleigh recalled Decker saying the private investigation firm for whom he worked might send him out of town for a while, but she presumed that meant a week or less, not two months. She had hoped he might stop by the museum, but he hadn't and it made her feel sad, lonely and disappointed.

Decker spotted Kaleigh near the bar and a lump formed in his throat. She was wearing faded bluejeans, a white peasant top that gathered off her shoulders and leather Buffalo sandals.

Amal must have felt the tension because she opened her eyes, pushed her body slightly apart and gazed up at him. It was clear to her the spell had broken. When the song ended, they returned to the table where Dogman had the three other women in stitches, telling stories about his childhood in a rural village hours outside the capital city of Santo Domingo, over impassable roads. Already they were flapping their arms like chickens as Dogman described his *abuela* chasing after the scraggly bird with a machete. Major was under the table pretending to be asleep at their feet.

Luddy seethed as he watched the wounded soldier entertain the women. He imagined taking the shepherd into the nearest alley and beating it senseless with a baseball bat. People and their fuckin' dogs, he bitched to himself. He eyed each woman at the table and his mind began to whir with anticipation. Did the tall giddy one in the jogging suit run alone at night? Were the two women in business suits who danced together unattached romantically and looking for boyfriends? Luddy cursed himself for even thinking they might be interested in him. And the one in the surgical scrubs, well, she was obviously interested in the I'm-oh-so-fuckin'-cool soldier who'd told him to take it easy after he

174

tried to kick the dog. Some day, he thought, the soldier would pay for that disrespect.

Luddy was on his fifth beer, annoyed by the dance music and Nemo's new wave of patrons when Sgt. Macusovich walked into the bar, his massive frame filling the entrance. The detective moved through the crowd with authority, his eyes probing the room until they fixed on Luddy.

"Hi there," said Bubby, who was wearing a green *Flashdance* headband to keep beads of sweat from falling into the drinks. "I thought you might be back."

Bubby glanced furtively at Luddy, who had dismounted from his bar stool and beat for the men's room. The sergeant followed him. Luddy was at the urinal and didn't look up.

"When you finish pissin', we're going to have a talk."

Luddy stared at the wall in front of him. "I don't have anything to say to you."

"It might be in your best interest."

"Talking to cops has never been in my best interest. Last time I did that, I ended up in Charles Street, but you already know that."

Luddy turned, zipped his fly and gave the sergeant his best tough-guy look. Macusovich took three aggressive steps forward, grabbed Luddy by the hair and tripped him onto the tile floor. He kicked Luddy hard in the ribs, waited for him to roll into a protective ball and then kicked him again in the buttocks.

"We know you killed Rose Cavelli. Your mother told us everything."

Luddy groaned in pain. "You got no right. I'm calling my lawyer."

Macusovich went down on one knee and gripped Luddy's windpipe with a vice-like hand. Luddy gasped for air and began kicking his feet on the tiles. The detective released his grip. "How's that feel, you fat fuck? Not so good, I bet. Now I want you to tell me about Rose Cavelli."

"I don't know nothing about that. I gave her a ride.

That's it," he coughed.

Macusovich drew a 9mm Sig Sauer semi-automatic from his shoulder holster, pinched Luddy's cheeks until his jaw released and stuffed the metal barrel into his mouth. Luddy's eyes were paralyzed with fear. The sergeant could feel the man's teeth vibrating against the blued metal.

"If you come clean about everything you've been doing, you might get 20 instead of life. I can convince the judge of that, but only if you cooperate," the sergeant threatened. "There's a lot of interest in the women who've turned up dead around here over the past year and I get the feeling you might have the answers."

Luddy shook his head, his eyes still wide with fear.

"Think about it, Shucker," the sergeant advised. "You might not get another chance. I hear other people out there are looking for you, people who might not give you any options."

The sergeant left Luddy sprawled on the men's room tiles just as the door opened and Jimmy Two Cubes entered.

"What the fuck's going on?"

"He slipped and fell. Be careful on these wet floors," said the sergeant, stabbing a finger into Jimmy Two Cubes' shoulder. "I'll leave you guys alone. You've probably got a lot to talk about."

Rane pulled Kaleigh out onto the dance floor. Decker could see she wasn't into it by the lackluster way she moved. Rane had his hands all over her model-thin body, trying to make her twirl, but she was dead wood. Kaleigh made for the bar as soon as the song ended and Rane followed closely, clamping down on her shoulder to slow her progress. From a distance, they appeared exactly like what they were, a couple having an argument.

Out the corner of his eyes, Rane saw Sgt. Macusovich storming out of the men's room. The sergeant was reading a message on his electronic beeper and it must have been urgent because he crashed through the crowd and went out the door.

When closing time approached, Dogman offered

to give the four women a lift home. Two were taking the Blue Line subway and didn't need a ride. Amal and Brenda accepted since it was late and they lived in Cambridge.

Once in the car, Dogman suggested they all have a nightcap at the apartment he shared with Decker since it was close by. Luckily there was beer in the refrigerator so they sat around watching an old movie. Dogman fired up a joint and passed it, but Decker and Amal declined. Clearly buzzed, Dogman attempted to stand and nearly fell over. Brenda quickly steadied him. "Got to let Major out," he said.

Brenda offered to go with him. When they returned five minutes later they walked straight into Dogman's bedroom and closed the door. Decker and Amal smiled. "I'll drive you home," he said.

Amal opened a cold beer and handed it to Decker. "We'll split it. I don't want a whole one."

She snuggled next to Decker on the couch and looked at him deeply with her dark almond eyes. Decker suddenly saw the beauty of Beirut, the piece he had missed. He sipped the beer, set it on the coffee table, put his arms around Amal and kissed her softly. She kissed him back and stretched out on the couch, turning on her side so that he could join her. Decker felt himself getting aroused as they kissed. His fingers momentarily fiddled with the drawstring on her scrub pants but then decided against it. He didn't want to lead her on because he wasn't ready for commitment. His life was anything but stable and if they had sex there would always be a weirdness or feeling of expectation between them. Decker didn't want to cause any hurt feelings.

Amal seemed to understand when Decker wrapped his arms around her and pulled her so close there wasn't an inch between them. She gave him a smile that was restrained by sadness just as Major plunked down in front of the couch.

When Decker awoke in the morning, Amal was at the stove making pancakes. Using the spatula as a wand, she pointed like a game show hostess to the stack on the plate. Major was parked at her feet. There was no sign of Dogman or Brenda.

"Your breakfast awaits," she said, smiling honestly. "I hope the coffee isn't too strong."

Decker seemed relieved. "I'm sure it's perfect," he said, pleased to see that she, too, had moved on.

CHAPTER 28

July 1986
Boston, Massachusetts

SPECIAL OPS, FEELY PROFS, AND
LITTLE DOLLS

Bill Carrington, Decker's immediate supervisor at
Executive Cover, laughed quietly as he hefted two olive-
green canvas duffle bags onto a folding table in his penthouse
office overlooking the Charles River.

"Help yourself," said Carrington, waving an arm
toward the goods.

Decker opened the duffle bags. Among the equipment
was a VHF handheld marine radio, police and fire scanners,
binoculars, flashlight, black duct tape, a night-vision Starlight
scope, a set of black BDUs, military ready-to-eat meal
pouches, a tape recorder with telephone microphone, tripod,
Nikon 35mm camera with telephoto lenses and 10 rolls of
film.

Beneath the table were a black-painted scuba tank,
wetsuit and other diving gear.

"What am I supposed to do with all this?"

"Go find out what happened to Jenny Lehman."

Carrington held out a set of keys. "Your
transportation. Brand new Jeep Cherokee. It's a loaner and
for this operation only so don't destroy it. In fact, don't even
dent it."

Carrington, an athletic man in his early forties with a full head of barber-trimmed blond hair, helped Decker lug the equipment to the elevator. When they reached the ground-level parking lot, Carrington gripped Decker by the bicep and handed him a .9mm Beretta 92FS semi-automatic pistol tucked inside a leather shoulder holster. Decker slipped the handgun from its holster, popped out the magazine and drew back the barrel slide to make sure no rounds were in the chamber. Satisfied the weapon was safe, he reloaded the magazine.

"And the carry permit for this? I'm a civilian, remember?"

"Already taken care of," Carrington said smugly. "And congratulations on your honorable discharge."

Later that day, Decker called Sgt. Macusovich. It took some doing to convince the detective to meet for coffee, but Decker was adamant it would benefit both of them. Since Macusovich was based on the North Shore, they met at Red's, a popular breakfast joint in downtown Salem a short walk from the district attorney's office and the courthouses.

Macusovich was glad to learn Decker had been an Army Ranger who had served in a combat zone. He mentioned the newspaper stories that had been published about a possible serial killer, referring specifically to those written by Tribune reporter Rane Bryson.

Ever the alert detective, Macusovich caught the uneasy expression on Decker's face when he mentioned the reporter's name. "You know him?"

"Who?"

"Rane Bryson."

"No. Not well. We've met. We both drink at Nemo's on the same nights sometimes. He was talking to people about his serial-killer stories. Apparently he's a good friend of someone that I know as well. Mutual acquaintances."

Decker had already explained he was working as a private investigator on the Jenny Lehman missing person case. When the topic came up again, he said, "Seems like she landed at Logan and then fell off the map."

Macusovich had been stationed at the airport's State Police barracks earlier in his career. He knew the airport and the key people who worked there. "We have a couple of suspects, but we can't get a judge to issue a search warrant for their homes. Not enough probable cause, I guess. Our request to search a suspect's boat was also denied by the same liberal-pussy judge."

Decker gambled on the detective's interest and willingness to partner, at least on some aspects of the investigation. He showed Macusovich the list of six suspects. The white index card looked tiny in the detective's massive hand.

"Did anyone check out the professor?"

"I'm doing that now."

"What about the landscaper?"

"Doubtful. He has an alibi."

"The backpacking buddy?"

"Ben Tillman. He's in Nepal," offered Decker. "That's the last time his passport was used. We await his return."

As Macusovich sipped his coffee, he asked, "And the cabbies?"

"I have two vehicles partially identified as possibilities but no information on who was behind the wheel that night. I have the names on the registrations, but that's about it."

"I may be able to help you there." The detective pulled a small spiral-bound notebook from his shirt pocket, opened the pad to a blank page and wrote down the names of the two cabbies. "Elroy McGuinness is a convicted sex offender who continues to be a source of complaints from female passengers, usually young women traveling alone. Luddy Pugano is a freelancer who served time for arson and has a reputation for torturing animals. People call him Shucker. He drives an older model Crown Vic, color dark blue."

"Nice fellows."

Macusovich was convinced Luddy had murdered Rose Cavelli and he told Decker as much. Decker recalled

Rane's graphic newspaper story along with the horror such details tend to leave in their wake.

"Luddy has a cabin cruiser, the *Sea Bitch*. It's sitting out there in Boston Harbor, but we can't find a judge who'll give us a search warrant. Same goes for the apartment where Luddy lives with his mother, Celeste. We'd also like to get inside McGinness' place in Jeffries Point, which from the outside looks like a real shithole."

Macusovich filled in Decker on Luddy's history of arson and car theft, street violence, and his penchant for torturing animals – dogs, cats, birds or whatever other living creature had the misfortune to cross his path.

Decker promised to get more information on Carson Pernell, the Tufts anthropology professor. Macusovich said Lt. Hannah Summers was leading the murder investigation and was the only person authorized to ask Nancy Perlman if she would be willing to talk to Decker. But frankly, said Macusovich, the medical-device saleswoman from Chicago was most likely still too shaken from her near-death encounter at Logan Airport.

Decker's demeanor changed completely at the mention of Summers. He wanted to know more about her, not just her investigative itinerary but personal background information.

Macusovich suggested he contact Summers himself, though he couldn't promise that she'd talk to him. She didn't like the news media and might feel the same way about a private investigator, he said.

Macusovich withheld the results of the autopsy on the woman in the red dress whose body had been found in a cornfield, as well as the latest on the corpse that washed up in Marblehead. The latter victim was a well-known nature photographer from Newton, a wealthy suburb west of Boston. The sergeant also knew the identity of the body found burned in the Revere quarry – marine science researcher Dr. Melanie Appleton, an academic nationally known for her environmental conservation efforts. Rapid response by the fire department had preserved some of the woman's teeth and bones. The charred remains lay on a slab at the regional morgue. It had been impossible to determine the cause of death due to the condition of the body, but Macusovich sensed the woman had died violently.

"More work by the Boston Butcher, or at least that's what the press has taken to calling our killer," the sergeant said.

Decker was fired up to work the case. He began by staking out Professor Pernell at the Tufts campus. He obtained a list of the professor's courses and the location of his office from the campus guidebook. The professor's teaching load apparently was light – one summer session course and advisor to students completing their senior thesis projects. The office was in a small, two-story, red brick building down a path off the green and there appeared a steady stream of co-eds visiting, presumably for academic purposes. Using the 500mm telephoto lens, Decker was able to see into a first-floor window. From what Decker could gather, Pernell was certainly the feely type, making a habit of touching each young woman while offering them a chair. When the meetings were over, he routinely embraced them, although Decker couldn't imagine why he needed to hug them.

On the second day of surveillance, he watched Pernell and a student with chiseled features and straight blonde hair to her waist get into a red convertible sports car. Decker's Jeep Cherokee was parked several blocks away so he couldn't follow them. Instead, he strolled through the campus, pretending he was a prospective graduate student interested in taking courses. He asked several young women if they knew anything about the Anthropology Department and the teaching capabilities of its faculty, particularly Professor Pernell. Only one student among those asked had taken anthropology courses. When the name Carson Pernell came up, she rolled her eyes. "He's highly intelligent and his courses are interesting, but he asks too many personal questions."

"Such as?"

"What do I do in my free time? Where do my friends and I hang out? Do I have a single or live with roommates? And even stuff like what novels I read, or whether I have any favorite poets?"

"I know this might sound strange, but has he ever made advances on you?"

"Advances?"

"Yes. Like sexual moves? Has he ever tried to hit on you?"

"Not me, except for the time he asked me about my bra."

"Your bra?"

"Yes, he apparently could see one of the straps sticking out from my blouse and told me it was a beautiful, warm pink. He claimed he didn't know much about bras but was interested only because he was planning to buy some expensive ones for his wife."

"What did you say to him?"

"I told him I wasn't comfortable talking about the subject."

"And what did he say?"

"He apologized and seemed really embarrassed. But I've heard he's done that to other students. He told one girl I know that he was doing a study of underwear in America from the Colonial Era to the present. He claimed that's why he had asked her what she was wearing beneath her dress. But why do you want to know?"

"I'm interested in knowing whether there's any truth to what's in his personnel file, which includes a disciplinary letter from the dean, warning him not to inappropriately fraternize with his students."

Just then, the two-seat roadster pulled up near the small brick building. Pernell and the young blonde were laughing and talking animatedly. Decker turned away and thanked the co-ed for her help. He crossed over the quad and took up a position where the brick building was still visible. Pernell got out of the car and opened the passenger door. He bowed deeply in a mocking fashion, which made the blonde laugh.

When she was out of the car she gestured for him to rise, as though she were royalty. Decker clicked four frames, the last two showing Pernell kissing the young woman on the hand and then on the cheek. He showed the photos to Carrington the next day.

"Doesn't prove anything other than the fact that he's probably a letch," Carrington said. "At this point, we don't even know if we're dealing with one killer or two."

Carrington tossed a sheaf of papers on the table where Decker was seated. "Credit card histories of all six names on the suspect list. You'll see why Skip Lehman was worried about the groundskeeper. The kid earns about $100 a week and spent almost $1,000 on flowers for Jenny Lehman."

Decker thumbed the reports. "Anything else jump out?"

"Your professor also has been buying a lot of flowers these days, though we're not sure for whom or what he does with them -- mostly your standard dozen roses and the occasional exotic orchid. He spent quite a few nights during the past year in different motels on the outskirts of Boston, but those were in the winter. I guess he couldn't get home because of all those snowstorms," Carrington said with a wink.

"Any evidence the professor wasn't alone?"

"No. His name is the only one on the registers. He could have had six coeds with him each time."

Decker smirked. "Are you fantasizing?"

Carrington rolled his eyes and slapped Decker on the back. "Goodbye, Decker. Get back to work."

Decker roamed East Boston's dilapidated industrial waterfront. He photographed the *Sea Bitch* at her mooring but the cabin cruiser was too far from shore to capture any details. He also snapped a few frames of Luddy Pugano working at the fish market, and others of Elroy McGuinness picking up female passengers at the airport.

The photographs were pinned and taped to a wall in Decker's apartment along with notes, maps and newspaper clippings. He called it the war room.

Dogman announced he was going on a real date with Brenda the fitness instructor. As he put it, they were about the same age, she was single, liked to laugh, loved dogs and didn't mind hanging around with a slow-moving cripple. Decker slapped him playfully on the back. "How does Major feel about this?"

At the sound of his name, the shepherd's ears stiffened straight upward and he cocked his head, waiting for instructions.

"Any more interest in her friend, the angel in the blue scrubs? You two seemed to hit it off."

"Maybe," Decker said. "As you know, she's Lebanese. Grew up in Beirut before her parents moved here. I don't recall seeing beautiful girls walking the streets of Beirut when we were there."

"Too many bullets flying. Probably ours. They wisely stayed indoors."

"I'll give her a call, but I think she works a lot at one of the big hospitals."

Dogman understood it was a half-hearted reply most likely related to the fact that Decker hadn't thought about a woman in years.

"Well, if you decide, maybe we can go on a double date to a concert or something," said Dogman. "I'm seeing Brenda tomorrow."

After dark, Decker drove back to the rickety docks and parked the Jeep in the shadows. For several minutes he watched the boat before donning his wetsuit and tank.

Once in the water, Decker took a compass bearing, estimated the distance at 50 yards and began swimming underwater toward the *Sea Bitch*. He surfaced 10 feet off the stern.

Decker tied the black-painted aluminum tank with buoyancy compensator and regulator to the boat's swim ladder, removed his fins and climbed aboard. Since Luddy's skiff wasn't tied to the transom, odds were good that the boat was unoccupied.

The glass and wood cockpit doors were locked but Decker used his SOG tactical knife to jiggle open the foredeck hatch. In the red beam of his waterproof flashlight, Decker could see the boat interior was a mess, with equipment and clothing strewn about the bunks, tables and counters. In the sink were two empty vodka bottles and a mound of crushed beer cans. Opened boxes of crackers and bags of potato chips littered the table.

Decker was looking for signs of struggle, blood, bodily fluids, broken glass, an unusual dent or puncture in the furniture and cushions. He checked the head, which looked as though it had been recently cleaned. A plastic jug of bleach was nestled behind the toilet. He got down on all fours and peered into the cabinets and storage lockers, hoping to discover an article of woman's clothing that might have belonged to Jenny Lehman. He searched the storage areas beneath the v-berth and in the main cabin where he found tools, cans of engine oil and transmission fluid, lifejackets and other items typically stowed aboard a boat. He thought it odd that there were no anchors, anchor chain or coils of rope in the anchor locker at the bow and made a mental note to mention it to Carrington.

After nearly an hour aboard, Decker exited the forehatch, using a short length of wire to pull the lock back into position. He was startled by the sound of an engine approaching and he flattened himself in the cockpit, his face against the teak floorboards. A few minutes later the sound died away and Decker peaked over the gunwale to see a fisherman in a bait-laden skiff aiming for a nearby lobster boat. As a final effort in his search, he lifted the panel of teak boards that covered the scuppers – the drains that channeled rain and seawater out of the cockpit. Atop the strainer on the starboard scupper lay a tiny, primitive doll, just smaller than his thumb. It appeared made of cloth, yarn and wire. Decker pinched the doll between his thumb and forefinger. He wondered, what would a guy like Luddy Pugano be doing with a folk art doll? Instinct told him to tuck it inside his wetsuit.

187

Carrington was impressed that Decker had made it aboard the *Sea Bitch* but he didn't have much to say about the miniature doll. "These things are made in Central America. They're a dime a dozen."

Decker left the office feeling discouraged. He was sitting up in bed drinking a beer and reading a novel when the phone rang. It was Carrington, asking him to meet at the office in half an hour. When Decker arrived, Skip Lehman was seated solemnly in a hardback chair near Carrington's desk. He was poking at the doll on which the yarn had dried and was coming unraveled.

"Do you recognize this doll?" said Carrington.

"Not this specific doll, but they do have a special significance to Jenny," Skip Lehman replied. "It's a worry doll. They're mostly handmade in Guatemala. Cheap little things really. Jenny traveled to Central America between her freshman and sophomore year of college. She and her dickhead boyfriend. I know Jenny can be all flowers and world peace, but this guy was even worse. Ben Tillman the pacifist. He was a click away from being a Buddhist monk, which is why I worried about them. I used to think, if they get into trouble down there, what the fuck is dickhead going to do? Nothing, that's what. I was glad she dumped him."

"Tell us more about Jenny and the worry dolls," said Carrington.

"When Jenny returned from Central America, she was so excited about these little dolls she'd purchased from some woman in a small village. The woman had filled her with all these crazy stories about how the dolls are magical and possess powers to ward off evil and that sort of thing." Lehman cupped the tiny doll in his fist, which Decker noticed was shaking slightly. "She told Jenny the dolls could help people erase their worries," said Lehman. "All you had to do was carry the doll in your pocket every day and life would be better."

"Hmm," said Decker. "Did you?"

"She made us all promise. Me, my wife and our other daughter, Sarah, had to agree to carry one of these dolls wherever we went."

"And?"

"No, Decker. I didn't. I don't believe in all that hocus pocus."

"But Jenny obviously did."

"Yes. During her last visit over Christmas, she asked me to show her the doll she'd given me. It should have been in my pocket, right?"

"And it wasn't?"

"No. It wasn't."

Decker pressed Lehman. "What about your wife and daughter. Did they carry the dolls?"

"I honestly don't know. It wasn't something we talked about."

"And what about Jenny, did she carry one of the dolls every day?"

Lehman paused. His voice cracked when he spoke. "Knowing Jenny, I wouldn't be surprised. Most of these dolls are mass-produced with little variation. But Jenny was convinced the dolls she acquired were different, made by an artist with a more refined sense of detail. The yarns were brighter and the dolls were given facial expressions. They weren't all exactly the same."

Lehman's fist closed around the doll. "That was Jenny. She always found the beauty."

CHAPTER 29

July 1986
Boston, Massachusetts

KEEPING AWAY THE NIGHTMARES

A few days later Decker phoned the Suffolk County district attorney's office and asked to speak with Lt. Summers whose face was burned into his brain. The receptionist put the call through to the major crimes unit. Within seconds a woman's voice came on and said, "Summers."

Decker quickly introduced himself as a private investigator interested in her thoughts on the disappearance of Jenny Lehman. Would she meet him for coffee? He promised to take up no more than half an hour and give her some useful information.

"It's an ongoing investigation. We don't talk about things like that," she said curtly.

"I thought maybe we could share some intel since we're both working toward the same goal."

"If you have information related to any crime, we would be glad to hear it. Do you have information about Jenny Lehman?"

"I may be able to save you a lot of legwork. Meet with me and I'll tell you what I know. I've already done that with your colleague, Sgt. Macusovich."

Summers kept silent, as if waiting for the caller to explain further, but Decker offered nothing more.

"If you'd like to come into the office, myself and another detective will interview you."

That wasn't what Decker had in mind. He wanted to meet with Lt. Hannah Summers alone to talk about the case, but more so he wanted to know if the vibe he felt when he first saw her photograph would be stronger in person.

"Just coffee. Not in the office."

"Thank you for calling, Mr. Decker. I have to get back to work."

And with that, Summers hung up the phone.

Annoyed by the outcome, Decker veered from his routine of stakeouts and showed up outside the museum just as Kaleigh was leaving. He needed a break from too many hours just sitting in the Jeep Cherokee with his binoculars. The temperature was pushing 90, the air still, the water barely moving along Fort Point Channel. Kaleigh was wearing a turquoise summer smock dress and matching flip flops, her long hair pulled back into a swinging braid that ended in a tiny white bow.

"Decker. What a surprise. I thought you'd run off with that pretty nurse, or was she a dental hygienist?"

"ER nurse. You married yet to that arrogant scribe?"

"Very funny. Where have you been? Why haven't you called me?"

"Busy. Working."

"Spy stuff? Top secret? Invisible ink messages? Smoke signals?"

"Let's go to the Perk and I'll tell you about it."

"I don't feel like coffee. I need something stronger."

"Nemo's?"

"No."

"Well, if you don't mind the mess, we can go to my place and talk in private. Dogman is out on a date."

Kaleigh raised her thick eyebrows. Twenty different thoughts raced through Kaleigh's mind as she envisioned Decker's apartment and the life he led there, none of which she was familiar with. She wondered, did he sleep in a single bed or a double? Did he sleep in the nude? Was his refrigerator a barren glow inside, the shelves stacked only with a variety of beers? How often did he bring women there? And if so, did they do it in his bed or on the carpet or the kitchen table? Did he have a kitchen table? Maybe there was just a counter with stools. One of her former boyfriends had used an industrial telephone cable spool and four wooden apple crates as a kitchen set.

Half an hour later they were climbing the stairs to Decker's apartment. He used two different keys to unbolt the three door locks.

"Heavy security," Kaleigh said with a slight tone of mockery.

Decker waited for the shepherd to bark but realized Dogman had taken the dog with him. He pushed the door open to unveil an orderly living room and open kitchen area. The walls were covered with paintings and posters, the largest of which urged recruits to become Army Rangers. The poster showed a soldier up to his neck in dark water, face painted black, rifle held above his head.

"Beer? Wine? Gin and tonic? Splash of bourbon on the rocks?"

"Gin sounds great."

"Have a seat."

Kaleigh was too antsy to sit. She gazed out the window at the street traffic before turning her attention to the war room wall. She began studying the photographs, notes and newspaper clippings, including those stories written by Rane about the recent spate of murders involving young women.

Decker emerged from the kitchen holding two glasses, each with a few ice cubes, a generous pour of Bombay gin, splash of tonic and a fresh slice of lime. She gave him a probing look as she clasped the glass. "You're a serial killer?"

"That's me."

Kaleigh raised her eyebrows. She spotted the empty duffle bags, radios, tape recorder and camera with long lens.

"What is all this?"

"My job. Tools of the trade."

Kaleigh touched her forefinger to one of Rane's stories on the wall, feeling suddenly guilty for being in Decker's apartment. "Do you believe what Rane wrote?"

"Are you asking me if I think there's a serial killer murdering women around here?"

"Yes."

"Well, nobody seems to know for sure."

"Why do you have all this on your wall?"

"Private client who's interested in the situation. But please keep that to yourself. I don't want to see my name in the papers."

"That's all you're going to tell me?"

"That's all I can tell you."

"I see. Do you mind if I use your bathroom?"

"Not at all. Just down the hall."

Kaleigh checked her appearance in the bathroom mirror, fixing her hair and touching up her lipstick. For just an instant, she let herself believe that Decker was actually a serial killer and that she might be his next victim unless she was very cautious. She might have to lock herself in this small room and hope that somehow help would arrive, though she had no idea how that might happen. Kaleigh again noticed the cleanliness of the bathroom, except for the bathtub that was filled with scuba gear. The equipment obviously had been rinsed, but traces of black mud and seaweed surrounded the drain.

"I didn't know you were a scuba diver," Kaleigh said as she returned to the living room. "Looks like it's still wet."

"I was using it in the tub," said Decker. "I get nervous if the water is too deep."

Kaleigh rolled her eyes. "Why can't I ever get a straight answer out of you?"

"Diving was part of my Special Forces training. I enjoyed it."

"So where did you go diving this last time?"

193

"In the harbor. I'm thinking of getting a recreational lobster license. I'll invite you over the first time I catch a few seabugs."

Kaleigh greedily sipped the freshened drink. "I know I have no right to ask, but I want to know if you're seeing anyone else steadily."

Decker guffawed. "I'm a pretty straightforward guy. You can ask me anything. Last time I checked, we'd already traded more than our fair share of intimate secrets." He paused and stared at her. "It's you who changed things between us."

"Decker, you know you mean something to me. You were there for me when I needed you, with the cat…"

"As any good friend would be."

"Oh, Decker. You know we're more than good friends."

"Then let's toast to more than good friends."

They clinked glasses.

"You still didn't tell me who the woman is in the surgical scrubs. She's very pretty. Did you meet her at the hospital?"

"No. Just met her that night. Her name's Amal. She's an ER nurse at Mass General. She and her friends sat at the table next to me and Dogman."

Kaleigh stared down at the floor. "You looked so comfortable with each other out on the dance floor."

"I didn't notice," said Decker, his impatience growing. Kaleigh remained motionless until Decker locked his arms around her. A warm summer breeze carried the salt air into the room. Decker inhaled deeply as he led Kaleigh toward the couch. They kissed hungrily, standing. Decker ran his hands over her bare shoulders and without warning pulled the loose-fitting dress over her head to expose her strapless bra. Kaleigh stood stock still, her lips open as though in disbelief. Decker nimbly unhooked the bra and kissed her nipples, edging her backward until she lay on the couch.

He gently gripped the waistband of her panties, slid them over her hips, down her thighs and past her ankles, taking off her flip flops as he went so that she was naked. She closed her eyes when Decker touched her with his fingers.

Decker cast his clothing aside in record time, lifted her legs so that her bare feet were around his neck, and plunged inside her. She moaned and he plunged again. He withdrew, kneeled on the carpet and swept his tongue inside her. He alternated plunging and kissing between her legs until she was nearly out of her mind with pleasure. A moment before she climaxed, Decker mounted her with renewed vigor, pushing her to a new level of joy as she felt his release inside her.

It was nearly midnight when they awoke, tangled in each other's arms beneath a blanket on the couch. Major was staring at them, panting. Dogman's bedroom door was closed but they could hear him snoring loudly.

In a single swift movement, Decker rolled off the couch, stood and lifted Kaleigh into his arms. He carried her into his room and gently laid her on the bed.

"You're staying here tonight."

"I can't."

"You can."

"People will wonder where I am."

"Rane?"

"Not just him. My roommates."

"Call them."

"It's too late. They're sleeping. They have to work tomorrow."

Decker kissed her neck and ears, tightening his arms around her. "If you're worried, you should call them, just in case it turns out I'm a serial killer."

"You do worry me."

Decker felt himself getting aroused. Kaleigh took him in her mouth until he was fully erect, then straddled him and abandoned herself to the occasion. When they awoke again, early morning light was streaming through the windows.

For the first time in months, Decker slept through the night without hearing the racket made by AK-47s and heavy machine guns, nor did he awaken in a cold sweat as an RPG came buzzing toward his sandbagged bunker.

CHAPTER 30

July 1986
Boston, Massachusetts

ON THE WATERFRONT

Paige Williston strode confidently into Nemo's in a white-and-black checked mini-skirt, dark red fishnet stockings, fluorescent green tank top and her Doc Martens. Three purple-gelled spikes of hair stuck up from her blonde tresses like a punk Statue of Liberty. Breathing heavily as though she'd been running, Paige grabbed hold of Rane's shirtsleeve. "Thank god you're here. I called the bar but Bubby told me she hadn't seen you tonight. I guess that chesty wonder thought she was somehow protecting you. The cops are heading out to Shucker's boat with a search warrant."

"Right now?"

"As we speak. Heard it on the police radio."

Rane looked at Kaleigh. "I gotta go. We can finish this conversation later."

Kaleigh's eyes bored into him, making it clear that they were engaged in weighty talk and that by leaving he was committing a serious infraction.

Paige ignored Kaleigh, keeping her hold on Rane's shirtsleeve. "Let's go. My car is double-parked outside," she said.

Kaleigh flipped her middle finger as they headed for the door. Luddy was among the few who noticed or cared.

He didn't like sassy, know-it-all women or those who would do something as disrespectful as flip a middle finger at their husband or boyfriend. Those were the kind of women who needed to be punished, he thought. She might not be so sassy with a sock stuffed in her mouth and an electrical extension cord wound around her neck. Luddy sipped his beer, imagining the possibilities and the joy he would feel watching the final breaths ebb out of her. Stuck-up bitch, he said to himself, but one day soon she would talk to him and come to know the meaning of fear.

Two marked Boston Police patrol cars were idling alongside the dock next to a State Police box truck and three dark-colored sedans bristling with antennae, vehicles that had ferried State Police homicide detectives from the district attorney offices in Suffolk and Essex counties as well as the Boston Police Department.

Since the *Sea Bitch* was in Boston Harbor, jurisdiction belonged to the Suffolk County district attorney. Detective Summers was heading up the search. Sgt. Macusovich's had been formally assigned as her counterpart from the Essex County district attorney's office because Rose Cavelli's body was found in the Peabody landfill in that abutting county. The going theory among investigators was that Cavelli had been murdered somewhere in Essex County and her body unknowingly carted to the dump.

Summers rapped Macusovich on the arm and gestured by cocking her head at the two figures rushing down the docks. "What do we have here?"

"Whoa, whoa," Macusovich called to Rane and Paige as they hustled toward the dock where a police boat was waiting. He shined his flashlight at them. "You two aren't going anywhere. By the way, what are you doing here?"

"Same thing you are," said Rane.

Summers stepped toward them and raked a hand through her lush blonde hair that was tamed by a ponytail. "Who's this?"

Rane flashed a smile and put up his hands in mock surrender. "Don't shoot."

Summers looked at her partner for explanation.

"He's a member of the press, but not the worst of them. They obviously got word that we were going to be down here."

Summers eyed Paige's outfit and spiked hair, in stark contrast to her own navy blue police polo shirt with sewn-on badge, snug bluejeans and white Nike sneakers. Despite the conservative outfit, the detective was magazine-cover pretty, physically fit, armed and dangerous. And she didn't play well with other women who were attractive but, in her opinion, too outlandishly styled and brash. "Well, I don't care who they are," Summers said. "They've got to get out of here."

Macusovich motioned with his head for Rane and Paige to move away from the dock. "I can't get you out on the boat, but if there's anything of interest out there that I can talk about, you'll be the first to know."

Macusovich genuinely liked Rane and was humored by Paige. He also enjoyed being in the media spotlight, which was almost assured through his acquaintance with Rane. Plenty of Boston newspaper stories had featured the heroics and ingenuity of State Police Detective Sgt. Andre Macusovich.

As Macusovich and Summers stepped aboard the police launch with several other Boston and State Police investigators and technicians, Paige yanked two nips of vodka from her camera bag. "Might as well enjoy ourselves while we wait."

Rane smirked appreciatively. "You're always thinking, Willi."

Paige clicked off a few shots of the police climbing aboard the boat, but she knew from experience that with a single streetlight providing the only illumination, the camera shutter speed would have to be slowed, producing grainy photos that in this case also lacked gripping content. Members of the forensic team came and went, carrying equipment bags and small Igloo coolers. It was a dull parade. Paige suggested they retreat to her car where they could get comfortable but still see some of the action.

"Oh, Willi, you are such a godsend," Rane said as he tipped another nip of vodka. Paige did likewise, untied her Doc Martens, tossed them onto the back seat and put her feet on the dashboard. Rane couldn't take his eyes off the red fishnets that encased her long, shapely legs. He rubbed a hand along her thigh, exploring until he reached the apex of Paige's pantyhose and cursed the fashion trend, thinking how much more erotic stockings and garters must have been to an earlier generation before they were phased out.

"You're being a naughty boy," she said, not flinching as Rane caressed her other thigh. She moaned softly as he rubbed his fingers against the nylon, creating heat. Paige pushed him back against the passenger seat, climbed over the console and straddled his lap. Rane responded eagerly, lacing his arms around her as they kissed with ferocity.

Paige reached between his legs and massaged him until he was hard. She fumbled with his belt buckle and zipper until her bare hand was around him.

"Push your seat all the way back."

Rane glided the seat to give them more room and felt his legs stiffen as he arched his back. Paige pressed against him, deftly slipping out of her pantyhose. She yanked on his trousers and underwear until they were around his ankles, then put her mouth around him, sucking savagely with her tongue and raking his skin with her teeth. Rane thought he would explode at that moment but Paige freed him just long enough to again straddle his legs and ease him inside her. She undulated her hips, wildly urging him to thrust upward and deeper, loudly crying out for more of him as she climaxed. Rane came seconds later.

Paige grew quiet, as though she was about to fall asleep, her eyelids struggling to remain open. "I'm sorry," she whispered in his ear.

"Sorry for what?"

200

"For making you do that."

Rane grinned appreciatively. "I wanted it as much as you."

"But you're with Kaleigh."

"We're not engaged or anything."

"But you're almost living together."

"No. Sometimes she stays over."

Rane was still inside her. He saw tears spill down her cheeks and he kissed them, moving his salty lips to hers. He moved his hands under her tank top and kneaded her breasts, rolling her nipples between his fingers. Paige began to rock slightly.

"No," she said. "We can't do this."

"Yes," he said. "We can."

The warm summer air caressed their faces as they kissed and Paige hungrily rubbed her high cheekbones against his blond beard and moustache. In the distance, the detectives were stepping onto the dock but Rane and Paige paid them no mind, lost in their lust. So it wasn't until the next day that Rane learned the search aboard the *Sea Bitch* had been unsuccessful. Macusovich told him the search warrant also included the Pugano apartment, but that might not happen for another day or two. Before Macusovich hung up the phone, he said, "By the way, there are a lot of motels around Boston."

CHAPTER 31

July 1986
Boston, Massachusetts

ALL IN THE FAMILY

Celeste was standing at the stove in the small kitchen, using her hand to shield her face against the spattering hot oil. "You know the police will be back," she said as she fried breaded calamari that Luddy brought home from the fish market earlier in the week.

"So what?"

"I'll have to let them in. They've already been to your boat."

"They won't find anything of interest there."

"You cleaned it up good?"

"There was nothing to clean."

Celeste shot him a look that showed she didn't believe him. "Good. Try some of this calamari. It's delicious."

"I'm not hungry. You eat it," he said, brooding as he sank deeply into the overstuffed chair and stared at the crucifix on the living room wall.

Luddy felt trapped. On summer nights like this, he often went to Revere Beach a few miles north and sat on the seawall where he could ogle the young girls in their bikinis and skimpy dresses. He'd eat an extra-large roast beef sandwich with special sauce at Kelley's, tossing the uneaten French fries onto the sand of America's first public beach where the gulls would fight over them. He hated the gulls with their raucous cries and thieving nature. Fuckin' air rats, he called them.

As a teenager he'd trapped two seagulls in a net near the East Boston docks. He stuffed a lighted cherry bomb down each of their gullets and grinned happily when their necks exploded. He'd done similar things to countless sea bass and stripers, enjoying the sight of them nervously swimming away until their insides were blown to bits. Cats and dogs were harder to kill, the method usually more complicated. Luddy was amazed at how much damage could be done with a baseball bat, poison, gasoline and matches. He particularly enjoyed lighting the dogs afire because unlike cats, they seemed willing to trust him.

"You sure you don't want some of this calamari? I made it for you."

"Ma. I don't want any calamari. I just want to think."

"What are you thinking about?"

"About how fucked up my life is. How fucked up your life is."

"We have a good life," she said, wiping her hands on her apron. "You have a job and a roof over your head."

"No. We don't, Ma. And you know that. You've hated your life since Antoinette died."

Celeste dropped the metal spatula she was holding. "Don't speak her name."

"For Christ's sake, Ma. You used to call me Antoinette when you were drinking heavily. You dressed me like a girl."

"I told you, don't speak her name." She plucked the oily spatula from the floor and wiped it on her apron.

"I wish to hell you'd tell me more about my father, more than he was a bastard who left you out on a limb."

"Your father, what's there to say? He gave me money for a doctor who could make sure you weren't born, but I wouldn't hear of it. And after he left, we got by, didn't we?"

Luddy was stewing again, his nearly black, deep-socketed eyes scanning the room as though it were the first time he'd seen it.

"No, we didn't get by. Every boy in my classes called me a sissy or a girl."

"I wanted you to look nice."

"No. You put me in her clothes, the ones you saved from the baby showers, and then you wheeled me around in a stroller under pink frilly blankets. Face it, you wanted your daughter, the one you had with God only knows who."

With surprising agility, Celeste took three steps toward her son and slapped him hard across the face. Luddy grabbed her wrist and began twisting it. Celeste whipped the spatula against the side of his head. It stung. Luddy cupped his ear with his free hand and when his fingers pulled away they were streaked with blood. He twisted Celeste's arm until she collapsed to the floor, then released her.

"You never wanted me," he shouted, looking down at her. "How many times did you wish I was dead? How many times did you wish I'd never been born?"

"You're right. I didn't want you. But I did everything I could for you."

"Did that include fucking Father Scarpino, or did you do that because you liked it?"

"You have no right to say that. Father Scarpino is a big-hearted man who helped us when I had no money to pay the rent."

"I guess I didn't understand at the time that your housecleaning duties at the rectory included getting into his bed."

Celeste shakily got to her feet. "We all do things in this life that we wish we didn't have to do."

Luddy sat back in the chair and braced his forehead as though in pain. "You used to leave me sitting alone in the hallway while you went into his room. I could hear you through the door. At first I thought they were animal noises, but then I realized it was him – and you. I can't believe that prick is still at the church saying Mass every Sunday and telling everyone they shouldn't sin for fear of god. What a son of a bitch."

"All that's past, Luddy. Let it go."

The next morning, after Luddy left for the fish market, Celeste pried the padlock off his bedroom door and stepped inside the forbidden sanctuary. Luddy had warned her never to set foot in his room. The walls were plastered with destination posters like those you might see at a travel agency – London, Paris, Rome, Athens, and smaller photographs ripped from magazines that showed the Australian Outback, the Mexican Baja, Patagonia, the Mariana Trench and the Sahara.

Celeste had expected to see pin-up girls and stacks of Playboy magazine, but there were only cardboard boxes filled with broken fishing reels, car parts and mechanic tools. A fishing tackle box shared shelf space with a varnished wooden case and perhaps a dozen books, including a Bible, a pictorial history of WWII, and how-to tomes on saltwater fishing, repairing automotive engines, boat navigation and running a charter business. Clamming rakes and pails were stacked in a corner. Luddy's clothing, which she routinely washed, folded and left in a basket outside his door, had been neatly placed in the bureau drawers.

Celeste got down on all fours and peered beneath the bed. A Little League baseball bat was coated with dust. She recalled buying it when money was tight and how happy it had made Luddy as he carried it over his shoulder to the park. The sight of the wooden bat also brought back the memory of a well-fed Luddy traipsing home that same day and announcing he had quit the team. It wasn't until hours later that she had learned about the fight in the dugout and how Luddy had struck another player with the bat after the boy called him a sissy pants. The boy wasn't badly hurt – a peach-sized contusion on the upper arm -- but the incident was enough to bring the coach to her door with threats of calling the police and the parents filing a lawsuit.

As Celeste scanned the room, her eyes locked on the varnished wooden box. She felt like a voyeur as she examined more than a dozen tufts of hair – mostly black or brown, but there were also two blonds and a red. Each snippet had its own texture and was gathered by a rubber band. A small white tag was tied to each by a short length of string. Luddy had written a name on each tag – Beach Blossom, Sweet Desert Girl, The Professor, Nature Girl, Wedding Slut, Flirty Gerty, Puppy Lover, Swedish Nanny, Street Corner Mary, Bible Jean, Morning Glory and Candy Land.

Celeste was afraid to imagine how these women had died but she presumed they had and that her son was responsible. Each hair sample was neatly tied and tagged, a show-and-tell of madness and death. She sat on Luddy's bed and prayed that it wasn't she who had led him down this path, but others with bad influence.

Celeste grabbed her purse and began walking at a brisk pace toward Saratoga Street where she hoped to find Fergus Cavanaugh. After thirty minutes she was out of breath but determined to talk to him so she marched on. It had been years since they had seen each other. She knew that Fergus, like other members of Boston's Irish Mob, regularly changed the location of their offices or used multiple locations to avoid police surveillance, especially electronic eavesdropping and hidden video cameras used by the FBI and the State Police Organized Crime Unit.

Celeste paced both sides of the street until she spotted three men smoking cigarettes and standing listlessly in front of a tenement doorway. As she approached them the men broke out their hardest stares, but that didn't stop her. "I need to talk to Fergus," she blurted out.

The shortest of the men tipped his tweed, snap-down brimmed cap. "Don't know anyone by that name."

"Don't fuck with me. I'm in a hurry," she said.

"Is that a fact? And who might we say is calling?"

"Celeste Pugano."

All three men snickered. The short man cocked his head toward the other two who disappeared into the building. A few minutes later, the door opened and Celeste was escorted inside.

Fergus Cavanaugh lay prone on a tattered couch,

watching a television talk show. Although he was indoors, he was wearing his trademark mirror aviator shades.

"Sorry to barge in like this," said Celeste.

Fergus never moved, nor did he look at her. "What can I do for you?"

Celeste glanced around the room. She recognized Stephen Flemmi from the newspapers. He was standing silently with his back against the wall. She recalled reading that he was called "The Rifleman" and that he had been involved in the killing of hitman Joseph "The Animal" Barboza in San Francisco ten years earlier. As the story went, Barboza was in the federal witness protection program after testifying against Boston's ranking Italian mobsters, but made the mistake of contacting a former pal from Lynn who then passed along the information regarding his whereabouts. Flemmi simply leaned out of a white van, aimed his hunting rifle at Barboza from 100 yards out and pierced his brain with a single shot. That was the legend and maybe even the truth, but so far the FBI had been unable to prove it, so Flemmi remained a free man.

Celeste was curious why an Italian gangster of Flemmi's stature would be hanging around in Fergus Cavanaugh's shamrock-festooned office. Two of the three thugs who had been standing outside on the sidewalk were now sitting in metal folding chairs along the wall, facing the TV. The short man wearing the cap was positioned near the door in a beach chair, reading the Tribune sports section.

"It's OK boys. Celeste and I will speak alone," said Cavanaugh.

Flemmi frisked Celeste on his way out, pinching her butt as a finishing touch. Celeste tried to slap him but he gripped both her arms with one hand as he patted her down.

"You pig," Celeste snarled.

Flemmi laughed uproariously. "Can't be too careful these days."

When the men were gone, Fergus sat up on the couch. "Your son is in trouble, but you already know that."

"I don't want you to kill him."

"Who said anything about killing anybody?"

"The police are going to search my house. They already searched Luddy's boat."

"And what did they find?"

"Nothing."

"So if they didn't find anything on the boat, why would they find something in your house?"

Celeste was momentarily silent. "I don't want Luddy to go to prison. I'm not sure he could take it. He was in jail when he was younger and it did bad things to him."

Fergus appeared to be mulling her words. "We don't want him in Walpole either. We don't want him anywhere that he might start blabbing. So how we going to do that?"

Celeste suddenly dropped to her knees. "Fergus, I've known you for many years. When your father visited from Ireland, I cooked him dinner almost every night. I made him feel like a king."

"And you got paid for it."

"That's not the point. I cared for him. I made his visit to America special, and he went home with a smile on his face. He left here knowing you were a boss who the people respected."

"Many thanks for that. It makes you part of the family."

"I guess you forgot that I almost *was* part of the family. If we had left things alone, you would have had a younger brother and so would Luddy, but that didn't happen. I used my own money to take care of it. Your father never knew and you didn't help me. And after that day, I never spoke of it, until today. So is Luddy part of the family?"

Fergus for once seemed tongue-tied, a blush of guilt and shame washing over him. "In some ways, he is, but you've got to remember that while I may be the underboss in Eastie, not everything in the city is up to me," he said.

"You mean Desmond O'Malley will decide whether to have him killed?"

Fergus didn't answer. He used the remote to click off the television and grabbed a can of Pabst Blue Ribbon beer

208

from the refrigerator.

"Can I offer you beer, wine, maybe something stronger?"

Celeste shook her head. "Just water, please."

"I promise you I'll put in a good word for Luddy. We don't forget about the people who have helped us, just like we don't forget about the people who have done us harm."

"I know Luddy has done whatever he was asked."

"True enough," he conceded, handing her a glass of cloudy tap water.

"He never told me exactly. But he did say he had to use the boat."

Fergus thought back on the foolish numbers runners who had stolen money from Doc Ragansky and a guy called Dumb Shoes, two of Desmond O'Malley's most profitable bookies. The thieves had spent every dollar on drugs and hookers and gone on to brag about it. And there was the scrappy Italian kid from the North End who decided to steal three cases of Scotch whisky, 100 cartons of cigarettes and a mink coat from a hijacked tractor-trailer that was under O'Malley's protection. The theft of the whisky and cigarettes hadn't angered the boss more than what was expected, but the missing mink had put O'Malley into one of his terror moods where being within pistol range was dangerous.

Fergus had been hard pressed to find a way to get rid of the three bodies. He was relieved to learn that a neighborhood kid named Luddy Pugano owned a boat and probably would be willing to assist. Fergus also knew that this kid had some minor credentials – an arrest for car theft and attempted arson and had done short time for his crimes.

"If whatever Luddy did for you has any value, then please consider it," Celeste said, digging into her purse. She held out a stack of cash. "There's eight thousand dollars here. It's all I got. But it's yours if you can get him out of the country."

Fergus listened to her plan with great amusement. The woman had evidently given it some thought or else she was just fast in a clutch situation. It really didn't matter. The issue

209

boiled down to whether O'Malley would approve it and if Luddy would cooperate.

"Put the money on the table."

Celeste set down the stack of bills, lamenting the loss of her remaining cash and security. It meant going back to housecleaning and sewing. But there was part of her that had to do this, to make up for all the anguish she'd caused Luddy because of her indiscretions. She was actually surprised by her own maternal instincts.

"When will I hear from you?"

"Tonight. Maybe I'll stop by while the cops are searching your place."

Celeste winced at the thought. "I've got to get home. I want to make sure nothing is there that might be a problem."

Fergus set the empty beer can next to the three-inch tall stack of $100s. "You want some advice? Next time you try to bribe somebody, bring the money in $20s. It'll look like five times as much."

Celeste didn't know whether he was being serious. "I won't be bribing anyone in the future. And I hope you don't think I'm bribing you now. This money is to pay for whatever it takes to get Luddy safely away."

"One of the boys will give you a ride home," he said, smiling wide enough to reveal a missing front tooth.

CHAPTER 32

July 1986
Boston, Massachusetts

THE POWER OF LATIN

Rane slammed the phone down and looked around the newsroom. A couple of reporters sitting nearby met his eyes and quickly went back to their stories.

After leaving two messages on Kaleigh's phone and receiving no reply, Rane's temper was flaring. He knew she was still riled by his departure from Nemo's with Paige.

Rane left another message on Sgt. Macusovich's beeper. When he finally got the return call, the sergeant was in a rush but quickly told him the Pugano apartment in Jeffries Point would be searched before nightfall. They'd talk later.

Rane watched the television news from his desk. The body of a Massachusetts woman had been found in Nevada -- more details to follow on the six o'clock broadcast. Typical TV story, he told himself – no names, scant details, lots of hype and swirling graphics. He drove his Triumph through the streets and alleys of East Boston, looking for familiar faces or anyone who might provide him with information that would link the deaths of these young women.

Jimmy Two Cubes was furtively walking along Bennington Street when Rane spotted him and pulled the motorcycle onto the sidewalk, blocking his path.

"Leave me alone," he cried, his legs jittery, hands rubbing his arms as though freezing cold despite the balmy

July temperature. "I don't want to talk to you."

"Jimmy, I'm just trying to help everybody find out who's killing these girls."

"We know who's killing them."

"Sure you do."

"I gotta go. Let me get by."

Rane dismounted and stared into Jimmy's eyes. "You're high as a kite."

Jimmy tried to push past him but Rane held him by the shoulders.

"Tell me who you think is doing this."

"Fergus knows."

"Fergus knows what?"

"That Shucker is responsible. The cops are all over the place. They shook me down three times this week."

"I'm sorry to hear that, Jimmy. I'm not here to shake you down. I thought we were friends," said Rane, opening his wallet and handing Jimmy a $20 bill. "You need to eat something."

Jimmy Two Cubes pocketed the $20 with no intention of spending it on food. "Look, all I know is what I hear. Fergus is angry and he's gonna make it so that Shucker can't do this anymore because it's causing too much heat."

"And how is Fergus going to do that?"

"He talked to me and Blade about it."

"Did he give you instructions? Orders to go out and kill Shucker?"

"No, but he will. Nobody crosses Fergus. He might not tell me or Blade to do it, but Fergus knows a lot of people who are lookin' for work."

Rane left a second message on Sgt. Macusovich's phone, relaying what he'd just learned, mostly because it would keep him in the sergeant's good graces since the information might be interesting to law enforcement but actually had little news value. The editors wouldn't run a story quoting an anonymous source saying Fergus Cavanaugh had put out a hit contract on a local fishmonger suspected of serial killings in the area.

212

Rane stopped by Nemo's on the chance someone might have heard a rumor worth chasing. He was surprised to see Luddy seated at the bar, considering there might be people looking to either arrest or kill him. He nodded, but Luddy didn't acknowledge him. The room was nearly empty – a half dozen locals long past retirement age nursing their beers at wooden tables along the far wall -- and for the first time Rane felt uncomfortable in this watering hole he knew was not truly his but part of another world. Bubby was clearly excited to see him so he ordered a beer and offered to buy a drink for Luddy and the other pock-faced man seated at the bar. The man accepted but Luddy waved off Bubby, shaking his head in refusal.

"Suit yourself," Rane said.

Luddy glared at him menacingly with his black, deep-socketed eyes. Rane drained his beer, left a hefty tip for Bubby and literally bumped into Decker on his way out the door. "Hey, Soldier Boy," he said sarcastically.

Decker scrutinized him through squinted eyes. "Shouldn't you be out chasing news stories instead of drinking in the neighborhood bars, or is that what journalists do these days?"

"I didn't want you and the other war heroes to feel alone."

"You're such an asshole. I don't know what Kaleigh sees in you."

"She has good taste," Rane said smugly. "But that's something a grunt wouldn't understand."

Decker exploded with pent-up anger and grabbed Rane by the front of his shirt, lifting him an inch off the floor. Rane kneed him in the groin and knocked Decker's arms away. Decker groaned but quickly recovered, driving the butt of his right hand upward beneath Rane's chin and sending him reeling into the entryway wall, knocking a beer sign from its nail. Bubby was out from behind the bar in seconds and standing two feet away, screaming for the men to stop fighting. But Decker and Rane ignored her as they traded punches to the head and torso. Decker was bleeding from the lip. He wiped the blood with the back of his hand. Rane took a wild swing. Decker ducked and Rane's fist slammed into the wall. He cried out in pain. Decker used the moment to twist Rane's arm behind his back and trip him to the floor. He grabbed hold of Rane's mane of blond hair and repeatedly banged his head on the tiles until Bubby jumped on his back and began pounding him. "Stop it. Stop it now! Both of you."

Luddy and the other patrons never moved. They watched the action as though it were happening on TV. Bubby pushed with all her strength against Rane's chest. "Get out," she yelled, opening the door to the bright light of day. "I don't need this kind of shit. And you started it."

Rane stepped onto the sidewalk. When Decker tried to follow, Bubby slammed the door closed and pointed toward the bar. "Not yet. You were just coming in when all this nonsense happened, so come in," she said.

Decker reluctantly sat at the bar and ordered a beer. None of the others dared look at him. They either gazed into their drinks or at the television set mounted over the bar.

The six o'clock television news was updating the story of a Massachusetts girl's body found in Nevada. The victim wasn't named. She was identified only as a 24-year-old Cape Cod resident. Her body had been covered with a pile of loose rocks in the desert just outside of Las Vegas. The police were theorizing she was killed in the springtime, most likely in April or early May. The news anchor, reminding her audience of the unsolved serial murders in metropolitan Boston, urged young women living in the city not to go out alone at night. Once again, Boston was in a panic. The anchorwoman credited the Tribune for its stories by reporter Rane Bryson that continued to provide details of the police investigation into the killings.

Wiping her brow from the scuffle, Bubby blurted out, "Hey, Shucker. That's about the same time you were out there in Vegas." She laughed, thinking she had injected a bit of humor into the room that was oddly quiet after the fight.

Luddy squirmed almost imperceptibly on his bar stool. For a fraction of a second he locked eyes with Decker,

214

but it was long enough for the soldier to realize Luddy knew more than the television news anchor did about the dead girl in Nevada.

Luddy didn't respond to Bubby. He simply swirled off the bar stool and headed for the side door near the restrooms.

Bubby stopped drying a beer glass and looked questioningly at Decker and the other man who was scratching Lottery tickets with a nickel. "What's with him?"

Both Decker and the gambling man shrugged. Decker left his unfinished beer, ran to his Jeep and began tailing Luddy. He ran two red traffic lights in order to keep him in view.

Luddy parked the Crown Vic in Maverick Square and pulled open the heavy doors to the Most Holy Redeemer Church. The interior of the church was dark and cool, a reprieve from the day's harsh sunlight and warm temperatures. As always, he had hoped to immerse himself in the mystical Latin phrases, even if only a fraction had survived the folk guitars and were still part of the ceremony.

Agnus dei, qui tolis peccata mundi. (Lamb of God, who takes away the sins of the world). *Sanctus, sanctus, sanctus.* (Holy, holy, holy). *In saecula saeculorum.* (Forever and ever).

There were so many phrases he yearned to hear, the ones that had entranced him as an altar boy. *In nomine Patris, et Filii, et Spiritus Sancti.* (In the name of the Father, and of the Son, and of the Holy Spirit). *Corpus Christi.* (Body of Christ). *Anima Christi.* (Soul of Christ). *Sanguis Christi.* (Blood of Christ).

But no Mass was being celebrated. The altar was empty. A few parishioners were standing in the confessional line. Luddy inhaled the aroma of Frankincense. He made the sign of the cross and prayed, staring fixedly at the gold crucifix upon the altar. When he had recited several Our Fathers, a Hail Mary and an Act of Contrition, he felt calm and on his way to being forgiven. He joined the confessional line and waited his turn.

Father Scarpino opened the sliding screen so that he was face-to-face with Luddy.

"Yes, my son?"

"Bless me, Father, for I have sinned," Luddy said, the rote phrase ingrained from his boyhood. "I think you know that I come to church, Father, but I haven't been to confession in a long time."

"God is here for you. Please tell him your troubles. Tell him what is burdening you and making you stray from his teachings."

"Some girls around here have been murdered."

"Hmm. And you have concerns about them?"

"I killed them."

Luddy heard a gulp as the priest tried to swallow and regain his composure.

"You know that Christ is against killing, that he forbids it. In the Ten Commandments, it says thou shalt not kill." The priest's voice was full of horror and disgust. "You have defied the Lord by breaking one of his most important rules."

"Yes, Father. That's why I'm here, to seek absolution for my sins. To have my soul wiped clean of the darkness. To be forgiven."

"The Lord cannot simply dismiss such heinous acts. Murder isn't something he can forgive," Father Scarpino answered in an imperious tone. "For these evil acts, you will burn in hell."

Luddy adjusted his posture as he kneeled on the thickly cushioned pad. "Are you saying God can't forgive me, the church can't forgive me?"

"Yes, my son. Your sins go far beyond what are considered forgivable offenses. There can be no redemption."

"What am I supposed to do now? I don't have anywhere else to go. You have to forgive me."

"There is nothing you can do but pray. Pray for your condemned soul."

Luddy suddenly felt claustrophobic in the tiny dark booth. He put his nose to the screen to get a closer look at the priest, who was sitting sideways, breathing heavily. "You can't forgive me for my sins, well, what about yours? You took my mother into your bed. Is that forgivable?"

Father Scarpino's aging muscles stiffened. "I did no such thing. How dare you say that."

"Oh, yes you did, Father. Whenever she went to the rectory to wash your filthy laundry, mop your floors and clean your toilet. As if that wasn't enough, you had to fuck her."

"That's about enough," the priest said with authority, though it was clear he was rattled by Luddy's accusations.

Father Scarpino was just about to stand and exit his confessional booth when Luddy's powerful arms thrust through the small screen and gripped the priest by the throat. The priest gasped for air but Luddy's calloused thumbs pressed the man's clerical collar until his body went limp and literally spilled out of the booth. The priest was coughing, struggling to breathe. He got to his knees. Luddy heard a woman shriek, "Oh my god!"

"Have mercy," Father Scarpino pleaded. "We're all sinners, and I'm an old man."

Luddy moved out of the confessional and stood over him. "You made my mother into your whore."

"She wasn't married. She was free to do as she pleased."

"But you weren't free. You were married to God, which makes fucking my mother an act of adultery. Thou shalt not commit adultery. That's one of the Ten Commandments and you broke one of God's most important rules."

As Luddy turned he could see those who had been behind him in line had scattered. Father Scarpino scrambled like a lizard toward the altar. Luddy was close behind, chasing him up the wide steps. The priest snagged on his cassock and landed face down on the stone, paralyzed by fear. Luddy tried opening the gilded tabernacle door but it was locked. He raised the small cabinet over his head and brought it crashing down on the polished marble. He reached through the cabinet's hinged door and grabbed the gold chalice, one that as an altar boy he had held many times. During those Masses, the chalice had been filled with wine into which white communion wafers were dipped before being placed on the tongues of each parishioner. But there was no Mass today, nor was there any wine or communion wafers that the priests would miraculously transform into the body and blood of Jesus. There was only the heavy metal chalice and Luddy slammed it down on Father Scarpino's forehead.

The priest rolled onto his back, his eyes dazed.

Luddy laughed aloud as he struck the priest three more times, shouting *"Corpus Christi, Anima Christi, Sanguis Christi."* When he was done, he tossed the chalice to the floor where it rattled down the three marble steps, finally coming to rest near the communion rail. Luddy stared at the dying priest. "I'll see you in Hell," he said.

As he turned to leave, Luddy nearly slipped and fell on the puddle of blood spreading across the polished marble. He burst out the entrance doors of the church into the blinding daylight and stood momentarily on the sidewalk, looking up at the sky.

Decker was stunned. Luddy's shirt was spattered red with what looked like blood. Luddy strode purposefully toward his Crown Vic and peeled out. Decker tried to follow, but Luddy lost him in the maze of streets and alleys near the waterfront. He stopped at a payphone to call Carrington, who answered the call in his car on a new Motorola DynaTAC mobile phone. Decker was impressed by the technology. He related to Carrington everything he had seen at the church and what he had heard on the TV news about the slaying of the Rev. Armando Scarpino.

Carrington listened without interjecting before voicing his disappointment. "We've already got all that. We watch the same TV news as you do. What do you have that we don't?"

Decker told Carrington how Luddy had reacted in Nemo's to the television news about a Massachusetts girl being murdered near Las Vegas.

"Yes. We've been following that case as well. Lot's of similarities that I'll explain later, but for right now, let's stay on Mr. Pugano. It's extremely important to Mr. Lehman," Carrington said in a tone Decker hadn't previously heard. "I'll do what I can on this end. We're running background checks and credit histories of everyone involved. We'll see if your gypsy cab-driving clam shucker charged any expenses in Nevada over the past six months."

CHAPTER 33

July 1986
Boston, Massachusetts

AFTER CHURCH

Five police cruisers were parked outside the Most Holy Redeemer Church and uniformed officers were posted at every entrance. Nearly an hour had elapsed since news of Father Scarpino's murder reached the community and spread across the city. Newspaper and TV reporters were staked out nearby, hungry for more details about the priest who was slain on the altar. The TV satellite trucks were arranged in a row along the curb, their dishes ready to transmit.

Several blocks away, Fergus Cavanagh was squeezing his phone handset so hard Blade thought he would break it.

"Find him," Cavanaugh barked. "If the cops get him, he'll squeal like a pig."

Blade gave Cavanaugh his most confident look. He unfolded and snap closed his switchblade. "I'm on it."

"If you get him, call me immediately. And don't kill him."

"Yes sir. I'll get him, Mr. Cavanaugh. Where should I bring him?"

"To the house on Webster Street. Finley will make sure the cops don't search that neighborhood."

Blade pointed to two of the men in the room. "Come with me. We'll pick up Jimmy Two Cubes at his house."

Sgt. Macusovich, FBI Agent Finley, two Boston Police Department homicide investigators and two technicians from the forensic team were sifting through the Pugano apartment when they heard about the murder of Father Scarpino. "You guys stay here. I'm going to look for Shucker," Macusovich told them. "He knows every square inch of this neighborhood. My guess is he won't go near his boat or the airport."

"I'm going with you," said Finley.

"Remember, Kevin, this is my turf. We need to make sure he's taken alive. He could help us wrap up a lot of cold cases and that would make my boss very happy."

Finley smiled. "I won't shoot him. I promise."

Macusovich glanced down at his beeper. The number belonged to his commanding officer at the Major Crimes Unit in Essex County. The sergeant used the apartment phone without asking Celeste's permission. When he hung up, he looked quizzically at Finley. "As you undoubtedly already know, the bureau has narrowed down the search to three areas – the airport, this neighborhood and the waterfront. The State Police are following the bureau's lead."

"So we should get going," said Finley.

Macusovich again used Celeste's phone to call Summers. The answering machine said Summers was unable to take the call and to leave a message. The sergeant also called State Police headquarters for an update on Summers' work schedule and possible whereabouts, which is when he learned it was her day off.

Luddy parked on a shaded Brookline street in view of Summers' apartment. It was approaching 8 p.m. and the young detective still wasn't home. He wondered if she had been called into work and chuckled at the thought that she was probably out searching for him.

Bitch, he thought as he swallowed three Dexedrine capsules and swished them down with a lukewarm can of Budweiser. He wanted to settle the score with her for pushing so hard to unveil the man he'd come to see himself as –

the Boston Butcher. It was because of her suspicions and theories that Trib reporter Rane Bryson had begun writing stories about a possible serial killer. She wouldn't be feeling so Goody Two Shoes with the rope he imagined around her neck, but Luddy knew that fantasy would have to wait. He was running scared. He had murdered a Catholic priest and from that there was no turning back. He knew there was no forgiveness. But he could exact some vengeance by kidnapping Summers. Besides, he wanted to rape and torture her for saying the things she did during the most recent televised news conference.

"Whoever is responsible for these murders is a sick animal, a monster," she had told the press, and her words were quoted on that evening's TV broadcasts and in the following day's newspapers. She deserved to suffer for being such a meddler and a troublemaker, he told himself, his brooding eyes scanning the street for movement like a predatory animal. He decided to drive the two blocks from Summers' Ivy Street apartment to Hall's Pond nature sanctuary where he had followed her on three different days and watched as she strolled the boardwalk around the pond, stopping frequently to admire the beauty.

Luddy's throat tightened when he spotted her in a yellow summer dress and sandals. He ducked behind a massive red oak tree. His heartbeat quickened and he felt himself getting worked up.

When a young couple holding hands appeared on the boardwalk Luddy pressed his body into the briers. The couple nodded to Summers but kept moving. The sun had already set and the light was quickly fading.

Summers opened her straw pocketbook and pulled out a Sony Walkman. She began swaying as soon as the headphones cupped to her ears. The cassette was filled with high-energy dance music so she didn't hear Luddy come up from behind her. He struck her hard on the side of the head with a leather blackjack and caught her as she fell. He deeply inhaled her perfume as he tossed her over his shoulder and trotted along the boardwalk toward his car in the parking lot,

222

surprised by how little she weighed. He felt oddly heroic, like a fireman carrying a smoke-poisoned woman from a burning building.

Once at the car, he flopped Summers' body into the backseat and expertly bound her hands and feet with telephone wire. A few drivers in passing cars slowed as though curious but none stopped. Luddy hoped they wouldn't call the police. He pressed a strip of duct tape over Summers' mouth and took a few seconds to touch her between the legs before driving away. He sniffed his fingers as he drove, his mind focused on the blood that was now staining the cheerful daisy pattern on Summers' dress. He carefully avoided the Expressway and other primary roads, sticking to the coastal routes. He headed for Orient Heights, guided by the towering illuminated cross that marked a holy shrine and could be seen for miles around.

"God wants a sacrifice. I'll give him one," Luddy uttered aloud as he checked the rearview mirror.

As deadline approached, Rane tapped out a few sentences about the slaying of a priest in East Boston and the in-progress police search for the suspect, a local man authorities believe could be linked to the serial killings.

The suggested headline read: Boston Church Horror.

The three words would likely cover most of the front page and below them, the subhead: Priest Slain on Altar.

Rane typed his byline, then added:

BOSTON -- Police are searching for a local clam merchant suspected in the brutal slaying of a Catholic priest earlier today at the Most Holy Redeemer Church in East Boston.

Investigators say they have not determined why the suspect, tentatively identified as Luddy Pugano, would have wanted to kill the Rev. Armando Scarpino.

Scarpino reportedly died of blunt trauma after being attacked on the altar. Law enforcement sources told The Tribune that Pugano's name appears on a list of suspects in

223

the so-called Boston Butcher serial killer investigation.
    Scarpino, an octogenarian, joined the parish shortly
after the end of World War II...

Rane finished the story and sent it to the city desk for reading, copyediting and final approval. He called Kaleigh's apartment several more times over the next half hour but her roommates swore they hadn't seen her since she left for work in the morning.

When his desk phone rang, Rane instinctively knew who was on the other end. He heard shallow breathing as though the caller was having difficulty filling his lungs with air.

"Hello?"

"Do you know who this is?"

"Yes."

"That's good. I'm calling to give you a news story."

Rane waved at his newsroom colleagues to lower their voices so that he could better hear the caller. He pointed emphatically to the phone handset and the noise level near his desk lowered almost instantly.

"Do you have her?"

"I do."

Rane's heart sank. A sheen of sweat glistened on his forehead, his hand visibly shaking as he held the receiver. It was his fault that Kaleigh was now in the clutches of a psychopath. He hadn't adequately warned her of the danger.

"I'm at a pay phone. I thought we could talk."

Once again waving to his colleagues to lower the noise, he said, "I'm not talking to you about anything until you put her on the phone."

"Sorry, but the lieutenant is currently indisposed, or should I say, tied up."

Rane suddenly realized that Luddy had abducted Lt. Summers. He selfishly felt relieved, but the guilt was still gnawing at him. "Put her on."

"It sounds like you don't believe me."

"Why would I believe you?"

224

"Because she's not at work at the DA's office and she's not at her apartment on Ivy Street in Brookline."

"Where is she?"

"Right here with me. We're having fun."

"You need to let the lieutenant go. Turn yourself in. Talk to the police, explain what happened…"

"Explain?" Luddy chuckled. "They won't understand. You yourself call me a butcher. The Boston Butcher. Isn't that the name you gave me? I really don't like it."

"The police are going to find you any minute now if your underworld friends don't find you first."

Luddy laughed deeply. "It's nice to be wanted."

"You're twisted."

"Some people might say that. I just have different tastes. We all have things that make us feel better."

"And by that, I suppose you mean killing people?"

"It does give me pleasure to watch women suffer, especially when they deserve it."

"What did Detective Summers ever do to you?"

"She's a whore like all women."

"I wouldn't know about that."

"If it weren't true, this wouldn't be her last day on earth. She's responsible for all that's happening to me right now."

"Shucker, listen to me. If Detective Summers is released unharmed, you can still turn yourself in and get through this."

"Don't call me Shucker."

"Mr. Pugano, sir. If Detective Summers is really with you and she's unharmed, then you haven't committed any crime that a jury wouldn't forgive."

"Don't lecture me about forgiveness."

"Sorry. I'm just trying to keep you from doing something that you might regret."

"I have never regretted killing."

"Then I won't argue with you. I'll just say that if the police had any hard evidence about all these allegations, all these killings, you would have been arrested years ago."

Luddy was silent. He dropped the handset so that it banged again the glass of the phone booth.

"Fuck," Rane said aloud, the colleagues surrounding his desk imploring him to share the content of the conversation. He looked around at them and shrugged, obviously under tremendous pressure. A few seconds later he heard the phone rattle.

"Miss me?"

"Where did you go?"

"To check on the detective. I want to make sure she's nice and warm before I kill her."

"If she's alive, let me talk to her."

"Why would I do that? I don't need to prove anything to you."

Rane held his temper. "Mr. Pugano, it isn't too late to do the right thing and let her go. If you do that, people will see that you're not the kind of man who was described in the media."

"You mean described by you."

"Yes, me too. I was quick to judge."

"You wanted a story. You wanted to see your name on the front page. So I'm going to give you a story that will definitely make the front page. I already gave you a good one at the church today."

"Why did you kill Father Scarpino?"

"He deserved to die."

"What did he do?"

Click.

"That was Luddy Pugano," Rane told the others gathered around. "He claims he has Detective Summers and is going to kill her. I've got to get to through to Macusovich."

CHAPTER 34

July 1986
Boston, Massachusetts

TAKING THINGS TO THE HEIGHTS

As the search for Luddy intensified, Sgt. Macusovich and Agent Finley prowled the city streets in an unmarked cruiser while listening to the police radio chatter and looking for any sign of the Crown Vic.

Macusovich read Rane's news desk phone number on his beeper. He stopped at the next payphone and called the Tribune newsroom. Rane picked up immediately and in a burst of details told Macusovich that Luddy very likely had abducted Detective Summers and was planning to harm her.

The sergeant explained it could take hours to trace whatever pay phone Luddy had used to reach the newspaper's main desk and by then he would be long gone.

"Did he give any indication where he was or where he was headed?"

"Nothing."

"Could you hear cars in the background? Planes?"

"No. He must have been in a phone booth with the door shut," said Rane. "Why did Luddy kill Father Scarpino?"

"We don't know," the sergeant said.

"What was he doing at the church?"

"Making his confession."

"Guess that explains it."

"Maybe not. There's always more," said the sergeant, who hung up in order to quickly radio the State Police dispatcher and request an urgent bulletin regarding an officer in trouble and to increase the number of units searching for Luddy's Crown Vic.

Finley had used the abutting payphone to call FBI headquarters in Government Center. "Nothing new from my end," the federal agent told Macusovich.

Finley had contacted FBI headquarters to get the precise location of their field units. He had then called Fergus Cavanaugh to relay that information and assure him the FBI would not be searching along Webster Street.

On the other side of the city, Decker peered through binoculars at the *Sea Bitch*, bobbing gently at her mooring near the docks. No skiff tied off to the transom. No lights on in the cabin. He sped to Logan Airport and weaved through the parking lots, looking for Luddy's vehicle. He spotted Elroy McGuiness parked in his gypsy cab near the American Airlines terminal.

Decker quietly approached the cab from the passenger side, opened the door and sat atop a brown paper bag that contained Elroy's dinner. Elroy's bloodshot eyes revealed his surprise.

The man sitting in the passenger seat was dressed completely in black – skull cap, longsleeve pullover, military-style BDU pants and lace-up boots. He shoved a 9mm Beretta FS92 semi-automatic into Elroy's ribs.

"Who the fuck are you?"

"Never mind who I am. I need some information."

Elroy nodded energetically. "You're sitting on my sandwich."

Decker pushed the gun barrel harder against Elroy's ribcage. "I don't give a fuck about your sandwich. I need to know where your buddy Luddy Pugano is."

"How would I know?"

"Because you guys are pals and you both take advantage of people who land at the airport."

Elroy feigned insult. "I run a respectable cab company."

"Cut the shit. You don't run any company. You drive people around in this battered old piece of shit, overcharge them for the ride, and if they're young and female you try to rape them."

"I don't know where Shucker is right now. Usually he works the airport but I haven't seen him today."

"Where does he hang out when he's not working?"

"Nemo's."

"Where else?"

"He stays home. He lives with his mother."

"I know that, you fuckhead. Where does he go when he's not working at the fish market, not at home and not at Nemo's?"

"He might be fishing. He could be out on his boat."

"I already checked. Where else?"

"The horse track – Suffolk Downs. He loves the horses. Or maybe Constitution Beach because he likes to watch the planes land and take off from Logan."

"Where else would he go to do that?"

"Maybe Belle Isle Marsh in Winthrop where he digs clams, maybe The Heights."

"Orient Heights?"

Elroy again nodded. "Shucker's weird. Sometimes he drives up to the Madonna statue and prays," he shakily explained, referring to the nearby shrine where a 35-foot tall, copper-and-bronze statue of the Virgin Mother stands perched on a hilltop in Orient Heights, overlooking the airport and the city. "I'll bet that's where he is right now. Why are you looking for him? Does he owe you money?"

"That's none of your concern. And if you tell anybody that a guy stuck a gun in your ribs and was asking questions about Luddy Pugano, I'll come back and cut out your tongue," said Decker, pulling up his jersey to expose a lethal-looking combat knife. "Don't make me come back."

With that, Decker slipped out of the cab and into the night, leaving Elroy cursing and rummaging through the flattened paper bag. He stopped the Jeep at a pay phone outside the airport and called Carrington. He provided an update on the search and requested more specific instructions on how to proceed.

"Mr. Pugano's travel record shows he arrived in Nevada by commercial carrier and three days later boarded the same flight for the return trip to Boston. He didn't rent a car or use a credit card during his stay," Carrington said. "But we're assuming he killed Suzie Milano, the girl from Cape Cod, because her car was found abandoned in Vegas."

"I see. Is that enough to connect him?"

"It may be. We talked to the bus driver who claims Mr. Pugano left the charter group during one of their rest stops and never returned. They waited several minutes and blew the horn a few times. When he didn't show, they left. We think that's when he crossed paths with Milano."

"Unless you have other instructions, sir, I'm going to drive past Suffolk Downs to see if Shucker's car is down there by the stables. If it's not, I'll check out Constitution Beach and then the Madonna shrine in Orient Heights."

"That's fine," said Carrington. "You might want to bring the Beretta."

"Already with me, sir. But I appreciate the concern."

Across town, Blade was driving wildly with Jimmy Two Cubes riding shotgun and two of Fergus' men in the back seat.

"Take it easy," Jimmy Two Cubes advised after the car bounced up on a curb and nearly clipped a fire hydrant. "You know you've got a bum leg."

"Shut up and let me drive. You sound like my mother."

"I just don't want any trouble. If we don't find Shucker, Fergus is going to go nuts. And if we get stopped by the cops, we're not going to find him."

"We'll find him. Eastie's not that big."

"You carrying?"

Blade tapped the left side of his thin windbreaker. "Not that we'll need it. We just grab the fat fuck, toss him in the car and get him to the safe house."

The car picked up speed at the airport entrance, passing an idling State Police cruiser while going well above the speed limit. Blade's eyes locked on the rearview mirror, realizing he was being stupid. They hadn't even made sure all the car lights were functioning before they took off. How many times had he heard stories of guys getting pinched because of a broken taillight? Dumb.

Decker drove the Jeep along the stables at the far end of the horse track. It was a gloomy place after dark. There was no sign of Luddy's Crown Vic so he headed for Constitution Beach, which looked across the murky water to the Logan Airport runways. The commercial airliners were so close he felt as though he could reach out and touch them, their navigation lights blinking and flashing. Vapor from the heated engines rose into the air beneath the wings. Decker could see the airport traffic control tower.

Constitution Beach was little more than a man-made, crescent-shaped strip of sand but it was reachable by subway and the locals seemed to like it. They called it Shay's Beach. Decker listened to the police radio as he drove along Bennington Street, hoping a transmission might reveal Luddy's whereabouts. From the sound of things, the FBI had beefed up its presence and the search was concentrated in three locations. Decker noted Suffolk Downs, Constitution Beach and the Madonna shrine were not among them. Through his binoculars he could see the beach was empty.

CHAPTER 35

July 1986
Boston, Massachusetts

A DAY AT THE SHRINE WITH LUDDY

Luddy parked the Crown Vic beneath a burned out streetlamp at the top of the hill that overlooked the airport and eyed the neighborhood until he felt certain his arrival hadn't attracted any undue attention.

Summers' sandals came loose and fell beside the sedan as he dragged her out of the backseat. She was groggy from the blow to the head but starting to gain consciousness. The tape was still across her mouth, the telephone cable binding her wrists and ankles. Blood stains spotted the front of her yellow flowered dress.

Except for two streetlamps about twenty yards away, the houses along the street were enveloped in a mix of darkness and eerie shadows. Luddy hauled Summers from the backseat and stood her against the car where she could see the Madonna statue.

"That's a pure woman," he snarled, roughly lifting her chin so that she was forced to look up at the towering 35-foot-tall bronze statue with its blue-and-white robes and gilded crown. "Every girl should come here and pray to the virgin."

Summers moaned, back pressed against the car, and slumped to the pavement, clearly in pain. Luddy grabbed her by the hair. "Shut the fuck up, you dumb cop bitch," he said.

"Kneel."

Summers tried to kneel but it was difficult with her wrists and ankles bound. Luddy glowered at her. "Say your last prayers, you slut," he said, kneeling beside her and making the sign of the cross just as a commercial airliner roared across the darkened sky, its altitude so low it was possible to see the details of each wheel.

When he had finished praying, Luddy gripped Summers beneath her right arm. "Get up," he said, hauling her to a standing position. "Let's go."

Luddy opened the back door of the Crown Vic and pushed her inside, striking her head on the doorframe and kicking her body repeatedly until she was flat across the seat. The duct tape muffled Summers' protests.

Luddy ignored her as he drove a few hundred yards to the 50-foot tall cross that had been erected in a grassy hilltop field in the same neighborhood of the Madonna statue. The cross, which most passersby assumed was part of the shrine, was originally wooden but had been replaced with steel. It was affixed with multiple lightbulbs so that it could be seen from miles around. Luddy imagined the crucifixion of Jesus might have looked like this on the hill at Calvary if electricity had been invented during the Roman Empire.

Luddy slipped the coil of rope he had taken from *Sea Bitch* over his shoulder, untied the telephone cord at Summers' ankles and pulled her from the car by her bare feet. "Stand up," he commanded.

Summers stood shakily. When she had gained her balance she tried to head butt him and but Luddy quickly clamped his big hands around her biceps, spun her around and slapped her hard across the face. Summers let out a muffled cry as Luddy grabbed a clump of her hair with one hand and with the other her wrists that were corded behind her back. He marched her forward through the tall grass toward the glowing cross. It took nearly ten minutes to reach the iron fence that surrounded the cross. Luddy easily found the damaged section where it was possible to squeeze through the bars. He knew from reading local history that the imposing cross was placed to mark the Battle of Chelsea Creek, the second military skirmish of the American Revolutionary War in 1775. The encyclopedias in his bedroom were not up to date, but in all likelihood, if a battle had been fought on this soil more than 200 years ago, then it was already a place of bloodshed.

Luddy took in the panoramic views of the airport, the harbor and the downtown skyline. The sight always moved him because he loved Boston and particularly Eastie. It had always been his home except for a brief period in Lynn as a baby. He had never been out of the country, although there were a few difficult months during the Vietnam War when he thought he might be drafted. An hour before his physical exam, he diluted a half pound of cane sugar into a quart of water and drank it, believing the tests would falsely indicate diabetes. But his ruse proved unnecessary because the doctors found he had clubfoot and suffered from heart murmurs. He wasn't shipping out for Southeast Asia.

"Get down on your knees," he shouted, pulling her hair downwards. "Stick your head through the fence."

Luddy nudged through the opening, keeping a hand locked around her left ankle. When they were twenty feet from the base of the cross Luddy ripped the duct tape from Summers' mouth.

Summers tried to scream but her throat was parched and what came out of her mouth was little more than a whimper. She was angry at having left her gun at home on her day off, though she knew it might not have made much difference.

"What are we doing here? Why are you doing this?"

"We're going to ask for forgiveness."

"Forgiveness for what?"

"For our sins. For all we've done to make God angry."

"What have I done?"

"You're a whore, like all women. You flirt. You lure men with your cunt and ruin their lives. And you're a cop. You fucked with me."

234

Summers began weeping. Luddy pinched her chin between his thumb and forefinger so that his dark brooding eyes were level with hers.

"Bitch," he said.

Summers tried to knee him in the groin but Luddy was too quick. He yanked on her hair until she fell into the tall grass, then kicked her in the ribs. Summers curled into a fetal position but Luddy clutched one of her ankles and dragged her to the base of the cross. The hem of her dress slid up to her hips. Luddy lifted her body by thrusting his hands into her armpits. He pressed her against the vertical post with his full weight as he wound the rope around her waist. When Summers began to struggle he punched her in the stomach so that she could hardly breathe. He undid the ties on her wrists and pulled her arms above her head, then lashed her wrists to the post. He did the same at her ankles, using the duct tape as an added measure to secure the rope.

"If you let me go, any judge will take that into consideration," she said.

Luddy slapped her again across the face so that her nose began to bleed heavily. He fished a folding knife from his pants pocket, opened the blade and rested the point against her cheekbone. Summers' eyes were filled with tears and fear. Luddy laughed madly, running his hand up her thighs and beneath her yellow dress. He inserted the knife into the dress material just below the rope that was tied around Summers' waist and ran it downward until the dress was split open, revealing white panties against tanned flesh.

"I'll bet only your special friends see you like this," he muttered in a voice so deranged Summers thought she would vomit.

Luddy sliced open the dress bodice, exposing a white bra trimmed with lace. He could feel himself getting hard. His heart was beating wildly. He cut through the bra between the two cups and gently fondled each breast.

"You like that, don't you?" He pinched her nipples so hard she screamed and he struck her again in the face.

Summers struggled against the ropes and tape but it

235

was of no use. "Please let me go. I won't tell anyone."

Luddy put his nose an inch from hers so that she could smell his sour breath. "No, you won't tell anyone, ever." He smiled mockingly, patting a fresh strip of duct tape over her mouth.

Summers watched him walk briskly toward a small grove of scruffy trees. Big commercial airliners, navigation lights blinking, roared overhead as they took off and landed at Logan. She couldn't stop herself from thinking about where those passengers might be headed, the great cities of Europe, the sandy isles of the Caribbean, or simply to visit family in a distant state? She tried to pretend she was one of them, Paris bound, perhaps. Anywhere but here, with him.

Jimmy Two Cubes was the first to spot the Crown Vic. "There," he said. "Definitely Shucker's. Dented trunk lid, spotlight on the driver's side."

Blade stopped the car. "I gotta call Fergus."

"No," Jimmy said. "We get him first. Bring him to the safe house and then call Fergus."

"But Fergus wanted to be there when it went down."

"Fergus said don't kill him. That's what I heard."

The two men in the back seat agreed with Jimmy Two Cubes. The one on the driver's side clutched a baseball bat. "Let's go get him," he said.

"I'm in charge," said Blade, dropping the transmission into drive and slowly pulling away from the shrine. "We need to call Fergus."

Luddy gathered a stack of dried twigs, two soiled paper plates and a crumpled cellophane potato chip bag. He returned to the illuminated cross wearing a boyish grin and carrying the trash as though it were a great treasure. The blood from Summers' nose had spilled down her breasts and stomach. She was exhausted from trying to pry herself loose. Luddy methodically placed the twigs near her bare feet, interspersing the wood with the paper shards and the greasy potato chip bag.

"Don't go away," he said, laughing as he stomped through the tall grass toward the Crown Vic.

Decker drove past Nemo's on his way to Orient Heights. En route he glanced down every alley in search of Luddy's car. He was surprised to see Dogman's Volvo parked outside the bar. He doubleparked the Jeep with its flashers on and went inside. Dogman was seated at a table finishing up a plate of steak tips and fries. Major was curled at his feet.

"Hittin' the town without me these days," Decker said.

Dogman gave him a thumbs up. "That's it. The cripple and the canine setting the world on fire."

Decker quickly explained he was searching for Luddy as part of his private investigation assignment and was headed for Orient Heights.

"Haven't seen him. But if you don't mind company, we'll tag along," said Dogman, leaving cash on the table for the bill.

The two friends and the shepherd piled into the Jeep Cherokee. "Nice wheels," Dogman said.

"It's a loaner."

"Possession is ninety percent of the fun."

Luddy returned carrying a plastic five-gallon gasoline container. Slowly he walked in a wide circle around the cross, purposefully leaving at least thirty feet as a buffer while drizzling the liquid into the high and dry grass.

When he had finished he threw down the container and struck a match. The flames followed the fuel, erupting quietly in both directions until the ends met. Luddy wondered what the airline pilots thought as they approached the airport runways. The dry grass burned easily, spreading upward and outward from the trail of gasoline. If the airline pilots didn't report the circle of flames, he knew it was only a matter of minutes before the neighbors in the nearest houses smelled smoke and telephoned the fire department.

"You deserve to die," Luddy said, setting fire to the small pile of debris directly beneath Summers' bare feet. He blew on the flames until the paper plates caught fire and impulsively ripped the duct tape from Summers' mouth. "I want to hear your screams."

Decker followed the spiraling roadway that led to Orient Avenue at the top of the Heights. It was the last place on his list of places to search. He quickly spotted the Crown Vic parked on the street. "I don't like it," he said, pulling the Beretta from its holster. Just then, as though on cue, the shepherd began to growl. The dog didn't bark, but his chest cavity was vibrating. He had picked up a scent they couldn't smell, or perhaps a sound they couldn't hear.

Dogman patted the dog on the head as they exited the Jeep. "*Buen chico*," he said, slipping two fingers beneath the collar. Seconds later they smelled the grass fire.

Decker scanned the open expanses with his binoculars. A gut feeling told him something bad was about to unfold.

Sgt. Macusovich was frustrated. He had phoned Summers a half-dozen times and left as many messages but she hadn't called back. He tried to hail her on the police radio frequency used by detectives but got no response. It appeared Luddy was telling the truth when he called Rane at the Tribune to say he had Summers.

There wasn't much they could do but search. Macusovich drove like a maniac through the airport terminal parking lots and service roads but there was no sign of Luddy Pugano or his gypsy cab. Based on Finley's recommendation from FBI headquarters, they headed back toward Jeffries Point where the forensic team was still taking samples under Celeste Pugano's watchful eyes.

Blade nervously explained to Fergus that they had found Luddy and would wait until the underboss arrived before making the grab. All four men heard the sound of

Fergus' booming voice emanating from the receiver.

"For the love of God, bring him to the safe house on Webster Street. Now."

"Yes Fergus. I mean Mr. Cavanaugh. Yes sir. Right away. I mean right now," he stammered, hanging up the pay phone.

"Get back in the car," Blade barked at the others.

Back atop the hill, Blade didn't recognize the black Jeep Cherokee. It hadn't been there when he left. But nobody was in sight. He parked a short distance away from the vehicle and attempted to look inside it but the tinted windows revealed nothing.

Decker momentarily thought he was delusional. Through the Leica binoculars he saw a ring of fire and within it a burly man built like Luddy Pugano hunkered down before a massive illuminated cross to which a mostly naked woman in a torn yellow dress was tied. The man was tending a fire near the base of the cross. It was reminiscent of a scene from the Middle Ages, or perhaps the Salem Witch Trials.

Ignoring the stiffness from his war wounds, Decker sprinted forward another 50 feet before peering again through the binoculars, knowing the reduced distance would afford him more detail. He was shocked to see Summers crying. Luddy Pugano was clapping and stomping his feet as though engaged in some private madman's dance.

Dogman and Major soon caught up with him at the fence. Decker handed off the binoculars, slipped through the bars and began running with a slight limp toward the ring of fire and illuminated cross. Summers was screaming in pain.

Decker saw the dog hurl past him in a flash, leap through the narrow circle of flame, jump four feet into the air and lock its jaws on Luddy's left arm. Decker charged through the flames that were rapidly spreading. He began stamping out the trash fire at Summers' feet and kicking the burning sticks aside. Summers' facial expression suggested she might pass out at any moment. Her feet were scorched and blackened. Luddy was screaming as Major's fangs sank deeper into his flesh. He tried to fend off the dog with little success. Decker aimed the 9mm Beretta at Luddy's head but he didn't want to chance killing Major. He pulled out his SOG combat knife and began cutting the ropes and duct tape.

Things were happening fast. As soon as Macusovich heard the radio crackle with a report of fire beneath the cross in Orient Heights, instinct told him that's where he would find Luddy Pugano. He attached the magnetic blue flashing light to the roof of the unmarked cruiser and raced toward the scene, sirens wailing. Finley sat nervously in the front seat, inspecting the magazine of his semi-automatic. Macusovich thought Finley looked worried.

Paige Williston also had been listening when the police and fire radios came to life in her compact sedan. She tailgated the fast-moving Engine 5, its red and white lights flashing, sirens wailing, horn blasting.

Luddy momentarily broke free of the dog and began running. He rammed Dogman full force with his shoulder, knocking him to the ground as he ran toward his car. The dog had released Luddy's arm and was tearing at his trousers, slowing his progress. Dogman lay in the grass, clutching his artificial leg in pain.

Luddy stabbed at the shepherd with his folding knife. Dogman heard the shepherd whine and a chill ran through his body. That dog was more precious to him than any other living creature. He shouted a command and the dog released its jaw lock on Luddy's leg. Luddy took another blind swipe with his knife just as the shepherd turned toward Dogman. The blade cut deeply into the dog's hind leg but the animal kept moving despite an obvious injury. Dogman thought he saw blood coming from Major's right side near the ribs. He yelled to Decker. "Medic!"

Summers had collapsed into Decker's arms and for a moment he stood there, holding her beneath the illuminated cross as a police siren warbled and blue lights flashed across the grass in undulating waves. She didn't recognize him but

240

was too weak to protest.

Seconds later Engine 5 came to a halt at the edge of the pavement. Paige parked beside it and started clicking away. She saw Macusovich sprinting across the tall grass. Agent Finley was close on his heels. Paige jogged after them, holding the two bulky cameras against her body. The sergeant, out of breath, was first to reach Decker and Summers. "Holy Christ. What the fuck is going on?"

Paige continued to shoot, the camera's motor drive whirring. Through the viewfinder she saw Decker holding Summers in his arms, the illuminated cross directly behind them, smoke still rising from the fire. Summers' long blonde hair spilled down from her limp body. Click. Click. Click.

"If you're looking for Luddy, he just took off in his car," Decker said.

Macusovich blurted the information into his portable radio before he called for an ambulance.

The firefighters on Engine 5 began dragging a hose toward the dancing flames. A large patch of tall grass was blackened near the cross and the ring of fire was still spreading. Paige captured the firefighters in action, silhouetted against the burning cross.

"I'll stay with her," said Decker. "You and Finley find Pugano. He can't be very far."

Macusovich weighed his options, decided he could trust Decker and handed him the portable police radio. He and Finley hustled back to the cruiser and took off with blue lights flashing. Decker pulled off his black jersey and used it to wipe Summers' battered face. He crouched in the high grass and checked her carotid pulse and respirations. She was alive and breathing. He carefully examined her feet.

Dogman shouted. "How is she?"

"She's breathing and her pulse is strong. Possible second-degree burns to her feet. I need to make sure she doesn't have any injuries that we can't see."

Decker roamed his hands quickly over Summers' entire body, looking and feeling for punctures, lacerations or dangerous contusions that might be hidden by what remained of the tattered yellow dress. "I need to roll her," he said.

Decker rolled Summers on her left side so that he could finish the trauma assessment. There were scratches and abrasions but nothing visibly life-threatening. Summers moaned but didn't speak. The ambulance sirens were getting louder.

Summers abruptly opened her eyes and despite her injuries asked Decker who he was and what he was doing at the scene.

"I'm Decker. You're going to be fine. Your partner and the fed have gone after Pugano."

"You're the PI who called me and wanted to talk?"

"That's me."

"How did you know I'd be here?"

"I didn't. I was looking for Pugano when I saw his car and then the fire."

Decker began talking into the portable radio. He contacted the State Police dispatcher, identified himself, explained the situation and updated Summers' medical condition for the paramedics who were en route. The radio transmissions were highly professional, Decker's voice completely in control without a hint of emotion.

"Be right back," Decker said, hurrying to Dogman's side where he examined his friend's leg. Dogman pushed him away and pointed to Major. "I'll be fine. Check on him."

The dog whimpered when Decker touched the two wounds. Decker spotted the roll of duct tape near the base of the cross. He took off his socks and used them as compress bandages for the rib cage puncture and the leg laceration, holding them in place with the tape. Dogman lay on the ground. Major crawled over and curled into him. "Just like old times," said Dogman, hugging the shepherd.

Click. Click. Paige was on autopilot, stopping only to thread on a new roll of film in her favorite Nikon F2.

Decker returned to Summers' side and again checked her breathing. She needed an IV and a blanket.

Decker gently pulled his black jersey over Summers' head and inched it downward so that it covered her arms and

242

extended to the middle of her thighs. An ambulance wailed in the distance, the sound getting louder with each passing second.

Paige squatted next to them and clicked off a few more frames with a wide-angle lens before she turned and left without saying a word.

"It really pisses me off when they do that," said Summers, who seemed suddenly more alert.

Decker smiled. "Glad you're still with us."

"You don't even know me," she said, her lips bruised and puffy.

"I've seen you on TV."

Summers scrunched her face as though she didn't understand.

"I saw you interviewed on the news a couple of times about Jenny Lehman's disappearance."

"Is that why you're trying to find Luddy Pugano? You think he can lead you to her?"

"You tell me. Did he abduct and kill Jenny Lehman?"

"I guess we'd all like to know that," she moaned, her head slumping off to one side.

The ambulance came to a halt, red and white lights flashing. The two paramedics rolled Summers onto a spine board, secured the straps, tucked a rolled towel beneath her head and lifted her onto the wheeled stretcher. They started a saline IV line and pain medication.

Decker followed the ambulance to the hospital in his Jeep Cherokee. A second ambulance was en route to the scene to transport Dogman, who had refused to leave without Major. His artificial leg had been twisted in the fall. He demanded the dog be brought to a veterinarian.

Three Boston Police cruisers were on scene at the top of the hill, one officer staying beside Dogman while the others strung yellow crime scene tape and directed traffic as the television news trucks began ascending the hill.

Decker asked one of the sergeants to radio State Police headquarters and request a K-9 officer be dispatched to take temporary custody of a victim's dog and to transport the injured animal to Angell Memorial Hospital in Jamaica Plain.

When the second ambulance pulled up, the EMTs assessed Dogman whose injuries were painful but not cause for alarm. They agreed to monitor him at the scene until the K-9 unit arrived. When it did, Dogman pleaded with the K-9 officer to take good care of Major.

Less than a mile away, Blade blocked Luddy's car on a narrow side street. Luddy blew the horn. "Get the fuck out of the way," he shouted.

Jimmy Two Cubes and the other two men got out of their car and walked slowly toward Luddy who was highly agitated. Luddy's knuckles were white from gripping the steering wheel. The man with the baseball bat wielded it menacingly inches from Luddy's arm that was now resting on the windowsill, getting ready to slide downward and open the car door in case the opportunity to bolt presented itself. The other man approached the passenger door, unveiled a short length of lead pipe and repeatedly slapped it in his palm. Jimmy Two Cubes flicked open his switchblade and pierced the left rear tire of Luddy's car, then the right. Luddy put the car in reverse and attempted to back up. Jimmy Two Cubes threw two metal garbage cans in its path while Fergus' men shattered the front and side windows. Blade put a knife to Luddy's throat and ordered him to lay off the gas pedal and cut the engine. Luddy did as he was told. Blade opened the driver's door and pulled Luddy out. Jimmy Two Cubes put a black cloth bag over Luddy's head and all four men hustled him to Blade's car, pushing him head first into the trunk. The smaller man struck Luddy on the head with the lead pipe just hard enough to keep him quiet. In seconds they were zigzagging across the neighborhood, headed for the safe house on Webster Street.

244

CHAPTER 36

July 1986
Boston, Massachusetts

SHARP AS A RAZOR, SOFT AS A PRAYER

The paramedics pushed the stretcher through the electronic doors to the Emergency Department at Massachusetts General Hospital. A clear oxygen tube ran from Summers' nose to the portable green cylinder on the back of the stretcher. Another surgical tube led from her arm to a clear plastic bag of saline hanging on a stainless steel post. Decker walked beside them, shirtless, Summers' dried blood on his chest and stomach from when he had taken her down from the cross.

At the emergency room, a nurse handed Decker a thin white blanket to put around his bare, bloodstained shoulders. Summers was wheeled into a curtained room. An ashen-faced doctor firmly instructed Decker to wait in the corridor. Seconds later, Macusovich burst through the ER doors.

"I need to talk to Lt. Summers," he bellowed. "The patient who was just brought in."

The doctor stood his ground. "You may be able to do that later, but for right now, she's my patient and my responsibility, so please let me do my job."

Just before the curtain was closed, Decker spotted Amal in her surgical scrubs. A mask covered her face so he wasn't sure if she smiled, but her eyes definitely saw him.

Frustrated by the doctor, Macusovich returned to his cruiser in the hospital parking lot where several uniformed and plainclothes officers were waiting for news and orders. According to Finley, Boston Police patrol units had located Luddy's car with its flattened tires and shattered windows. But Luddy was gone. Macusovich sensed the Boston Butcher was most likely in the hands of those interested in keeping him quiet.

In the middle of the night, a bleary-eyed Macusovich again entered the emergency room. He looked haggard and defeated. Decker was seated in a straight-back chair a few feet from the curtain that divided Summers' bed from the corridor. His eyes were closed. Macusovich tapped him on the shoulder in a way that showed he appreciated Decker's presence. An overworked nurse appeared and informed both men they could not stay with the patient.

"She's still very weak and traumatized, but her vitals are stable," the nurse reassured.

Decker spoke softly to the nurse. "Are there any other injuries we should know about?"

"Are you family?"

"No."

"Then I can't discuss her condition with you."

Macusovich flashed his State Police shield. "Please try to be cooperative."

The nurse frowned. "She has a fractured cheek bone, lacerations to her lips and left ear, possible concussion, abrasions to the knees and elbows, and second-degree burns to her feet. There are ligature marks on her wrists and ankles. And, she has been traumatized. Anything else you'd like to know?"

"Is there anything else we should know?"

The nurse pursed her lips. "We won't have any lab results until late morning."

"Thank you so much," Macusovich said in a surly voice as he turned to leave. Decker followed and slept for a few hours in his Jeep in the parking lot. Shortly before dawn he slipped into the ER again, hoping the nursing staff had

246

changed shifts and would be less apt to challenge him. When the nurses seemed busiest he made his way to Summers' bedside. She was groggy but awake. Decker held her hand and was suddenly reminded of Beirut where he'd done the same on many occasions for dying soldiers.

"I guess I have you to thank," said Summers, looking at Decker and then at his hand holding hers. She didn't pull it away. "Did they get that bastard?"

Decker shook his head. "I don't think so."

Summers tried to sit up but Decker gently pushed on her shoulders until she was again resting on the pillows. He still had the hospital blanket folded over his shoulders. Summers studied his bare torso. It was muscular and unblemished, except for the scars on the left side near his ribs.

"Where'd you earn those?"

"Lebanon."

"Marines?"

"Rangers."

"Where's Mancusovich?"

"The nurse booted us out. I'm sure he'll be back."

"What time is it?"

"Let's just say most people haven't had breakfast yet."

"How did you get back in?"

"I waited for the right time."

"How long am I going to be in here?"

"Until your wounds heal. You've got some bruises and a black eye that any prizefighter would be proud of."

Summers seemed suddenly self-conscious of her looks. She reached back for her hair that was spread across the pillow. The nursing staff had cleaned most of the blood streaks but the strands were a tangled mess.

"Looks good on you," Decker said.

"What's that?"

"The hair. I've never seen it down."

Summers blinked in surprise at the compliment. "I don't wear it that way very often."

"Why not?"

"Because some perp might try to grab it while I'm arresting him."

"Got it."

"If I had a cup of coffee I'd be good enough to get out of here."

"Spoken like a cop," said Decker, flashing her a warm smile.

"I'm serious."

Decker wore an amused grin as he thought, she's just had a near-death experience and she's ready to rejoin the fray. "I'd be glad to get you one, but only if you have the stomach for hospital cafeteria coffee."

Summers smiled with bloated lips for the first time. "It can't be any worse than the coffee at the DA's office."

Decker avoided the doctors and nurses as he left the emergency room and headed for the cafeteria. When he returned he set the coffee cup on the wheeled table next to the bed.

"The nurse just left. She saw you come in even though you thought she didn't. She seemed to know you. I could tell by the expression on her face. I told her you were a good friend and that it was all right for you to stay. She told me I was lucky to have such a good friend."

Decker had brought along two sugar packets and two single creamers. He removed the plastic top from the Styrofoam cup and said, "It just occurred to me that I don't know how you take your coffee."

"Three creams and three sugars."

"Well, I've failed my mission."

"Two will be just fine. Now tell me why you're so interested in Luddy Pugano."

"I've been tailing him for weeks. Private surveillance job."

"What's your client's interest?"

"Now you're interrogating me."

"Sorry."

"Seems a lot of people are interested in him."

"Like Fergus Cavanaugh?"

"I'd definitely put him on the list."

"Where do you think Pugano is now?"

"If I knew, I'm not sure I'd tell you."

"And why is that?"

"Because even though you probably want to kill him, you'd probably arrest him and he'd stand trial. It would become a big media circus and in the end, you never know, twelve fuckheads might feel sorry for him, recommend psychological counseling and get him a job at a sheltered workshop next door to my apartment."

"Got it," she said, mimicking his response to her explanation about why she doesn't wear her hair down. "And you'd be opposed to that, presuming he was found not guilty?"

"I never said that."

"But it was implied."

"From all that I've seen, heard and read, there's good reason to believe that Luddy Pugano, aka Shucker, aka the Boston Butcher, has tortured and murdered several young women. As a taxpayer, I don't like the idea of providing him with food and shelter for the rest of his life, even if it is in a maximum security prison."

"What other choice is there?"

"Sit back and see if Fergus Cavanaugh takes care of the matter when we're not looking."

"You think the Irish Mob wants him dead?"

"That's very possible, and maybe the Italians are thinking the same thing," he said. "I'm sure you're aware that the mob has a way of cleaning its own house."

Summers sipped the coffee, grimaced and pushed the cup to the middle of the table.

"It's that good?"

"It may have needed that third sugar after all."

Summers nestled her back into the pillows and studied him with her lively greenish-gray eyes. He did the same. Neither uttered a word, but they were communicating. Decker was completely intrigued and he admired her spunkiness, particularly given the medical monitors to which her body was attached. Summers felt inexplicably drawn to him and quickly attempted to expunge the thought. After about two minutes, which seemed much longer to both of them, she said, "I don't think this coffee is going to get any better."

"You may be right."

"Is there a mirror in the side drawer?"

Decker opened every drawer but there was no mirror. "Another failed mission," he said, giving her a close-lipped smile, his eyes flirtatious. "I guess you'll just have to take my word for it that you look beautiful, despite a few bumps and bruises."

Summers was taken off guard by the flattery that was loaded with possibilities. She gathered her thoughts and tried to return his smile but found those muscles hadn't been used in a while. Besides, her lips were puffed from the beating.

As Summers lay back, she imagined kissing Decker, a notion she immediately dubbed preposterous and attributed it to the effects of the painkillers she'd been forced to swallow. She chided herself for having such thoughts. They were luxuries she couldn't afford because they only led to heartbreak.

She reminded herself, you're a cop, Summers. You carry a gun, you practice martial arts, you have a high-functioning brain and you don't take shit, all qualities that most men find unsettling, undoubtedly including Emmett Decker. Certainly Dr. Chandler Hughes had been unable to handle the pressure.

Their two-year relationship had gone down the tubes because the remains of each day, moments she often referred to as the dregs, were not enough to sustain it. Far too frequently their beepers had sounded in the night, pulling them apart, she to a crime scene, he to the operating room.

Decker had similar musings. Summers was undeniably attractive. He'd heard people say she reminded them of a movie actress, though they could never decide which one. And she was brave and resourceful, but she was probably a pain in the ass and undoubtedly had a guy in her life. He wondered what those sensual lips would feel like pressed against his own. He sensed that beneath that standoffish exterior was a treasure and it made him think of a line from a Tom Waits song, '*She was sharp as a razor and soft as a prayer.*' He thought about that softness and flashed her a boyish, full-tooth smile that was straight from the heart.

"What?"

"Nothing."

"You're thinking something," she said. "Tell me what it is."

"I was thinking this has been a great first date," he said, snugging the blanket around his shoulders.

Summers almost laughed. "Can't recall when I've had a better time, Decker. Nothing like spending quality time together in the ER. Could you make sure my IV drip is still working?"

The medication was making Summers sleepy. Twice she said Decker's name as she dozed off but her other words were indecipherable. Decker hoped if he was subconsciously in her thoughts that it was for good reason.

The first TV news truck had arrived in the hospital parking lot. Beside it two hospital security guards were in a heated discussion with a newspaper reporter who had tried to enter the emergency room. Decker walked past them, cringing at the thought of phoning Carrington with the news that Luddy had escaped. When Carrington answered, Decker gave him the blow-by-blow of what had transpired during the course of the evening. The story was interesting but it didn't matter to Carrington. The bottom line was far more important: Luddy Pugano was a fugitive instead of a corpse and Carrington was lamenting the task of conveying that information to Skip Lehman, his immediate superior at Langley. The phrase "Don't shoot the messenger" came to mind but Carrington suppressed it and a few minutes later rang Lehman's private number.

Lehman's first question had already been anticipated.

"Why didn't Decker shoot him when he had the chance?"

"He was afraid he'd hit the dog."

"Who cares about the fucking dog? We're talking about terminating a monstrous serial killer."

"Apparently Decker cares, as does his friend who owns the dog. Their ties go back to Beirut. They were in Sandland together."

"You mean to tell me Decker, the ace marksman, couldn't get off a round when the target was fleeing?"

"I asked him that."

"And what did he say?"

"He said the round would have been in the back and that would have been hard to explain. There was also no assurance that it would have been fatal, and that could have caused more complications down the road."

"So now what?"

"We stop, look and listen. It's only a matter of time before one of our operatives gets word on whether the target is alive or dead."

"Frankly, I'd prefer the latter," said Lehman.

"I know you would, sir."

CHAPTER 37

August 1986
North Atlantic Ocean

PASSING THE TIME ABOARD SHIP

Luddy was frightened when he heard voices and the sound of the metal latch being undone on the shipping container. His muscles tightened and ached after what he figured was about 14 hours. His head still pounded from where he had been struck with the lead pipe.

There was little fresh air inside the container and no light. The men who had stuffed him inside it spoke no English and didn't give him a flashlight, food or water.

Luddy knew they were at sea by the pitch and roll of the big ship, so much different than his days aboard *Sea Bitch* on the relatively protected waters just beyond Boston Harbor. He had no sense of which direction they were heading but he didn't care. To stay in Boston would have been a death sentence. Surely he would have been arrested and stood trial before a merciless jury. Twelve people would have voted to put him behind bars for life – the maximum in a state with no death penalty. The Boston Butcher. The nickname conjured ferocity and brutality, but what would that get him behind the thick walls of a state prison? Most likely, the nickname would only have encouraged the meanest of inmates to challenge him at every opportunity and before long he would be lying dead on the wet shower floor, his body pierced by a handmade shiv. Or maybe he would be hanging from the bars of his cell, a bed sheet knotted around his neck.

"Out! Come!"

A brown-skinned man wearing faded tan work pants, a Boston Bruins T-shirt and white knee-high rubber boots was pointing to a metal door that was visible from the canyon made by shipping containers that rose upward for sixty feet. The big boxes were painted different colors and many were emblazoned with foreign language labels that offered little clue to their contents.

"You go," he gestured emphatically.

Luddy made his way to the heavy door. Another crewman opened it and pushed him through. Luddy tripped over the steel threshold and fell, unable to get his contracted muscles under control. The crewman laughed, folded his arms and waited for Luddy to stand.

Luddy thought, if you did that to me in Boston, I would have killed you. Together they climbed a series of metal stairwells to the bridge deck where an older man, presumably the captain, was peering out at the ocean through large plateglass windows. Luddy estimated the ship was moving at 20 knots, far faster than *Sea Bitch* could ever do on a calm day. He wondered what would happen to his boat now that he was gone and never coming back.

"Good morning, Mr. Martin Campbell."

Luddy scrunched his eyebrows at the unfamiliar name. "Who is Martin Campbell?"

"That's what it says on your Canadian passport and work visa. Mr. Martin Campbell of Toronto, Canada."

The captain gave Luddy a knowing smile and handed him the forged passport. "Welcome aboard the freighter Maersk Athena Express. You are probably hungry. I will get our cook to prepare a meal."

"Where are we headed?"

"What have you been told?"

"To Ireland."

"Then that's where we are going."

"When will we get there? Who am I supposed to meet?"

"All I can tell you is that we are going to Cork. The sea conditions often dictate how long our passage will take. But I can assure you, the fewer questions you ask, the better for everyone involved. One of the crew will show you to your berth. If by some chance we are boarded, you must quickly return to the container. We will give the necessary warning."

Luddy nodded. The thought of returning to the shipping container depressed him. They hadn't even provided him with a bucket, so he had urinated on the floor and tried to remember the spot so that he wouldn't sit in it. He followed the cook to the wardroom and drank a cup of tepid coffee while waiting for scrambled eggs and toast. His head pounded, which he presumed was from the lump he'd received, but also from dehydration. He declined a second cup of coffee.

Being at sea gave Luddy time to reflect. He admitted to himself that he missed working at the fish market, a place he had cursed daily. He imagined the feel of the cold, slippery fish in his hands -- haddock, tuna, sword and other prime species. He enjoyed the way his favorite filet knives cut through the flesh and separated it from the bones. Even the customers he had told himself were an annoyance suddenly found a place in his heart. He wondered who was sitting on the corner barstool at Nemo's and what was happening there on this sunny day. Was Bubby pouring a chilled draft beer right now or swirling some crafty vodka drink? He realized he was homesick.

To pass the time, Luddy tried to remember the faces and bodies of the women he had murdered, going all the way back to the first one in Boston's Combat Zone in the early '70s. It seemed like an odd mental exercise, but he enjoyed it and soon ran out of fingers on which to count them. He'd never been college material and floundered through trade school where he learned about plumbing but was more interested in auto mechanics. Working at an autobody shop on Bennington Street had given him spending money, but his weak lungs couldn't take the fine sanding dust, fiberglass particles and paint fumes. Every day he coughed for an hour after work. He didn't have a girlfriend and he'd not thought much about the world of pimps and hookers until a nattily-dressed man stopped by the shop to get the dents removed from his Cadillac.

When Luddy pointed out that the dents in the grill and hood resembled those often resulting when a moving car collides with a human body, the shop owner pulled him aside and explained that no questions were allowed. If somebody brings in a car with a dent, we fix it. And if they're paying cash, we fix it faster.

Luddy was about to say tattered bits of clothing and what looked like chunks of flesh were stuck in the grill, but he decided not to mention it. When the man picked up his car a few days later, he praised Luddy for a job well done. The car owner was accompanied by two leggy young women who wore heavy makeup and were provocatively dressed in glossy boots to the mid-thigh and short dresses with plunging necklines. The women were abundantly perfumed and toyed with him. One asked if he could repair a couple of her parts that were wearing out from over use. Everyone laughed at that except for Luddy who seemed to miss the meaning.

Later that summer he began driving through the Combat Zone that was lined with strip clubs, massage parlors and seedy restaurants. He was astonished that women dressed similar to those who'd come to the autobody shop brazenly approached his car. While he was at a stoplight, one woman lassoed her fake feather boa around his neck and blew him a kiss as she retrieved it. Had his mother done that to the men in Scollay Square? He had collectively pieced together their family history over the years, with the exception of his father whom he knew little about. It was a sorry bunch, he thought.

On weekends the Combat Zone was more alive and grew wilder after dark. The number of women on the street tripled. Luddy obeyed when a young Nordic-looking woman told him to open his passenger door. The woman got inside the aging Chevy sedan and slid across the bench seat until she was snuggled against him. For $20 she would give him relief, for $50 whatever he wanted within reason – no kinky stuff, no animals and definitely not overnight.

Luddy opted for the first choice. The next day he went to church and prayed for forgiveness. He didn't go into the confessional, but he inserted $5 into the metal box near the candles and lit a votive in his own behalf. When Father Gallagher crossed the main aisle without genuflecting, Luddy cringed. It was a church rule. If you crossed before the altar, you were supposed to get down on one knee as a show of respect and adoration. But Father Gallagher, he knew from experience, was a rule breaker and a pedophile. The priest saw Luddy sitting in a pew near the front entrance but didn't acknowledge his presence.

After their first encounter in the Combat Zone, Luddy never expected to see Gertrud again, given the number of women vying for customers, but there she was on the corner, smiling and transmitting come-fuck-me looks to the drivers of passing cars. When she recognized Luddy she simply opened the door and hopped inside.

Luddy wanted to talk before they did anything, which is when he learned she preferred the name Gerty. She had been born in Sweden and for the past year had been earning money as a nanny for a wealthy family in Back Bay. She actually worked very little in the Combat Zone because the children got up early each day and she had to be alert. But the money was far better, she explained, and soon she'd have enough to pay for college tuition.

Flirty Gerty was a dreamer, telling Luddy she could imagine them married with children, living in their own house and both of them with good-paying jobs. She had asked him if he, too, could imagine it.

Luddy had been speechless. He had only met her once before, but she was closing in on him, drawing him into her world or, more likely, trying to become a part of his. She must think I'm stupid, he told himself. They drove around until Luddy parked the car beneath the elevated expressway that snaked through the city. Gerty climbed over the seats and urged him to join her. By the time Luddy opened the rear door, Gerty was naked, sprawled across the seat. Luddy opened his wallet and began pulling out $10 bills but Gerty raised her hand in a gesture telling him to stop. Luddy clumsily got inside and closed the door. Gerty giggled at his uneasiness, which made him flush with anger. She undid his belt and pulled down his pants, engulfing him with her mouth. Luddy came almost immediately, which made Gerty smile impishly. When she mentioned that he seemed nervous and hurried and that she'd have to work on getting him ready again if they wanted to have more fun, Luddy's mood began to change. The little slut was laughing at him, he had surmised, and it was then he reached for the tire iron on the floor of the back seat and struck her across the face and head. Gerty cried out, shocked by the blood on her hands. Luddy dropped the tire iron and gripped her neck with both hands, pressing his thumbs against her windpipe. He felt the cartilage crush. Gerty twitched but Luddy kept squeezing until she was silenced, her sparkling blue eyes had rolled back in her head so that only the whites showed.

Luddy recalled the elation he felt upon witnessing the life leave Gerty's body. He had felt amazingly powerful yet calm as he touched her breasts and the straw-colored hair between her legs.

As apprehension set in, Luddy backed the car farther beneath the expressway on-ramp to keep it out of sight until he figured out what to do next. A homeless man was asleep in a large cardboard box, his arms and legs spread across his worldly possessions. Luddy kicked him in the stomach and told him to beat it. Dazed by alcoholic stupor, the barefoot man cradled a few items and ran away into the night.

Luddy was frantic. He needed time to think. He knew he wasn't willing to go jail for killing Gerty. She was nothing. A slut. The way he saw it, she had brought this problem upon him and now he had to deal with it.

Luddy flattened a sheet of the hobo's cardboard and tucked it into the car trunk, then set Gerty's limp body atop it and covered her with a canvas tarp. He drove slowly, almost trancelike, toward a stretch of abandoned piers on the East Boston waterfront. He parked the car next to a loading dock between two dilapidated and boarded-up brick warehouses, switched off the engine and waited to see if anyone else was around. His heart was beating faster than he'd ever felt it and beads of sweat had formed across his brow.

Luddy spread Gerty's body on the ground beneath the loading dock. He had to hunch over as he used the hacksaw in his toolbox to saw off her feet and hands, making quick work of it. Although he was strong, the head proved more difficult and he cursed as he sawed until, finally, the cervical column gave way. He was relieved to see Gerty didn't have any tattoos because he would have had to cut those off as well.

Luddy collected the body parts in the canvas tarp and tossed them into the car trunk, astonished that a human head was nearly as heavy as a bowling ball. He lifted Gerty's torso, staggered to the water's edge and let it fall into the water. He heard the splash in the dark but when he looked down from the wooden pier he couldn't see it. His shirt and pants were a bloody mess. He was sweating heavily and short of breath.

Acting on pure adrenaline that night, Luddy had driven north on Interstate 95 and exited at Newburyport. He followed the road leading toward Amesbury and stopped the car on the Chain Bridge, a 225-foot suspension bridge that spans a branch of the Merrimack River. He quickly tossed Gerty's hands, feet and head into the fast flowing water, praying the current would carry them to the ocean on the next tide.

Just thinking about that night more than a dozen years ago made him shudder as the massive container ship rolled and pitched in the waves. Chills ran down his spine and goosebumps spread across his arms. Gerty's disappearance remained a mystery. Unsolved. In police parlance, it was a cold case. And once the newspapers reported that she was known to work the streets, the political pressure on the police to find the killer slacked way off. After all, it wasn't as though she were the daughter of some senator or millionaire businessman. She wasn't even a U.S. citizen. Her death wouldn't cause a ripple.

After the first slaying, the others came easier. Like any other skill, it was all about making mistakes and learning to correct them. Luddy told himself that soon he'd be a pro. The hooker in the red dress that he'd left in a cornfield somewhere north of Boston had been the easiest of all – eager to earn her drug money and get back to her squalid apartment to shoot up. Only she never got there. Instead, she got an ice pick to the heart. Luddy scolded himself for not burying her body.

CHAPTER 38

August 1986
Boston, Massachusetts

A SECOND DATE

Decker was sitting on the stone steps with two cups of coffee when Summers exited the Superior Court building in Government Center lugging a heavy leather briefcase.

It was just after 4 p.m. and the criminal case in which Summers was testifying had recessed for the day. Her blonde hair was confined to the top of her head by an elegant French braid. She was wearing a knee-length maroon skirt, white cotton blouse and conservative pumps.

Decker, clad in white painter's pants, green short-sleeve pullover and casual loafers, stood and held out the coffee cups. "I swear I didn't get these at the hospital cafeteria," he said, flashing a smile.

Summers laughed. She hadn't seen him since their dramatic evening atop Orient Heights and the following morning in the hospital emergency room. Even though she had ignored the three messages he had since left on her office phone, she was happy to see him, her heart revving at a beat she hadn't felt in years. She accepted the coffee and they stood talking on the steps.

The past two weeks had been a whirlwind, she said, with mandatory counseling for trauma, a slew of medical appointments and all sorts of paperwork, not the least of which was a detailed account of her being held captive by a

261

suspected serial killer. Her left eye was no longer blackened and many of the contusions from the blows she suffered had turned yellow and were fading. Her lips, too, had returned to their perfectly sensuous shape.

Summers had chosen to return to work far sooner than would most people faced with the same circumstances. As she put it, "I didn't want to just sit around feeling sorry for myself and having people look at me with that oh-that-poor-girl expression. Luddy Pugano is still out there and I want to find the son-of-a-bitch."

Decker asked plenty of questions about her recuperation but tip-toed around the sexual assault. He knew from the lab reports that Summers wasn't raped, but Luddy Pugano had touched her in ways that might leave behind emotional scars.

As for Luddy, there were two theories being bantered about by the State Police – he was hiding somewhere along the East Coast between Maine and New Jersey, probably in a motel under a phony name, or was already dead, eliminated by organized crime figures who feared he might talk about their exploits if captured.

"Do you buy either one?"

"I'm not sure. I spoke again with Celeste Pugano who claims she hasn't seen him or heard from him. Of course she isn't going to tell us even if she did, but I got the sense she was telling the truth in her own way. She was very embarrassed that I was the one he abducted."

Decker was about to ask her another question about the investigation but instead said, "Why didn't you return my calls?"

Summers hesitated before answering. "Because you're a private investigator and I'm a police officer. We may be working on the same case, but we have significantly different interests."

"If we weren't working on the same case, would you return my calls?"

"That would depend on what you were calling about."

"A second date."

Summers laughed pleasantly. "That's right. Our first one wasn't so spectacular."

"So you'd consider a second one?"

Summers lifted the heavy briefcase. "I need to get home."

"For what? To feed your cat?"

"I don't have a cat."

"But if you did, you wouldn't need to rush home to feed it if you'd already done that in the past 24 hours."

"Why are we talking about a cat that I don't own?"

"That's a good question. Let's talk about something else. What about dinner?"

Summers rolled her eyes and started walking with her briefcase. Decker caught up and took it from her.

"I'm going to my car."

"I'll walk with you."

"If you insist."

The car was parked behind the courthouse. Summers locked the briefcase in the trunk. She was about to get into the driver's seat but Decker held the door closed.

"Just dinner."

"You are persistent."

Together they walked to the Oceanaire Seafood Room on Court Street, an old-style steakhouse with an interior décor that evoked a 1930s luxury liner. Summers instructed the waiter to bring water with no ice. When asked if she would like something stronger before ordering from the menu, she politely declined, telling the waiter it was too early in the day and there was still work to be done. Decker smiled as he ordered a bottle of Amarone, announcing he was in the mood for something Italian because it was well past the working hours of those who had toiled since sunup. Summers frowned disapprovingly. The waiter cautiously backed away, returning a few minutes later with the bottle and two wine glasses. He looked to Decker for guidance.

"We'll have a dozen of the featured oysters. You can just uncork the bottle and leave it," he said.

"What if I don't like oysters?"

"You don't like oysters?"

"I didn't say that. But you didn't ask me if I do or don't."

"I'm sorry. Do you like oysters?'

"Are you always this way?"

"I thought you'd like them."

"You hardly know me."

"I'd like to get to know you. Will you have some wine?"

Decker lifted the bottle but Summers spread her hand over the mouth of her glass. He feigned sadness, rubbing his eyes as though he was wiping away tears. "Our second date is already going down hill."

"We're not on a date, Decker."

"What do you call this?"

"A meeting. We're eating."

Decker poured himself a glass of wine and made much of how delicious it tasted. The waiter set the plate of oysters on the table along with two smaller plates. "We'll have two bowls of the bouillabaisse," Decker said.

Summers just shook her head, astonished by his brazenness. "What if I don't like bouillabaisse?"

"You don't like bouillabaisse?"

"I didn't say that."

"Then you like bouillabaisse?

"Pour me some wine."

Summers momentarily lowered her guard, making it plain to see she was overwhelmingly attracted to the handsome young man across the table. As Decker poured, her face lit up with a 1,000-watt smile and he basked in its glow.

Decker proposed a toast. "To our second date."

"To our second date."

After the third glass of wine, Summers admitted she enjoyed studying Decker's face with its light stubble that lent him a distinctly roguish look.

"Roguish?"

"Yes. Roguish."

"Well, I like your French braid. I think it makes you look like royalty."

"Royalty?"

"Yes. Royalty."

Nearly two hours had elapsed since they entered the restaurant and the wine was gone. The dinner conversation had run the gamut from childhood memories to family histories to what each wanted out of life. The September sun washed across the Public Garden, enveloping them in late-summer warmth as they strolled the paths amid the flowers.

The wine had made Summers light-hearted. She was having fun. She wanted to forget about Luddy Pugano. She wanted to ride the swan boats but they were already closed for the day. Instead they walked and talked along Commonwealth Avenue, enjoying the European flavor of the tree-lined boulevard with its bronze monuments to the famous. It was evening when they returned to the courthouse where the mood turned awkward. They hugged briefly and ended their outing with a handshake.

Over the next week, Decker led their return to the Public Garden where they glided across the lagoon on the swan boats and later dined at a Thai restaurant in Chinatown. Both acted as though they were just friends, ignoring the sexual tension. After work one day, Summers on a whim bought three summer dresses at a Downtown Crossing boutique, three pairs of thin-strap feminine heels, a small pile of bras and underwear from Victoria's Secret, and forced herself to put on lipstick.

Although both were aware their respective bosses were interested in the whereabouts of Luddy Pugano, neither brought it up in conversation. It was a fact that just got in the way.

Summers knew for certain she was finally over her breakup with the charming, renowned and frequently obnoxious Dr. Chandler Hughes. The split had occurred nearly a year ago and she seldom missed him. At first she'd found herself riding the Men Are Dogs Bandwagon, swearing she'd never again get involved in an intimate relationship.

Eventually she conceded to going on a few dates, but those were with cops and the subject of discussion was usually limited to law enforcement. Some of those cops were really good guys but she was bored by their black-and-white view of life, the good-versus-evil with no room for gray. Now, her every thought was of Decker. If she were clairvoyant, she would have known that Decker's mind was awhirl with thoughts and visions of Hannah Summers.

Decker had never met anyone so down-to-earth, with a tell-it-like-it-is attitude. Even more surprisingly, Summers was strikingly beautiful but seemed to pay her looks little attention. She seldom wore makeup and not once had he seen her gazing blissfully in a mirror.

After six years of combat experience, Decker instinctively knew whenever he was in a dangerous situation, and that now included his heart because it beat faster whenever Hannah Summers was around. Emmett Decker understood without a doubt that he was in love.

CHAPTER 39

August 1986
County Cork, Ireland

CORK AND A BOTTLE

From the rail of the massive ship, Luddy's eyes absorbed the rich texture of the city, the church spires and bell towers, the lighthouse, the busy harbor, the quaint streets and the green hills beyond.

"You must return to the container while we unload," the captain instructed. "Once we are on land, you can go."

"I thought my passport gave me permission to be in the country."

"It does. But you do not have permission to be aboard this vessel. You are not listed on the passenger manifest. So technically, you would be a stowaway and the authorities would arrest you."

"How long do I have to stay in the container?"

"Until it has been offloaded. When we reach the terminal, the containers will be lifted off by crane. Don't be alarmed if you feel it rising because in a few moments it will be set down securely on the dock."

"You still haven't told me who I'm supposed to meet."

"It has all been arranged," the captain said. "We on the ship are to deliver you to Ireland, and that we have done. I'm certain you will soon meet your hosts."

Luddy looked worried. He reluctantly gathered the sea bag they'd given him and shuffled toward the bright orange container. A smiling crewman held the door open.

"Bon voyage," the crewman said, latching the door so that Luddy was again left in total darkness. "We'll be sure not to leave you at Spike Island." Luddy heard the crewman laugh.

The Port of Cork was a flurry of activity. As the container ship passed Roche's Point Lighthouse, ferries churned the harbor where freighters and cruiseships were anchored, awaiting tugs that would nestle them into their berths. The Shandon Church steeple could be seen from nearly all around.

Luddy felt a pit in his stomach as the orange container went airborne and then banged to a landing, the metallic clanging filling the confined space. An hour passed, then two, before he heard the latch squeak and squeal and a shaft of light entered the dark cavern. Luddy squinted at the two faces aimed in his direction. The men chuckled. "Fergus will be glad to hear he made it to Cork alive," commented the lanky one in his early twenties.

"Let's go, Mr. Campbell," said the older man whose face was a map of wrinkles. "Come on now, time's a wasting."

Luddy hoisted the sea bag on his shoulder and followed them to a brown panel van. "In you go," said the wrinkled man. "I'm afraid you won't be in Cork long enough to kiss the Blarney Stone."

"A shame," remarked the younger. "I climbed those castle stairs when I was a mere, tongue-tied lad of 18. But once I kissed the stone, I became an eloquent poet."

The older man shoved the lanky kid toward the driver's side of the van. "You never stop talking, that's for sure."

Luddy didn't know what to make of them. They didn't seem liked hardened underworld professionals. The van wove through the narrow streets of Cork until it reached the outskirts of the city and picked up speed. The men offered

Luddy a can of the local beer. It was warm but he drank it. He felt suddenly rejuvenated. He was off the ship and in Ireland. He repeated the country's name to himself aloud. "Ireland."

Luddy was thrilled by the prospect of foreign travel. Just the sound of the phrase was enough to make him smile. "I'm a foreign traveler," he said to himself aloud. He had waited more than 40 years to see a country besides the United States. He didn't care if it was Ireland or Antarctica.

Luddy often felt unsophisticated and he bristled in Nemo's whenever the newcomers engaged in conversation about all the places they'd visited – London, Paris, Rome. Some of them had been on African safaris. The only safaris in Eastie were pub crawls, as when the men informed their wives or girlfriends in the local slang that they were "going out on safari."

Nearly three hours later, the van stopped at a scenic overlook that framed the Blackstairs Mountains. Luddy was hungry. They entered a pub and ordered beer and mutton stew. Luddy relaxed and looked around. The pub wasn't all that different from Nemo's, but it exuded more of a slow-paced calm and serenity. If there was a television set, it wasn't in view. Before they had finished the stew, a tall, thin, angular man with penetrating blue eyes, reddish hair and a ruddy complexion entered the pub and sat down at their table. He introduced himself as Sinn Fein, which made Luddy's two companions roar with laughter.

"Actually, it's Sean Fitzpatrick," he said, extending a hand to Luddy who hesitantly gripped it. "I'll be your, what should we call it? Your guide until you're settled. You'll be staying with me until we make other arrangements."

Fitzpatrick had been given no information about the man he agreed to hide other than he was from Boston and on the run from the law. It was simply a favor to Fergus Cavanaugh and showed his loyalty to the IRA.

Fitzpatrick grabbed a chair, ordered a beer and explained the local geography. The Blackstairs Mountains were part of a remote, rural setting that resonated with hardy tourists willing to pay money to stay and hike the rugged trails. Other than that, the mountains were in the boondocks where there wouldn't be much to do, which is why they made a great hideout.

Luddy made himself at home, feeling a bit like a celebrity. Fitzpatrick catered to his every whim and the host's 16-year-old daughter, Molly, seemed excited to have such an unusual visitor. She'd never met an American. Luddy noted the way the girl sashayed through the small house as though it were a castle.

Bright-eyed Molly Fitzpatrick left for school each morning and upon her return began cleaning the house. Luddy gazed at her as she scrubbed the kitchen floor on her knees, her reddish hair hanging down so that the tresses nearly swept the surface. She was perspiring when she raised her head and caught him staring at her.

Luddy was charming and flirtatious and the teenage girl reacted in kind, pleased by the attention. He told her stories about Boston and fishing, about eating so many boiled lobsters that he could hardly walk. She laughed robustly so that her breasts jiggled. For the second day in a row she offered him beer, which he gladly accepted.

Luddy memorized the girl's full figure, each curve of her taut body as she swept the livingroom carpet and dusted the side tables. After his second beer, he began to relax. He playfully pinched her on the butt as she moved past him carrying a mop and pail. The girl jumped and shrieked, feigning pain while looking coyly back over her shoulder. Luddy felt himself getting aroused and wondered what she might do if he tried to tickle her, maybe wrap his arms around her and pull her body into his. He didn't know what time her father would be home but his reverie ended because Sean Fitzpatrick walked through the front door before the girl returned from dumping the pail of soapy water.

Luddy's first week in the Blackstairs Mountains passed uneventfully. Except for his interactions with Molly, he was bored, but as he reminded himself, he wasn't behind bars or, worse, dead. He was surprised when Fitzpatrick excitedly entered into his room before dawn and told him

270

to gather his things, they were leaving immediately. They needed to get to a cabin nearer to County Carlow before daybreak.

In the car, Fitzpatrick explained that there was a rat in the organization, someone who had informed the police of Luddy's whereabouts. When he found out who it was, he'd kill him with his bare hands.

CHAPTER 40

September 1986
Boston, Massachusetts

THE IRISH JIG

Decker felt sickened when he found out for certain that Luddy had managed to leave the country aboard a container ship. It had taken hours of painstaking research and some physical coercion, but he finally obtained the name of the ship, a cargo manifest, crew list and sailing schedule. Then he called Carrington who had been awaiting an update.

"Where is he?"

"Ireland."

"Jesus Christ. I need you to find him. Skip Lehman was just here. He wasn't in a jovial mood but he believes Mr. Pugano is hiding out somewhere on the East Coast. When I tell him our target is in Ireland, he's going to go ballistic and I don't blame him."

"I know the Maersk Athena Express reached Cork after a 12-day crossing and spent four days unloading. There must have been a contact waiting for him at the dock. Any suggestions?"

"Skip Lehman isn't the type of guy to let things go, and that's especially true in this case. I need you to come into the office for a briefing with some Executive Cover employees who are familiar with the country and the key people who can get things done there."

"I don't think the IRA is going to help. Fergus Cavanaugh was one of their rock stars before he relocated to the United States. But the British will certainly do their part to help capture and extradite him."

"I don't think Mr. Lehman is interested in obtaining assistance from the IRA or the British judicial system. He's not interested in extradition."

Decker mulled over what he was hearing. "Mr. Lehman feels certain his daughter is dead?"

"That's correct."

"Were your people ever able to track down Ben Tillman in Nepal? He might be able to provide some insight into the worry dolls, like which village made them in Guatemala and where they were purchased. If those details and the artistic style match the doll found on the boat, then Mr. Lehman has good reason to believe his daughter won't be coming home. But if there isn't a match, then there's always the possibility that…"

"Stop shitting rainbows and unicorns, Decker," Carrington snarled, cutting him off in mid-sentence. "Jenny Lehman is as dead as all the other young women Luddy Pugano murdered."

"Sorry, I just…"

"Don't be sorry. Just be realistic. We're dealing with a madman, an unpredictable wildcard bent on inflicting pain in the lives of innocent people. And yes, we located Ben Tillman in the Himalayas. He was certainly surprised to see our team. He cried when he found out Jenny was a likely murder victim. He actually had one of those stupid fuckin' dolls in his pocket. We have it here."

"Does it look like the one from the boat?"

"Just come in and we'll get you on a plane. You won't need a ticket."

"Yes sir."

Within hours, Decker had sent several coded messages to a small group of ex-military friends and boarded a private Gulfstream jet bound for Cork International Airport. He left Summers an apologetic voice message, saying he was leaving Boston immediately and would be in Ireland until further notice. He was the only passenger aboard the plane.

Studying the map he'd been given, he knew the Cork airport was approximately six kilometers south of the city near Farmers Cross. The plane landed at a private airstrip where Decker was met by a black Land Rover carrying three men clad in black tactical gear. He was glad to see his old pals – Memphis, Claymore and Poker Face. Claymore handed him a duffle bag filled with lethal devices and an M16 rifle. "To help you get a good night's sleep," he said cheerfully.

By the way they talked and carried themselves, it was obvious Decker's companions were most likely ex-special forces -- Delta or Rangers, possibly Navy SEALs. Over the next two weeks, the small tactical team scouted a succession of remote villages, but Luddy's handlers always seemed to know when the posse was scheduled to arrive. It was frustrating. When the team members described Luddy Pugano to villagers, it became evident he had been there and was long gone, the trail cold. It reminded Decker of missions in Lebanon when he had been assured the person of interest would be hiding at a certain location, but when he and the other soldiers arrived, it became obvious they'd been played.

Decker was perplexed by the situation. When he called Executive Cover on a scrambled phone line to report another failure, Carrington was beyond angry, threatening to come to Ireland himself and finish the job if Decker was incapable. Decker sensed there was a security leak, but he had no idea where to look. He knew only that Fergus Cavanagh, who from all accounts on the street had arranged Luddy's getaway, still had strong connections to the die-hard IRA. Among the toughest, most dedicated IRA soldiers, Cavanagh was legend. If he needed something from them, they considered it done.

The underground information network was proving more efficient than the intelligence reports flowing from Carrington's new-fangled fax machine.

Decker sent Carrington a coded telegram, suggesting he take action to find the leak because until then, capturing the target was highly unlikely. Carrington knew Decker was right, but he wasn't going to admit it. He did, however, share the suggestion with Lehman, who immediately contacted the company's Security Division and ordered that all forms of communication related to the Irish Mob be closely scrutinized for a possible breach.

CHAPTER 41

September 1986
Boston, Massachusetts

YOU CAN'T TRUST THE IRISH

Macusovich and Summers had agreed to request
assistance from Interpol, which in turn had contacted
Ireland's primary police force, An Guarda Siochana or The
Guard. Agent Finley had been against the decision, saying
internal security would be weakened if too many agencies
were apprised of the situation.

"You can't trust the Irish, and I'm Irish," he declared,
trying to make a joke of it once his professional opinion had
been rejected.

During a late-September meeting of the district
attorneys in Suffolk and Essex counties, the decision-makers
scraped up enough funds to send Macusovich and Summers
to join the search for Luddy Pugano in Ireland, at least for a
couple of weeks. The FBI paid for Finley's travel expenses.

When they arrived at Sean Fitzpatrick's home,
accompanied by a heavily-armed Irish police tactical team,
they felt confident Luddy would be captured. They were
disappointed to find him gone, the rooms still warm from the
woodstove. Finley made a show of complaining that Irish
law enforcement couldn't keep its mouth closed long enough
to allow capture of the suspect responsible for the murder
of at least a dozen American women. It was unacceptable
and a disgrace, he claimed, but the others weren't listening.

Both Macusovich and Summers telephoned their respective commanders in Massachusetts to report the mission had been foiled.

Back in Eastie, Fergus was pleased to learn that Luddy had not only reached Cork without incident but had managed to escape the first of what were to become a series of police raids. He instructed Jimmy Two Cubes to personally relay the news to Celeste. Before the month was through, he would send Celeste two similar reports, in each case Luddy having escaped in the nick of time. It appeared the $8,000 she had put up was being well spent, he said, tossing the latest telegram from Finley into the top drawer of his desk. The FBI agent's message had been terse and to the point: *Dogs sure to bark before intruders arrive.*

Fergus understood Finley had access to the classified intelligence reports that popped up whenever Luddy or somebody who looked like him was spotted, which inevitably led to plans for another police raid. Fergus' friends in the IRA gladly passed on the information that allowed Luddy to stay one step ahead of the police. It was a dangerous game, but until the police gave up the search in frustration, Finley knew he had to keep playing.

Rane was spending most of his before-and-after work hours making amends with Kaleigh who was still smoldering about his questionable relationship with Paige. Kaleigh had also unveiled to him her feelings for Decker and her intention to continue modeling for art students at the museum, whether he approved or not.

Kaleigh had driven to Connecticut to visit her parents on a whim while Luddy Pugano was stalking Summers at the nature sanctuary in Brookline. She was upset, confused and needed to get away from Boston in order to think, to sort out what was important and what should be cast aside. She hadn't even called in sick at the museum or told her roommates where she was going. She just left and it wasn't until she returned that she heard about Decker's dramatic rescue of Hannah Summers. She felt jealous of the pretty police lieutenant.

During the following weeks, Rane wooed Kaleigh's roommates in an effort to solicit their support, frequently bringing them pizza, wine and pastries from Bova's Bakery in the North End, which he knew they would devour.

Rane had grudgingly written the story of Decker's rescue, focusing mostly on how the police had allowed a serial killer to escape. The news story had described Decker as a fledgling private investigator who coincidentally had been working in the neighborhood and spotted Summers being assaulted by the Boston Butcher on a hill in Orient Heights.

Rane had no desire to tell Boston Tribune readers how Decker saved the day, but even slightly ignoring the end result would have been seen as pettiness by those in the know and exposed him as unprofessional. He was forced to admit that Soldier Boy had cut Summers down off the burning cross with his knife, held her in his arms and tended her wounds. Besides, several of Paige's photographs accompanied the story, including what would become the award-winning image of handsome Decker holding the beautiful, almost-naked Summers in his arms with the illuminated cross in the background. The editors had the photograph enlarged so that it covered the entire front page. The spot news excellence had earned Paige plenty of kudus from her colleagues who were already talking about a potential Pulitzer, but Rane chose to act as though she barely deserved the recognition. "Good eye," was all he said when they passed each other in the corridor just outside the newsroom.

Paige had stopped at that moment and looked at him in an imploring way as though she anticipated something more, perhaps an explanation. She asked herself, was he really holding this against her, the fact that she had done her job and done it professionally? Did the photograph make him feel like a loser? A cuckold? Was he really angry that it wasn't him who was the hero, but Decker?

Rane kept walking down the corridor outside the newsroom without looking back. It was as though he had become a complete stranger.

CHAPTER 42

October 1986
County Wicklow, Ireland

SPENDING TIME WITH THE NATIVES

The three girls were clearly having a grand time, sipping pints of Guinness in the dimly-lit pub at the edge of Baltinglass Village, a small settlement in County Wicklow with an abundance of ancient ruins, including Baltinglass Abbey and stone passage tombs that dated back to the Stone Age.

Luddy listened to them telling stories and giggling. He guessed they were of post-secondary-school age but not much older than 20.

Luddy studied them as they talked and drank. Twice he heard one of the girls say, "Tess, you're awful. You shouldn't even be thinking things like that."

All three girls broke out in shrill laughter. "It was so small, a little bitty thing, no bigger than my pinky finger," observed Tess, smoothing her shoulder-length auburn hair and gathering it with an elastic band. "I told the lad, 'What do you plan to do with that?' I wouldn't have said a word, but he'd been so cocky all night."

"What did he say?"

"Yes, tell us."

"He told me it was more than enough because he knew how to use it. I nearly spit up my beer."

The two other girls shrieked again and ordered

another round of Guinness from the waitress who demanded to know what they had found so funny. Tess held up a hand and waved her pinky finger. Her two companions looked at the waitress as if to say, don't mind her, she's bonkers.

The tallest girl, whose spiked white hair and dark-rimmed eyeglasses gave her face an owlish appearance, acknowledged she had the opposite problem – a boyfriend with no interest in bedding her.

Luddy heard the tall girl, who the others addressed as Brigid, announce loudly, "I'm going to my grave a virgin unless I can get out of this village."

I'd like the opportunity to change that, Luddy thought, inching his chair around to get a better look at the three of them. He ordered an Irish whisky and avoided small talk with the other patrons, just as Fitzpatrick had advised. He had been warned not to strike up conversations or encourage them with anyone who might question his identity, and to stay out of the local pubs. Fitzpatrick had bluntly said, 'Loose lips sink ships, and alcohol has a way of loosening people's lips. So stay the fuck out of the pubs.'

"We're all going to get out of this place," vowed Myrna, who raised her glass to her two companions. "To Prince Charming and not dying virgins."

Myra facetiously pressed her fingers to her lips and rolled her eyes toward Tess. "I guess I'm only speaking for myself and Brigid."

"Now don't be spreading lies about me," Tess said with a smile.

When the waitress returned, the girls ordered food. "I think some bangers would be appropriate," said Brigid. "Preferably big ones."

"Yes," Tess heartily agreed. "Give it to her take-a-way so she can enjoy them later at home." Again the girls giggled merrily.

The waitress guffawed. "You girls are having a devilish time. Better get something into your stomachs."

They all ordered the Dublin Coddle and continued their good-natured bantering well into the evening. When

Tess burped loudly, the girls all broke out into tears of laughter. Brigid tried an imitation but couldn't manage to bark up the air. They were being silly.

Luddy nursed two more pints of Guinness and ate a plate of flounder, which made him think of Boston. The waitress twice attempted to engage him in conversation but Luddy didn't respond so she quit trying. When the waitress announced last call, the girls ordered a final round of beers.

Luddy ignored them and stepped out into the cool evening. He leaned against an ancient limestone wall and trained his eyes on the main road. An occasional passing car broke the quiet. The place was truly remote, the River Slaney gently flowing through the village that seemingly hadn't changed in a thousand years.

On the way to the most recent safe house in County Wicklow, just south of Dublin, the driver had prattled on for half an hour about the Vanishing Triangle, which is the name the locals used for this region near the Wicklow Mountains because several young women had disappeared there over the past decade.

"Supposedly there's a serial killer out here in these parts, but I don't think that's anything you need worry about," he had said.

Luddy wasn't certain whether the driver was an IRA operative and just being coy, or truly didn't know about his passenger's criminal background.

"I'll lock my doors and windows," Luddy had wryly replied.

But now, as he leaned against the stone wall and gazed up at the night sky, he wondered who had killed those women, and whether that person was still alive, perhaps among those enjoying a Guinness this very night at the comfortable pub in Baltinglass.

One by one, the customers departed. The three girls were the last out the door. Luddy heard the waitress bid them goodnight and watched the pub owner dim the lights and lock the door. The girls chatted for a few moments, their laughter carrying across the stillness.

When the girls split up, Tess headed off alone toward the village center while Myrna and Brigid stayed together as they walked the darkened road. Luddy followed at a distance, halting only when the two girls entered a modest house whose front door opened directly onto the road. He was about to head back to the hideout when Brigid reappeared and starting walking along the road at a quickened pace. Twice she looked back over her shoulder as though she sensed the presence of an animal.

Luddy could see the road followed the curve of a cemetery. He hoisted himself over a low stone wall and ran through the cemetery to the entrance where he waited behind a pillar. He listened closely for Brigid's footsteps. When he was sure she was only a shadow's length away, he stepped out from behind the pillar, his hands ready to grip her by the neck. The girl screamed loudly. Luddy punched her in the stomach, knocking the air out of her. As she struggled to regain her breath, he dragged her into the cemetery and pounced upon her, tearing her cotton dress. The girl tried to fight but Luddy's weight held her in place. He cupped one hand over her mouth and explored her body with the other, ripping away her underwear. The girl bit down hard on his fingers, drawing blood. Luddy punched her face, breaking her horn-rimmed eyeglasses, pummeling her head until she was borderline unconscious. She groaned in revulsion as he tried to force himself inside her but he couldn't get hard.

Disappointed in himself, Luddy pulled up his pants and cinched his belt. The girl had rolled over on her side between two gravestones. Moonlight reflected off her white hair. Luddy picked up a loose rock bigger than his hand and hammered it until the girl's skull was cracked, then tossed it aside. Her whitish hair was turning dark before his eyes. He dragged her body into the nearby woods and covered it with brush and downed tree branches, knowing the police would find it quickly once she was reported missing, but he didn't know what else to do. He hoped Fitzpatrick would move them to another safe house before a search got under way and that Molly would be with him.

CHAPTER 43

November 1986
Boston, Massachusetts

COMPANY RULES

Decker was eager to share the news with Carrington that a girl from Ireland's County Wicklow had been murdered, perhaps by Luddy Pugano. He felt badly for the girl and her family, of course, but the information provided by her death might put them back on the trail that had gone cold. When Decker and other members of the search team had returned from Ireland empty handed, Skip Lehman lapsed into an inconsolable tirade. He threatened to end their careers, Carrington's included, by putting negative assessments in their personnel files at Langley.

Decker, who at that point didn't know he had a personnel file with the spy agency, was standing near the window when Carrington entered the Executive Cover conference room, watching the college crew teams row along the Charles River. It was November, but there was no sign that winter was coming.

Without preface, Decker tossed a manila folder labeled Interpol Report on the table. "Open it."

As Carrington read the cover sheet and highlights, Decker provided his own narration. "Brigid O'Brien, age 19, disappeared after drinking in a small rural pub with friends last month in Ireland. Death by blunt force trauma. Attempted sexual assault evident. A lock of hair cut away."

Decker waited for Carrington to speak. When he didn't look up from the report, Decker asked, "Sound familiar?"

"Do we have an approximate date of death?"

"We do," said Decker. "Late October."

"Any witnesses?"

Decker shook his head slowly as a disappointed expression formed across his face. "The police have talked to people who regularly frequent that pub, but nobody seems to recall much. Too many alcohol-rattled brains, I imagine."

"Interpol knows we're privy to their intelligence gathering but we don't want them to know we're directly involved. They're already sharing information with the two Massachusetts State Police detectives, Andre Macusovich and Hannah Summers."

Carrington stopped speaking, as though waiting for Decker to comment. But all Decker said was, "Hmm."

Carrington locked eyes on Decker. "We know you've become involved with Detective Summers, at least as friends, which is understandable considering all that's happened. But we're not looking for partnerships, so you should be careful in that regard. As I explained earlier, what we do is private," he said.

Decker bristled at the professional jab. "I already have assets on the ground in Ireland," he said curtly. "They're interviewing villagers, grocery clerks, anyone who might have pumped petrol and noticed a man fitting Mr. Pugano's description."

"So what's our next course of action? I need to know what you're thinking because Mr. Lehman will be joining us in a few minutes," Carrington said. "He wants to reassure himself that you're the right man for the mission."

Decker joined Carrington at the window where they discussed the merits of crew competition and the beauty of the river that wends through Boston.

Lehman opened the door without knocking. There were no greetings exchanged.

"Sorry I'm late." He tossed his briefcase on the nearest chair. "This is good news. Now maybe we can find him."

"I'm certain we will, sir. The game is already in play," said Decker, who suggested they all sit at the round table in the middle of the room.

Carrington was clearly nervous. "Decker was just explaining that we already have boots on the ground," he said. "I'm sure you'd like to know the details."

Skip Lehman cleared his throat before he spoke. He locked eyes with Decker. "As you may have guessed, Executive Cover doesn't always operate in the same way other investigative services might."

Decker remained pokerfaced, nodding, elbows on the table, his palms pressed together as though in prayer.

"We have a situation here in which a madman has been allowed to go free. And now he's apparently started killing again, only in a new country. We can't let that continue," Lehman explained.

"Once we lock down on his position, we can snatch him, if that's what you want."

"That's not exactly what I had in mind."

Decker narrowed his eyes and focused on Lehman. "No *habeas corpus*, is that what you're saying?"

Carrington interjected so that his boss would have the option of not answering the question. "In most instances, our organization conforms to both domestic and international law, but occasionally the procedures must take a different route. And this is one of those occasions," he said.

"By our organization, you mean Executive Cover?" Carrington looked at Lehman for permission to continue.

"It's fair to say Executive Cover is part of a larger organization," Lehman said.

"Exactly," said Carrington.

"And I'm to assume both of you are members?"

"You may assume what you will," Carrington said.

"Should we be concerned that Luddy Pugano is simply a murderer and not a threat to national security."

Lehman's face flushed red. Carrington squirmed in his seat. When Lehman composed himself, he looked directly at Decker. "That miserable fuck murdered my daughter."

"Understood, sir. No need to explain."

Carrington seemed relieved. "So you're with us on this, no matter what the situation requires?"

Decker nodded. "I am," he said, looking first at Carrington and then Lehman, where his eyes lingered. "But one final question."

"Shoot," said Lehman.

"Where's the leak? Or should I say, who's the leak? Because we may start following a trail of fresh bodies and get there only to find the target has been relocated."

"We've got some theories and some evidence, neither of which I can discuss right now," said Lehman. "That's precisely why we didn't want to involve Interpol, the FBI, the State Police or any other agency for that matter."

"I'd like to leave as soon as possible," said Decker. "My men are waiting for my instructions."

"I fully agree. This is the best break we've had in over two months. You should leave tonight," said Lehman. "Start in Baltinglass and see where the trail takes you."

Once again, Decker left Summers a phone message saying he was headed to Ireland with no forewarning. He offered no other information, knowing that he couldn't, but his heart beat a different rhythm.

During the days in Boston between trips to Ireland, Decker and Summers met for lunch at Maison Robert, an elegant French restaurant with an outdoor café in Boston's Old City Hall. They ate shrimp cocktails, drank champagne and basked in New England's waning autumn sunshine. Summers was soaking up the rays, Wayfarer sunglasses perched on her head, as she turned to Decker and said, "This is just too freakin' perfect . I don't know what to do with it."

And Decker, his lips shaped into an amused grin, had responded, "You don't need to do anything with it. This is your life. Just live it."

On another afternoon, they visited the Museum of Fine Arts and wandered for hours through the Impressionist galleries. Talking about the artists and paintings was an easy way to spend time together without having to talk about their respective jobs or where their feelings for each other were headed.

Although both had been on separate assignments to Ireland, neither shared specific details. Instead, they dwelled on the superficial – the green Irish countryside, the friendly people, the slower-paced lifestyle. In some ways, their inability to be honest drove a wedge in their blooming romance, but neither wanted to acknowledge it.

CHAPTER 44

December 1986
County Wicklow, Ireland

THE GUEST FROM HELL

Decker sat at a tiny table and sipped Jameson as he tried to envision Luddy in the quiet pub. He asked himself, where would Luddy have chosen to sit? To whom might he have talked, and about what?

"You're definitely not from around here," observed the waitress, exposing a smile of crooked teeth. "Come to Baltinglass looking for excitement?"

Decker grinned. "I'm doing exactly what I came to do. Vacationing. A little R&R. Time off from work."

"And what is it that you do?"

"Sales. Plastic storage containers, mops, brushes, window squeegees, that sort of thing."

The waitress cocked her head sideways and screwed up her face. "What gives me the feeling that your telling tales?"

"Actually, I'm an accountant."

She playfully wrenched her thumb and forefinger around his muscular bicep and smiled. "I can see that."

"Colleen, let's hurry it up," the cook shouted from the kitchen's swinging door at the rear of the room, leaving no doubt someone's dinner was ready to be served.

"Seems you're being paged, Colleen," said Decker, emphasizing her name. When the dinner rush slowed, Decker

289

invited Colleen to sit and have a drink. She gladly accepted.

Small talk soon shifted to more serious matters, namely the recent murder of Brigid O'Brien. Decker revealed he was a private investigator attempting to gather information about the case in the event it was related to similar murders in the Boston area.

The waitress remembered the sullen man who had ordered a few pints of Guinness and a plate a flounder on the same night the O'Brien girl disappeared. The man was heavyset with dark piercing eyes that gave off an animal-like intensity, but he had hardly spoken to her. She thought it odd that he had asked why the beer wasn't ice cold.

"Gave me the creeps," she said. "He left the pub maybe ten minutes before those girls departed and we closed up. You're not the first one to come in here asking about what happened that night. The others were police – Americans, I think -- two men and a younger woman. The woman was polite, blonde and very pretty. They were with two of our local investigators who were rude and expected a free meal."

As Decker prepared to leave, she called out. "The fellow you're interested in, he paid in American dollars. I remember that because he left such a small tip."

Decker relayed to Carrington every bit of information about the creepy man who had dined in the pub on the night of the murder. He also interviewed Brigid O'Brien's two friends. Both described the teenager as fun, outgoing, trusting, but not someone who would go off with a stranger. Brigid sang in the church choir. She had a sheepdog named U2 that she loved. She visited her ailing grandfather nearly every day, bringing him soup and news of the outside world, at least as it pertained to Ireland. Neither girl had left her house since the killing.

Sean Fitzpatrick sent word to Fergus that Luddy was becoming disenchanted with his situation. The foul mood seemed ever present and on some days difficult to handle.

Fitzpatrick didn't realize Luddy was brooding in part about not being physically able to rape Brigid O'Brien before

290

her death nor make any headway with his host's teenage daughter, Molly. But his fatherly instinct sensed Luddy would harm Molly despite being a guest in his home. He asked himself how any man could be void of honor, which he valued, but he knew from past experience such people were out there in numbers.

Fitzpatrick knew they'd soon have to move to another safe house, farther from Dublin, perhaps all the way to the northern border. He had plenty of IRA contacts in Belfast but didn't want to call in any favors. So for now, he'd try to do whatever was necessary on his own rather than get members of his cell involved. He was the designated Boston liaison for all business and political matters and he wanted to keep it that way. There were deals in the works that would bring him a new level of prestige and perhaps some extra income.

Fitzpatrick was in the small market picking out cheeses and fresh vegetables for the upcoming move when he spotted a good-looking blonde coming toward him at a determined pace.

"Mr. Fitzpatrick?"

"Yes?"

"I'm Detective Summers with the Massachusetts State Police," she said, flashing her gold shield. "I'd like to talk to you."

Fitzpatrick quickly glanced in every direction as though preparing to flee. He spotted two men who looked like cops standing at the front door to the market. There were two more at the side entrance.

"What can I do for you?"

"Can we go outside and talk?"

"Frankly, I'd rather not be out on the street with you," he said, stepping slowly toward a quieter corner of the shop. "And could you please put that badge back in your pocket?" Summers came straight to the point. "We believe you're hiding Luddy Pugano who is wanted by the police in Massachusetts for a series of murders."

Fitzpatrick acted surprised.

"Cut the crap, Mr. Fitzpatrick. We're talking about a sadistic killer who rapes and tortures young women before he kills them. There's a very good probability that he killed Brigid O'Brien right here in your beloved country."

Fitzpatrick's thoughts went immediately to Molly. He looked at his watch. He knew she was back at the safe house with Martin Campbell, who apparently was using an alias.

Fitzpatrick's face paled with concern.

Summers continued. "He's wanted for murders in Massachusetts and most likely New Hampshire, maybe in Nevada, and there are probably bodies buried in other places as well."

Summers knew it was time to set the hook.

"We know your daughter accompanies you on some of your travels. She's a very beautiful girl and from everything I've been told, she's a caring person with plenty of love in her heart. You're a lucky man."

Fitzpatrick understood precisely where the detective was headed and why she had offered such high praise for his daughter. He inhaled deeply and held his breath, trying to control his emotions. "How many women do you think he's murdered?"

"At least ten, maybe more. Many more."

Fitzpatrick's face turned ghostly white. "Love of god," he muttered, dropping the bunch of carrots he was holding. He picked up the carrots and distractedly set them back in the wooden basket, stood completely upright to his full six-foot-three and cleared his throat. "I'm really not sure what you're talking about. I don't know anyone by that name."

Summers frowned. "Look, I asked my partners if they'd let me speak to you first. They wanted to come in here and take you away in cuffs, but I don't think it needs to be done that way."

"There's nothing I can do."

"You mean you won't do anything."

"No. I mean there are powerful people in Boston who have arranged for his protection."

292

Summers didn't want to force the issue for fear of spooking him. "Maybe Luddy Pugano is no threat to your daughter. Maybe he looks at her differently because she's yours and you're his host. You're his protector and that makes her untouchable. I guess you can always ask your daughter if he has made her feel uncomfortable. Is she home alone with him right now?"

Fitzpatrick had noticed slight changes in the man he called Martin Campbell, since that's what was written on the passport and work visa. He hadn't been told much more than the man was a fugitive from the American justice system and a friend of those in control of Boston's Irish underworld, namely Desmond O'Malley and Fergus Cavanaugh. Of late there had been a bit of a swagger to his guest's step and he had taken to wearing a tweed snap-brim cap like those favored by men in the Irish countryside. Since they hadn't been shopping, Fitzpatrick knew Luddy had either borrowed or stolen the lid.

Just thinking about this man at home alone with his daughter made his blood pressure rise. He inadvertently bumped Summers as he headed without warning for the shop entrance.

Summers nodded to Agent Finley and one of the Irish police officers to let him pass. The two men stepped aside as Fitzpatrick ran to his car.

Later that afternoon, Finley called Fergus to give him the news that Summers had tracked down and talked to Fitzpatrick and that they needed to move Luddy to a new safe house immediately. He also called FBI headquarters in Boston to tell them Luddy was most likely holed up in a tenement house just south of Belfast, the address of which they were very close to identifying.

Finley suggested his colleagues at the FBI office make a courtesy call to the Massachusetts State Police, provide them with the same information about Luddy being in a Belfast tenement, and tell Detectives Macusovich and Summers to focus their attention on that northern city rather than waste time elsewhere. He preferred the intelligence report go through official channels rather than have it come directly from him.

Finley told the team he was opposed to raiding the present safe house in the Wicklow Mountains just over an hour's drive south of Dublin, contending they couldn't be sure if the public chat with Fitzpatrick in the market had already compromised any possibility of success. He also made it clear the FBI did not want blood on its hands in the event Fitzpatrick or his daughter were caught in the crossfire. After all, Luddy Pugano's police file indicated the man was adept with firearms and other weapons. And Fitzpatrick was an alleged IRA operative who undoubtedly had access to guns.

Macusovich disagreed. He believed the intelligence was solid and he wanted to raid the house before the occupants had opportunity to flee. The two Irish police detectives were on board with Macusovich and suggested they call for a tactical team.

It took an hour for the squad to assemble and devise a rudimentary plan that was mostly designed to keep the police from shooting each other. Another hour elapsed as the convoy of armored police vehicles sped toward the Wicklow Mountains. By the time the 20 officers surrounded the house and the command was given to move in, the occupants were gone.

Macusovich, Summers and Finley – each of whom had been given an expensive second chance to track down Luddy Pugano in Ireland -- were a day away from packing for the return flight home when a boy on a bicycle delivered a letter. The boy had done as instructed and waited until the woman police officer was alone. He handed her a white envelope and pedaled away as fast as his short legs would take him.

Summers tucked the envelope into the back pocket of her bluejeans, crossed the street from the small hotel where she, Macusovich and Finley were staying, and ordered a tea. Making sure nobody could see the contents, she opened the envelope and read the message: "Do not trust your friends. Meet me in Sligo tomorrow. Come alone. The courthouse steps on Teeling Street at noon." She inserted the sheet of paper into the envelope, casually walked to the fieldstone fireplace and tossed the envelope into the flames.

Summers knew Decker was still in Ireland but she wasn't sure how to reach him. She assumed any phone call would be monitored so she went to the telegraph office and sent him a message, care of Executive Cover in Boston. Carrington was puzzled by its arrival. The dispatch read: "DECKER. GOING TO SLIGO ALONE TOMORROW. COURTHOUSE ON TEELING STREET AT NOON IF INTERESTED. HANNAH."

Carrington used a scrambled line to call Decker's hotel room in Dublin and convey the message. "Do you know what this is all about?"

"Not really. But if Detective Summers is going to be there tomorrow at noon, she probably has good reason, so I should meet her."

"Do you trust her?"

"I do."

"You don't think she's the leak?"

"Absolutely not. She wants Luddy Pugano behind bars more than anyone I know."

"Then report when you get to Sligo."

Summers departed Dublin and drove along Route N4 with the morning light pouring over her shoulders. She left word at the hotel's front desk for Macusovich and Finley that she was feeling whimsical and would be renting a car, shopping, touring the countryside and making the most of her last day in Ireland. Privileges of being a woman, she wrote, adding a smiley face. She'd meet them at the airport.

The road trip took just over three hours with traffic, leaving her time enough to study the layout of the city square and the narrow streets leading to it. She noted the height of the surrounding buildings, the respective fields of fire and places that would afford cover in case she was walking into a trap.

Ten minutes before noon, she began making her way down narrow Teeling Street toward the ornate Sligo Circuit Courthouse with its multiple spires and turrets. Decker watched her from the street corner where he was hidden in the shadows. At noon, Summers found herself alone amid the pedestrian traffic that moved through the square and entered and exited the courthouse. She stood on the courthouse steps, tapping her foot anxiously and fidgeting with her black clutch purse. Decker had almost overlooked her. She was wearing a knee-length gray wool skirt, white blouse and black open-front cashmere sweater that contrasted nicely with her blonde tresses. A black lamb wool jacket was slung over her shoulder. Instead of the usual cop shoes or flats she wore low gray pumps and a single string of pearls highlighted her lovely neck. Decker thought the fashion-model clothes dovetailed nicely with her magazine-cover face. She was certainly a looker. The sun lent a reddish tint to her blonde hair that swept across her forehead and spilled onto her shoulders.

Sean Fitzpatrick was walking fast with his hands in the pocket of his coat. He was hunched over as though trying to hide his height. "Follow me," he quietly ordered as he passed in front of her.

Summers looked around for Decker. Maybe he hadn't received the telegram, or had chosen to ignore it, she thought. She followed Fitzpatrick down the narrow street and into an alley. Fitzpatrick was obviously nervous, his hands trembling and unable to light his cigarette.

"You were right. When I got back to the house yesterday, my daughter was crying. She claimed he tried to touch her, the pig. Of course he denied everything when I confronted him, but I know my daughter."

"I'm glad you got there before something awful happened."

"I, too," he said. "My daughter is waiting for me at a tea room a few doors down from the courthouse. I would

296

never leave her alone with him again. I feel such a fool."

"So where is he now?"

"He's back at the house in the Wicklow Mountains that I have the feeling the police already know about, but they may get thrown off the trail. I'm here trying to find another house in the northwest near the border. It's easy to come and go from Sligo," he said. "This city is a small port and there are plenty of boats willing to take you wherever your heart desires."

"Please tell me what it is that you want me to do."

Fitzpatrick paused a moment as though unsure he actually wanted to say what he was about to say. "I'd like to give him to you."

"Won't that put you in danger? Didn't you tell me you were following orders from very powerful people in Boston?"

"That's correct. I am. I'm protecting this man as a favor, but I'll not be sacrificing my daughter for the likes of them."

"Will they come after you?"

"It's hard to say. This man we're holding can do a lot of damage if he's allowed to go free. And if that happens, there are business matters in the works that very likely will not go forward as planned."

"Care to elaborate?"

"I've already said enough. But if you're willing to take him, he's yours."

"And after that?"

"I try not to think about it. My wife died in childbirth when Molly was six. Now she has only me."

"When would you like to surrender him?"

"Tomorrow. But we need to be careful. We're close to the northern border so there may be certain IRA men about who would like to take custody of him as much as you do. It would give them some clout with the Irish mob in Boston."

"How is that?"

"We know for fact that Fergus Cavanaugh doesn't want this Martin Campbell or whatever his name is to be running his mouth to the authorities back in The States. As long as the IRA can hold him here, they can threaten to release him at any moment, like a time bomb. He becomes a weapon."

"I understand," she said, keeping her eyes focused on the alley entrance. "I did as you suggested and came alone, but why here? Why Sligo? Why couldn't you tell me all this in Dublin?"

"Too many eyes in Dublin. I'm here looking for another safe house. And I wanted to see if you could be trusted."

"And why did you say that my friends can't be trusted? What do you know about them that I don't?"

"Only that the federal officer, the one from the FBI, stays in touch with Fergus Cavanaugh. If we move to a new safe house, he tells Fergus. If the cops are planning a raid, he tells Fergus, and off we go again. Now you know why every time you planned a raid, we knew you were coming hours in advance, sometimes days in advance."

"That fucker."

"That's one way to put it."

"What about my other partner?"

"We have no reason to suspect that the big fellah is on anyone's payroll except for the U.S. government's. He seems like a fine copper."

"That's good to hear. Why didn't you contact him instead of me?"

"Because my gut told me you were the best bet and the least likely to start shooting instead of talking."

"So do you have another safe house near Sligo?"

"No. It didn't work out. Not everyone wants to take a risk, even if they're poor and can make a bit of cash. But I have another idea."

"Just get me to Luddy Pugano and I'll take it from there."

Fitzpatrick nodded his willingness. "By tonight, my daughter and I will be back in the mountains. I'll explain to him that the IRA men are coming to take him away to hold him hostage and that he must come with me to a hideaway where nobody will find him. I'll say we will only be in this new place for a day, two at most, but no more, just long enough to arrange for a new safe house farther west near Galway."

"So where is this hideway?"

"Back the way you came, a short drive north of Dublin. It's called Knowth."

"What's so special about Knowth?"

"It's an ancient passage tomb. Ireland is full of them. Imagine grassy hillocks and massive rocks and a doorway leading into the bowels of the earth," he explained, handing Summers a tourist map with additional notes and sketches in his handwriting. "Supposedly they were used for holy ceremonies and to bury the dead. For all we know, they could have been built for food storage. Some people believe these chambers are clocks that tell the time by allowing light to pass through holes in the rock during various phases of the moon."

"And you plan to hide Luddy Pugano in one of these ancient tombs?"

"Knowth is the largest. Dowth and Newgrange are in the same vicinity. All part of the netherworld beneath this green land," Fitzpatrick said with a smile. "Almost all have chambers off the main tunnels where it would be easy to hide, at least for a short while. But the real reason for Knowth is that I have a friend who works there on staff. Once the public part of the tomb closes for the day, he's free to guide us to the lesser-known tomb that I've marked on the map."

"Can you trust this friend?"

"Absolutely. We grew up together throwing rocks and Molotov cocktails at the British soldiers. He knows the area better than most. There's a maze of connected underground chambers close to the main tomb in Knowth that are still under excavation. My friend says the archeologists only dig two or three times a year because they lack funds. They won't be back for weeks."

"How long do you plan to stay there?"

"Until you come for him."

"And when will that be?"

"Tomorrow at sunset."

Summers was pleased by the answer. "I'll be there."

"Do you think you can handle this alone?"

"I can call for backup."

"If you do that, tongues will wag and the IRA will be there before you get off the phone. At that point, you can say goodbye to Mr. Pugano."

CHAPTER 45

December 1986
County Sligo, Ireland

A MEETING OF EQUALS

Decker was waiting at the end of the alleyway. He was dressed in a long-sleeve, red plaid shirt with button-down collar, khaki trousers, leather loafers and a moss green overcoat that hid his shoulder holster.

"I didn't know if you were coming," Summers said, hesitantly, not knowing if he had received her telegram.

"I've been here awhile. Didn't want him to see me."

"Why is that?"

"Because he trusts you, Hannah, not me. Why don't we get a drink and you can fill me in on what Fitzpatrick has planned. Oh, and by the way, you look absolutely beautiful."

"I'm trying not to look like a cop," she said wryly.

Decker chuckled. Summers relished the compliment. She felt feminine, sophisticated, and exalted by the fact that she was working a foreign assignment. She was also thrilled to see Decker.

They walked until they saw a sign for Hargadon Bros, which claimed it was the oldest or second-oldest pub in Sligo. Perhaps because she was paying undivided attention to Decker, Summers didn't notice the three muscular men clad in dark military-style clothing crouching in the shadows, watching them enter the pub.

Decker's eyes rolled when Summers set her menu on the table and blurted out, "I want pudding."

"Nobody goes out to eat and orders just pudding."

"It's right here on the menu. Pudding. P-u-d-d-i-n-g."

Decker smiled, amused by her insistence. He raised an eyebrow when Summers tossed her clutch purse on the table where it landed with a heavy metallic clunk.

"Make that two puddings," he told the waitress. "And two Jamesons, on the rocks."

The waitress looked at Summers quizzically, as though seeking to confirm the dinner order wasn't a prank.

"Jameson it is," Summers said enthusiastically. "Whisky and pudding."

When the waitress had gone, Summers asked, "By the way, what kind of wine do you think goes with pudding?"

"Guinness," he said.

"Got it."

They ate pudding and ordered a second whisky. Summers quietly explained the plan and showed him the map sketch. Fitzpatrick would drive to Knowth and park the car at a distance so as not to attract attention. He and Luddy would then walk to the secondary tomb. Fitzpatrick's friend would hang a black bandana at the entrance as a sign all was clear.

Each man would carry a sleeping bag, flashlight and enough provisions for two days. Once they selected a chamber and settled in for the night, Fitzpatrick would find cause to retrieve some additional piece of equipment from the car – flashlight batteries, a jug of drinking water. He would urge Luddy to accompany him and that's when the arrest would take place, just outside the tomb.

"Sounds pretty straight forward," Decker said.

"And you'll be with me, so that you can tell your client Luddy Pugano has been taken into custody and will be brought back home to face a jury?"

"I'll be with you."

Summers affectionately rubbed the back of Decker's hand where it rested on the table. She was glad he didn't pull away or look at her like she'd done something weird.

She raised her glass, her eyes unwavering. "To working together," she toasted.

They clinked glasses and gazed deeply at each other. Decker turned his right hand so that it lay flat on the table, palm up, the fingers separated and relaxed. Summers eyed the gesture, clearly not the offer of a handshake, yet an invitation to make contact. She allowed her fingers to lace with Decker's, sensing a current between them that made her nervous yet excited. Decker felt it as well and knew in his heart she was right for him.

"I feel good about this plan," she said.

"To the best-made plans," said Decker, his eyes lingering on their clasped hands. "Just for record, I've never held hands with a cop before."

"What's it feel like?"

"Arresting."

"Maybe you need to be cuffed," she said, emboldened by the whisky yet surprised by her own brazenness.

"I think I'd like that."

"I thought you would," said Summers, smiling, her cheeks reddened. "Your hands are rough. You have callouses."

"I missed my manicure this week. Next time I'll soak them longer."

Summers released his hand and began studying each finger. "I think I like this one the best," she said, pinching the forefinger of his right hand.

"Why is that?"

"It's your trigger finger. The range instructor at the police academy used to call it digitus secundus. Supposedly means second finger. I like to picture you at the range, empting one magazine after another from your beloved Beretta."

"You have an odd sense of appreciation for certain things," he said, knowing that same finger had also fired his high-powered sniper rifle with devastating results.

Decker gently lifted both her hands. "They're warm, soft and very feminine, with lovely fingernails, even if they aren't painted."

"You like them painted?"

"Not necessarily."

"Good, because I don't have time for weekly manicures. Cops don't get to take breaks like some private investigators do."

There was an awkward silence as Decker slowly rubbed her fingers. Summers was surprised that such a simple gesture could seem so intimate. She imagined them in bed together, Decker deeply inside her. Decker did the same. The Jameson worked its magic and left them feeling buoyant.

"I'm so full of pudding. I don't think I'll ever eat again," said Decker.

"What would you have preferred, meat and potatoes, as if I couldn't have guessed?"

"That sounds good, but pudding with you is better than meat-and-potatoes by myself."

Summers glowed. It was an odd compliment but she found it endearing. Better than meat-and-potatoes. What more could a girl ask for? She grinned, thinking of all the things she liked about Decker, from his looks to his taste in clothing and his overall manner that was direct yet playful.

It was late afternoon when they emerged from the pub into the chill winter air. Decker put an arm around her shoulder and pulled her close. She nuzzled her head against him as they walked. Decker had never felt happier.

"I guess I'll drive back to Dublin now," she said. "I didn't exactly tell my partners where I was going."

"Will that be a problem?"

Summers hesitated to tell Decker what she had learned but she decided to trust him. "Sean Fitzpatrick thinks my partners, or at least one of them, may be playing for the other team."

"I presume you mean Agent Finley?"

"That's right. How did you know?"

"We've been trying to identify the leak. We have good reason to suspect the FBI agent is responsible. That explains…"

"Why the people hiding Luddy Pugano know about our raids before they happen," she said, finishing his sentence.

"You can't go back to your hotel. You need to stay clear of Finley."

"We're scheduled to fly home tomorrow."

"But now you have other plans."

"I do."

"And this is our sixth date."

"Will you stop counting," she complained, punching him in the arm.

"I have a room at the Clarion. My office made the reservation in advance once I told them I was going to Sligo."

Summers went suddenly silent. When she spoke, her voice faltered. "You rest here and drive back in the morning. I'll head back now and meet you early afternoon so that we can still get to Knowth before sunset."

Decker took her into his arms. "Stay here tonight. We'll both take separate cars back in the morning."

"I should go," she said, hoping he would protest.

"There are two beds in the room. I've already checked in."

Summers gave him a skeptical look.

"I insist. You've had two Jamesons, or was it three, and the first one was a double. And now you're planning to get on the road. What if you're stopped by the police? Imagine the headline," he said, waving a hand through the air as though setting the type on a news page. "*American police detective busted for drunk driving on road to Dublin.* Your colleagues at the State Police will hate you because you just ruined their chances for a foreign assignment."

"There are really two beds?"

"Yes. Two. And they're nearly eight feet apart. You won't even hear me snore."

"You snore?"

"Only after I've had three Jamesons, or was it four?"

Decker paused just outside the hotel. "You never explained why you decided to contact me. I'm not wearing a badge."

"Just a feeling I got. But it wasn't women's intuition, just the standard variety. I asked Macusovich about you. He gave me most of your background, at least the military part of it and your new career as a PI."

"And what did he tell you?"

"You know Macusovich. He's a man of few words and big fists. But he told me you seemed top shelf," she said. "Now don't let this go to your head, but he described you as good looking, intelligent and unafraid."

"I hope you disagreed."

Summers flushed red. "In fact, I did. I told him he must be partially blind and a poor judge of character."

Decker took her hand and held it firmly as they entered the lobby. The concierge gave them a knowing look as they passed by the front desk and headed for the ancient elevator that slowly deposited them on the third floor.

"The penthouse," announced Decker, smoothly withdrawing his Beretta as he unlocked the door. He glanced back at Summers and smiled appreciatively when he realized she was already holding the compact semi-automatic that had filled her clutch purse.

"Like minds," he said, crouching and sweeping the gun side to side.

"That's a scary thought," she answered.

When they were certain the room was clear, Decker tossed his overcoat and shoulder holster on a side chair and kicked off his leather loafers. He set his Beretta, wallet and passport on the nightstand, vigorously fluffed the two pillows, flopped on the ornate bed nearest the door and stretched his body the length of it. With his back pressed against the headboard, he crossed his legs at the ankles and stared longingly at Summers who had gone into the bathroom and left the door open. He watched as Summers studied herself in the mirror and splashed water in her face.

306

"I don't even have a toothbrush. Everything I brought is in the car," she said.

"You can use mine."

"That's gross. Who knows what sort of diseases you may be carrying?"

"My employer doesn't allow diseases."

"I should have known."

Summers slipped off her pumps and curled her toes into the thick carpet. She pushed back the heavy velour curtain and peered out the tall windows, though there wasn't much to see in the fading light. She could feel his eyes boring into her, undressing her.

"Are you nervous about tomorrow?"

Summers glanced over at him, questioningly. "Do I look it?"

"No. You seem very at ease." Decker thought she looked magnificent, so different than the all-business Detective Hannah Summers in jeans, navy windbreaker and polo shirt, a gold badge clipped to her belt. He liked that Hannah Summers, too, but this one was the stuff of dreams.

"Well, I'm not."

"Not what? Not nervous? Not at ease? If all goes well, and it will, it'll be a big boost for your career."

"What do I do about Finley? He's a rat."

"Let's see how tomorrow goes. Then we'll worry about how best to handle Finley."

"I'm just so pissed at the thought of him doing that. I hate deceitful people. I guess the pay must be pretty good."

Summers picked up Decker's wallet and passport from the nightstand and opened them.

"Emmett Decker," she announced, comparing the information on both documents.

"That's my name. Same as my granddaddy's. What did you expect?"

"I just wanted to make sure it hadn't changed since the last time we talked."

"First you accuse me of potentially carrying a disease and now you suggest I may be using an alias. I can't imagine what you'll say I've done next."

Summers smiled, amused by the handsome ex-soldier about whom she knew so little. She tossed the wallet and passport back on the nightstand and literally collapsed prone onto the other bed, cuddling the pillows. She had shed the lambs wool jacket, scarf and cashmere sweater.

"Mattress to your liking?"

"I could sleep on a sack of potatoes."

"You're in the right country for that."

Decker turned over on his side, head propped up on his elbow, and studied her curves beneath the long woolen skirt, the way the pearls draped across her neck, and how she pursed her lips when she was thinking about something specific. He could feel himself getting aroused. He recalled how her body had felt when he cut her down from the burning cross. It had been a strange night. She was traumatized and nearly unconscious, so there had been nothing sexual about her torn summer dress and all that it exposed. To her, on that fateful evening, he was a stranger coming to her rescue, a faceless first responder, someone she might never see again.

Decker couldn't imagine never seeing her again. She was certainly a different kind of woman. He felt she could be his equal. When Summers rolled onto her back, Decker thought he would explode from desire and anticipation.

Summers reached toward the nightstand and switched on the radio. Van Morrison, native son of Northern Ireland, was belting out a spirited rendition of *Moondance*, but Decker immediately shut it off.

"Pardon me," said Summers, taken aback by his abruptness. "I guess it isn't a fabulous night for a moon dance."

"Sorry. I'll put it back on if you like."

Summers was puzzled but knew it wasn't the right time to figure it out or challenge his impulsiveness. Decker vanished into the bathroom and closed the door. He leaned against the sink and stared into the mirror, trying to rid his memory of the humid afternoon when he expertly shot a big-time Colombian drug lord through the head from 600 yards out and spent two days running for his life through the jungle. Van Morrison had been crooning *Into the Mystic* through his headset as he pulled the trigger and watched the man's head literally burst into fragments. He turned on the water, cupped his hands and drank from the sink, getting control of his breathing.

When he emerged several minutes later, Summers was standing near the drapes, looking out at the street. She appeared deep in thought. She was also completely naked. Her black bra and panties lay on the floor at her feet.

Decker was tongue-tied. For a moment he suspected he might be hallucinating. Summers turned and wrapped her arms around his neck. Decker gazed into her eyes and kissed her ravenously. She kissed him back with equal fervor, her hands unbuttoning his shirt and finding their way to his belt buckle.

He pulled her close and she responded by arching into him. Summers felt her entire body come alive, a sensation of electrifying chills that seemed to converge between her thighs. She had never felt this aroused.

Decker brushed her hair back so that he could kiss one ear and then the other, making his way to her neck. She closed her eyes and let out a soft moan as he nibbled at the sweet flesh.

Decker led her to the bed and nudged her gently backward so that she rested on her back, her blonde hair spilling across the pillow. She looked so beautiful Decker knew then that he had found the soft prayer.

Decker slipped off his clothes and lay next to her, feeling a mix of joy, fear and passion. Summers reached out and traced the lines of his scars. Decker trembled at the warmth of her fingers. Her touch was healing.

Decker was fully aroused as he began kissing her shoulders, his lips following a path to her breasts. His tongue swirled around one nipple and then the other, clamping each lightly with his teeth. Summers moaned and the sound made Decker feel like the luckiest man alive. She gripped his hair as he moved lower and kissed her hips. She began to writhe as he continued the path downward until his tongue reached a downy patch of blond.

Decker breathed deeply, wanting never to forget this moment. Her scent was intoxicating.

"I never thought I would meet someone like you," he said.

Summers pulled him to her, hugging him tightly as though she wanted to fuse their bodies. "Kiss me, Decker."

They kissed wildly.

Decker felt he would burst but he didn't want the moment to end. "I won't stop kissing you. Ever."

Summers knew she was almost over the edge. She could feel herself flowing, melting beneath his touch. She used every bit of strength to push him onto his back. She straddled him, pinning his wrists against the sheets and slowly lowered herself onto him, rocking her hips until he begged her to stop.

"No stopping now," she said, smiling lasciviously.

Decker gently held her by the waist, their eyes locked in an unfathomable embrace. She wanted him more than she had ever wanted any man.

"You're beautiful," he said.

"You make me feel that way."

Decker thrust deeply inside her and she responded by arching her hips, moving faster and faster. She shuddered, crying out in pure joy as he exploded inside her.

Decker gathered her in his arms, holding her against his beating heart, where she quickly drifted off to sleep.

"I wish we could stay just like this forever," he whispered. "I've never felt anything so perfect in my life."

CHAPTER 46

December 1986
Dublin, Ireland

NIGHT OF THE TOMB RAIDERS

Summers dropped off her rental car in Dublin and tossed her luggage into the rear compartment of Decker's Land Rover. She noticed the M16, the canvas case that contained a long-barreled sniper's rifle, military field packs, sleeping bags, canteens, binoculars and other equipment, including a satphone. "You come prepared," she said, still reveling in the memory of their night together but slowly morphing back into cop mode. Blouse. Slacks. Sensible shoes.

"We should be all set," he said, leaning in to kiss her. "But all I can think about is you. We should be going on vacation somewhere – Tahiti, Bora Bora -- not on a manhunt."

Summers distractedly returned the kiss. The soft prayer was gone and the sharp razor was back. She had tamed her hair with a ponytail. She was already thinking of what she would say to Luddy Pugano and how it would feel to slap the cuffs on him and crank down so hard that the metal cut into his wrists. Once inside the Land Rover, she turned her face away from Decker as he drove. "I never wanted to be a cop," she said, looking at herself in the window. "It just sort of happened."

"Roger that," he said. "I came back from Sandland and the next thing I knew, I was working as a private investigator, only it turns out the firm was a lot bigger than the storefront that hired me."

"You still haven't told me why your client is so interested in Luddy Pugano. He's a two-bit Eastie scumbag. If he hadn't killed all these young girls, he'd be nobody."

"I'd rather not get into it right now. Let's just drive."

Summers studied the map that showed the route to Knowth – M1 motorway straight north, then a few side roads. Less than an hour drive time. She identified route options, the land elevations and possible escape routes, pointing out each to Decker as he drove. He was impressed by her map-reading skills that surpassed many of the soldiers he had fought beside in the deserts and jungles.

Once they arrived, Decker parked the Land Rover behind a grassy mound and changed into his woodland green-and-black camouflage fatigues. Another Land Rover that had been following at a distance also came to a halt and pulled off the road. Three men in black BDUs quickly grabbed their weapons and spread out prone in the roadside ditch.

Decker did a 360-scan of the terrain, not pleased by the lack of foliage. "I hope there's cover. Anything that's green in this country is mowed down to a nub," he said. "The Irish are so damn anal."

"Let's not be prejudiced," said Summers, releasing the magazine on her Sig Sauer to make sure it was fully loaded before slapping it back into the handle.

"My mother likes to garden in a natural way," said Decker. "Our neighbors freaked out when she decided to let the front lawn grow as high as a hayfield and asked my dad not to mow it."

"Did he comply?"

"Not willingly. He was always more concerned about what other people thought of our house and our family."

"And what about you? Are you more like your mother or your father when it comes to what other people think?"

Decker didn't answer the question. He blackened his

face with smudge paint and pulled on a black skullcap. He slung the heavy Barrett M107 with scope over his shoulder and carried the M16 rifle by its handle.

Summers smiled at him, trying to sound gung ho.

"Lock and load," she said.

Decker slipped a hefty .50-cal. round into the breech of the Barrett M107 sniper rifle.

"Hey mister, that's a big bullet you got there," she said, trying on a Mae West accent that didn't fit and actually made her laugh at herself. She was trying to quell her nervousness.

Decker chuckled. He liked the fact that Summers had a sense of humor in addition to an appreciation for weapons. Not many women he knew had either. He'd met too many narcissists, anti-gun because they were living in a country that had never known war on home soil in their lifetime. Guns were for cowboy movies.

Decker walked the perimeter of the tomb until he was satisfied he had found a suitable spot from which he could cover the entrance and at least forty yards to either side of it. His ears perked up at the sound of a helicopter in the distance. It made him jumpy, a reflection of his hyper-vigilance since returning from the war zone.

"What's wrong?"

"Did you tell anyone else that you'd be here besides me and Fitzpatrick?"

"Absolutely not."

The *thwap-thwap-thwap* of helicopter blades momentarily got louder and then stopped.

"What was that?"

"I'm not sure. But if any of Fitzpatrick's unfriendly IRA buddies show up, you get out of there. Understand? Come back to this position."

Summers nodded. "Like you told me, it's all going to work out fine," she said, holding up a set of metal handcuffs. "And when we get back home, I may use these on you."

Soft as a prayer, he thought, looking into her eyes.
"Go."

"Yes sir," she said, saluting.

Summers crawled her way closer to the entrance to the tomb, flattening out on the ground behind a few scraggly thorn bushes. She could see the black bandanna fluttering in the breeze. The sun had begun to set, bathing the tomb in a mystical orange light.

Decker saw Fitzpatrick and Luddy trudging down the grassy slope toward the tomb. Fitzgerald wore a large backpack and carried two suitcases. Luddy had sleeping bags tucked under each arm, his hands gripping a lantern and a large spotlight. They stopped just outside the tomb entrance where Fitzpatrick switched on the spotlight. He shined it on a hand-drawn map that Decker could see through his riflescope. The map showed the Eastern Passage, the stonewalled primary corridor with a series connecting chambers like a spinal column that went deep into the earth for at least 40 meters.

Decker framed Luddy's head in the crosshairs and adjusted the scope. His index finger twitched. He wanted to hold his breath, squeeze off a round and put this mission to bed. Game over. He knew the .50-cal. round would take Luddy's head off. There would be no question about whether the target was killed or wounded.

Fitzpatrick and Luddy entered the tomb as darkness descended. Summers tried to see Decker but he was completely invisible, part of the landscape. The inside of the tomb was cold and damp, stone on all sides. Fitzpatrick followed the map and found the chamber his friend had recommended. It was spacious enough for them to spread out the sleeping bags. Luddy foraged in the large backpack, hunting for food.

"No cookies?"

"No. You'll have to make due with a lamb sandwich."

"I hate lamb."

"Then don't eat."

314

Fitzpatrick envisioned Luddy trying to touch his beloved daughter, his 16-year-old angel and love of his life. The thought of this repulsive man's hands on her filled him with rage. He slipped his fingers into the pocket of his overcoat and rubbed the chill metal of his .22-cal. Ruger pistol. It didn't pack much of a wallop but when fired from close range it could be lethal. He considered shooting Luddy through the head and leaving his body.

Luddy scowled at Fitzpatrick. "What the fuck's with you today?"

"Just tired."

"How long do we have to stay here?"

"Tonight and tomorrow night, then we'll go to Sligo."

"Where's that?"

"About three or four hours from here, due west. There's a lovely home overlooking the sea where we'll be staying."

"Is it safe?"

"That's why I picked it."

Luddy found a bag of M&Ms in the backpack and ripped them open. He dumped half the bag into his mouth and crunched. "We should have brought a few beers," he said.

"There are some in the car. Left them in the boot."

"The what?"

"The trunk. I'll go get them. Do you want to come or would you rather stay here?"

"If you're leaving, I'm not staying here, that's for sure. It's a goddamn cemetery."

Decker instinctively turned and pointed his Beretta at the sound of high grass moving out of synch with the steady light breeze. His forefinger finger rested on the trigger as he silently released the safety. He nearly let off a round when he heard his name.

"Decker. Over here."

Twenty feet away, Carrington and Lehman in jungle camouflage and three operatives in black BDUs were crouched in the underbrush. Carrington crawled toward Decker on his elbows. Lehman, similarly dressed, was right behind him. Although Carrington was in his early-forties and Lehman in his early-fifties, they moved like men half their age. Decker was relieved to see the accompanying commandos, their faces were painted black. Claymore, flanked by Poker Face and Memphis, flashed him the OK sign.

Summers saw Fitzpatrick and Luddy exit the tomb and start walking toward their car. She could feel the hatred pulsing through her bloodstream. This was the moment when she was supposed to spring from her cover and arrest Luddy Pugano. She was just about to expose her position when a battered stake truck roared up the road and came to a screeching halt. Several gun-wielding men dressed in street clothes, their faces covered by balaclava masks or bandanas, began running toward the tomb.

Decker looked for Summers through his riflescope. She hadn't moved, obviously confused by the additional players. She was aiming through the sight on her Sig Sauer. Decker hoped she would stay put until they figured out what was going on. He again framed Luddy in the crosshairs.

Lehman nestled beside Decker in the grass. "You have him?"

"I do, sir."

"Is it a clean shot?"

"It is, sir."

"Then shoot the bastard."

Just then, the six men who had arrived in the stake truck spread out and dropped to their knees, rifles and shotguns aimed at Fitzpatrick and Luddy.

A brawny man in an Irish knit sweater was shouting orders and appeared to be in charge. He stood slowly, lowered his shotgun so that the barrel faced the ground and took a few steps toward them. He loosened the balaclava so that it dropped and hung from his neck like a kerchief. Fitzpatrick recognized the pockmarked face. Cormac O'Hagan -- once a stalwart member of the Provisional Irish

316

Republican Army and now the force behind a renegade faction.

"Good day, Sean. And where might you boys be goin', for a little nighttime stroll?"

Fitzpatrick tried to play it cool. "For a moment, I thought you were the pigs. Glad to see some friendly faces."

"Why did you leave the safe house?"

"The pigs are onto it. They were planning a raid."

"And how might you know that?"

"I've got my sources, Cormac, as we all do."

"What are you doing here?"

"We thought we'd ask you the same question."

"Sometimes valuable cargo needs extra protection. We're here to help. I've got men who can stand guard and provide extra firepower if we need it."

"I don't want your help. This man is under my protection. Fergus Cavanagh personally arranged his passage from Boston. I think you know what happens to people who cross Fergus."

Cormac O'Hagan backed off, his tone becoming less aggressive. "How long do you intend to stay in this graveyard?"

"Until we can find another safe house."

Luddy's face showed his surprise. "I thought you said we had a safe house in Sligo?"

"Shut your mouth," Fitzpatrick said.

"If you come with us now, we'll keep you safe. We have a house in Belfast that even the British army won't go near."

The others laughed. "Tuck you both into bed at night," another man quipped.

"Thanks for the offer, but we'll be on our way," Fitzpatrick said. "Come on, Mr. Campbell."

O'Hagan raised his pump shotgun to waist level and aimed at Fitzpatrick. "How can we be sure you aren't planning to turn him over to the authorities?"

"Why would I do that? Fergus isn't the forgiving sort. Maybe you've forgotten that when he ruled this part of the land, there were no renegades. We were all one. We were brothers. Besides, he and I are friends. We fought side-by-side together for years until he left for America."

O'Hagan didn't look convinced. "If this man ends up in the hands of the Guard, it'll be your ass. We won't cover for you."

Decker framed the man doing the talking in his riflescope. Lehman squinted through his binoculars. "Who are they?"

"IRA from the far north. Hardcore, but there's no way to tell who they're working for. I'm guessing they want Luddy Pugano for themselves."

"What value would he have?"

"Insurance. They can threaten to hand him over to the U.S. Justice Department if they don't get what they want. His testimony about certain crimes could be a knock-out punch for the Irish mob in Boston."

"And why do they need this insurance?"

"So that whatever business deal they're involved in will proceed as planned. Holding Luddy Pugano increases the odds that they'll get paid for whatever they're selling, or receive whatever it is they've already paid for."

Lehman pursed his lips as though in deep thought. "You may be right, Decker. We've been hearing rumors about an arms shipment that's supposed to leave New England for Ireland, but the details are sketchy. All we know is that it involves a transaction in millions of dollars and a freighter full of military hardware."

Lehman quietly ordered Carrington to fall back along with the three other operatives and attempt to outflank the IRA men. "There's a friendly in those bushes to the left," Carrington whispered to the first man. "Detective Summers. Massachusetts State Police. Make sure the others are aware."

Fitzpatrick's patience had come to an end. He had no intention of turning his guest over to these men whose loyalty was uncertain. If he did, Fergus Cavanagh would have him

318

killed. He grabbed the shotgun barrel that was pointed at his abdomen and pushed it sideways, betting O'Hagan and the others would relent. The gun discharged, the buckshot ripping into the nearest man who howled in pain and began writhing on the ground, clutching his bloody left boot where part of the foot was missing.

O'Hagan cradled the shotgun and fired at Fitzgerald, striking him in the stomach. Luddy raised his hands in surrender. Another IRA man held a vintage revolver to Luddy's head.

"You two, take him to the truck," O'Hagan barked, instructing a third man to assist the wounded. The two IRA men grabbed Luddy by the arms and began muscling him toward the stake truck. Luddy's feet were dragging on the rocks and grass.

Fitzpatrick lay groaning on the ground, his body curled, a hand beneath his coat exploring his fatal wounds. O'Hagan stood over him. "You were never very smart, Sean. You never learned that doing the right thing will get you killed."

Fitzpatrick used the last of his strength to roll on his back and fire the small-bore semi-automatic Ruger twice before O'Hagan's shotgun again discharged, killing him instantly.

Claymore, Poker Face and Memphis opened fire with their silencer-equipped rifles, eliminating the six IRA men. Decker watched the scene unfold through his riflescope. He saw Summers carefully emerging from her hiding place in the bush. Decker focused the crosshairs on Luddy who was prying the shotgun from O'Hagan's dead hands. When the gun broke free of the man's grasp, Luddy crouched on the ground, not knowing whether to run or hide. When he spotted Summers fifty feet away and moving in his direction, her Sig Sauer clasped with both hands and pointed at him, he backed toward the tomb entrance.

"Stop," she shouted. "Police."

Luddy disappeared into the tomb.

Lehman was still prone on the ground next to Decker. His face was puffed with frustration. "For Christ's sake, shoot," he said.

Decker got to his feet. "Let's go."

Lehman was perturbed by what seemed an act of insubordination but followed Decker down the long hill. Carrington and the others had gathered around.

Summers ran toward Decker and hugged him. She seemed unsure of what everyone was thinking but she didn't care. Decker coiled his arms around her. He was proud of her bravery, her intelligence and her restraint.

"He went back inside," she said. "I'm going after him."

"No," Decker said. "You're not."

Decker looked directly into Lehman's eyes and nodded, cocking his head toward the tomb entrance. The man understood what was being offered.

Decker said, "We'll wait for you out here, sir."

Poker Face offered his night-vision goggles. "Please take these, commander." But Lehman suspected they would be useless in the tomb's total darkness.

Lehman handed Carrington his rifle and radio. He pumped the slide on his Beretta, pushing a 9mm round into the firing chamber. He felt deeply in his pocket for the thumb-size worry doll and rubbed it between his fingers, then withdrew his Ka-Bar fighting knife from its sheath.

Summers' jaw dropped. "You can't just…"

"Yes," said Decker. "We can. Some things are personal."

"It's personal for me too," Summers said sulkily.

"Do you trust me?"

"Yes."

"Then believe me when I say this is even more personal."

CHAPTER 47

December 1986
Knowth Tomb, County Meath, Ireland

A FATHER'S REVENGE

Lehman didn't look back as he entered the tomb's central passage. He crept forward to where the first chamber opened onto the narrow tunnel. It was empty except for clumps of soil and ash. Lehman darted to the next chamber on the opposite side, slowly making his way forward, staying low and sweeping the Beretta right to left. The ambient light from the sunset was quickly fading, leaving the chambers farther down the tunnel in total darkness.

As he cleared the next two chambers he allowed himself to think about Jenny. She had been everything a father could ask for even when as a teenager she did a few things that had riled him.

Some days, as he sat at his desk in Langley, he still couldn't believe she was gone forever. He remembered how thrilled she had been on a visit to Boston, browsing the aisles of the F.A.O. Schwartz toy store and finding the perfect white stuffed bear. She had carried it that day on the swan boats and through the Public Garden and later to an outdoor restaurant on the harbor where she drank three Shirley Temples with fifteen cherries before eating a plate of chicken nuggets. The bear was still on her bed at home in Maryland.

Lehman felt the tears brimming and they distorted his vision. He stopped for a moment to repeatedly blink and clear his eyes. He felt his rage welling up inside and he squeezed the Beretta's handle for comfort. He imagined squeezing Jenny's small hand as they wandered the Washington Mall and later the Smithsonian, recalling her love for the abstract canvases whose meaning he often found elusive.

What was it that made her crave black raspberry ice cream? Did he ever say he was sorry for yelling at her after she dented the family car? She'd only had her driver's license for a week. He should have been happy that she wasn't injured. And then there were the arguments over wearing makeup, especially the thick blue eye shadow. He had made a big deal over that. Just like he did over the cost of ballet lessons. Jerk.

Lehman's ears caught what sounded like metal clanking against stone. He stopped and counted to five before peering around the corner. It was cool inside the tomb but he was sweating. He tried to force the thoughts of Jenny out of his mind. She was dead and there would be no more shared delight, no new memories. Right now he was a hunter, a predator seeking out his prey, but the thought of hunting only brought up another vision of Jenny, this one at a birthday party when Curious Creatures transported several reptiles to their home, including a white boa constrictor that hadn't eaten in nearly two weeks and was eyeing his small daughter as possible lunch.

Predator and prey. Stop thinking. Concentrate. Pet turtles. Goldfish. Braces. The family traveling through Italy, France and Spain. Jenny eating gelato in Florence. Jenny smiling from atop the Eiffel Tower. It was no wonder she had been eager to explore Central America, even if it was with that dickhead Ben Tillman. Worry dolls. Guatemala. That's where they'd bought the worry dolls. He clenched the knife in his teeth, freeing his left hand to again rub the small cloth doll in his pocket. Jenny had this with her when she died. He could feel her presence.

Daddy, daddy, can we catch fish from the sailboat today? Do you think they'll bite on popcorn if I put some on my hook? It's so pretty here on the ocean.

What happened on that boat in Boston Harbor? What did you do to my daughter? Did you kill her there, or did you kill her someplace else and drag her body onto your evil vessel so that you could dispose of her at sea? Did you torture her? Did you rape her? Questions that will forever go unanswered.

Lehman's temples were throbbing. He had counted the chambers on the hand-drawn map. Four more, two on each side. He was at least 25 meters from where he'd started. Another 10 and he'd run out of tunnel. After that, it was a dead end. Bedtime stories. Taking off the training wheels. Be careful riding your bicycle on the street because Mrs. Perkins has cataracts and won't even see you coming. If you're going to the prom, you'd better be back here by midnight, one o'clock at the latest. And tell that fellow not to drive fast.

You bastard. You did this. And for what? To satisfy your sick mind? You have made a zombie of my lovely wife, Cornelia, and filled my daughter, Sarah, with fear of the world. You did not even give me opportunity to bury my daughter.

Payback is a bitch, Lehman told himself, but it will never equal the anguish you have caused. He saw a narrow spotlight beam cross his path about 20 feet ahead. The beam passed through the chamber entrance and created a round circle of light on the far wall of the tunnel. Then it went dark.

He tossed a fist-size rock down the tunnel. The shotgun blast that followed was deafening in the confined space and left a ringing in his ears.

Outside the tomb, the commandos started toward the entrance. "Stop," Carrington shouted, holding up his hand. "We don't interfere. He has to do this his way," he said. Summers looked the other way. Decker put his arm around her shoulders and she made an effort to rest her head on his chest. He could feel her whole body tensed and pumping with adrenaline.

"This isn't what they trained me to do," she said. "It doesn't seem right. You could have thrown a flash-bang grenade into the tunnel and then brought him out."

Lehman's ears were recovering from the shock. He heard the next shell being pumped into the action. He guessed the shotgun had a five-round magazine. Three of those had been spent outside the tomb and a fourth inside.

"That shotgun won't do you much good once you've emptied it," Lehman shouted. "You've got one round left. After that, I'm coming for you."

"Who are you?"

"I'm the avenger."

"What do you want?"

"I want you."

Lehman listened closely as Luddy moved around inside the chamber that opened to the left no more than 10 feet away. He heard him stumble over a piece of equipment and curse.

"Why don't you turn on the light so you can see?"

"Why don't you get the fuck out of here and leave me alone?"

"Are you nervous, Mr. Pugano?"

"How the fuck do you know my name?"

"I know a lot about you."

Luddy attempted to muster some bravado but his voice was trembling. "I'm under Fergus Cavanaugh's protection. If you mess with me, you'll be a dead man. He'll kill you."

"You are under no one's protection," Lehman hissed. "You are here alone, in the dark, which is where you will die."

"Who the fuck are you?"

Lehman silently moved forward, his back pressed flat to the rock wall. It was time for vengeance. In the pitch dark he crossed in front of the chamber from where the beam of light had come. He took cover behind the stone arch, curled his arm around it and blindly fired twice into the chamber, the bullets ricocheting wildly in the small room.

Luddy cried out in pain. A fragment of lead or stone had struck him. "Why are you doing this? Are you fuckin' crazy?"

324

"Are you afraid, Mr. Pugano?"

Lehman again crossed in front of the chamber entrance. Two more rounds from the Beretta slammed into the stone, the ricochets sending Luddy scurrying along the floor like a crab. Luddy screamed loudly, "You fuck. Tell me why you're doing this?"

Lehman momentarily considered telling him that he was about to die because he had murdered his daughter Jenny, but he didn't want to give him that satisfaction. He simply wanted revenge. He wanted to torture and kill this man to make himself feel better.

It sounded to Lehman as though the shotgun was being dragged on the stone floor. He felt around for another loose rock but couldn't find one. He needed something to toss into the chamber so that Luddy would spend what he hoped was the last shotgun shell. And even if it wasn't, Lehman knew he was ready for action. He was ready to die.

Daddy, look what I drew for you today. It's a sailboat. And I made paper flowers for mommy. It's beautiful, honey. I'm going to frame it and put it on my desk at work. I love you, daddy. I love you, too, sugar plum.

Lehman could barely swallow. His mouth was cotton.

"I can see you," he taunted from behind the archway. "I'm standing right in front of you. All you have to do is turn on your spotlight and you'll see me."

Luddy shouted. "Go to hell."

Lehman hurled the Beretta into the chamber in the direction of Luddy's voice. The shotgun roared as soon as the handgun clattered along the stone floor. The heavy buckshot blasted the archway and sent bits of stone and soil flying in all directions. Lehman felt a stabbing sensation in his ears. He pulled a chemical light stick from his cargo pocket, broke the cylinder and tossed it into the chamber. In the eerie green glow he saw Luddy upright and bracing himself with his back against the farthest wall, the darkened spotlight in his left hand, the shotgun pointed downward in his right.

Lehman let out a primitive war cry as he charged with the Ka-Bar. Amid the light stick's green halo he saw Luddy pump the shotgun but it didn't fire. He rammed the K-Bar's seven-inch steel blade into Luddy's stomach and twisted it. Luddy cried out and dropped the spotlight, one hand on the wound, the other trying to swing the shotgun like a club.

Lehman picked up the spotlight and switched on the beam. Luddy was bleeding heavily.

"I want to watch you die," Lehman growled. "Slowly."

Luddy again swung the shotgun like a club but Lehman ducked, grabbed it by the barrel and threw it aside. With a surge of adrenaline coursing through his body, Lehman powerfully slashed the Ka-Bar across Luddy's face. The blade left a bloody gash from the left eye, through the fleshy part of the nose and split the lips. Luddy instinctively brought the palms of his hands to his face, then tripped backward over the sleeping bags and fell to the floor. Lehman pounced on him. He pried open Luddy's clenched teeth with the Ka-Bar and forced the heavy pointed blade down his throat, just far enough to cause great discomfort but not kill him immediately. Blood trickled from Luddy's mouth and he gagged, his eyes centering on the protruding knife handle.

"You're no longer the predator. You're the prey. How does it feel knowing that you're going to die in this cold, miserable tomb?"

Words came out of Luddy's mouth but they were unintelligible. He gazed at Lehman as though trying to match a face. He wanted an explanation for what was happening. Who was this avenger and why did he want him dead? Lehman kneeled beside Luddy and without warning repeatedly stabbed him in the testicles, taking care not to slice the femoral arteries.

Luddy let out a horrific groan.

"Does that hurt? I'll bet it does," said Lehman, turning the Ka-Bar sideways and forcing it between Luddy's ribs until the blade was half buried in a lung. Luddy gasped. Lehman made a similar puncture on the opposite side, then inched backward on his knees until he was satisfied with the view, like a sculptor studying a slab of carving stone in order

326

to decide where to strike the next chisel blow.

Luddy attempted to sit up, clutching his stomach. His pullover shirt was soaked with blood but he wasn't in complete shock. His heart was still pumping and his lungs were holding just enough air to keep him alive.

"How are we feeling tonight?"

Lehman sat back against the rock wall and shined the spotlight directly on Luddy's face. This is the beast that killed my baby girl, he said to himself and then began laughing uncontrollably. He brought his knees to his chest and looped his arms around them, rocking his body as though trying to calm himself.

Lehman felt exhausted. He knew if he closed his eyes he'd fall asleep. He crawled toward Luddy, set the Ka-Bar's sharply-pointed tip over the man's heart and slowly eased it through the skin and muscle, coaxing the blade deeper until it reached the beating heart. Luddy's eyes went wide as the knife sent a searing pain through his body. He felt his heart flutter and begin to beat irregularly. Lehman leaned his full body weight onto the knife handle until the blade sank to the hilt. Luddy's body reflexively stiffened with the pain and then he went limp. Lehman had expected some cathartic moment, some spiritual cleansing, maybe even a feeling of pure joy. Instead, he felt hollow. He had sought vengeance and found it but inflicting pain and killing the man responsible for his daughter's murder would not bring her back.

"Commander?"

It was Carrington. "Are you all right, sir?"

Carrington and Decker shined their flashlights along the tunnel, zigzagging in the tight quarters but moving quickly, unsure of the situation. They took cover behind the archway to the last chamber. Lehman was in a trancelike state. Luddy's body was still, the handle of the combat knife sticking up from his chest. Carrington and Decker each grabbed an arm and lifted Lehman to his feet.

Decker examined Lehman for wounds through his bloodied fatigues. "Medic! Medic! Memphis, we need you," he shouted.

They looped Lehman's arms around their shoulders and led him out of the tunnel. Memphis helped lower Lehman to the ground and inserted an IV saline line to push the meds. Carrington had radioed for the helicopter and the *thwapping* blades could already be heard in the distance.

"We'll get a crew in here to take care of this mess," he said.

CHAPTER 48

December 1986
Boston, Massachusetts

THE REAL STORY -- ALMOST

Rane appreciated the phone call from District
Attorney Sanders, giving him a heads up on the death of
Luddy Pugano and the pending public announcement that
would follow within a matter of hours. It was a favor that
afforded Rane some precious lead time as he prepared his
story for the morning edition.

According to the written statement that was released,
suspected Boston serial killer Luddy Pugano had been fatally
wounded in Ireland during a firefight between two rival IRA
factions.

Sanders relayed to the reporters precisely what he
had been told by the U.S. State Department, that Pugano had
gone there to help broker a multi-million-dollar arms deal
between one of the IRA factions and Boston's Irish Mob. The
story left the false impression that Luddy Pugano was both
cunning and intelligent, a big-time player masquerading as a
gypsy cab driver.

Sanders was eager to hold the press conference
at which he emphasized, "If not for the hard work of
State Police Detective Lt. Hannah Summers, who almost
singlehandedly tracked down Mr. Pugano in Ireland, he
would still be a fugitive from justice and a menace to
society."

A practiced politician, Sanders paused to allow the reporters to digest his words, then added, "Our investigators have determined that Mr. Pugano was responsible for the deaths of at least 20 women, primarily in eastern Massachusetts. He was also the key player in what was an ongoing weapons deal with the Provisional Irish Republican Army." He reminded the news media of the previous year's mortar attack by the IRA on the Royal Ulster Constabulatory police station in Newry that left nine officers dead.

The television cameras zoomed in on Summers. Blue polo shirt, gold detective shield clipped to her belt, hair pulled into a coil beneath the State Police cap, the visor pulled down to her eyebrows. Before the press conference, the district attorney had asked that she remove her hat and let her hair down as the cameras rolled to show she was an exceptionally good-looking young policewoman, but she had ignored the request.

As the reporters asked questions, Sanders stressed that the sale of guns and other weapons by Boston's Irish Mob to the IRA, including rocket-propelled grenades, would have undoubtedly led to the death of more British soldiers and innocent civilians and continued to fuel the Irish rebellion.

Sanders briefly mentioned State Police Sgt. Andre Macusovich during his formal statement, but only in the context of having assisted Summers. He offered no information on precisely how the burly detective had contributed to the case. Macusovich acted like he hadn't noticed the snub, but he understood the politics. His State Police homicide unit was assigned to a different elected official, the district attorney in neighboring Essex County. And that made him of little value to Sanders, whose jurisdiction included Suffolk County and the city of Boston within it.

The reporters were already familiar with Summers as victim, having covered the story of her abduction. Now they were being given Summers the hero as the district attorney described how the detective had arrived at the scene of the shootout while the gun smoke was still rising, only to find the dead bodies of Luddy Pugano, Sean Fitzpatrick and Cormac O'Hagan.

Summers wasn't taking questions from the press so Sanders didn't have to concern himself with her potentially spilling the truth. If that's what the U.S. State Department claims happened at Knowth, then that's what happened, he told himself. Sanders was a survivor and he wasn't about to pick a fight that he couldn't win. Besides, Summers was the star of the show, the golden girl of the moment, and she worked for him. He'd just put her on display and made sure she kept her mouth shut.

Despite the divide in jurisdictions, the press had already begun referring to Summers and Macusovich as Boston's IRA Strike Force. The name had a nice ring and adopting it made the headlines more interesting. No mention was made at the press conference about FBI Agent Kevin Finley or the bureau's involvement in the case.

It was only a matter of hours after the first breaking news television broadcast about the death of Luddy Pugano and the foiled arms deal that the Irish press picked up on the story. And from those ranks came plenty of speculation that the shootout had left other IRA members wounded or dead, but since there were no witnesses and no additional bodies, it remained just that. As one Irish television news commentator put it, "There's no telling how many others from both factions were shot and seriously wounded in the gun battle yet made it back to their hiding places to avoid police detection."

The more enterprising Irish reporters, trying to milk another day or two out of the story, tenuously tied the violence to the 1981 hunger strike by IRA soldier Bobby Sands, whose starvation death at age 27 inside an Irish prison prompted strong recruitment to the rebel cause. Five years may have elapsed since the martyr was buried, but the men whose bullets struck Luddy Pugano could very well have been some of those recruited as a result of his sacrifice. It was a story the readers might be willing to believe.

Carrington and Decker read the newspaper stories and watched the TV coverage in amusement as they sat drinking coffee in the Executive Cover conference room. Summers had been invited to join them after the press conference but she continued to have mixed feelings about the way the situation was handled. She had been singled out for heroism and bravery, but she knew that soon she would resign from the State Police. After all, she had witnessed the fatal shooting of six IRA operatives by what she could only surmise were former Special Forces soldiers. She had also allowed Skip Lehman to murder Luddy Pugano without lifting a hand to stop it. But worse than that, she had submitted a politically-charged report to the top-ranking Massachusetts State Police colonel that alleged an FBI agent was working for Boston's organized crime families, and cops don't testify against cops, at least not if they intend to stay on the job.

The report had been immediately stamped as classified and a series of high-level emergency meetings were taking place as she sat on a park bench along the Esplanade watching a fleet of small sailboats tack toward the Longfellow Bridge.

Lehman telephoned while Carrington and Decker were monitoring the fallout. He had done as advised and rested at home for two days, which was about all he could endure. He was back at his desk at Langley and wanted to express his thanks to both men. Carrington said there was no need for thanks, just doing his duty. So Lehman asked him to put Decker on speakerphone.

"Your understanding of the situation in the field was much appreciated, Decker. I'm grateful. We usually don't do business that way."

"Thank you, sir. I'm glad it all worked out."

"It wasn't what I thought it would be, but it's over and now my family and I can move on."

"I'm happy for you, sir."

Lehman then unveiled the more pressing reason for his call. "Decker, I hope you'll join us on a more permanent basis. You would continue to work with Bill, who I'm sure would have no objections. You probably know that he likes you. You're a natural."

Carrington saluted Decker with two fingers but didn't take his eyes off the TV.

"It's an intriguing offer, sir. If you don't mind, I'd like to give it some thought. I need to talk to Hannah, I mean Detective Summers. She's in a bind and I feel like I'm the one who put her there. I need to do whatever I can to help her."

"We all had something to do with putting her there, but I'm sure there's a solution."

Decker was already aware that Lehman had used his contacts at the State Department to ship Luddy's body back to Boston. The body had been cremated on the premise that the firefight left a corpse so bullet-riddled it seemed the only decent course of action. The U.S. government had paid the shipping costs, which Carrington rightfully suspected would come as a relief to Celeste Pugano.

The bodies of Sean Fitzpatrick and Cormac O'Hagan were laid to rest in Ireland where they were accorded near celebrity status. Carrington had made certain the story of their deaths was properly leaked in Boston. The story had a simple-to-understand thread, which Carrington knew was ideal for the television news and easy for the viewing audiences to digest. The gunplay of two rivals and their gangs had ended the life of Luddy Pugano when he was caught in the crossfire. The story even came packaged with the sweetener that suggested Luddy was not only a cunning serial killer but a savvy businessman sent to Ireland to make sure the weapons deal went smoothly. In essence, fate had taken a hand.

"Poetic justice and all that," Carrington said to Decker. "The media will love it."

Decker knew Carrington's assessment was accurate. He privately smiled when he spotted Rane on live television amid the crowd of journalists raising his hand and struggling to ask questions at the press conference. The hotshot journalist no longer had an exclusive story and it showed on his face. His media colleagues were having a feeding frenzy more focused on who could report details faster rather than whether the truth was being unveiled. In that battle, television was always the winner. It was a media circus that would have exploded out of control had Luddy Pugano survived and come home to stand trial. Decker envisioned the hell Kaleigh would have faced if Rane realized he had been used as a political pawn.

Desmond O'Malley and Fergus Cavanaugh celebrated Luddy's death because it eliminated the possibility that he might return to Boston one day and testify against them. Carrington had not only fabricated the arms deal story, he named the two Boston mobsters as alleged participants. The news accounts attributed that information to "a highly-placed source familiar with the investigation." Carrington knew the reporters he trusted wouldn't publicly identify him as the source because that would mean only their competition would receive news tips in the future.

Since there was no hard evidence, Desmond O'Malley and Fergus Cavanaugh would never have to worry about being arrested in connection with Luddy's death or the rumored weapons deal. But their celebration was short lived because Summers' report had been unsealed by a judge and given to the Suffolk County district attorney who presented it to a grand jury as evidence of Finley's corruption.

Sanders understood it was dangerous to take on the FBI, but he was betting Finley would be convicted. If that happened, Sanders would become known as the prosecutor who cleaned up police corruption in Boston and put him in the running for a judgeship or state attorney general.

Sanders instinctively knew that word of the secret grand jury inquest would soon leak out of the courthouse.

Rane and other journalists who covered crime as part of the Boston press corps would be eager to report that the indictment of Finley was imminent. Meanwhile, the FBI Special Agent-in-Charge of the Boston office repeatedly declined comment when asked if Finley's allegedly traitorous acts had jeopardized other agents in the field, especially those working under cover.

CHAPTER 49

December 1986
Boston, Massachusetts

A MOTHER MOURNS -- SORT OF

Celeste sat in her favorite stuffed chair staring transfixed at the day-glow rosary beads hung around the neck of the Virgin Mary statuette on the credenza near the door. She had often prayed on each bead but it always left her feeling that she was no closer to god, if one existed.

Her son was dead but it didn't make her sad. In many ways, it was for the better, she thought, because he was driven by demons that had ruled his life since birth. He was a cursed child, she told herself.

Celeste poured a double shot of anisette, setting the bottle on the floor beside the chair. She opened her Bible and pulled out the tuft of Antoinette's hair, gently rubbing it between her fingers. The feel of her daughter's hair soothed the turmoil inside her. She was glad Luddy hadn't come home in a handmade wooden coffin like those the Irish were so fond of, nor did he arrive in a steel casket. What remained of Luddy was enclosed in a one-foot-square, gray metal box with a chrome hasp lock, and inside was a ceramic urn that held his ashes.

The funeral director didn't seem surprised when she told him there would be no visiting hours. Celeste had looked him in the eye. "Who's going to come to see ashes in a pot?"

The funeral director was aware the U.S. government

had paid for the cremation and the urn. He asked, had she considered a burial plot in one of the city cemeteries?

"I'll take him home with me," she said.

Luddy's urn shared space on the credenza with the Virgin Mary and two lighted candles. Celeste chortled to herself, thinking she might use the ashes in her tomato plants out on the fire escape.

Since Luddy's death, the neighbors had been standoffish. Celeste didn't care. She had little use for them and they for her. If she died alone in her small apartment, she knew it could be weeks before anyone checked on her, unless of course the stench wafted to the other floors.

Celeste had hoped that one day before she passed away she could make up for her misdeeds, for wanting Luddy to be someone he was not, for wanting him to be Antoinette. She knew in her heart that it was she who had taught him cruelty and resentment. As a boy he had seen her poison cats and dogs, shoot pigeons and streetlamps with a BB gun, break windows by throwing rocks, and knock heavy icicles from the roof edge with a broom handle just as the neighborhood schoolchildren passed beneath them. She had known Luddy was watching as she put pins and metal chips from a broken razor blade into candy bars and apples that she distributed to children during Halloween.

Celeste went to the kitchen sink where the varnished wooden box she had rinsed was nearly dry. After the police visited the first time, she had hidden the box in the grimy sewer in the alley behind the apartment. Now she set the hinged box on her lap and admired the contents. The locks of hair were lovely – mostly dark browns but a few blond and an unmistakable red. She picked up each one and felt the texture, putting them to her nose and inhaling deeply. These were the women in her son's life and, in some odd way, each had the potential of becoming her daughter-in-law. She read the names on each white tag.

"Antoinette, these are your sister-in-laws," she said aloud, placing the tuft of Antoinette's hair in with the others. "Now you have a family."

As she dozed off in the chair, she dreamed Nello Franchi was on his way to her from New York with flowers and a bottle of French champagne. She had to find the right dress and a pair of nylon stockings.

CHAPTER 50

December 1986
Boston, Massachusetts

THE PARTNERSHIP

The district attorney's press conference was long over but Summers still hadn't shown up at Executive Cover where Decker and Carrington were tracking and analyzing the media response to what was being referred to as the Irish Tomb Shootout.

Decker had left a message on her office phone, inviting her to join them after the dog-and-pony show was finished. Summers had not responded, but Decker hoped she would come. It would give Carrington an opportunity to meet her in a less stressful situation than what they'd faced in Ireland.

Summers' phone answering machines at the prosecutor's office and at her apartment were both recording messages. Decker began to worry. He tried calling her several more times but with no results so he reached out for the district attorney, hoping he might shed some light.

Sanders, who agreed to speak with Decker only if off the record, told him Summers had left the office in a huff after the press conference and hadn't been heard from since. According to Sanders, she had made a few disturbing comments about justice in America and physically pushed aside another assistant prosecutor who had attempted to stop her from leaving the building.

Decker drove to Brookline and sat in the Jeep Cherokee for four hours outside Summers' apartment, thinking of what he would say when she returned. But she never showed.

The following morning, Decker telephoned Carrington. "I need to find her. Can you help?"

"If she uses a credit card, we'll find her," Carrington responded reassuringly. "I don't want to ask the cops to put out an APB because too many of them may be pissed off at her right now."

Decker paced the rooms of his Eastie apartment where Dogman was sprawled on the couch with Major. The shepherd was still limping from the aftermath of the knife wound.

Dogman, whose artificial leg was repaired, grabbed two beers from the refrigerator and handed one to Decker. "I don't know the true story myself about what happened over there, so I'm sure Hannah is feeling a bit confused," he said.

Decker clinked his bottle to Dogman's. "She didn't deserve this," he said. "She trusted me and I let her down, made her do something she wasn't prepared to do."

"Don't beat yourself up. You know what happens once the shit starts flying."

Decker spun around at the knock on the door. It was Brenda in her workout clothes carrying two white paper bags from Burger King that got the shepherd's attention. "Not for you," she said to the dog.

"I already promised him a Whopper," said Dogman, maneuvering his artificial leg so that he could sit comfortably on the couch.

Brenda handed him a double cheeseburger, an order of French fries and a fist full of napkins. "Because you're such a slob," she said, leaning down to kiss him on the cheek.

Holding up the cheeseburger and fries, Dogman grinned goofily at Decker. "You see. There is a god."

Major sat at attention, his keen eyes brimming with hope. Dogman hadn't told Brenda the backstory of what had happened to Decker in Ireland, but she'd been around

340

both men long enough to sense that not all was well. They were usually joking with each other, but a serious mood had overtaken the apartment.

Brenda spoke softly and sincerely. "Girl trouble?"

"You might say that," said Decker.

"Do you love her?"

"More than I ever thought possible," he said.

"Does she love you?"

Decker didn't answer, so Dogman added, "Maybe not right at this minute."

"Did you try flowers?"

"I don't know where to find her."

"I guess that rules out flowers. Where do you think she went?"

Dogman explained that Decker had already gone to Summers' workplace and home and called her enough times to wear out the phone wires.

"Decker has been pacing for hours. He's like a tiger at the zoo."

Brenda made a sad face. "What about her parents? Do they live around here?"

"Kansas City, Missouri," said Decker, who realized he knew very little about Hannah Summers, yet his desire for her was overwhelming. He certainly missed the feel of her between the sheets and in his arms, but he was experiencing something far more powerful. He missed her wit, her intellect, her smile, her confidence, the way she easily slipped her gun into its holster, how she seemed to have an uncanny way of anticipating his thoughts and movements. He missed the sound of her voice and the way she walked with a slight and unconscious sashay. He'd never felt this way with any other woman, simultaneously in sync on so many levels. They had a similar sense of humor and the laughter they frequently shared was an aphrodisiac. The fact that she holds a black belt, understands forensics, speaks three languages, and may be able to match him on the firing range, just added to his attraction.

I can't get enough of her, Decker told himself.

Most men he knew were not nearly so brave, yet Hannah Summers had tracked down hardcore criminals with little thought about her own safety. She was fierce, relentless and single-minded.

Decker pictured her in his bed at the Clarion Hotel. He hadn't expected it. Yet she was there by choice, the blankets partly pulled back. A complete surprise and he hadn't seen it coming. Sharp as a razor, soft as a prayer.

"I'm going to find her."

"Well, at least take a cheeseburger," said Brenda, tossing him one as he walked out the door. Major followed the arc with his head as it left Brenda's hand and landed in Decker's.

Decker scrambled down the stairs and energetically muscled through the front door. If Summers hadn't reflexively stepped aside, she would have been knocked to the pavement. She watched as Decker gained control of his momentum.

"Whoa! I've been looking all over for you. I wasn't sure if you knew where I lived."

"Took some real detective work," she said. "Freddie Morales is listed in the phone book."

Decker was panting from his descent. "I was just going back out to see if I could find you."

"Well. You found me. I had some thinking to do. Were you going to offer me a cheeseburger?"

Decker reached out with both hands as though he planned to embrace her but decided against it. After all, he thought, she might have come to say she couldn't go along with what happened in Ireland and wanted to give warning that she was about to tell all.

"I'm sorry. I should never have put you in that position."

Summers brushed her thick blonde hair from her eyes. It was no longer in a ponytail. "I tried to imagine myself as Lehman. What does it feel like to have such power in your job, and yet somebody completely unknown, some loser like Luddy Pugano, comes along and takes away one of the most precious things in your life? I'm not a mother, so I really can't say what it feels like from a parent's perspective, but I can imagine."

"I felt the same way when it was happening. I wanted Lehman to get some payback. I wanted you to get some payback. I felt like I was depriving you of the chance to get even with Luddy for what he did to you. But I deceived you from the start. I made you trust me. All the while, it was my mission to put a bullet through Luddy Pugano's head. When you told me he was going with Fitzpatrick to the tomb, I never intended to let you arrest him. So I'll understand if you can't forgive me for that."

"After the press conference, I went down by the Charles and just sat there, watching the river go by, watching the fucking ducks. I wanted to hate you, but I couldn't, so I drove south and spent the night at a little cottage in Newport. The whole time I was there I kept thinking how much better it would be if you were with me."

Decker felt as sad and lost as he looked. "Would you mind if we walked?"

"Not at all," she said, lacing her arm through his and turning him toward the street.

"When I came home from Sandland, I was a mess. Dogman showed me what it means to be courageous. Compared to him, I'm a wimp."

"We all have our crosses to bear."

"You told me once that you never wanted to be a cop. What was it you wanted to be?

"I got my first taste when I was a college student, working part-time for campus security, mostly helping with the files and other office work. Lots of things went down that never got reported, even though they should have been. Money talks. Rich parents intervene. College endowment accounts get fattened. That's when I got a glimpse of how the system works, that justice is a commodity based on how much you can afford."

"Is that when you decided to become a real cop?"

"No. I initially thought I could fix the system so I went to law school. I wanted to become a prosecutor, an assistant district attorney, be the one responsible for making sure the bad guys get put away once they're arrested. At that point, I'd already done an internship with a prosecutor's office where I worked with the victims. I sat with them as the court made a mockery of what they'd endured. It wasn't much different than what I'd seen on campus. The young girl who wore her skirt too short deserved to be raped. The 18-year-old kid who stole a six-pack from a convenience store was beaten so severely by the cops it left him paralyzed for the rest of his life. They said he was a punk who had it coming. The police officers weren't even reprimanded."

Summers knew the words were rolling off her tongue in a rant but she needed to vent. "Justice is a fucking illusion," she said.

Decker reached for her hand as they slowly navigated the chipped and broken sidewalk. She squeezed his palm and didn't let go.

"So you took a turn from law school to law enforcement?"

"I thought I could be more effective as a cop, get more done on the street than I ever could I the courtroom."

"Is that why you turned away when Lehman went into the tomb?"

"I don't know, Decker. I guess I wanted to see justice done for once."

"Lehman told me it didn't make him feel any better."

"Then maybe it's not about him, it's about his daughter. It's about making things right for Jenny."

"You may be right."

Decker told her that Lehman had asked him to stay on at Executive Cover, but he wasn't sure how he felt about it.

"What did you tell him?"

"That I'd only come back if he took both of us."

"Me? Why me?"

"Because I think you and me together could be unbeatable."

344

Summers looked at him in disbelief. "You want me to be your partner?"

"Exactly. We're both good at what we do and, well, we're learning to trust each other."

"You mean I'm learning to trust you."

"Yes. That's what I meant. I already trust you."

"You should. I've never given you reason to think otherwise."

"So what do you say?"

"I guess it depends on whether Lehman is game."

"Is that a yes?"

"Yes. That's a yes."

Decker pulled her close. "I'll make the pitch and if he doesn't accept it, we both walk away. We get jobs as ticket takers at the movie theater or as crossing guards at the neighborhood school."

Summers knew she couldn't go back to the State Police. Her written statement against Agent Kevin Finley was enough to black ball her from membership in any law enforcement organization. At this point, she told herself, it would be tough getting a job as a mall security cop.

"If you can sell the deal, I'm in," she said, pushing him away and extending a business-like hand to shake. "Partners?"

"Partners."

"Good. I'm hungry. Let's go eat," she said. "I can smell Santarpio's from here."

Decker and Summers walked arm-in-arm along Chelsea Street, heading for the legendary pizzeria. They sat at a corner table, ordered two beers, a large pizza with plenty of Italian sausage and a Caesar salad, which Summers insisted upon.

"If we're going to be partners, you'll have to eat your vegetables," she warned, raking a pile of salad onto his plate.

Decker grinned. "Yes ma'am."

Decker thought if he smiled any wider his lips would tear, but he was happier than he'd ever felt in his life. Later that evening they returned to Decker's apartment where

Dogman, Brenda and Major were watching a cop show on TV. Decker made the introductions and the two women quickly sized up one another.

"Decker was out of his mind when he couldn't find you," Brenda ventured.

Summers immediately showed interest in the subject. "I didn't know that," she said.

"Well, I thought you should," said Brenda. "Isn't that right, Decker?"

Decker blushed.

Summers smiled. "Out of your mind were you?"

"I was worried. That's all."

"It's nice to know somebody was worried about me."

They all had a beer after which Decker and Summers retreated into his room and didn't come out for two days, except for morning coffee and to answer the door when the Chinese takeout was delivered.

Decker first ran the partner idea past Carrington who was lukewarm about it. "How can you be a field agent acting in the company's best interest when you're working with someone you care about? What if you have to make a decision that you know will lead to their death? Would you be willing to do that?"

Decker countered. "Hannah is a professional. She understands the risks, but more so, she has what it takes to get the job done."

Carrington vowed to discuss the proposal with Lehman but couldn't make any promises. "Lehman won't like it. I can tell you that for certain."

"It's both of us or none," said Decker. "I just wanted to make that clear. I'm going to call him myself."

Over the next month, Agent Kevin Finley was indicted and Lt. Hannah Summers resigned from the State Police. Sanders demanded a reason but Summers stayed with the story that she was just tired of being a cop. He requested she keep a low profile while the case against Finley remained in the news.

CHAPTER 51

January 1987
Mexico

TEQUILA AND THE MEXICAN SUN

Decker and Summers were relaxing on a beach south
of Cancun when a hotel staffer informed him of an important
message awaiting this attention at the front desk.

"I'll go see what it is," said Decker. "If the waiter
comes around, tell him two more margaritas with *añejo*
tequila on the rocks."

"Salt?"

"No."

"Do you want me to come with you?"

"I want you to relax. That's why we're here. We need
to rest up for tonight's New Year's Eve party."

When Decker returned to their beach chairs, it was
obvious from his glowing smile that he had news. "That
was Lehman. He's in Mexico City on personal business. He
wanted to let us know we have our first assignment. Sort of a
trial run."

"Now that's what I call a great start to 1987. And
to a wonderful partnership," said Summers, hip-checking
him as she let out a *woo-hoo* and toasted with the ice-cold
margaritas. "I haven't been this excited since my dad brought
home a puppy when I was six. Did he give you any details?"

Decker looked around for unwelcome eyes and ears
before speaking.

"Not many. He mentioned Earth First, which is apparently a group of fringe environmentalists who have been destroying government equipment and cutting power lines that feed some important defense facilities near the Washington-Oregon border."

"What about them?"

"Lehman wants us to make friends with them and join the fun. We'll have separate covers. He sounded stressed so we didn't talk long. The full briefing won't happen until he returns to Langley. This will be a strictly intelligence-gathering mission."

"Do we need to leave right away?"

"No. He's not due back for two more days. He told me to give you his best regards and to tell you welcome aboard."

"Well, if we only have 48 hours, we'd better go back to the room to start packing," Summers suggested with a captivating smile.

"I think you're right, but not before we take another swim."

Decker lifted Summers in his arms and carried her into the turquoise waves, tossing her just as a frothy one crashed over them. They played in the surf and exchanged salty kisses, their bodies rubbing together at every chance.

Decker felt himself getting aroused. He ran his hands beneath her surprisingly skimpy bathing suit as another wave crested. "I definitely need to start packing," he said.

Summers rested her hands on his shoulders and gazed into his eyes. "I'll help you."

Back in the room they left the balcony doors open so that the sea breeze swept over the bed. Summers tuned the radio to an American top-40 station, threw her bikini on a chair, leaped onto the bed and began dancing to *Let's Go All the Way* by Sly Fox.

For the first time in longer than he cared to remember, Decker didn't mind the music. He was mesmerized by the sight of Summers gyrating her hips and provocatively urging him to join her. Decker started to climb atop the bed but

Summers shook her index finger.

"No bathing suits allowed."

Decker dropped his suit to the floor and began dancing on the bed. It was difficult to stand securely on the spongy mattress so they bumped into each other until finally Summers began jumping straight up and down, laughing as her hair billowed in the breeze. Decker did the same and like two kids on a trampoline they bounced until they were exhausted.

CHAPTER 52

January 1987
Mexico

THE NEXT MISSION

Lehman understood the risks of traveling alone to Mexico City to meet Nikolas Ruskoff, but the man sounded as though he wanted to put the past behind them. At one time, they had been more like brothers than professional colleagues. But 11 years had gone by since the American helicopters had evacuated them from Saigon. If he was successful, it would mean no more threatening calls and written messages, no more concern that his daughter, Sarah, might be targeted for revenge. It was enough that Jenny was gone and his wife transformed into a medicated droid. He had experienced enough tragedy.

Lehman waited as instructed until just after sunrise to begin his planned walk through Alameda Park with its statues and fountains. Birds were chirping overhead in the lush trees but Lehman had no idea what species they might be. He sat on the edge of a stone fountain, listened to the water cascading and waited. It was the first day of the new year, perfect time to set things right.

Lehman pretended to read a newspaper as the sun edged over the trees. A jogger trotted past followed by a young couple pushing a vintage baby carriage. He expected Ruskoff to arrive at any moment. Time, he reminded himself, had a way of healing things. Those last days in Vietnam had been a nightmare and every day since he lamented having to make the decision to leave Ruskoff's family behind. If he hadn't, the embassy staffers with the most sensitive information would all be dead or in a North Vietnamese prison camp, himself included.

The last thing Lehman saw was a metallic glint in the window of a building overlooking the park. His body toppled backward into the fountain where the cleaning crew found it the next day.

It was the middle of the night when Carrington called Decker's hotel. Groggy from tequila, the New Year's Eve dance party on the beach and a long night of lovemaking, Decker didn't pick up the phone until the fourth ring.

"Call me back at this secure number in five minutes," he said, rattling off a series of digits that Decker scribbled on a hotel desk pad.

When he called, Carrington answered immediately.

"Lehman is dead," he said. "He went to Mexico City to meet with a former colleague and patch up their differences. Looks like a sniper. I doubt if their meeting ever took place."

Decker was stunned by the news. Summers covered her breasts with the bed sheet and moved closer so that she could listen.

Carrington was all business. "I'm on my way there now. My flight leaves DC in a few minutes. I need you both to meet me there later today. See if you can book an early flight from Cancun," he said, giving Decker the address of a company safe house near Plaza Garibaldi. "I know Lehman offered you and Summers an assignment. You can start working on that after we find out what happened in Mexico City. That's priority. We're not expecting a lot of cooperation from the Federales."

Decker was about to ask if Lehman's wife and daughter had been told but Carrington hung up without saying goodbye.

Decker gently returned the receiver to its cradle, staring at the phone as he digested what he'd just been told. Summers draped her arms around his shoulders. She didn't know what to say. These people were playing hardball.

Decker looked at his watch that showed 3 a.m. in Cancun. "Well, partner. I guess it's time to roll."

Summers lay back languorously on the bed and gave him her most sultry look. "There are no flights until six. Are we finished packing?"

Decker smiled. "I might have a few more things that need to go into my suitcase."

"I was hoping you'd say that," she said, pulling him beneath the covers.

THE END

ACKNOWLEDGMENTS

A heartfelt thanks to my wife, Christine, and daughter Julie, for their unwavering support throughout the writing of this book. Not only did they keep me on track, they're responsible for eliminating errors that readers will never see and for making me look like a better writer. My gratitude extends to my son, Zack, for his encouragement to follow my dream.

I'd also like to thank all the law enforcement officers who, over the course of my career in journalism, taught me how the criminal justice system works and, sometimes, doesn't.

ABOUT THE AUTHOR

DAVID LISCIO is an international, award-winning journalist whose lengthy experience covering crime stories led to the writing of his debut novel, the serial killer thriller *Deadly Fare*.

An investigative reporter, David's work has appeared in dozens of magazines and newspapers. The recipient of more than 20 journalism honors, his feature stories have earned first-place awards from the Associated Press, United Press International and many regional news media groups. He has reported extensively on organized crime in both the United States and abroad, in addition to writing about environmental and military subjects.

David is an avid sailor, outdoorsman and adjunct college professor. A father of two, he lives with his wife and dog on the Massachusetts coast, where he is a volunteer firefighter and Ocean Rescue team member.

He's currently working on a second novel. You can contact him on his website: *www.davidliscio.com*

Made in the USA
Middletown, DE
07 April 2021